To C[...]
with best wishes
Susannah Campbell.

ACKNOWLEDGEMENTS

I thank the guests who were brave enough to
Bed and Breakfast with us during our own particular financial crisis,
many of who became, and remained, good friends.
I'm sorry we weren't able to offer
the same exciting services as the characters in the book!

Thanks to Dr Ian Campbell and his wife Averil
for their hospitality and medical expertise.
To John and Tessa Robson for their insights into Lloyds of London.
To Alan Rix of Barclays Bank for explaining
the process of Bankruptcy.
To Donald Le Strange Campbell for the shooting anecdotes.
To my friends, Robert and Penny Wood,
Linda Moore, Margaret Goddard, and Liz and Woody Littlefield,
for their long years of encouragement.

And special thanks to Pauline and
Jeff Jessop without whom this book would never
have been published.

SUSANNAH CAMPBELL

Fat birds don't fly

DESIDERATA PRESS

LONDON & CAMBRIDGE

Published by Desiderata Press

Copyright ©Susan Campbell 2001

First published in The United Kingdom in 2001
by Desiderata Press
London & Cambridge
PO Box 112
Cambridge PD0 CB4 3SU

ISBN 0 9541678

Typeset in Bembo
Printed and bound by CPI/Bookcraft,
Midsomer Norton.

For BGC

FRIEND

MENTOR

LOVER

PROLOGUE

The Rev James Laughton dumped the white plastic carrier bag down on the kitchen table. Taking the two bottom corners, he shook the contents out onto the table and spread them out with his broad podgy hands. He was a short, rotund man, with a corpulent belly, a balding head, and a rounded, sagging jaw.

He took a wooden chopping board and a willow-patterned plate from the dresser and, slitting open the vacuum packed smoked salmon, he transferred all of the contents onto the board. He peeled off the cellophane leaves that separated the slices. Then he spread each slice with a thick layer of cream cheese. With the palms of his chubby hands he rolled each slice into a sausage shape and, taking a sharp knife, chopped them into manageable sections. He laid the salmon and cheese wedges, in an ordered pattern, on the blue and white plate.

Then he took a cut glass champagne flute from the dining room, opened the bottle of champagne and filled the glass to the brim. Taking a sip of the foaming liquid, he turned up his nose and consulted the label. He had set his heart on champagne and this was the best that the wine merchant had to offer; but somehow James felt a little cheated; he would have liked a rarer vintage.

He put a white linen tray cloth onto a wooden butler's tray, added the salmon and champagne and carried his supper through to the dining room. Seconds later he returned to the kitchen, broke off a small sprig of parsley from the pot growing on the windowsill, took it back to the dining room and added it to the plate of smoked salmon.

James sat at the head of the table, as he always did, whether dining alone or with friends. He slipped his white linen napkin out of its delicately engraved silver ring, tucked the starched white square into his clerical collar, and surveyed his supper. He was in no hurry: this was a meal to savour.

He rubbed his hands together. He was almost enjoying himself and felt as if a great burden had been lifted from his shoulders. He had made a decision, and was at last doing something to ease his pain.

They'd open him up, of course. He imagined the contents of his stomach spilling out onto the mortuary table. The macabre vision was strangely comforting. 'The condemned man ate a hearty meal,' he said, and laughed. He placed the first roll of smoked salmon into his mouth and chewed it slowly. Sipping the champagne, he washed it around his teeth before he swallowed. He was thinking of nothing in particular beyond the sensual taste and smooth texture of the food, he was concentrating on making every mouthful last as long as possible.

His meal completed, he took the tray back to the kitchen, washed his plate and his glass, and restored them to their places. He staggered a little as he made his way through to the sitting room. He had drunk a whole bottle of champagne, and eaten almost a pound of smoked salmon. James Laughton's overweight body betrayed and confirmed his gluttony, but at this point in his life it no longer mattered.

He lit the gas fire, turned it up to full heat, and sat down heavily, causing the legs on the little chair to scrape on the highly polished wooden floorboards. As a child, James had been nursed in this very chair; it was of great sentimental value to his mother. But his upbringing, and youth were of little consequence now. He fished into his pocket, produced a silver cigarette case, and ran his fingers over the inscription. Darling Jimmy, it read, yours forever, Russell. 'Forever' had meant two years, seventeen days and four hours. He knew, because he had calculated every hour and every minute, and had feasted on the good times and wept over the bad.

He lit a cigarette and drew in the smoke with a slow deliberate air; widening his nostrils as he exhaled. He'd intended to give up, but that was yet another thing that didn't matter anymore, another responsibility lifted from his shoulders. He was a dead man already.

He wondered briefly what his mother would feel, and his sister. What would Victoria say? He smiled to himself. Victoria would probably be pleased; his sexuality had always been an embarrassment to her. He imagined the headlines in the local paper. Would it say, 'Gay Vicar Commits Suicide'? Or maybe, 'Vicar of St Faiths Loses Everything in Insurance Gamble'? What other reason could they find? They certainly wouldn't say, 'Man of God Loses His Faith'.

He took another long pull on the cigarette, and looked at his watch. It was almost six o'clock on Saturday evening, twenty-four hours since he'd argued with Russell, thirty-two hours since he'd spoken to his agent and been told that his Lloyds losses far exceeded anything he possessed. He ought to write a note, explain the reasons; explain that he had lost his faith both in mankind and in God.

With an almost violent movement James stubbed out the cigarette, went over to the bureau, and snatched up a pen and some writing paper. He stared at the blank sheet for some time. Then he pushed them both back into the cubby hole, picked up the telephone and dialled his mother's number. An answering machine told him that she was out playing bridge and would be back by nine o'clock.

9

He was tempted to leave a message, saying that he was the local burglar and that it was kind of her to advise him of a convenient time to rob her blind, but his heart wasn't in it.

'Mother,' he said, 'it's me.' But he said no more, and replaced the receiver.

Next he telephoned Victoria.

Andrew, his brother-in-law, answered: 'Hullo.'

'Hello, Andrew. It's James. Is Vicky in?'

'I'll go and see,' Andrew replied in a surly voice.

'Hi, James,' Victoria came on the line.

'Vicky?'

'James, is it important? I'm awfully busy: Alice has to be in the village hall in ten minutes – the ballet class are putting on a concert – I can't really talk now.'

'Russell has left me,' he blurted.

She sighed. 'James, I'm really not interested in your sordid little affair.'

'I just wanted to— '

She interrupted him. 'For God's sake, James,' she hissed, 'I have children in the house, I can't talk about it now.'

'Talking to me on the phone won't contaminate the kids, Vicky. Look, I'm feeling very low. I don't suppose I can come round, can I? I could watch my niece in her show.'

'James, you know how Andrew feels. Thomas is at

a very vulnerable age.'

'Vicky? What are you saying? My nephew's safe enough with me! You know that.'

She sighed again. 'I know that, but Andrew's doesn't. He doesn't feel comfortable about it, he doesn't want ... well, you know. Your ... ' she gave a little cough, 'your friends mentioned in front of the children.'

'I don't want to talk about Russell. It's Lloyds. You know they've crashed? Vicky, I've lost everything.'

'Look, James. I really can't talk now. Alice is waiting to go. Ring me early next week, we could maybe meet for coffee.'

'Next week may be too late, Vicky.'

'Oh, for God's sake, James, cut the melodrama. Phone me next week.' She replaced the receiver.

James sat for some moments listening to the dead line. Finally he gently replaced the instrument into its cradle. He pushed himself up by the arms of the chair and went upstairs. The vicarage had a large square hall with a solid oak staircase. He went into his bedroom and sorted through his ties and belts, but could find nothing suitable for his purpose. He went back downstairs and out into the garage, where he found a stout nylon rope. He took it back into the house and up the stairs.

The rope was coarse, and for some absurd reason he was appalled by the thought of the rough fibres biting into his flesh. He went back into his bedroom and, from his tie rack, he selected a silk cravat – a present from Russell the previous Christmas, but he didn't think of that. He removed the white clerical collar, and bound the soft material around his neck. Then he went into the bathroom and emptied his bladder; he did not want to be found soaked in his own urine.

He made a crude loop with one end of the rope, and tied the other end around the banister rail. Slipping the noose over his head, he climbed over the balustrade, balanced precariously for a few seconds, then allowed his weight to topple forward. He put out his hand in a half-hearted attempt to save himself, and plummeted down toward the black-and-white tiles of the hall floor.

James Laughton's last mortal thought was: that his act would show Russell, Lloyds – and God – exactly what he thought of them.

Death did not come quickly.

James was not plunged into instant oblivion; his neck did not break with a sickening crack. The rope tugged and bounced as his weight extended it to its full length, before, slowly and mercilessly, strangling him to death.

CHAPTER ONE

'It won't do, Toby. It simply won't do.'

The keeper shifted his weight from one foot to the other. He touched the peak of his well-worn cap. 'Sorry ma'am. But they're not—'

She interrupted him:

'Don't tell me that they're not old birds.' She shook her head. 'Do you think I can't tell, so long as they're minus their feet and feathers? Those birds have been around for a good few winters. It's plain from the thick layers of fat around the breasts. And look at them, they're full of shot! We'll all get lead poisoning if we eat those.' She pushed her fingers through her hair. She wore no makeup and felt, but did not look, every one of her forty-four years. Moving her delicate hands with a light fluid gesture, she brushed a small piece of lint from the front of her sweater. Her skin was pale and she had a spattering of granny spots; soft blotches of discoloration on the backs of her hands. Her nails were varnished in a very pale pink, and elegantly manicured.

Toby bit into his bottom lip. 'Well, shall I leave them? Or not?'

Lavinia sighed. 'Of course you must leave them, but next time, young birds, remember?' Her face was strained; she was taking all the problems of the day out on the gamekeeper. 'And I'd like them a little sooner, too. The last shoot was well over a week ago.'

'They was in the fridge,' Toby said defensively.

What was the man playing at? The lady of the house ought to have the very best birds, not the rejects – and she could think of no apter way to describe the present offerings.

'I've a good mind to make you show me the birds before you pluck and draw them,' Lavinia continued.

It seemed that Toby could find no answer to that.

Lavinia reached forward and snatched the pheasants out of his hands. She closed the door in his face and leaned her back against it, wondering why she had made such a fuss over such a trivial matter. Suddenly calm, she smiled. 'There's more flies caught with honey than with vinegar,' Mrs Jarvis would say, and she was right. Losing her temper with Toby would only ensure that her next lot of pheasants would be even older and tougher.

Feeling guilty for her curtness she opened the

door again. She intended to call Toby back. She wouldn't apologise, but she'd charm him; she'd ask him about the next day's plans. Josh, in his usual understated manner, had said that it was to be an important shoot. He'd invited his bank manager, Brian Bamford, and he'd told Lavinia that he was 'determined to put on a good show', although for the life of her she couldn't understand why he was so concerned. She frowned. Josh saw an awful lot of Brian these days. What was it Josh had said about the shoot? That he wanted to 'appear in charge' of his own destiny. To show the bank manager that old money went a lot further than new money and that 'traditions would go on and overcome all adversity'. Lavinia shook her head. What did it matter what a country bank manager thought? Why should Josh bother to impress Brian Bamford? Josh's finances were stable enough.

She called after the gamekeeper, but he had already climbed into his Land Rover and was noisily revving the engine so that her voice could not be heard.

Lavinia frowned. It was all Mrs Jarvis's fault, going sick the day before a shoot – how could she? Given more notice, Lavinia could have called caterers in. As it was . . .

'Damn.' She dumped the pheasants in the refrigerator, slammed the door; took a despairing look around the chaotic kitchen, and laughed aloud. 'To hell with it all,' she said, her shoulders suddenly relaxed and her face

15

looking lighter and less troubled, she made her way up to her bedroom.

She ran herself a bath, added copious amounts of sweet-smelling oil and immersed her slight body in the fragrant water. The last of the autumn sunshine poured through the bathroom window and played upon her collection of cut glass and crystal bottles, sending dazzling patterns over the walls and ceiling. It was a collection started long ago on their honeymoon in Venice. She lay back and enjoyed the bright colours, and wished for all the world that she and Josh could return, be it very briefly, to those first happy carefree days before the children had come along, and before she'd had to deal with the whims of cooks and gamekeepers.

After her bath she pulled on a silk robe and lay on the heavily draped four-poster bed. She drew her knees up to her chest and enjoyed the sensation of warmth and well being that inevitably came to her at that time in the day. She massaged body lotion into her legs and thighs and idly wondered how long Josh would be. This was the time that Lavinia enjoyed the most; soon Josh would bring her a drink and they would chat about their day and more than likely they would make love. They would then dress for the dinner Mrs Jarvis had prepared – only tonight there would be no ready meal. They always dressed for dinner, always made an occasion of it, even when the children weren't home. It was what people like them did; it occupied the time, it marked off the sections of the day and it gave their lives order. Josh's parents had had the same routine and probably his grandparents before them, although Lavinia doubted they made love with quite such passion and regularity as their heir. She giggled at the thought of them lying under that same canopy doing the things she and Josh did — but then but why not? They too were of the leisured class; they had had the time and the energy just as she did . . .

Sometimes Lavinia thought she had too much energy, too much time, to indulge in her pleasures and fantasies. She felt her breasts though the soft silk of her gown, her nipples were hard and raised. Where was that husband of hers? She pushed her hand between her legs. Resting her middle finger on her clitoris, she pressed hard and then released the pressure. 'Come on Josh,' she said aloud. 'Otherwise I'll have to start without you.'

CHAPTER TWO

It was almost dark when Jocelyn Elliot returned from his walk. He had walked almost to Applegate Farm, across the ridge nearly as far as the ancient gibbet, and cut down by the Lady Well. He had been checking the pegs that the keeper had placed to mark where the guns would stand on the following day.

The October evening was crisp and bright, and the leaves in the park crunched under his feet as he made his way homeward. He looked at his watch. 'Drat this silly idea of putting the clocks back,' he muttered aloud. 'We lose a good hour of daylight every evening.'

Thinking that Josh was talking to her, the black Labrador pricked up her ears, and trotted a little closer to her master's heels, almost tripping him up. Her dark brown eyes stared up at him, and the gently curved tail wagged so vigorously that the rear end of the dog swayed from side to side.

Josh smiled. 'Well? What do you think, Fen? Hey? What do you think, girl? We'll have a short day's shooting tomorrow because of this dratted winter time, you know.' The dog responded with even more exaggerated tail wagging.

'Come on old girl. Let's get home. The Missis will wonder where we are.'

He entered Hulver Castle by the gun room door. The dog, Fen, knowing that her suppertime had come, bounced up and down on sinewy back legs that looked far too frail to support such a hefty rear end.

'Calm down, old girl, calm down.' Josh opened a tin, smelt it, turned up his nose, and prised the dog meat into a large stainless steel bowl. He added a handful of dog meal, and mashed it all altogether with a bent, discoloured fork.

'Sit,' he then commanded.

Fen, who had already anticipated her master's orders, sat back on her haunches. Her tongue darted in and out of her mouth, and a trickle of saliva left her soft lips and formed a bead of liquid on the quarry-stone flags.

Josh placed the bowl at her feet. The dog shook with excitement but made no move toward the food. Josh waited for a few seconds more before lifting his hand in the air and giving Fen permission to proceed. 'Good dog,' he said. At this signal, the dog jumped to her feet and began to devour the contents of the bowl in huge greedy swallows. Before Josh had hung up his coat and changed out of his outdoor shoes, the food had disappeared, and the dog had picked up the empty bowl in her gentle mouth and had carried it off to her basket, settling down with a contented sigh.

'You silly old thing,' Josh said, stroking her head as he padded out of the gun room in his socks. The dog waddled after him. He made his way across the marbled hall, down the long ornate library corridor and on into the kitchen. The warmth of the room engulfed him. Lavinia had left the lid of the Aga up; he gently replaced it. The kitchen was in complete disarray. He remembered that Mrs Jarvis, their cook, had telephoned that morning to say that she was sick and couldn't come in. So Lavinia had started to prepare the shoot lunch for the following day. Huge amounts of steak and kidney were cooling in an earthenware bowl and a cookbook lay open on the table. Beside the book were weighing scales and the basic ingredients for making pastry.

Josh called out his wife's name, but she did not reply. He glanced at the kitchen clock.

'Good Lord,' he said, half to himself and half to the dog. 'Is that the time? It's well past six o'clock.' Speaking directly to the dog he said, 'I know exactly where your Missis will be.'

The *City Post* was lying open on the edge of the kitchen table and a headline caught his eye.

Lloyds Blamed for Vicar's Death, it read.

Josh paused and scanned the print. 'Good God, Jimmy Laughton! I'd no idea that he went into the Church. Well, I'll be blowed.' He shook his head and smiled. 'Always was a funny one, was Jimmy. I'm not surprised he took up the cloth – he'd have felt at home in a frock.' He continued to read.

The newspaper explained that James Laughton's losses had been heavy and that it was assumed that he'd taken his own life because he had no hope of ever paying his debts.

Josh shivered. Surely things weren't that bad? Anyway, even if they were, ending it all didn't exactly solve anything. Lloyds' debts went on even after death. If you weren't around to pay, then your heirs would have to cough up. He read to the very end of the article and then skimmed the print again. James Laughton had left a mother, a sister, a niece and a nephew; there was no mention of a wife. That figures, thought Josh. He nodded sadly. Poor old Jimmy Laughton. Always was a misfit. And always would be, even in memory. He frowned. 'Please God,' he murmured. 'Let me never get that desperate.'

Josh looked round at the chaos in the kitchen, shrugged his shoulders, and made his way into the old butler's pantry. The dog sighed and, with her head resting on her front paws, she settled herself in front of the Aga. Josh found a small silver tray; onto that he gathered two glasses, ice, and a bottle of malt whisky. Carrying the tray carefully, he proceeded through the marble hall and up the great staircase.

He pushed the door of his bedroom open with his foot, and smiled as his wife's handsome face greeted him. She was lying on the bed, and was clad in a deep wine coloured silk robe. He knew that under the robe she was naked and he smiled as he caught her eye. Poor Jimmy Laughton, he had no one as wonderful as Lavinia to live for. He offered up a silent prayer of thanks, then added an amendment, praying that his loses would never be great enough to effect the love of his life.

'Darling,' she said, 'I thought you were never coming.'

'And I thought, as you'd got this lunch on tomorrow, there was no rush,' he replied.

She laughed. 'I'm not going to let a silly little lunch spoil my evening. I'll get up early tomorrow and finish off. I've cooked the steak and kidney, and I've stewed the apples. I've only got to make the pies.'

'I could take them to the pub, you know.'

'Darling, I know. You said. But they do expect to come here. Don't fuss, I'll manage, there's really nothing to it.' Her face belied her words.

He sat down heavily on the bed. 'You left the lid of the Aga up.'

'Whoops! Oh, God, I'm sorry. Did you close it?'

'Of course.' He handed her a drink and leaned toward her. He was a pleasant looking man of sixty-three, well built, with a square face and brown eyes. His once mousy brown hair was now grizzled with grey and his face was lined and weather-beaten. His smile was wide and generously given, his chin held the slightest suggestion of a dimple. His hands were rough and broad, for although Jocelyn Elliot was Lord Hulver of Hulver Castle, he did not see himself as an aristocrat – indeed, he had never once occupied his place in the House of Lords. Josh preferred the role of country gentleman; nothing made him happier than his hours spent shooting and fishing and organising the wonderful estate that he had inherited on his father's death.

His wife Lavinia was the daughter of Clarence Seabrook, one-time First Lord of the Admiralty. Now into her forties she could no longer be described as pretty, for her looks had matured; she was an elegant, beautiful woman, slim and lithe. She had light brown, almost hazel eyes, an oval face, straight nose, full lips and high cheek bones. Her not completely natural hair colour was deep and brown, and she wore it somewhere between ear and shoulder length in a sweeping bob. But her most striking asset was the way that she moved. Her mannerisms had a cat-like sensual flow; she had the ability to make even the most mundane action look fluid and exceedingly sexy.

'Did you see that article in the paper?' Josh said. Even as he asked the question, he was praying that she hadn't.

'Darling, I haven't had a minute! I haven't even glanced at the paper.'

'Jimmy Laughton hanged himself.' Josh conjured up a mental picture of the hanged man. The image portrayed a spotty adolescent, a vulnerable, unsure, rather chubby boy of sixteen. The sadness and hopelessness of his contemporary, made him shudder.

'Should that mean something to me?'

'I was at school with him. I was never his friend , he was as queer as a clockwork orange. There was some scandal concerning him and a younger boy. All the same, to have killed himself . . . it's unnerving.' He shook his head as if trying to shake the image from his brain

'Why'd he do it?'

Josh avoided her eyes. 'Doesn't really say. No suicide letter.' He made a mental note to remove the newspaper before Lavinia could read it. One mustn't upset

24

the womenfolk if one could avoid it. That had always been his father's maxim and, against Josh's better judgement, he had always tried to live by it.

'Probably fell out with his boyfriend.'

'He was a vicar.'

'It doesn't mean he didn't have a boyfriend,' Lavinia said.

'No, I suppose not.' He smiled. 'Oh well, nothing to be done, is there?' He studied her face, somehow hoping that Lavinia might have an answer. That she might reply that, yes, there was something to be done. His wife was a wise woman and he relied upon, and trusted, her good sense.

One of Lavinia's knees was poking out from between the edges of her robe. Idly Josh ran his finger over it and, almost absentmindedly, pushed his broad strong hand up and over her thigh.

He took a long sip of his scotch, placed it on the bedside table and tugged at the cord on her gown. Lavinia rolled over onto her back. As the gown fell open, she drew up her knees and let them fall apart.

'God, you're beautiful,' he said, pushing all thoughts of his one-time acquaintance from his mind.

'Then worship me in the time-honoured fashion,' she said and laughed.

He didn't have time to remove his heavy corduroy

25

trousers or his thick vyella shirt before Lavinia had unzipped him and pulled him close to her.

'Just exactly how long have you been waiting up here for me?'

'Long enough,' she giggled as she ran her hands down her body and lifted her hips toward him.

'Hey, give a chap a chance, you seductress, you! It's cold out there, a chap needs a little warmth and stimulation—' but before he could say more, Lavinia's moist warm mouth was clamped around his penis, causing it to spring into life.

Josh saw his wife as filled with virtue. In truth she was no more virtuous than the next woman, but she was tender and loving. He had never ceased to be thrilled and amazed by her lusty sexual appetite, and he'd loved her from the first moment they'd met. She was a deep thinker and she understood people. Josh didn't understand people but he understood business and the running of the estate. They were, he believed, equally balanced and perfectly matched. She was beautiful and sexy and he loved her, and she was his wife; what did anything else matter? What complaints could he possibly have? Compared to the lonely desolate life James Laughton had led, his was on a different plain. And things would work out; didn't they always?

Afterwards, as they lay in the warm afterglow of sex, sipping their drinks and delaying the moment before they had to get up and dress, Lavinia said, 'Josh, I was thinking, maybe this autumn, for our wedding anniversary . . .' she hesitated. 'Well, maybe we could go back to Venice. You know, have a sort of second honeymoon?'

He nuzzled into her neck. 'There's nothing we can do in Venice, that we can't do here,' he said.

She kissed him full on the lips. 'You can't have forgotten the Danielli,' she said. 'Nor how we came by our coloured-glass collection?'

He chuckled. 'I gave you a glass bottle every time we made love in a different position.'

She pushed her hand between his legs. 'Not quite! I seem to remember that there weren't enough different patterns and colours to cope with the demand.'

He chuckled again and eased her over on to her side, coming up close behind her. 'Do you think they might have more in stock?'

She pushed her hand between her legs and rested his flaccid penis between her thighs.

'Expecting a bit much aren't you? I'm not as young as I was then.'

'Then you won't need to buy quite so much glass!' She felt him stir. 'On the other hand . . . ' She wriggled close to him. 'Can we, Josh? Can we plan to go to Italy in the autumn?'

'Vinnie, I...'

'Yes?'

How could he tell her? 'Not next year darling. You know how busy I am with the shoot in the autumn.'

She pulled away from him. 'Mustn't let your marriage interfere with the shoot, must you?' she said sulkily. She rolled out of the bed.

'Vinnie, don't go. I didn't mean what you're implying. It's just that . . . ' His voice trailed away.

She sat back down on the edge of the bed and, tilting her head to one side, she ran her hand down his body, stopping at his lower abdomen and cradling him in her hand.

'Please?' she said.

He moistened his lips and smiled. 'If it's at all possible, then yes, of course I'll take you to Venice.' He knew it was an empty promise, but the problem was a whole year away. She'd probably forget all about it. Suddenly Josh felt sickened by the thought of what the next year might bring. He pushed the horror of it from his mind; her touch was beginning to excite him.

'Vinnie, come back to bed,' he said.

She slipped back onto the bed and, taking her from behind, he made love to her again.

'I'm going to start counting from now,' she said.

'Counting?'

'Positions. That's two pieces of Venetian glass you

28

owe me already.'

Dinner consisted of a microwave meal from Marks and Spencer, served on fine bone china with silver cutlery and cut glass crystal, in the small dining room. The room was one of the many later additions to the house, which had originally been built in 1135 for Edmund, the first Lord Hulver. The room formed a major part of the north-west wing and contained the original 17th century oak panelling and solid oak doors, crowned with exuberant cresting surrounding the Hulver coat of arms. Although the room was generally known as the small dining room, its proportions were still quite magnificent. The Elliots ate their meal illuminated by warm candlelight, with Lavinia chatting excitedly about their forthcoming holiday.

At ten o'clock, they watched the news on television. At ten-thirty Josh let Fen out for a final run. Standing in the cold frosty garden he called:

'Now old girl, don't you choose tonight to chase a late night rabbit. It's cold and I want my bed.' Within ten minutes the dog returned and with a fond pat and a promise of good things on the morrow, her master settled her in her basket and left her to sleep.

By eleven-thirty the Elloits were soundly asleep, their legs and hands intertwined and Lavinia's, if not Josh's dreams untroubled.

CHAPTER THREE

The day of the shoot dawned wet and misty.

Lavinia Elliot pulled a Harris tweed skirt up over her narrow hips, wriggled into a cream silk blouse, and topped it all with a bottle-green cardigan. She slipped her feet into a pair of tan leather loafers and stood back from her bevelled mirror to survey the whole effect. She ran her hands over her thighs and hips. Not bad, she thought, for four children, the last two of which, were twins. She turned this way and that, decided that she looked unattractively frumpish and peeled the whole ensemble off again, throwing the discarded garments on a chair for her daily help to put away.

She was standing in her underwear flicking through the clothes in her wardrobe, the hangers grating loudly on the metal rail, when Josh, dressed in plus-fours and a check shirt, came up behind her. He kissed the back of her neck.

'Good morning, Lady Hulver,' he said. 'Did I mention that I love you?'

She turned to face him and put her slim arms around his neck. 'I love you too, Lord Hulver. And yes, Josh, you've mentioned it every morning for the past twenty-two years.' She smiled up at him.

He kissed her neck again. 'Ah yes, but did I mention that I've loved you a little more, every single one of those years?'

She snuggled up to him. 'Oh Josh, we are so very, very lucky. We have so much to be thankful for.'

Had anyone asked Lavinia if she loved Josh, her answer would more than likely have been: 'of course, he's my husband', as if the one naturally went with the other. She would not have gone as far as to say that it was her duty to love him. Nevertheless, that's what she felt. Lavinia knew all about duty: it was her duty to give to local charities, both with her time and with her money. She dutifully went to church, not so that people might see her there – she cared nothing for what people thought of her – nor for any religious compulsion, but she considered it right that she went; it was her duty. So it was with many of her habits, they were performed out of her sense of duty, and for no other reason.

The married state suited her well. Sex too had been both enjoyable and comfortable. But love? Love had been ungrudgingly but only gradually given. Lavinia had plighted her troth and given her body, but love had not

31

come naturally. And now, as she stood in her husband's arms she thought: he loves me so much more than I love him, I wish I felt his passion. Not sexual passion, her relationship with Josh had always been rich in that. But that extreme state of love, that feeling of being actually in love. Lavinia was not certain of the exact nature of this elusive emotion, for she had never experienced it. It was a sort of fancy to her; something she knew existed but constantly evaded her and taunted her. She was like a child at Christmas leaving notes for the unseen Santa Claus, convinced that he, in the generally accepted form, did not exist; but sensing, rather than knowing, that he had a somewhat better substitute. Was that it? Had Lavinia something better than extreme love? She loved Josh but she wasn't in love with him. Perhaps, she thought, I'm oversexed – perhaps my carnal desires choke love away.

Perhaps it was better to love rather than be in love? The love she felt for Josh was both comfortable and comforting – an undemanding, decent, safe feeling; an emotion that dwelt a thousand miles away from obsessive love. And yet she felt sexual passion. That was the trouble of course; she felt the two should be combined, as if half of the pleasure was missing. The heady lusty feeling she had when making love, the all-consuming bodily need she felt when her naked flesh touched Josh's, seemed to bear no relationship with the safe gentle married life she led.

Lavinia frowned.

Dear Josh, why had she never fallen in love with him? Why had love come so quietly, as if it were an unimportant, inferior emotion? She felt she had been cheated. True love, she thought, was the one thing she had gone without.

Josh's hands were firmly placed on her buttocks, gently rotating, slipping over the fine silk of her slip. She ran her fingers over the course tweed of his plus-fours. She pushed back from him so that she could see his face. Not meeting her eyes, he pulled her close to him burying his head into her neck. 'I have to go and let Fen out. She'll pee herself with excitement if I leave her any longer.'

They kissed, and Jocelyn left the dressing room to exercise his dog. She turned and watched him leave. What was wrong with him? He seemed forever preoccupied these days, as if he carried a guilty secret. But Josh was hopelessly transparent, perhaps the worst liar she had ever met. He could hardly keep a Christmas surprise, let alone tell a guilty lie.

Lady Lavinia Elliot of Hulver Castle continued to slide the hangers along the rail. She finally decided on a short, brown, corduroy skirt, and a green-and-cream checked blouse. She tucked a pale green silk cravat into her neckline and, with her unique fluid movement, ran down the wide marble staircase.

Steve Jarvis, Jocelyn's odd-job man, had already lit

a fire in the huge open fireplace in the hall below. The wood coughed and spluttered, sending sparks over the black-and-white marble floor.

Lavinia made her way to the kitchen, where Josh was standing next to the deep ceramic sink. He had The Financial Times spread out on the work top, it being the only surface in the entire kitchen not effected by Lavinia's lunch preparations. He cradled a cup of tea in his left hand and he adjusted a pair of gold-rimmed glasses with his right.

She bustled into the room. 'Have you had breakfast? Shall I do you some toast?' She didn't wait for him to reply, but put two slices of bread into the toasting rack and slammed the Aga lid down onto it. She looked at her watch, ran her fingers through her hair and, with an exasperated sigh, she surveyed the chaotic kitchen.

Josh, as if to read her mind, said, 'What's wrong with Mrs Jarvis anyway?'

'God knows,' Lavinia replied. 'Cold or something. She must be quite sick, I've never known her miss a shoot day before.' Lavinia didn't add that this would be the first shoot lunch she had ever cooked all by herself.

'I can take them to the pub, you know. I have offered.'

Lavinia looked irritated. 'Cool it, Josh. I can manage,' she ran her fingers through her hair again. 'Doris will be here in a moment. She'll soon clear this lot up and she'll set the table.'

Josh was gazing out of the window. 'Just look at the weather. The birds will never get off the ground, and it'll be dark by four.' He spoke in a voice loaded with gloom.

Lavinia looked at her watch again. 'Shouldn't you be getting ready? They'll be here in fifteen minutes.'

'I thought you were making me some toast.'

Lavinia turned sharply in the direction of the Aga. 'Oh shit,' she said, rushing over to rescue the toast. She flicked the Aga lid up and thick blue smoke bellowed into the kitchen. The smoke alarm situated just outside the kitchen door gave out a series of piercing screeches.

'Oh shit,' she said again.

'Vinnie, you swear in such a lady-like way,' Josh laughed. 'I've never heard anyone pronounce "shit", with quite such a refined accent.'

Lavinia ignored him. She was busy trying to scrape the carbon from the toast, but the burnt square disintegrated and crumbled into ragged pieces.

'Oh shit,' she said yet again.

The smoke alarm gave one last piercing bleep. Josh was still laughing. 'Don't worry, old thing. I'll have a liquid breakfast today.' He tapped the silver hip flask that he'd filled earlier and placed it in the pocket of his Barbour jacket.

Lavinia frowned at him. 'Why the "old thing,

" Josh?'

'What?'

'The "old thing" – the P.G. Woodhouse mode. You sound like your father talking, and that means that there's something worrying you.'

He raised his eyes to the ceiling. 'Vinnie, oh Vinnie, you should be a psychologist only you wouldn't be a very good one. I have no worries,' he shook his head to emphasize the fact, 'except whether the birds will get off the ground.'

She noticed that he avoided her eyes as he spoke.

He whistled, and Fen appeared at his heels. He picked up his gun and cartridge belt, rechecked his pockets and walked down the library corridor to the hall.

'You coming to say hello?' He called to Lavinia over his shoulder.

Lavinia brushed her hands on her skirt, pushed her fingers through her hair and followed him between the long cases of books.

The huge front door stood wide-open and cold damp air rushed in, causing the logs in the fire to roar and spit. Steve Jarvis stood to the right of the door, almost to attention. He was twenty-four, broad and handsome. He too was dressed for shooting, although the only gun he would hold that day would be Lord Hulver's, when it was time to reload.

Hot toddies were lined up on a side table. The game cart, although parked at a discreet distance, was in full view of the open door. Several Land Rovers and Range Rovers were parked on the drive, and little groups of men and dogs greeted each other. Fen, in a state of ecstatic excitement, ran around in a circle sniffing the ground and looking as if she were doing a very useful job.

As the stable clock struck eight-thirty several more vehicles arrived. Lavinia and Jocelyn stood just inside the door and greeted each of their guests as they entered. The first was Rupert Seabrook, Lavinia's younger brother.

At forty-two he was as plain as Lavinia was handsome. He had a round fleshy face, exaggerated by his completely hairless head. His ears were rather prominent and he wore narrow oval-shaped glasses to aid the sight of his dull hazel eyes. His nose was broad and fleshy, his lips thin and covering small even teeth. Although short of stature he was a little taller than his sister. He was a nervous, clumsy man, always bumping into things and forever apologizing.

'Vinnie, darling,' he said, kissing his sister on both cheeks, 'you look ravishing.'

She laughed. 'Oh please, Rupert, I'm harassed and disorganized and, all in all, pretty dowdy. Ravishing, I am not.'

'To me you look pretty ravishing,' he said and

kissed her cheek a third time.

In one swift movement he gulped down the drink Josh proffered, causing Lavinia to raise her eyebrows. He went over to the side table and helped himself to another. Seeing that Lavinia was watching him he said, 'Uh-uh. Big sister's monitoring me, I can sense it.'

'Take it easy, Rupe. You've got a long boozy day ahead of you.'

He gave a rather tense laugh. 'You sound like my wife,' he said.

Lavinia made no reply.

He turned to Jocelyn. 'Talking of wives, Josh, are we shooting right through? It'll be dark by four-thirty.'

Josh looked at Lavinia. 'Would that be a problem? It makes sense.'

'That would suit me well. The more time I have the better. What time do you want food?'

Josh pulled a face. 'What? Say . . . three-thirty?'

Rupert looked at his sister, 'Be a sweetie, Vinnie? Go and phone Rosie and let her know what time to come.'

Lavinia looked alarmed. 'For lunch? Is Rosemary coming for lunch?'

'Well, Josh did say – last week when we were shooting at the Andersons – he invited all the wives. Shame you weren't there, Vinnie. You missed a really good day.'

Lavinia fought back her angry words.

'Josh?' She said.

Josh was flustered. 'Didn't I mention it?'

'You know damned well you didn't. What's the matter with you, Josh? You no longer communicate with me.'

'We could go to the pub,' he said weakly.

'It's not a problem.' She tried to smile but the expression was more of a grimace.

She folded her arms in front of her. 'So, who's coming? I mean, how many?'

The hall had become quite crowded, and there was a high-pitched buzz of conversation.

'Let's see.' Josh started to count on his fingers. 'There's Rupert and Rosie. Then Major Hunt – he won't bring anyone. The McTodds – I expect Ailsa will come with Philip. The Miles-Joneses – Hillary usually comes, she doesn't trust George to drive home. The bank manager, of course. Smile sweetly at him, darling, but don't get involved in a conversation. Not only will he bore you rigid, he'll try and confuse you with meaningless figures.' Josh took a breath. 'The Osbourne-Penningtons – I see Brooke is already here. Julian and Ursula Henchforth and a couple of young city chaps – you don't know them, David Trevelyan and Richard Brown-Cummings. I expect they'll have girl-friends and— '

Lavinia was desperately trying to count up on her fingers as Jocelyn had long since given up. 'Josh you've lost me. Just tell me how many?'

'Well, nine guns of course, and I expect everyone will have a wife, or . . . what is it they call them these days? A partner, yes . . . that's right, a partner – except dear old Bill Hunt . . . so that's? Let me see.'

'Eighteen including me, although I doubt that I'll have time to eat anything.' Lavinia was not smiling.

"I'm sorry," he said.

'I don't mind,' she insisted, 'but the least you could have done is given me warning.'

'How was I to know that Mrs Jarvis would go sick? I've offered to take everyone to the pub.'

'Josh, for goodness sake, that's not the point. You're deliberately missing the point.'

'Hullo,' boomed Major Hunt. 'I say, Lavinia, jolly nice of you to put up with us all like this! What?' He put his arm around her and kissed her, not on the cheek but fully on the lips. 'How are you, me dear? You're looking jolly well, I must say.'

Josh raised his eyebrows and, walking backwards, he merged into the gathered party.

The clock on the stable block struck nine. A whistle blew from somewhere in the courtyard and, gradually, the buzz of conversation moved toward the stout oak doors and out to the front of the castle.

William Hunt, the retired major, gave Lavinia

another full-lipped peck and joined the others. He was a frail old man of seventy-five; he had a square, worn looking face, brown rheumy eyes, very black bushy eyebrows and snow-white hair. His neck was exceptionally thin and scrawny, the collar of his shirt standing a couple of inches away from his flesh. He was always immaculate in both dress and manners. He'd seen active service in North Africa, and frequently said that the battle of El-Alamein compared favorably with a shoot day on the Hulver Estate.

Lavinia stood with her arms folded in front of her and watched them go. She gave a rather weak wave as the trailer and game cart left by the East drive, accompanied by the barks of excited dogs.

From the corner of her eye she could see Brooke Osbourne-Pennington packing things into a basket and generally organizing the Range Rover that she and her husband Sir Henry had arrived in.

Lavinia was in a bad mood; she had neither the time nor the inclination to converse with Henry's tiresome American wife. Brooke Osbourne-Pennington was just too enthusiastic, she, just adored, everything, and what she didn't, just adore, she, just loved. Lavinia rather resented a foreigner marrying into one of Britain's oldest families. Pennington Manor was one of England's finest houses, set in a beautiful traditional farming and sporting estate. It was a world that Brooke Osbourne-Pennington couldn't possibly understand.

Lavinia was different – she knew the ways of country life, she'd been brought up in the county set. She was the right wife for Jocelyn, the right woman to care for the Hulver Estate, she was from the right kind of family background. In other words, she was a suitable match for Lord Hulver. When she'd first met him she had felt sorry for him. He was in his late thirties and had been left both a widower and a grieving parent after his wife Celia and his beloved son, also named Jocelyn, and heir both to the title and the estate, had been killed in a horrific car crash.

Rumour had it that his wife had been drunk at the time – certainly she had a reputation for drunkenness – but her husband had never confirmed that as the truth. Josh showed neither bitterness nor regret, but entered into his marriage with Lavinia with passion and loyalty. And a kind of love had grown, just as her father had said it would. When at nineteen she had met Josh Elliot, her only emotions were ones of compassion, and she determined that she would compensate for all his sorrow. She had done well; she was as perfect a wife as Josh could hope for. She ran the house smoothly, and lovingly cared for their children; both motherhood and marriage had suited her well. Her first two pregnancies had not produced the longed-for son and heir, but her third had brought forth not one, but two bouncing boys, and Jocelyn Elliot's life had once more felt complete. Had the twins been girls, then Lavinia would have carried on producing baby Elliots until she had presented Josh with a boy to inherit the estates and title. She considered it her duty, it was part of the deal, and the way things were meant to be. How could a woman like Brooke, an American reputed to have met Henry in a New York bar, possibly understand all that the title Lady demanded of her? What did she know about sacrifices and tradition, how could she possibly hope to fit in?

It irritated Lavinia that Josh didn't share her views. He thought the American woman charming, 'A breath of fresh air,' was how he described her. And, 'Wasn't it clever of Henry to chose a wife that wasn't part of the establishment?' And, 'Everyone can see how very attractive and intelligent Brooke Osbourne-Pennington is.'

Lavinia had once seen a T-shirt with the logo "Natural Blonde, Please Speak Slowly" emblazoned on the front, and she had rather bitchily told Josh that she thought it might make a suitable present for Lady Brooke.

Remembering her tiff with Josh, and seeing Brooke looking absolutely stunning in plus-fours and a fitted tweed coat, Lavinia decided that she actually hated the woman. Continuing to pretend that she hadn't noticed her, Lavinia turned abruptly into the now silent hall and pulled the big oak doors closed behind her.

CHAPTER FOUR

Lavinia threw another log on the fire and made her way into the great dining room. The room was a later addition to the original tenth-century building, as indeed was much of the rest of the castle. This particular room had been added by the fourteenth Lord Hulver in the early 1770's, and had been designed by Robert Adam. The room was of splendid proportions, with a huge square bay window overlooking the deer park. Four fluted pillars topped with Ionic capitals supported the bay. A deep classical cornice ran around the tops of the walls, which were painted in a subtle green wash, the cornice and dado rail being defined in matt ivory. The mahogany floor, polished to a high shine, showed around the edges of a huge rare eighteenth century Turkish carpet, on which stood a magnificent dining table surrounded by twenty-four Chippendale chairs. The fireplace, one of Adam's finest, had full door-cases on either side, the left-hand one being blind, added purely in deference to symmetry. William and John Adair, two of the master craftsmen of the time, crafted both these cases in 1787.

Lavinia looked around, it was so cold in the room; Josh had turned off the radiators. She tutted. Why, oh why, did he go around turning down the heat? 'Save on the pennies and the pounds will take care of themselves,' he'd say, if ever she should complain. It was ridiculous; the room was freezing. She started to turn the radiators on, but then decided that the room was far too formal and unfriendly for such a dismal day and for such an occasion.

She went back into the hall. The log she had placed on the fire had already burned through and she placed another on the red embers. She opened a door on her right and walked down the long dreary passage that led to the castle's third dining room. This was a much later addition and had been built by Josh's father in the early 1900's, although why he had felt the need for yet another dining room was a mystery to Lavinia. The room was panelled and had three elegant sash-windows that descended to the floor, and served as French windows during the summer months. In the center of each of these windows her late father-in-law had placed a stained-glass panel depicting the Elliot coat of arms; a decoration that Lavinia thought rather vulgar. The room was, however, light and airy. The dining table was designed to seat fourteen but was extremely roomy and Lavinia decided that she could easily squeeze in the extra places. Here too the heating had been turned off. She checked all the radiators and turned them fully on, flicked an imaginary speck of dust off the sideboard and went off in the direction of the kitchen.

She heard voices before she'd reached the end of the library corridor and she pushed the door open tentatively.

Brooke Osbourne-Pennington was seated at the kitchen table sipping coffee, whilst the efficient Mrs Jarvis bustled about tidying, and organizing the shoot lunch.

'Oh! Mrs Jarvis – how are you? I didn't expect you in today – I mean, you said — '

Betty Jarvis interrupted her. 'I couldn't let you down, Lady H.' She gave a loud sniff. 'Only don't get too close to me, my woman. I've got the very devil of a cold. I told our Steven to tell you I'd be in. Didn't he let you know? No? Well, the boy's got air for brains. He was too excited about the shoot, was that one. He's not beating today, you see. He's loading for his Lordship. I said to him, I did, "You be careful, our Steven. Don't go shoot one of them there Lords, will you!"' Mrs Jarvis gave a peel of laughter.

Brooke Osbourne-Pennington looked amused and Lavinia was quite mesmerized.

'No,' Mrs Jarvis continued. 'He's gone up in the world, has our Steven. He went off on Saturday and

46

brought himself a load of fancy kit, he did. I said to him, I said, "What do you want to go and spend all that money on fancy kit for, our Steven, when a pair of jeans and a parka would do as well?" "Well Mum," he says to me. "If his Lordship thinks I looks all right, he'll maybe take me with him on some of them there big shoots, I'll maybe go up in the world," he says. And now look at all this rain. His good kit'll be ruined. Anyway, I says to him, I says, "You're daft," I says. "The likes of you don't mix with the likes of them."' Mrs Jarvis paused just long enough to give a noisy blow into a none-too-clean hanky. 'He's got ideas above his station, Lady H. He has indeed.'

Lavinia had caught Brooke's eye during Mrs Jarvis's long speech, and both women exchanged amused glances.

'Well, I thought he looked very nice, Mrs Jarvis,' Lavinia said.

'You did? Yes, well he's a handsome boy, is my Steven.' She hesitated for only a moment before adding,

'So do you think he will?'

'Who? Will what?' Lavinia said, her brow creased.

'Take him with him? His Lordship, you know, when he shoots away? Can I tell him he will, then?'

'Oh, Mrs Jarvis, that's up to his Lor – I mean, my husband. That's up to him, I couldn't possibly – '

Mrs Jarvis interrupted her again. 'But you'll put in

a good word, won't you?'

'Of course. But I mean, I'll do what — '

'It's as good as done then.' Mrs Jarvis cut her short. She sniffed loudly and tipped a large bag of Brussels sprouts into a bowl.

Why was it, Lavinia wondered, that the staff treated her as one of them? Admittedly a very influential one of them, but even so, they didn't give her the same status as they gave Josh.

Lavinia smiled at Brooke, and, trying her best not to sound sarcastic, she said, 'Hello Brooke. I see you've made yourself at home.'

'Hi,' Brooke gushed. 'Yes indeed, your cook has kept me highly entertained. You know this is excellent coffee. Do you buy it locally? It's absolutely wonderful. Can I get you a cup?'

'No. No thank you. I can get my own.' She spoke sharper than she intended. But Brooke didn't seem to notice.

Lavinia put the coffee pot, milk and sugar, on a tray and led the way through the library corridor into the morning room, calling to Mrs Jarvis, as she left, that she should send Doris in to see her as soon as she arrived.

The morning room was another of Josh's father's light, airy additions, but it had been redecorated by Lavinia not long after her marriage. Facing south, it too had long sash windows down to the floor, its chaste walls were decorated in a pale yellow, the curtains and the carpet were cream, and the deep comfortable sofas were upholstered in a beige and cream tapestry. Devoid of heavy pattern the room was probably Lavinia's favorite. It had an open restful air. The very few paintings dotted about the walls were ones that she and Josh had collected themselves and were light, modern watercolours. Lavinia was relieved to find that Josh's heating economies had not extended into here.

'Gee, I just love this room!' Brooke announced. 'It's like a little oasis amidst all the business of castle life.'

'Castle life?' Lavinia said, raising an eyebrow.

'Well, yes. The rest of the castle is so ... well, it's so old. So ornate. So, well, so busy. This room's so plain and peaceful. You know, Lavinia, you are so, so clever. You must come and advise me. Run your eye over Pennington Manor?'

'I don't think your smart London designer would welcome my opinion.'

'Nonsense, Lavinia, Charles Lavery is a pussycat. He'd welcome your ideas. After all, you have been at it so much longer than me.'

Lavinia gave Brooke a rather cool look, wondering if the woman was just tactless, or if she meant to be rude and ill-mannered.

But she could see what Josh and the other men

49

saw in her. Brooke Osbourne-Pennington was, at forty, a very pretty woman. She and Henry had been married for fourteen years and had patiently waited for twelve of those years to inherit both the title and the Pennington Estates. Brooke had spent the last two years, and a deal of Henry's inheritance, completely refurbishing the Manor House. She was blond, with a smooth, peaches-and-cream complexion. Her hair waved in a delightful, abandoned manner, but always looked untamed, as if it needed a good brushing. 'As if she'd just rolled in the hay,' Josh described it. She was slim, almost to the point of thinness. She had gray eyes, full lips, and dimples appeared in her cheeks when she smiled, which she did often. She was always well dressed, and wore her clothes with such ease that she looked smart even in the most ordinary ensemble. She seemed terribly casual and relaxed about everything. She and Henry had two children, both boys; Henry Jnr, the heir, who was twelve; and Thomas, who was three.

Even Lavinia, for all her dislike of the American, was forced to admit that Brooke was an excellent wife to the twelfth Baronet of Pennington, and a good mother to his children.

'Betty's quite a character, isn't she?' Brooke said

Lavinia frowned. 'Betty?'

'Your cook.'

'Oh, Mrs Jarvis.'

'Mrs Jarvis!' Brooke laughed. 'Tell me, why do you call your daily help Doris, by her Christian name, and your cook, by her surname?'

'It's tradition, Brooke. The way it's always been done.'

'Gee, is that so? Boy, that's really quaint. I never knew that.'

'How could you have known?' Lavinia said, once again rather coldly.

'You must come to Pennington when they shoot next week, Lavinia. You could put me right on so many things. Everyone's coming. I know, why don't you and Josh stay over?'

Lavinia shrugged her shoulders. 'We live so close. We'd love to, of course. But there's the dog, and everything. She's used to her routine.'

'But the keeper will look after the dog. She can stay with everyone else's. He's very good, Lavinia. Quite a wonderful man, in fact. Oh, do stay over, I'd so like your advice on the house. The Henchforths and the McTodds will be staying. It'll be such a fun party. They stayed with us last night, you know. It's such a long drive for them.'

Lavinia felt immediately guilty for not inviting Josh's shooting guests to stay at the castle, and she muttered as much.

'Oh, I don't think they were at all offended. Henry asked them to stay with us months ago, as soon as Josh put the day together, in fact.'

The conversation wore on; they talked about domestic matters, and about their children. Lavinia's younger children, the twins, Sebastian and Quentin, were the same age as Henry junior, and all three were preparing to sit their Common Entrance exam the following year.

'Where is Henry junior going next September?' Lavinia inquired.

Brooke sighed. 'Oh Lavinia, don't ask. I think he should go to Eton, it's such a very English establishment. But Henry insists on Edgeford. You know it's really too bad. Just because Henry went there, he thinks his son should do the same.'

'Not just Henry, surely? His father and his grandfather before him, just like Josh's.'

Brooke rolled her eyes. 'Tell me about it! That's all I ever hear. It seems to me a pretty poor reason – to send your son to a particular school just because your ancestors went there.'

'It's a lovely school, Brooke. Have you seen it?'

'We've driven through Edgeford of course, but I've never actually been round the school. We're booked for the grand tour next month, as a matter of fact.'

'You'll love it. Mark my words.'

'Well, Lavinia, if you say so. But I still wish Henry would consider Eton. The boys look so cute in their little penguin suits.'

Lavinia shook her head and laughed. 'Frankly, Brooke – and I don't mean to be offensive – but I think that's a really bad reason for sending a child to a particular school.'

Brooke frowned. 'What?'

'Just because you like the uniform.'

The American woman did not take offence, but smiled. 'Oh, oh, I see what you mean. You're teasing me! But you must admit, they do look adorable all dressed up, don't they?'

Lavinia softened. The woman seemed to say exactly what she thought, without trying to make a good impression, and without fear of making a fool of herself.

She was open and unafraid, and part of Lavinia both admired and envied her. Despite her prejudices she was beginning to like Brooke Osbourne-Pennington. 'I remember taking Zoë up to London, to buy her prep school uniform. She stood in the school outfitters flicking through the rack, trying to choose her public school, which she informed me, could only be chosen on the strength of the school uniform. She, like you, decided that it was the only reliable way of choosing a decent school.'

They both laughed.

'There, you see! Your daughter and I obviously have sound judgement in common.'

CHAPTER FIVE

The first drive was a disaster.

The beaters were not at all synchronized and the birds flew in every direction, with only a few very low ones flying over the guns who, in any case, had barely reached their stands when the birds were disturbed. A few half-hearted pot shots were taken, but only a handful of birds were brought down. The second drive wasn't much better. This time the guns stood in the cold wet drizzle for over half an hour, shivering. Their fingers were blue with cold, and their shoulders soaked in the downpour before the cry 'Your bird!' was heard, as a great covey of partridges flew overhead, followed by the still low-flying pheasants.

It was almost twelve o'clock when the guns gathered for the third drive on the slopes above Applegate Farm, facing Applegate Wood.

Because of the terrain, Josh found himself sharing a stand with Philip McTodd, an old friend who'd driven down from the borders. Once again, it seemed an interminable length of time before there was any sign of a bird, and the rain was still falling in a steady drizzle. Josh knew it made sense to abandon the day, but he had arranged it months ago and was doggedly opposed to cutting it short.

The men stamped their feet and rubbed their hands together; a rivulet of water ran down Philip McTodd's lined face and dripped off the end of his aquiline nose. Philip was sixty-one but looked much older, his full head of hair was iron gray and his jowls sagged. He had a permanently sad expression and looked always to be full of care. Philip had only one eye on the wood and seemed very distracted.

'Penny for them,' Josh said.

Philip's brow furrowed. 'You're in Lloyds, Josh. What agency are you with?'

'Smith and Benson. Why?'

'It just doesn't look so good. The whole Lloyds thing, that is. Had your fingers burned have you?'

'Hardly. A few thousand, that's all. It's just a blip, Philip. What one expects. It'll recover, you'll see.'

'Few thousand, Josh? What's a few thousand?'

'Six or seven,' Josh lied. You have to look at the sort of money it's been bringing in, Philip. I'm still well in pocket.'

'So am I but, well, rumour has it — '

'Rumour, rumour! Come on, Philip! You're such a pessimist.'

'I hope you're right, Josh. Ailsa's none too pleased. She wants us to get out right away.'

'Even if you did, you'd still have the next three

years' loses to weather. More if you've got open years.'

'I know. But Ailsa calls it damage limitation.' He laughed a rather nervous laugh. 'You don't seem at all concerned, Josh. You really don't think there's anything to worry about?'

'It's a blip, Philip. Just a blip.' Josh was clenching his teeth, pushing the thought of disaster away from his mind. The last thing he wanted was for Bamford to get wind of his liabilities. He was relying on the bank to extend his loans.

'But you see, I borrowed heavily for the Business Park. It seemed such a winner. But now, what with this recession taking hold . . . ' Philip looked down at his boots for a moment. 'You see, Josh, we couldn't take a big loss. We're mortgaged up to our necks. I have no capital at all. All I have is tied up in the land and the house. If Lloyds lean on me, I'll lose everything. Every last bit of it. And that land has been in Ailsa's family for generations.'

Josh patted him on the back and laughed: 'Philip, Philip! Cheer up, old man! When you join Lloyds, I know they tell you it's down to, "the last shirt button and safety pin", but you don't seriously think it will come to that, do you?' But Josh's mouth had taken on a peculiar dry taste. Christ, he thought, I hope Philip's wrong.

Philip gave his friend a weak smile. 'Are you in the know, Josh? Or are you not facing up to the truth?'

Josh leaned back on his shooting stick and laughed

a hollow laugh. 'It's nothing, Philip. You mustn't go around talking like this. Next thing you know the ladies will get wind of it and you know how upset they'll be if they think things are out of our control.' Josh looked him straight in the eye and tried to swallow the metallic taste of fear away. 'It's nothing, Philip. Nothing that won't come right, given time.' He hesitated for a moment. 'Look here, old chap, I'd be grateful if you didn't burden Vinnie with all this scare-mongering. Not good to upset the ladies, don't you know.' There he was again, talking like his father.

'I expect you're right, Josh,' Philip said without even a trace of conviction. 'But Ailsa's probably said something already.'

A cry went up.

'It's yours!' Josh called as a high bird flew out of the copse.

At 2.30, with one last damp drive, the men returned to their vehicles and made their way back to Hulver Castle. The fire in the hall welcomed them, and caused thick steam to billow forth from their wet clothes.

Josh handed Steve his gun. 'Clean that, Jarvis,' he said, 'and then take the beaters round to the kitchen door. Lady Hulver will no doubt have some beer and soup for you all.' He pointed his index finger at Steve. 'But clean the gun first, mind, and lock it in the gun cabinet.' He handed Steve a pair of keys. 'And bring the keys back to me.' Then, as an afterthought, 'Oh, and shut Fen in the gun room, will you? Make sure she has water, and dry her off a bit. You'll find a towel next to her basket.'

'Yes sir,' Steve said, his hand jerked up almost to mid chest height as if he was about to salute.

The cold wet morning had emptied most of the men's hip flasks and everyone, with the exception of Philip McTodd, was very merry, and in Rupert Seabrook's case, rather more than merry. This, however, prevented none of the party from downing the hot toddies handed out by Lavinia and Brooke.

'We're early, I'm afraid, darling,' Josh said.

She was holding a tray of drinks in front of her and Josh was, without any sign of embarrassment, rubbing her buttocks with the palm of his hand as he spoke.

'Josh, dear, I think you've drunk enough,' she said

'Quite right, my dear,' he replied and downed the drink in one.

Lavinia sighed, but smiled. 'You're hopeless,' she whispered.

'Not what you said last night,' he hissed back and winked.

Still smiling, she moved on round the room. Wives and partners had joined the men, and the conversation was thick and occasionally punctuated by a high-pitched laugh or an exclamation; the gathering seemed very loud and very happy. At precisely three-thirty Lavinia announced that the meal was ready and everyone filed into the dining room, although not before Lavinia had repeated the announcement several times.

Doris had done a valiant job with the long mahogany table. Candles glowed in the waning light, and a huge bowl of frosted fruit and nuts acted as a centerpiece.

The extra chairs fitted in without difficulty and the meal commenced. The steak-and-kidney pudding was served with copious amounts of rich fruity claret, the apple pie was laced with brandy and cinnamon cream, and the meal got noisier and noisier the longer it proceeded.

On several occasions Lavinia seized the opportunity to whisper to Josh that perhaps he was drinking a little too much, and at one point she actually accused him of being drunk. Josh replied with thinly veiled and rather schoolboyish sexual innuendoes.

Doris came in to clear the pudding things away, and Lavinia got up to fetch Stilton and fruitcake. Josh followed her to collect the port. He caught up with her at the bottom of the library corridor and he grabbed her from behind, kissing her neck and fondling her breasts.

'Josh, you're drunk.'

'Drunk, am I?' his speech was slurred. 'Come with me,' he said. 'I want to show you something.'

'Josh, I can't leave our guests. What is it?'

'Come with me. It won't take a minute.'

He led her back up the corridor, across the main hall, and into the cloakroom.

'Josh, what are you doing? You're drunk. No! Let me get back to our guests.' She snatched her hand away from him.

He grabbed her hand again. 'Just give me one minute, just one.'

Inside the room Josh slid the bolt across the door.

'Josh!' She was becoming irritated.

He heaved her up onto the marble stand that surrounded the wash-hand basin, he pushed her skirt up over her hips and literally ripped the thick brown tights away from her.

'Josh! What on earth are you doing!'

'Proving I'm not drunk,' he said. 'I couldn't get it up if I were pissed, could I?' He unzipped his plus-fours and exposed his penis; he was purple and swollen and wanting her.

Lavinia was perched at a perfect height.

She began to giggle. 'You've gone mad,' she said, but Josh was exciting her and she wriggled a little toward him. 'I must go and serve the cheese.'

'Let me help you to a little cream first,' he said.

'Josh Elliot you've gone mad! Quite, quite mad!'

'Ah, but you love it, don't you?'

Lavinia swallowed, she was loosing control of her

breathing.

'There's only ever been one way to silence you,' he chuckled.

Lavinia took a sharp gulp of air. She gripped the edge of the marble with her hands.

Josh pulled her panties to one side. 'You're a deceitful woman,' he said, pushing his fingers inside her.

'Pretending you want to go and serve cheese, when here you are all ready for me.'

She giggled, then gasped as her husband thrust into her.

Josh's drunkenness made him just a little rougher than usual, just a little less inhibited, and for Lavinia, just a little more exciting. Her back was being driven into the basin taps and the edge of the marble cut into her thighs, but she was finding this new aggressive Jocelyn unbelievingly exciting. She was almost enjoying the pain in her back as the taps connected harder with each forceful movement. Josh smelled of damp hair, gun oil and wine, and Lavinia was intoxicated by the aroma. She loved the feel of his rough tweed on her inner thigh and she thrilled to his big hands on her hips pulling her forward and further onto him.

Josh's face was extremely red, his breath was so sharp and short that he was actually grunting. Sweat was running down his face. Lavinia had her head thrust back against the mirror, which swayed on its hook as she moved back and forth with Josh's violent movements.

The familiar sensation began slowly in the pit of her stomach and radiated out to her furthest extremities. It gained momentum and brought wave after wave of hot pleasurable impulses rippling through her body, bringing an intense and caressing warmth in its wake. She made a soft gurgling noise as Josh exploded inside her. But her sounds were lost in Josh's cry of. 'Oh, my God, my God, my God.'

'Blessed is he that cometh in the name of the Lord,' Lavinia giggled.

Then there was total silence as Lavinia leaned forward and rested her red perspiring face on Josh's neck. They stayed like that for several moments, their breath short, their hearts beating wildly.

Eventually, Lavinia, her voice soft and weak, said, 'OK, you're not drunk. And I hope you get, not drunk, very often!'

Josh pulled away, and she felt his warm fluid gush away from her. She put her hand down into the creamy liquid that had spilled over the marble top, and brought her fingers up to her lips and pushed them into her mouth. Josh smiled at her and with his own hand he copied what she had done. They held each other's gazes.

'Oh God, Vinnie, I love you so much.'

She curled her legs around his back and held on to him.

After a while, he said, 'I suppose we'd better serve the port and Stilton?'

She discarded the tights in the bin, straightened her skirt, and ran her fingers through her hair.

They returned to the dining room.

No one seemed to have noticed their absence, just as no one noticed the dark stain that had appeared on the front of Josh's plus-fours. Lord and Lady Hulver couldn't take their eyes off each other. From the other end of the table, Lavinia smiled at her husband and nodded her head. They were talking a language that had no need of words or even touch. Yes, she thought, I love him. I'm not in love, but I love him and I desire him. He makes it happen for me; I have the best sort of relationship. I love him and I need him, and he loves me and he needs me in return. She looked down at her plate and reflected that there probably weren't that many married couples who had what she and Josh had. They were very, very lucky people.

It was gone eight before all the guests departed. Josh and Lavinia had promised to attend the Pennington shoot the following week and Lavinia was already dreading the hangover that Josh was sure to experience after the revelry.

CHAPTER SIX

'What's this then?' Betty Jarvis muttered as she entered her son's bedroom. 'Hammer House of Horror?' She yanked the curtain back with a forceful snap.

Steve was lost in a magnificent dream. He was on the slopes of Applegate Hill, his hand-crafted Purdy poised, when hundreds of pheasants flew over, and with perfect aim, and deadly results, he emptied both barrels of the twelve bore. Swiftly, he handed his gun to his loader – who happened to be Lord Hulver himself – and swapped the gun for its fully loaded, perfectly matched twin. Once again he brought down the birds, whilst the Peer of the Realm reloaded the first shotgun.

'*Hoi!* Wake up.'

Betty prodded her son with her chubby, dimpled elbow.

Steve opened an eye and pulled the pillow over his head. 'Aw, Mum! Watcher do that for? I was fast asleep.'

'I knows that boy. But you've no right to be sleeping. It's gone seven. You promised his Lordship you'd be in by seven-thirty.'

Steve rolled over onto his stomach, letting his arm dangle from the side of the narrow bed onto the dusty floor. He had a thumping headache. After leaving the castle he'd spent the evening in the King Charles with some of the keepers and the beaters. The guns had given him a generous tip and he'd drunk his way through most of it. The landlord had thrown him out at twelve and he'd gone back to his girlfriend Tracy's house, where, on her parents' ancient settee, he'd fumbled his way into her underwear. Tracy, terrified that her parents might wake at the sound of their whispers and giggles, had been tense and uncooperative.

'Come on, Steven. Get up.' Betty wiped her nose on the back of her hand. 'Where's me bloody hanky?'

'Language, Mum, please. What would Lady H say if she heard you talk like that?'

'Buggar Lady H. God, did you see her and that other one, Lady Osbourne-Pennington?' Betty pursed her lips. 'Osbourne-Pennington, what sort of a name is that? I tell you, the longer the name, the more hoity-toity they are. Do you know I crawled into work yesterday morning, on me knees I was, and you should have seen the state that kitchen was in when I got there. Lazy cow hadn't even cleared their prefab dinner cartons away from the night before. What they'd do without me, heaven only knows.

She can't even make a piece of toast without burning it.'

Steve lifted his head. 'She seems all right to me – and that other one, the one from Pennington? Real nice piece of skirt she is. Cor, what I could do for her!' He thrust his hips down into the mattress.

'You'll be doing nothing for nobody if you don't get up and go down to the castle my boy.'

'Okay, okay — '

'Come on then.'

'I'm not getting out of bed while you're standing there. I've got no clothes on.'

'But I'm your mother.'

'That's just what I mean. So go! I'll be down in a minute.'

Betty tutted and went down to the kitchen, where she blew her nose very loudly. Then, taking the damp tissue she'd used on her nose, she absentmindedly wiped the kitchen table with it. A few minutes later her son appeared, picking his way barefoot through the messy kitchen, and wearing only a pair of worn faded jeans.

Having inherited few of his mother's visible attributes, Steve Jarvis was dark and swarthy. His hair was almost black and curled into the nape of his neck. His eyes were nearer black than brown; he was smooth skinned, straight-nosed and square-jawed. Betty Jarvis – a small, round, pink woman – was barely five feet tall. Her son was over a foot taller. He was lean and athletic, and not at all generous with his smiles. There was an almost menacing, brooding look about him. In all his twenty-four years he had never once asked his mother about his father. It wasn't that he wasn't curious; he was. The village gossiped about gypsy blood and bad ends and Steve had an image of his missing parent that he didn't want altered. He had romantic ideas about his parentage, and his looks lent some credibility to those ideas. For Steve Jarvis was broad and handsome, strong and fearless; neither his features nor his stature could be faulted.

Had Betty told him the truth – that his father was a car worker from Coventry, whom Betty had met on a day trip to Maplethorpe – Steve's dream would have been shattered, and so he had never pinned her down. Thus, an unspoken agreement of silence had been established in his youth and was even now adhered to.

A few moments later Steve came out of the lean-to bathroom. The room, tucked on the end of the kitchen, was of single brick construction. Always cold, even in the height of summer, it was never free of a black mould that thrived in the cold damp conditions.

Steve grabbed a shirt from the clotheshorse that stood to the right of the stove. The kitchen was warm and damp; steam from a constantly boiling kettle condensed on the metal window frames and ran in long rivulets onto the sill. He tucked the shirt into his jeans, pulled on his socks and boots, and grabbed the fried-egg sandwich his mother passed to him.

He looked at his watch. 'When are you in, then?'

'Not until two, today. Lady H is out to lunch so his Lordship said he'd fend for himself – as I was so late finishing last night. Young Zoë's home from school tomorrow, so Madam wants me to bake a cake.'

'Mmm' said Steve, thrusting his hips forward and rubbing his hand over his crotch. 'Wouldn't mind baking Zoë Elliot's cake myself!'

His mother playfully clipped his ear. 'I'll have none of that talk, Steven. If his Lordship heard you say that, you'd be out on your ear – make no mistake.'

'His Lordship won't hear me, Mum. Not unless he spent the night here with you, and he's now hiding under the table!'

'Walls have ears, Steven.'

Steve looked up at the ceiling. 'Yes, Mum,' he said, then paused. 'She's not a virgin, you know.'

'Who?' asked his mother.

'Zoë.'

'What?'

'Girls that ride all the time aren't virgins.'

'What?'

'Girls like Zoë.'

'It's Miss Zoë to you.'

He raised his eyebrows. 'Well, Miss Zoë isn't a virgin.'

'How do you know?'

'Because she rides! It breaks the hymen.'

'The what?'

'The hymen. When they're riding. That's why they do it. They like to straddle all that warm horseflesh, and they like hitting their fannies on all that polished leather. You watch their faces when they're doing it. They're in ecstasy.'

'Steven! Don't talk so filthy.'

'Well, it's true.'

'Miss Zoë's a lovely girl. I don't believe a word of it.'

'I didn't say she wasn't lovely – she certainly does it for me. I just said — '

His mother interrupted him. She was cutting a loaf of bread and she stopped and pointed the knife at him as she spoke. 'Listen Steven, you behave yourself. You've got in too much trouble with girls already. You've got good prospects down at the Castle, don't go and spoil it all.'

'I'm hardly likely to do that – am I, Mum?' He finished lacing his boots. 'By the way? Why do you always say: down?'

'Down?' she sniffed, wrinkled her nose and smeared mucus over the back of her hand.

'Yeh. You always say: down at the castle, when it's uphill to us here.'

'Oh, be off with you! And behave yourself.'

Steve looked out of the window. The rain still fell in a cold damp drizzle. He grabbed his coat and without saying goodbye he was gone, slamming the door behind him.

For all his vulgar talk, Steve really liked Zoë Elliot. He could remember her being born, even though he was only six at the time. A great party had been given to celebrate the child's arrival. He also remembered her sister being born two years later and another party for her; though the joy on that occasion had been more muted, when the longed-for son-and-heir failed to appear.

Four years after that, the party thrown to commemorate the birth of the twins – both boys – had been a celebration surpassing all others. A marquee had been erected in the deer park, and even the tenants had been invited to partake of a festive glass of beer.

Steve climbed into his battered red Cortina. Zoë was coming up to eighteen now, which must make Tiggy almost sixteen. He smiled to himself. He'd break-in one, if not both of those fillies, or his name wasn't Steve Jarvis.

CHAPTER SEVEN

The weather cleared and a watery winter sun replaced the endless rain of the past few days. On Saturday morning Lavinia, as usual, went into Norwich to have her hair styled and her nails manicured. Josh spent the morning in his office sorting through bills and reading The Times. Pete, the Elliot's chauffeur, went off to Cambridge to drive the girls home from their public school. The boys' exeat wasn't until the following weekend.

It was mid afternoon before the girls and their parents finally got together. They were gathered for tea in the mahogany-panelled library, a room in which Lavinia never felt quite comfortable, but a room that Josh loved. Like any good country-house library, it was filled from floor to ceiling with unread, leather bound, books. The furniture was of solid Victorian mahogany and the sofas and chairs were covered in blood-red leather. The curtains were made of heavy brocade and fringed with braid. Three long casement windows overlooked the Deer Park.

They were drinking tea and eating Mrs Jarvis's

fruitcake in front of a roaring log fire. Tiggy had her legs curled up under her, and was asking her parents if they'd allow her to accompany a school friend on a trip around Europe in the summer holidays. Lavinia said that she didn't see why her daughter shouldn't go, but Josh became agitated, and said he thought it senseless to spend money on travelling abroad when Tiggy had a perfectly good home to enjoy.

'Why don't you bring your friend home for a week or two? There's lot's of things to do here.'

'Such as?' Tiggy said. Making her question sound like an accusation.

'Well, there's lots of nice walks,' Josh said weakly.

'But Josh,' Lavinia said. 'We're going on a wonderful holiday next autumn. Don't be a meanie. I'm sure Tiggy's trip won't cost very much.'

'Where are you going?' Zoë asked, obviously intrigued. 'You never go anywhere, except to Scotland at New Year.'

Lavinia gave Josh a rather shy smile. 'Your father's taking me to Venice in the autumn,' she said, and Josh's heart sank.

'Wow, what a very un-Elliot thing to do,' Tiggy said.

'Not so very un-Elliot,' said Lavinia. 'We've been before. In fact, we spent our honeymoon there.' She gave

Josh another rather shy smile. 'We're going to be there for our wedding anniversary. Aren't we darling?'

ßJosh coughed, he felt uncomfortably hot. How was he going to tell her? She was building the thing up into a huge event; so much for hoping that she'd forget his promise. He'd even overheard her telling Mrs Jarvis about it. He ought to alert her now, warn her that it might not be possible.

'But what about us?' Zoë wailed.

'You'll be at school.'

'I won't. Not if I go to Uni. I won't start until October.'

Lavinia put her arm around her elder daughter. 'You're quite old enough to look after yourself. It'll be fun for you. Won't it, Josh?'

Josh gave a weak smile. 'Well, hang on, old thing. Perhaps we ought to put it off for a year or so. Not right to leave the young on their own, and all that.'

Lavinia frowned. 'Josh? Please don't talk like that.'

'What'd you mean?'

'Like your father. You keep doing it.'

'I don't know what you're talking about.'

'All these, "old things" and, "don't you knows".

The next thing we'll get a sprinkling of "what ho's". What's the matter? Are you completely regressing into the past? What's troubling you? Are you worried

73

about something?'

'Worried? Lord no!'

'There you go again. You talk like that when you're trying to escape from the present. You talked like it for a solid twenty-four hours when I was in labour with the twins.'

'Well, I was concerned about you. They were big babies, don't you know.'

The girls burst into a fit of giggles.

Josh sprung to his feet. 'I told you the other day, Vinnie. It's the way I talk – it's the way I am. Stop trying to read things into it.'

Her eyes were still full of concern. 'But everything is all right, isn't it, Josh? You haven't changed your mind about the holiday?' Her frown deepened. 'We can afford it? Can't we?'

'Oh, Lord. Vinnie, of course I haven't changed my mind.' Then, as if to confirm the situation, he said, 'In fact, I'm really looking forward to it.'

Josh had, of course, not mentioned his conversation with Philip McTodd. But Lavinia had lunched with Ailsa the day before, and Josh hoped that Philip had played his part and asked Ailsa not to mention her worries to Lavinia. At least now he was pretty sure that Ailsa hadn't told Lavinia. Josh wasn't worried, or at least that's what he fervently tried to tell himself. It was unforgivable of Philip to worry Ailsa. That was the golden rule, one did not discuss business with the womenfolk. There was no need to distress them. Philip should realize that women were temperamental creatures; their brains were not geared to the cut and thrust of business life. Hadn't his own father drummed it into him from a very early age? Don't upset the ladies; don't burden them with your troubles. Not that he was really troubled of course. It was just a blip. He was on good terms with his bank manager; Brian would see him through all right. And next year would be better, despite what his agent said. There had to be a mistake, it would all come right. It always did.

'By the by, how did your lunch with Ailsa go? Did she mention anything?'

'Anything? Oh yes,' she moistened her lips, 'I was meaning to ask you. About Lloyds? Apparently the outlook is very bad for them. Thank goodness we're not in the same syndicate. We're not, are we, Josh? You'd have told me, wouldn't you?'

It was as if those few confident words of Lavinia's had opened a tap and all his good intentions drained away from him, to be replaced by an urgent need to confide. Perhaps his fears, once voiced and shared, would fade into oblivion. That familiar dry metallic taste invaded his mouth again.

He gave a little cough and despite his resolve not

to alarm Lavinia he said, 'We're in a similar one, Lavinia.' The words once said seemed so simple, so harmless, so unthreatening.

'Yes, but we're not losing money, that's the difference. Philip and Ailsa have had to pay out thousands. Josh? Is that what's worrying you?'

Josh saw the alarm in Lavinia's face, and was strengthened again. He swallowed the fear away and gave a weak smile. 'Good Lord, I'm not personally worried. But yes, Philip told me how worried he was. I tried to tell him it was just a blip, but the poor chap's always been a worrier, and he's worried to death about this one.'

'And is it?'

'What?'

'Just a blip? Is it just a blip?'

'Of course it is. The market's always been up and down, you expect a little loss here and there.'

Lavinia frowned. 'Have we lost, Josh?'

Josh looked at the girls. He had a not–in–front–of–the–children look on his face.

'Don't look like that, Josh.'

'Like what?'

'Like as if you're discussing our sex life in front of the family.'

'Lavinia!' He was both alarmed and amused. A feeling of love spread over him. I'll never let you down

76

Lavinia, he thought. I'll never give you any unnecessary worry. Not if I can help it, I won't.

'They do know we have a sex life, Josh,' Lavinia said.

Josh and Lavinia's vivacious younger daughter began to giggle.

'What are you laughing at, Antigone?'

Tiggy giggled a little more, and Zoë shook her blond head and nudged her sister's arm.

'Well?' said Josh. 'What's so funny?'

'You and Mummy are.'

Josh nodded his head up and down and tapped his fingers on the arm of his chair. 'Really?'

'Well, Mummy said that we knew you had – but I certainly didn't.'

'Had what?' Josh was pretending to be confused.

'A *sex* life!' Both girls collapsed into helpless laughter, dropping cake crumbs all over the red leather chesterfield.

Josh shot Lavinia an exasperated look, only to find that she too, was curled up in uncontrolled mirth.

'Would you like me to show you the cloakroom?' She spluttered between helpless giggles.

At this Josh felt a stirring in his loins. Oh, how he loved this woman. She was such a jolly good sport, so sexy, so dear and so funny. He too, began to laugh. At the sound of their father's laughter, both girls abruptly stopped giggling and turned to each other with a look of incomprehension.

'I don't get it.' Zoë said. 'What's so funny about the cloakroom?'

But both Josh and Lavinia were too hysterical to give a sensible answer.

Zoë looked annoyed and rapidly changed the subject.

'Daddy,' she said, 'if you can stop laughing long enough, perhaps you'd tell me exactly what Lloyds is?'

Josh wiped a stray tear from his eye and blew his nose. He surveyed his offspring with a fond parental eye. Zoë, the elder of the two, was tall and quite well built, having inherited his build rather than his wife's; she had long blond hair, a pretty round face and mischievous brown eyes. Her sister Antigone was shorter and slimmer; her hair, although also blond, was more of a honey colour, and she wore it layered to just below her ears, encouraging soft waves to frame her exceptionally pretty face. She looked more like Lavinia than Josh. Her eyes were an indefinable colour, not quite gray and not quite blue. She had a sprinkling of freckles on her nose and she was forever laughing and finding the brighter side to life, whereas her sister looked at the world in a more sober way.

Josh was carefully composing his answer as he gazed on them. He found it difficult to believe that his two bright babies were growing into women, women that asked questions, women that insisted on knowing everything. Girls in his day left business matters to the men and concentrated on running the home and making sure they were good wives and mothers. 'Well . . .' he said at last. He was a little out of breath from his uncontrolled laughter, and he paused for a moment. 'Well, like a lot of landowners, I'm capital-rich, but income-poor, and so I'm able to use the capital as a guarantee. Underwriting, it's called. In exchange for the risk I take with my capital, I get a share of other people's premiums.'

'Guarantee for what?'

'Insurance.'

'Oh, so if there was a disaster, you would have to pay?'

'Me and a lot of others. But, put simply, yes.'

'But if you've no income, how would you pay?'

This was something Josh didn't want to think about. He gulped: the thought was frightening him. 'With the capital, of course.'

'But what is the capital? You said you haven't got cash,' Zoë said.

'The capital is here.'

'The estate?'

'But you couldn't sell Hulver, Daddy.' Tiggy protested.

'Of course not, I'd have to borrow on it.'

'But that's stupid! Why don't they just save up all the premiums to pay for any claims?'

'They do with some of it, but there wouldn't be nearly enough if there were to be several big claims in one year.'

Zoë lifted her arms in the air. 'It sounds stupid to me.'

'Stupid or not, it's paid your school fees for a good many years.'

'But what if there's a really big disaster? The *Titanic* or something?'

Josh laughed. 'My dear, the *Titanic* would be chicken feed, compared the sort of money these boys deal with.' And once again, the taste of fear crept into his mouth, that sour metallic taste that could not be washed away. He took a gulp of his tea but the taste remained. He blushed and glanced at Lavinia, afraid that she could somehow sense the panic that had flooded his mouth. He could lose everything, – his estate, the castle; everything. His whole way of life could change. Jimmy Laughton must have experienced this self-same feeling of fear, and he had dealt with it in his own tragic way. Josh shook his head. Poor old Jimmy, he thought, unconventional life and unconventional death.

Zoë shrugged impatiently. 'Well, it still sounds

pretty stupid to me.'

Josh decided that it was too hard for him to explain. They wouldn't understand, and besides, Lavinia was looking definitely alarmed, and that was the last thing he wanted. He was relieved when Zoë and Tiggy got up and announced that they were going to take Fen for a walk.

After the girls had left the room, Lavinia said, 'There really isn't anything to worry about, is there, Josh?' He kissed her, 'Nothing at all, my darling, nothing at all.' *Never upset the ladies*, he heard his father say.

'But have we lost money, Josh?'

'Everyone has lost a little.' He gave a light-hearted laugh, but his heart felt suddenly heavy. Zoë had said it, it was stupid, he'd gambled away his inheritance and now the chips were down, he was finding it hard to face the consequences.

'How much is a little, Josh?'

'Not enough for you to worry about, my darling.' He patted her hand and smiled at her sheepishly.

He looked up out of the window and across the deer park, desperate to change the subject. 'I find that a deal more worrying,' he said.

Under a row of ancient beech trees Zoë could be seen talking to Steve Jarvis. 'I don't like Zoë messing about with young Jarvis.'

81

Lavinia came and stood beside him. 'I know what you mean, he's fearfully good-looking, isn't he?'

Josh raised his eyebrows; he'd never thought of Jarvis as being good-looking, and was surprised that his wife thought in those terms. Lavinia's comment made him mentally dislike the boy.

'I don't trust him,' Josh said. 'He doesn't know his place.'

'Oh Josh, she's going to meet lots of young men like him at university.'

Josh felt angry. 'No, Lavinia. That's where you're wrong. The young men she'll come into contact with will be better educated, and have damn-sight higher intelligence.'

'Josh, that's terribly unfair. Steve is a very, very bright lad.'

'He's too cocky, Lavinia. Look at them – have a word with her would you?'

'That's the thing most likely to drive her into his arms.'

'Good God, you don't think — ?'

'No I don't think.'

'Vinnie, you're taking this very lightly. It worries me to death.'

'Josh dear, worry about the orphans in Romania, by all means, but don't start worrying about something

82

that hasn't happened. In fact, if you leave it alone it will just fizzle out. Zoë's got her head screwed on. Besides, you're overreacting – he's a nice enough lad, and he's by no means dim.'

'I want you to speak to her.' He bit into his bottom lip.

Lavinia just didn't understand; that was the trouble, women didn't understand. He conceded that the world was a constantly changing place, but even so, some things never changed. Zoë and Steve Jarvis could never be just friends; it didn't work like that. It would always be a question of them and us. They weren't equals, and they never would be. The Elliots were the leaders and the Jarvises were the followers. The old of the village understood; they showed respect for the people at the castle. But his children's contemporaries resented them for their privileged upbringing, and Steve Jarvis was no different. Class still existed, and it still mattered just as it had in the past – only, in the past, people knew their place.

It seemed that Steve Jarvis didn't.

The Elliots were needed to guide the rest. It was ever thus; where they led, others followed. The Elliots, and families like them, had always been in the front line. Not for nothing had Burke's Peerage been late for publication after the Great War. It was men like Jocelyn Elliot's grandfather that had led the way forward into battle. They were then, as now, the ones in the direct line of fire. The leaders looked after the ordinary foot soldiers. Steve Jarvis would survive a relationship with Zoë, but Zoë might not be so lucky.

Josh looked out onto his parkland. What would become of them if they lost everything? Where could he and his family fit into society? How could they survive in a world that favored the underdog? How would he bear to see other people occupying his land? His rubbed his cheek; all the values he held dear were being threatened, he had nowhere to go for guidance, and no one he dared turn to for sympathy.

Zoë was sitting on the post-and-rail fence that ran round the edge of the home meadow. Tiggy and the dog were nowhere in sight.

'So, are you coming or not, then?' Steve had asked her to go to the disco at the King Charles that evening.

'I might do,' she said.

'See you there, then.'

'You might do,' she said again.

CHAPTER EIGHT

'But you brought us up not to be snobs. You've always quoted that bit in the Bible, the bit about all men being equal in the sight of God.'

'Yes, Zoë, in the sight of God, but not in the sight of your father.'

'So it's no, then?'

'Yes, it's no.'

'But it's only a disco, for God's sake.'

'Don't blaspheme, Zoë.'

'You do, all the time.'

'That doesn't make it right, or proper.'

'Right and proper! Oh God, I despair of this family.'

'Despair or not, you're still not going to the pub with Steve Jarvis.'

'You can't stop me,' Zoë said. 'I'm nearly eighteen.'

She was so angry that little red blotches had formed on her cheeks.

'Can't I?' Lavinia replied.

Zoë's mind flitted through several apt replies but she voiced none of them. If Lavinia wouldn't give her consent, then she would jolly well go to the disco without it.

'Do you want me to set the table?' Zoë said, her tone ungracious.

'Yes, but it won't make me change my mind.'

'I never for one moment thought it would.' She felt extremely hard done by, but no matter, she was already forming other, more exciting, plans. At her age she did not need parental approval. She stalked out of the kitchen and into the small dining room where she set the table for dinner. Her mood was considerably lighter, but she knew better than to let her mother see that.

That conversation had taken place late in the afternoon, well before dinner, which had been eaten almost in silence. At nine-thirty, Zoë crumpled her linen napkin and placed it on the table. 'I'm sorry I was such a pain earlier, Mummy,' she said.

Lavinia glanced at Josh. She had already explained what the argument had been about.

'And you were quite right, Mummy.'

Lavinia patted her daughter's hand.

'I've got a frightful headache, do you mind if I go to bed?' She gave her mother a weak smile. Better go the whole hog. 'It's my own fault: for shouting at you.'

'Poor darling. Of course I don't mind. I'll come up and see you later.'

'No, no, please don't. I'll take a paracetamol and go straight to sleep. I'll say goodnight now.' She got up and kissed her mother on the cheek, she went round the end of the table to her father and kissed him on the top of his head. 'Night-night, Pa. I'll see you in the morning.'

'Night-night, darling. I hope the head gets better.'

Tiggy got up. 'If no one minds I'll go up too. I'm really, really tired.'

Once out of the door the girls suppressed relieved giggles.

'You must cover for me, Tiggy. If Mummy comes up, tell her I've gone for a walk, to clear my head or something.'

'Can't I come with you, Zoë?'

'Tiggy!' Zoë sounded very annoyed. 'You promised! Anyway you'd only be in the way.'

'Thanks a lot.'

'Tiggy, you know what I mean.'

Once in her room, Zoë slipped off her formal red dress and pulled on jeans and a tight fitting black top. She knew she looked good. Her breasts looked large and shapely, her waist slim. She ran her fingers through her hair using exactly the same mannerism as her mother.

'You're not going like that?' Tiggy said.

'What's wrong with it?'

'Well, it's supposed to be a dance, isn't it?'

'*Disco*. It's a disco, and it's at the King Charlie. Hardly the dressiest of places.'

Tiggy conceded that her sister was probably right. 'But you can see the shape of your nipples through the material of the top!'

Zoë giggled. 'Yes,' she said. 'I know.'

By ten o'clock, breath short and heart thumping, Zoë had cut across the north drive, braved the Castle Wood and was standing at the bar of the King Charles, sipping an Archers and lemonade.

In fact Lavinia did not look in on Zoë that night, she merely listened at the door and was then distracted by the sound of Tiggy's television set. She chastised her daughter for staying up so late, suggesting that Tiggy might do well to follow her sister's good example and get some sleep.

Tiggy did not betray her elder sister; loyalty, or perhaps anger at her parents' criticism, forbade her to break Zoë's trust.

CHAPTER NINE

In contrast to the Hulver shoot, the Pennington shoot was held on a perfect late autumn day, bright and crisp; ideal weather for a day of sport. Josh, still disturbed by seeing Zoë and Steve Jarvis together the previous Saturday, decided that he would take matters in hand and have a word with the boy. He therefore arranged for Pete the chauffeur to drive Lavinia to Pennington in the Bentley, whilst he drove himself and Steve Jarvis in the Range Rover.

Once they were well on their way, Josh approached the subject that was causing him so much unease.

'I saw you talking to Miss Zoë on Saturday, Jarvis.'

Steve, who was much too clever for the likes of Lord Hulver, knew exactly what was coming and immediately took evasive action. 'Yes, yes, she was asking me about my girlfriend.'

Josh raised an eyebrow.

'Yes, Tracy, my girlfriend. She's training to be a social worker.' Well, didn't Tracy say often enough that her job was a cross between bloody marriage guidance and social work? 'And Miss Zoë was asking me about her work, for that project she's doing at school for her A-levels.'

Josh, who hadn't a clue which particular A-levels Zoë was studying for, nodded sagely. Psychology? Yes that was it; Zoë had said something about it, hadn't she? He frowned. Or was that Tiggy? But then, as if he'd just remembered that Steve had asked Zoë to go to the pub, he said, 'But I thought you asked her to some sort of dance at the public house.'

'Oh yes, well, you know, it was to meet Tracy – she was home from college this weekend.'

'Josh nodded again. 'Oh, I see, but you know Steve . . .'

Steve smiled at the mention of his Christian name —

'With all the good will in the world, the village pub is hardly a place for Miss Zoë to frequent.' He studied the boy's profile. Vinnie had said he was good-looking. Well, Josh supposed he was; in a boyish, immature sort of way. But why a woman of Vinnie's age and experience should find him attractive was a mystery to Josh. He knew men of his age often looked at younger women, but the other way round? No, surely not; it wasn't quite decent.

Steve shook his head submissively. 'I realize that now, Lord Hulver. I was thoughtless, and I do sincerely apologize both to your Lordship and to Miss Zoë for any embarrassment I may have caused.' God, he thought, this was taking boot licking a little too far. It wasn't as if Saturday had been that much fun; the King Charles had been crowded, and Steve had spent his time simultaneously flirting with Zoë and pacifying Tracy. The two occupations had not married well. 'Whad'yer have to be buying her a drink for?' Tracy had asked. 'She's bloody well-heeled – why can't she buy her own?'

'Because,' Steve had replied, 'she's me boss's ßdaughter, and I'm saving browning points for a rainy day.'

He'd been relieved when Zoë had said she thought she should go home. He'd given her a lift to the castle gates. And it wasn't him that had kissed Zoë; it was she who had kissed him. He smiled now when he remembered the chaste peck she had offered him; his smile broadened when he thought how he had clung on a little longer and gently parted her lips with his beer-scented tongue. He'd part her legs too before very long, or his name wasn't Steve Jarvis.

The evening had had a bonus as well, for when he'd returned to the pub to pick Tracy up after her evening stint behind the bar, she'd been very obliging to him in the back of his steamed up Cortina. He'd rather it had been Zoë – lovely tits Zoë had, made Tracy's look like pimples – but then a bloke had to take what was on offer at the time. Funny that, though; the worse you treated women the keener they were on you.

Josh nodded in apparent satisfaction. 'Why don't you bring your friend? Tracy? Why don't you bring her up to the castle one day when Miss Zoë's home. What university did you say she was at?'

'Er, Cambridge,' Steve improvised; it was really the

only university he'd heard of. 'She's in her second year.'

Josh nodded his approval. 'Cambridge, eh? And she's your girlfriend, you say?' Josh sounded doubtful.

Steve compressed his lips together. In for a penny, in for a pound, he thought. 'Yes, she's a clever girl, is Tracy. That's what I'm saving up for, as a matter of fact.'

'To get married?'

Steve gave one of his rare smiles. 'No, no. To go to college. I want to study estate management.'

Josh too was smiling. 'Oh. Oh, I see! Well done you. Let me know if I can help in any way.' He'd misjudged the lad; that was clear. As usual Vinnie was right.

And when, later, he repeated the conversation to Lavinia, Steve Jarvis had become 'a man to look out for'. Steve Jarvis would, thought Josh, go a very long way, and Steve Jarvis would not only be a credit to his mother, but a credit to the Hulver estate as well. And if Josh could give the boy a leg up, he jolly well would. And Lavinia was to get all that nonsense about Jarvis and Zoë out of her head. There was nothing going on there; even a fool could see that. 'And by the by,' he added. He'd taken a close look at the lad, and he didn't think he was that good-looking.

Lavinia smiled sweetly but contributed very little to the conversation; very soon she had waved goodbye to Josh and the rest of the shooting party, and returned to her hostess, Brooke Osbourne-Pennington.

CHAPTER TEN

Pennington Manor, unlike Hulver Castle, was not a hodgepodge of different additions carried out over many periods, but was a huge, handsome, Victorian pile. It had been built in the 1880's on the sight of the original fourteenth-century house. The present Manor had five large public rooms, a huge two-story Victorian conservatory, billiard room, gun room, fifteen bedrooms, ten of which had dressing rooms, and ample servant's quarters. It had a large stable complex, keeper's house and kennels, tennis courts and croquet lawn. The shooting extended to over 10,000 acres, 1,000 of which were woodland. The rest divided equally between pasture and arable land. There was anchorage for boats under a mile from the house, from which direction Pennington Manor was originally approached. The interior of the house had a wealth of rich dark panelling, wooden chimneypieces and leaded-light windows.

Much to Lavinia's surprise, Brooke had not changed the nature of the place, but had embarked on her refurbishment with a sympathetic eye, and was in the process of restoring the Victorian interior to its original glory. She was meticulous in her efforts, and vowed she would make the house as splendid as the Victorian Osbourne-Penningtons had intended it to be.

The day looked to be as successful as the Hulver day had been disastrous; the bag was huge and Henry Osbourne-Pennington was well pleased.

After Brooke had shown them around the house the women spent the rest of the morning at the Osbourne-Pennington's shooting lodge, which stood on a high promontory and overlooked the North Sea. The lodge was used for shooting parties in the winter, and in the summer it became a beach house and tended to change its name along with the seasons. A long single-storied building, constructed of Carrstone, it had been built several years before the main house and the architecture differed enormously. It had one main open-plan room with a yellow flagstone floor, a huge open fireplace and primitive cooking facilities. The lodge was furnished with a jumble of items, which Brooke referred to as 'the junk of ages'; an old leather chesterfield, a bentwood rocking chair, a cane chaise-longue. Colorful rugs covered the floor and a very large pine table, surrounded by mismatched chairs, stood to one side of the fireplace. On the eastern side of the lodge, overlooking the Pennington's private beach and jetty, ran a long wooden veranda. In recent times the veranda had been enclosed with large glass picture windows; and it was here that Brooke had placed a row of steamer chairs, and to each she had allocated a tartan rug to keep the winter draughts at bay. The ladies were seated in these chairs when the men joined them at noon for thick vegetable soup and crusty bread rolls.

At three the ladies made their way back to the Manor and, retreating into the drawing room, they waited for the men to return from the last drive of the afternoon. They had been talking all day, and Lavinia was heartily sick of hearing about other people's children's schools and the price of a decent haircut.

Hillary Miles-Jones, wife of Lavinia's second cousin George, was not joining in the conversation. She was two years older than her husband, being in her late sixty's. She was a heavily-built woman with pale skin and once-blonde hair, that now hung grey and lank around her deeply lined face. Her lips were thin and her nose large, with wide, almost flared, nostrils. Her eyes were sunken and she seemed depressed and remote.

Lavinia went over to her and sat down by her side. 'Hillary, we haven't seen each other for ages! How are you?' The other women were deep in conversation, admiring the material that Brooke had had especially woven to replace some original Victorian brocade.

Hillary smiled, the coral corduroy dress she was wearing only seemed to make her face look paler and, in turn, emphasized the dark grey rings under her eyes. She pushed her hair behind her ears.

'Lavinia, how nice . . . Josh looks well, and you . . . You look positively blooming, and how's my Goddaughter?'

'Hillary, I asked you how you were?'

'Me? Oh . . . I'm fine, just fine.'

'You look tired.'

'Yes. Yes, I must admit I am a little tired. But I mustn't complain. You know . . . ' Hillary glanced at her watch and then at the door.

'What is it, Hillary?'

Hillary forced a smile. 'Oh nothing, I just . . . wish George would get back. That's all.'

'He's all right! Isn't he?' An alarm bell sounded somewhere at the back of Lavinia's mind.

'George? He's fine. He's . . . ' To Lavinia's horror, Hillary began to cry. She fished a handkerchief out from her sleeve and sniffed as she tried to stifle the tears.

Lavinia looked around at the others. No one was taking any notice of them.

'Come on, Hillary. Let's go into the conservatory,

and you can tell me all about it.' She led the older woman by the hand.

Once in the magnificent glass house, surrounded by orchids and other rare plants, Hillary stopped sobbing. 'Lavinia, I'm so sorry. I don't want to burden with my problems. You have enough to worry about.'

Lavinia covered Hillary's blue-veined hand with her own. 'What is it, Hillary? I might not be able to help, but at least I can listen, and I've got a good wide shoulder for you to cry on.'

Hillary gave a weak tearful smile. 'I'm just a silly old woman and that's all there is to it. We all have to get old, don't we?'

'That won't do, Hillary. I need to know more precisely what's troubling you.'

'That's it, you see, George and me . . . we're getting old.'

Lavinia cocked her head to one side and raised her eyebrows to encourage the other woman to enlarge on her statement.

'We've been very lucky, George and I. We've always kept very well, and we've the children and the grandchildren to be thankful for.'

'But?'

Hillary's eyes flooded with tears. 'He's got . . . oh, Lavinia. I can hardly bear to say it.'

'What?'

'George has Alzheimer's. Oh, Lavinia, sometimes he doesn't even know who I am. I can't bear it. He used to be so . . . so, well, so alive. And now it's as if part of him is already dead. And it's the most precious part. All our memories, all our happiness . . . gone. All gone.'

Lavinia looked alarmed. 'But he seemed all right at Hulver last week.'

'He does, a lot of the time he seems fine. If you didn't know, you wouldn't guess. George never was the sort of man that drew attention to himself. He's always been content to be in the background. But if you paid attention to him, you'd realize that all is not quite as it should be.'

Lavinia thought back to the previous shoot. She had a vivid recollection of George sitting in the dining room, a bread roll in front of him and his soup left to get cold. He hadn't even eaten the roll, but had shredded it into little bits and chased the crumbs around the table-cloth. In the end Doris had removed the soup, still untouched, as the rest of Lavinia's guests were getting restless and the meal had to continue.

Lavinia frowned. 'How long has he been ill?'

'I don't really know. You see, it was all so gradual, and some days he seems almost normal. At first he was just a bit forgetful, always loosing things and forgetting what he was doing. I didn't take much notice. I'm forever going to

98

the pantry myself, and forgetting what I've gone there for. But now he forgets even the most recent past, but oddly enough, not the distant past. He'll suddenly start telling me about things that happened in his youth, and sometimes he calls me Mother. At other times he's so confused he forgets to put his shoes on in the morning, and he'll lose his way, even in the house – and God knows the house isn't that big. I mean, it's not like here, or like Hulver, is it?' Hillary sighed. 'Last week I found him urinating in the tumble dryer – he insisted that it was a urinal.' Hillary blew her nose. 'I'm sorry, Lavinia. It's unfair of me to burden you with this. You've quite enough to worry about with this Lloyds thing.'

Lavinia knitted her brows together. 'Lloyds?'

'Yes, I know Josh is in the same syndicates as George. And that, of course, is another thing I'm having to deal with on my own. George, bless him, is no help whatsoever.'

Lavinia was about to delve deeper into what Hillary described as the Lloyds thing, when a thought struck her. 'Hillary? If George is as forgetful as you say, is it all right for him to be out with a gun?'

No sooner had the words left her mouth when Henry appeared at the drawing room door, he whispered something to Brooke, who left with him. Moments later she went through to the two women in the conservatory.

'Hillary, I think you had better come, there's been a bit of an accident.' Seeing Hillary's alarm, she added, 'Oh, it's all right now, no one's been hurt.'

The men were all gathered in the hall. The rich dark panelling seemed oppressive and gloomy. Josh was giving Rupert Seabrook a drink and there was a low buzz of conversation. Henry was trying to persuade George to let go of a handful of cartridges. When Henry saw Hillary he rushed over to her. A neat, handsome man who had never been adverse to speaking his mind, Henry spoke it now loud and clear. The muffled conversation was silenced as he said:

'What the hell do you think you're doing? Why didn't you tell me he'd lost his marbles? He could have killed us all. He missed Rupert by inches – just inches. You must be as mad as he is, to let him go out like that.'

Hillary was trembling. 'What? What happened?'

'You might well ask. He'd been behaving strangely all day – then during the very last drive he suddenly bloody turned on us! Thought he was back in the war, and decided that we were all bloody Krauts, so he thought he'd better bloody well shoot us. If Josh's chap hadn't disarmed him, God knows what might have happened.' Henry too was shaking, either with fear or with rage.

Hillary collapsed into tears.

Lavinia, who had followed her through, put her

arms around her. 'For goodness sake Henry,' she snapped. 'This isn't solving anything. As long as everyone's all right, that's all that matters.'

Although still enraged, Henry spoke with less vehemence and less volume. 'With the greatest respect in the world, Lavinia, that is not all that matters. It was your brother that nearly got killed, remember? God, what if the press get hold of this? Think what they would make of it. Blood sports get a bad enough press as it is.'

Brooke had entered the hall. 'Henry, darling, there's no harm done. The press haven't got hold of it, and I suggest you have a word with Josh's man. Reward him generously for his presence of mind, and suggest to him that George's unfortunate lapse of memory is nothing to sensationalize.'

Henry let out a great sigh. It was a well-known fact that he took notice of his very sensible wife.

She went over to him and rubbed his shoulders. 'Shouting at Hillary isn't going to help,' she said softly. 'It's kind words, not cruel accusations, that she needs.'

Henry looked at Brooke's soft gray eyes and then down at his shoes. He turned abruptly to Hillary, who was still shaking violently. 'I'm sorry, Hillary,' he said, tenderly touching her arm. 'I guess I was in shock. Brooke's right. Shouting at you isn't helpful to anyone.' He looked up at the ceiling and played his fingers over his lips. 'I think you

101

should take George home now though.'

Hillary looked crestfallen.

'Henry!' Brooke snapped, 'Have you taken leave of your senses?'

She turned to Hillary, who now had a very benign-looking George by the hand. 'Hillary, why don't you take George upstairs and get him to have a rest before dinner. We don't eat until eight so there is plenty of time. And, Hillary, dear, don't worry. We'll help you with all of this.' She gestured expansively. 'We're your friends – yours and George's – we won't let you down.'

Henry sighed heavily and practically stamped his foot as Hillary led George away. 'Come on, everyone,' he said. 'I need a drink, but for Christ sake lock your guns away before you come through.'

Lavinia pulled Brooke to one side as the others left the room. 'Brooke, I could kiss you,' she said.

Brooke smiled; she put her arm around Lavinia's shoulders. 'Don't take too much notice of Henry. He doesn't always think about what he's saying.'

Lavinia returned Brooke's embrace. 'You know, Brooke? I've believe I've misjudged you.'

CHAPTER ELEVEN

For all Brooke's kind and welcoming words, Hillary begged to be able to take George home. She felt awkward, she said, after what had happened; besides she felt George would fare better in his own home.

She was right to take him home; the party would have fallen very flat had they stayed. As it was, crude jokes were made at both Hillary's and George's expense – jokes not intended to be cruel, but the jesting somehow helped to ease the tension and fool everyone into thinking that the episode had not been as serious as it actually was.

In the end, only three couples stayed the night at Pennington, despite Brooke's protestations and her generous invitation for them all to take the horses out on the following day. For most of them the day at Pennington had been spoiled. They saw the episode with George as a black cloud on an otherwise perfect horizon, an omen perhaps, that heralded the end of their cosseted lifestyle.

Josh and Lavinia, although they hadn't intended to stay, stayed, and Steve Jarvis stayed too, although not, of course, at the big house. He was invited to stay with John Felts, the Pennington's keeper, an invitation that both Henry and Josh encouraged; perhaps, they said, he might like to help with the horses on the following day. Steve, who passionately believed in his Gypsy blood, had an equal passion for horses, convinced that his imaginary ancestors had passed on a special equestrian gift. Sure enough he proved to have a way with the creatures, whether by blood or misplaced confidence.

Philip and Ailsa McTodd stayed, as did Lavinia's brother Rupert and his young wife, Rosemary.

But on the following day only Ailsa opted to ride.

The men cloistered themselves in the billiard room; they had, they said, business to discuss. Rosemary stayed in bed nursing a hangover – not an unusual occurrence. Lavinia and Brooke, who had sat late into the night discussing Hillary and George, both felt far too tired and jaded to take to the saddle.

Try as she might, Lavinia could not get close to her sister-in-law. She was often heard to mumble that she couldn't see why Rupert had married her, which, of course, was a thoughtless remark; because everyone else could see that Rupert and Rosemary's marriage had been a very well balanced arrangement. Rosemary, a sexy, not very successful, ex-model, had traded her youth and beauty for money and position. It was simple and unquestionable, and the arrangement seemed to suit them both very well.

Rosemary at twenty-eight simply oozed sex appeal. She was not the most intelligent and well educated of girls, but she gave what she had. In return, forty-two-year-old Rupert was plain and steady and boring; he was also very, very generous to his lovely wife. Indeed, she openly referred to him as her 'Sugar Daddy' – a name which amused Rupert but alarmed both Lavinia and the rest of his family.

They had no children, not, Rupert assured everyone with a wicked grin, through want of trying.

Ailsa, in borrowed riding habit, set off at eleven with Steve Jarvis as her groom and companion, leaving Brooke and Lavinia smiling, and saying amongst themselves, that they hoped young Jarvis would be safe in her hands, for Ailsa McTodd had a reputation for flirting with younger men.

Ailsa was forty-three but looked ten years younger. She was a woman with a hobby. A hobby that tennis coaches and golf professionals all over the world would immediately recognize. A hobby that even Steve Jarvis recognized the first time he met her.

Holding out her cool manicured hand, her first

words of greeting had been. 'Hello, Steve, I'm Ailsa McTodd.' Then, running her eyes over him from the top of his head to the tips of his toes and back again, she said, 'My, you're a fit young man. Do you work-out?'

For Ailsa had also recognized Steve for what he was, a recognition that was confirmed when he didn't answer her, but simply returned her laughing stare with a black eyed, brooding look of his own.

'I see we understand each other perfectly,' she said. Her borrowed jodhpurs were very tight and her white blouse, under the tweed riding-jacket, was open almost to the waist. Her hennaed hair was tied back in the nape of her neck and a black riding hat completed her ensemble. She had a square face with full lips and wide apart eyes. She always looked slightly amused as if she could read her companions' minds and found the sentiments expressed there trivial and rather petty.

They trotted out of the cobbled stable yard and broke into a canter across the open parkland. At one point Ailsa lost her hat and sent Steve back to find it for her. He did so, and handed it back to her with a haughty, defiant air, as if to tell her that he too could read her mind and knew all she planned, and it was he, not she, that had a full hand of cards.

They rode up onto the cliff top and eventually arrived at the Osbourne-Pennington shooting lodge. No words were spoken, not one. They dismounted and tied their horses to the gun-rack outside the entrance. Ailsa produced the key and led the way inside. A few red embers from the day before still glowed in the huge open fireplace. Steve took newspaper and twigs and added more wood, and soon the fire burst into life.

Ailsa stood a little apart watching him. As she watched, she slowly removed first her jacket, then her blouse, never letting her eyes leave his face. She smiled when Steve gave an involuntary gasp as, just as slowly, she removed her bra revealing her large, slightly pendulous breasts. She removed the pin from the back of her head and shook her hair lose over her shoulders.

She spoke then. 'So,' she said, 'what do you have to offer?'

'Plenty,' he replied, his voice thick and rather gruff. 'But let's see the rest of the goods first.'

She shook her head, her red hair cascaded around her shoulders. 'No,' she said. 'I want to see if it's worth my while.'

Steve unzipped his Levi's; he was so hard it was difficult to pull his penis through his fly.

Ailsa, still perfectly in control, smiled. ' I guess that will have to do – poor old McTodd hasn't got much to offer these days.' There was genuine regret in her voice.

She pointed to the hearthrug. 'Down there,' she

said, and obediently Steve lay down on his back in front of the fire, his erection sticking up like a beacon.

Ailsa removed her riding boots, her jodhpurs and her panties. Then she replaced the boots so that she was completely naked apart from her lower legs and her feet. She was big breasted with a slim waist and rounded hips. She stood above him with her legs either side of him.

'Okay groom-boy. Let's go for a ride.'

She lowered herself none too gently onto him, and rode him, her hips moving with force and vigor, and she cried out as if she were leading a field of hunters and a pack of excited hounds. Her nipples brushed his cheeks as she bent forward, and left Steve gasping for air.

When both she and Steve were satiated, she stood up, pulling herself away from him very slowly. He watched her thigh muscles tense as she lifted her body. Slowly she replaced her clothes.

Steve lay still on the hearthrug, breathless and slightly dazed. 'Christ,' he said. 'I didn't need to move a muscle.' He shook his head, about to say more, but Ailsa spoke first.

'Come on,' she said. 'We'll be late for lunch, and I'm starving.'

Steve got to his feet and zipped up his jeans; once again he tried to speak.

She laughed at him. 'Whatever you were going to

say, Jarvis, don't. You're no more than a hunk of well hung horse flesh to me.' She walked over to him, unzipped him, and encircled his penis and testicles in her hand. 'This is the only part of you that I'm interested in,' she said.

His face showed no emotion, his eyelids didn't even flicker. 'Funny,' he said. 'That's the only part of me that's interested in you.' He touched his forelock with his hand, 'My lady,' he added, and bowed.

If Ailsa was unnerved, her face didn't show it. They left the lodge, mounted their horses and galloped at full speed back to Pennington Manor, arriving in the stable yard with their mounts frothing and sweating as profusely as they themselves had done thirty minutes before.

CHAPTER TWELVE

On the following Wednesday, the first in December, Lavinia set off to visit Hillary. Brooke and Lavinia had agreed between themselves that if possible one or the other of them would visit the Miles-Joneses every week. A visit was, they thought, the kindest act they could do to help. The sunshine of the week before had deserted the countryside and the air hung damp and heavy. Stillness descended on Hulver Park and the black skeletal trees dripped great globules of moisture in the dull foggy atmosphere.

Hillary and George lived twenty miles from Hulver in the little village of Glowers Boothby, having sold their house in Kensington and retired there five years before. George had worked in the city all his life. He had earned a good income and invested well. A small rotund man with receding hair, bushy eyebrows and a full beard, he had a reputation for complete integrity and was admired for his quiet and calm approach to life. He had loved his new life at Glowvenders Barn, a barn converted only a few years before the Miles-Joneses bought it.

Glowvenders stood close to the river Nene; it was a successful contemporary conversion married into a beautiful historic building and set in an idyllic rural environment. The house had been created within the shell of a magnificent six bay 18th century barn. The architect had used flare and imagination to create a home that was both unusual and functional. The bedrooms were on the ground floor, the first floor reserved to house a huge drawing room flooded with light. The views from the windows not only encompassed the river but also stretched far into the distance. It was a light, airy property that, even on a dull day, felt warm and inviting.

Hillary was leaning forward, her elbows on her knees.

'You see, I thought it would be all right. He was all right – at Hulver, I mean, at Josh's shoot – he was all right then, wasn't he?' Her eyes pleaded with Lavinia for comfort and reassurance.

In fact after the Pennington incident Josh had told Lavinia that George had been far from all right. The once levelheaded man had acted both irrational and preoccupied. But Lavinia felt it would be of little benefit for Hillary to be told of this.

Hillary was still speaking. 'You see, I keep thinking that if we keep doing the old familiar things it will make him well again, sort of jog his memory into action, if you see what I mean?'

At that point George came into the room. Lavinia noticed that his fly was undone; Hillary gave her a weak smile.

'George, dear. Look who's come to see us.'

George smiled; his smile was warm but childlike.

'Hello, my dear, how nice to see you.' He turned his puzzled gaze toward his wife.

'It's Lavinia, darling. Your cousin – Josh's wife, from Hulver.'

George nodded his head. He took Lavinia's hand. 'How nice to see you, my dear,' he kissed both her cheeks. 'I haven't see you for a long time.' Then he added, 'Have I?' And there was an emotion written on his face that Lavinia found hard to read. Profound sadness? Weariness? Panic even? George still had hold of her hand. 'Now, just refresh my memory, my dear. Where is it you live?'

My God, Lavinia thought. How could things be this bad and me not have noticed?

'Hulver,' she said brightly.

'Ah yes, Hulver, of course. Do you know the . . . er . . . er . . . ' He frowned and shook his head as if the movement itself might dislodge a memory. 'The . . . er . . . um, you know, I'll get it in a minute. The, er . . . the . . . Oh, you know, the people at the castle. Yes, that's it, the castle. Do you know them? They're good friends of mine. I can't quite think of the name, but they are good friends of mine. I haven't seen them for ages though . . . not for ages. But they're really good friends of mine. Where was it you said you lived?'

Lavinia was almost reduced to tears by her cousin's ramblings. 'They'll always be good friends of yours, George,' she said softly.

He smiled at her in his delightful benign way.

'Why don't you come and sit down and read the newspaper, George?' Hillary said.

George, like a small child, allowed himself to be led over to the sofa and dutifully picked up the newspaper and stared at it. A few moments later he started to tap the arm of his chair with his fingertips, and then he began a rhythmic humming of a long forgotten tune.

Hillary smiled a weak, sad, smile. 'If it wasn't so sad, it would be really funny,' she whispered. 'We have those sorts of conversations a dozen times a day.'

Lavinia covered Hillary's hand with her own. 'Don't fall apart, Hillary. George needs you. Wherever would he be without you? You know, you ought to get some help with him, a nurse or a home help. You're looking awfully tired.'

A weary, forlorn smile creased Hillary's face. She shook her head.

'It's out of the question, Lavinia. We're practically

cleaned out now, we have a few stocks and shares, but if the predictions are correct I'll have to sell them soon. The bank have already made it clear that they won't see us through the crisis. George has a good pension, of course, but most of that has to go toward paying the bank for what we've borrowed already.'

It was then that Lavinia asked the question that had started as a slight concern but had grown to a full-scale worry over the last two weeks. 'What crisis, Hillary?'

Hillary looked at her blankly. 'The Lloyds thing, of course – Josh has told you?'

'Lord yes,' Lavinia said rather loudly. 'I just didn't realize George was in Lloyds.' This was a lie, she knew full well, but she didn't want Hillary to clam up on her.

'He's in the same syndicates as Josh, so you must know how bad it is. I must say, Lavinia, I envy you your rational approach. Maybe I could be calmer about it if I had George to help me. I know you must be worried sick but you don't show it. To the outside world you don't seem a bit concerned.'

Lavinia smiled, but a little seed of fear had crept into her chest. A little seed that was taking root, and would, she knew, grow strong and tall, blossom, and eventually reproduce.

'Nor should you be worried, Hillary. Josh say's it's just a blip, the profits have always been up and down.'

She patted Hillary's arm again. 'Look, I can tell you just how confident Josh is that things will even out. He's planning to take me to Venice in the autumn, a sort of second honeymoon. So you see, he can't be that worried, now can he? He'd never have planned a holiday if he was worried about money, would he? You know Josh.' But the fear in her heart wouldn't go away. It spread over her body, seeping down into her fingertips and her toes. Her mind became a sponge, soaking up the fear until she was totally saturated by it. She opened her eyes wide. Josh hadn't promised her Venice, it was she that had suggested it. What was it that Josh had said? She clenched her fists – she couldn't remember. But she did know that he'd made some excuse before she'd finally persuaded him. Even then, his promise had been edged with a series of get-out clauses – like fine print on an insurance document. Josh had never refused her anything, and he had never burdened her with his worries. There was that time when his Hunter watch had been stolen from his London club; he'd never even mentioned it until the thief had been caught and the watch returned. But surely this was different?

Hillary's words brought her back from her thoughts.

'You're very sweet, Lavinia, but you know, I'm a realist. I know how bad things are, and I know you're in it much deeper than we are. Dear Lavinia, you are so very kind to worry about us, when you yourself have far more at stake than ever George and I have.' Hillary looked around the big room. 'I'd be so, so sad to leave this place, Lavinia. But it's fairly new to us, it's not like you. If you have to leave Hulver, well, it will break all your hearts.'

Lavinia tried to keep calm. 'Hillary, just how much has George lost?'

Hillary let out a great sigh. 'Eighty thousand last year, forty in ninety-one, more I fear will be due next year.'

Lavinia's mouth felt dry, a taste had invaded it, the taste that, unbeknown to her, her husband knew so well. A taste of airplane food and snacked meals; a taste of disorientation. George and Hillary were poor in comparison to her and Josh, so if the Miles-Joneses had lost that much, how deeply was Josh wounded?

With a tremendous effort, Lavinia brightened. 'Let's not talk about it anymore, Hillary. It's all too gloomy for words – something will turn up. Josh isn't too worried, so why should we be.'

'With the greatest respect in the world, Lavinia, you and Josh have a little more behind you than we have.'

Lavinia patted the older woman's hand. 'Don't worry, we won't see you starve, you know. We'll help you out, we won't let you down.'

Hillary stared down the drive and watched Lavinia drive

away. The car's brake lights engaged as she reached the gates, and with their red glow, gloom descended on Hillary like a thick black mantle. Lavinia was making very light of the Lloyds thing, she and Josh must be better placed than she thought. She put her hand up to her head, her feeling of isolation complete. She turned sharply as she heard a noise behind her. George was sitting on the hearthrug tearing up newspaper, making strange paper patterns and spreading them out on the floor in front of him. He smiled at her, a little boy's smile, a dependant, trusting smile, and Hillary felt overwhelmed with love for him, the sort of love a mother feels for a helpless child.

She seated herself at the piano. 'Shall I play something for you?' she asked.

George looked up at her again, his head on one side as if already hearing the notes she was about to play. For Hillary, her music was her solace, her friend, and her bridge to sanity and reality. She began to play Chopin. She played the notes slowly, drawing the piece out and making the music seem immeasurably sad, reflecting her mood, and adding to her air of melancholy. Meanwhile George, with his meaningless grin, began to hum a totally unrelated tune.

CHAPTER THIRTEEN

Lavinia drove through the castle gates and proceeded up the long, slightly twisting, drive, purposely made that way so that the visitor could view and admire the house from a variety of interesting angles. Not for the first time she wondered who had decided to call it a castle; it had neither dungeon nor castellation, nor was it surrounded by a moat. Indeed the McTodd's house in Scotland was far more of a castle, being stout sided with a flagpole and turrets. Today, in the gloomy November air, Hulver Castle looked dour and unwelcoming, thick mist brooded around the roof, and rain dripped unrelentingly from the guttering and windowsills. The castle was built of yellow sandstone, which looked warm and welcoming in the bright summer sunshine, but on a dull dismal winter day the stone seemed to absorb the moisture, turning it to dirty dull ochre and adding to the air of gloom. Lavinia's visit to Hillary had depressed her, the wet day, and the view of her home in the rain, only served to dampen her spirits a little more.

She threw her coat onto the sofa in the marble hall. The house felt cold and she shivered. The day being Wednesday, a team of cleaners could be heard vacuuming somewhere in the bowels of the house. The arrangement was that Doris came in every day except Sunday, and several village women came in once a week to do what was described as the rough work, although with the aid of modern appliances the description wasn't entirely appropriate.

Lavinia went through to the kitchen and stood for a moment or two warming her back on the Aga. From there she went into Josh's office, calling his name. She felt desperately in need of confiding her worries concerning her cousin and his wife, and felt quite tearful when Josh was nowhere to be found.

Doris had piled the mail up on Josh's desk. The room was so cold that Lavinia's breath condensed as it left her nose. She shivered and folded her arms around herself as she idly flicked through the pile of letters, bills and circulars. She pulled out three letters addressed to her and Josh, picked up a Sotherby's catalogue that was lying on Josh's desk, and made her way back to the warmth of the kitchen, feeling various cold radiators as she progressed through the house. Doris was in the kitchen making coffee; she was a plain, masculine looking woman with tightly permed hair, and dull brown eyes.

'Ah, Lady H,' she said brightly. 'Would you like a cup of coffee? Gawd. It's as cold as charity today, ain't it?'

Lavinia accepted the coffee and agreed that it was indeed, as cold as charity, and said that she thought the heating must have broken down again, and did Doris know where Lord Hulver might be found?

'He's gone out with the dog, Lady H, went about an hour ago – said he didn't think you'd be home for lunch. Thought you were having it over at Glowers Boothby.'

Lavinia was glad that Hillary hadn't suggested she stay for lunch. She'd found the morning quite depressing enough without prolonging the agony. But if she felt that way, how on earth did Hillary feel?

Once Doris had left the kitchen, Lavinia opened her mail. There were two thank-you letters from guests of the previous week, and an invitation to the New Year's Day Shoot at the McTodd's. This was an event that Josh and Lavinia hadn't missed in fifteen years; they'd even gone the year after the twins had been born, determinedly carting nannies and nappies up the Great North Road and back again. She put the letters on the kitchen dresser so that Josh could see them when he got back. She glanced out of the window; it was raining heavily now and Lavinia shook her head, wondering what could have possessed her husband to walk the dog on such a foul day. Surely he'd be home soon. It was almost half-past-one, where was he?

She went to the fridge and got out the ingredients for making a sandwich, shivered, changed her mind, and opened a tin of soup instead. She poured the soup into a jug and warmed it in the microwave. She put two bread rolls in the Aga to warm, set the table and sat down to wait for Josh, feeling by now almost angry. She needed to share Hillary's pain with him, only by sharing it, could she hope to reduce her own. Josh would have some bright idea; he'd know a way in which they could help the Miles-Joneses.

The clock crept around to two. Lavinia was warm at last, but the discomfort of being cold had been replaced by the discomfort of hunger, and still Josh did not come. She flicked through the Sotheby's catalogue, a gun sale, really not of much interest to her. She pushed it to one side. As she did so a small white compliment slip fluttered to the ground. She bent over and picked it up. It had the auction house's name, address, telephone and fax number written on it, and page 89 typed in the center. Lavinia turned to page 89. A pair of fine Purdy Shot Guns the caption read. Lavinia sighed. Surely Josh wasn't interested in buying? Josh had a wonderful set of Purdy shotguns, guns that had belonged to his father and his grandfather before that. Lavinia frowned. Her hunger forgotten she got up and went back to Jocelyn's study. She opened his top desk drawer, felt to the back and took out the gun cupboard key. Then she returned to the kitchen and took the other key from the top of the kitchen dresser, from there she went to the gun room.

Kicking Fen's basket to one side with her foot, she opened the false mahogany front to the gun cupboard, and turned the keys in the locks of the reinforced steed cabinet. The door swung open to reveal three guns. Lavinia sighed. For a moment she had thought that Josh was about to sell his Purdys. She didn't hear Josh enter the room and she started violently when he said, 'Vinnie! What on earth are you doing?'

'Oh! Oh, Josh. I nearly jumped out of my skin.' She laughed then. 'Isn't that the most revolting saying? I mean, can you imagine anyone actually jumping out of their skin?'

Josh gave an awkward smile. 'What are you doing, Lavinia?'

'Doing?' She shook her head. 'I was just looking at that Sotherby's catalogue. First of all I thought you were going to bid for a couple of Purdys,' she laughed. 'And then I got the mad idea that you were selling yours.' She laughed again, unable to interpret the look on her husband's face. Josh didn't speak.

'You see,' she said. 'Hillary spoke about Lloyds this

morning and I thought, well, to tell you the truth.' She drew in a deep breath. 'I thought that you'd been holding out on me, and that you were selling the guns to make ends meet. But they're still here I see, so – Josh? Josh? What is it?'

Her husbands jaw was working back and forth. 'I didn't want to worry you, Lavinia. I didn't think I'd need to worry you, you see. I thought I could sell the guns and, well, they are worth a lot of money, you know.'

'But they're still here,' Lavinia said.

Josh leaned over her toward the gun cabinet. He took out the first gun. 'Sixteen bore,' he said. 'My father taught me to shoot with this, and I'll teach the boys with it one day.' He stared straight ahead of him. His eyes, whilst not actually watering, held a promise of tears. 'That's if we have any land to shoot over.'

'Josh, you're frightening me.'

He reached over for the next gun. 'This is a two-two rifle, very dangerous bit of kit this, the boys must never be allowed to touch it.'

'Josh, you're frightening me,' she said again.

As if he hadn't heard her, he reached over for the last gun. 'And this, this is a twelve bore – made inSpain especially for the export market. Cheap but effective, kills just as efficiently as a Purdy and the insurance is far more reasonable.' He put the guns back, shut the metal door with a clang and turned both the keys simultaneously. He stared straight ahead of him, twisting the keys around in his hand.

'Josh,' she whispered. 'You're frightening me.'
Still he didn't meet her eyes. 'I'm frightening myself, Lavinia.'

'How bad is it, Josh?'

He drew a very deep breath and followed it with a long sigh, and now he met her eyes. 'You know, Vinnie. I haven't thought of it in those terms. Funny that, don't you think? My greatest concern has been not to upset you, not to get you involved.'

'Well, how bad is it?'

He shook his head, 'I can't say, Vinnie.'

'Can't, or won't?'

'For Christ sake, Vinnie,' he shouted. 'What do you want me to say, that we're ruined, that we're broke? OK. We're ruined – we're broke. We'll sell up and, and, and go and live in a terraced house in Coventry.'

Somewhere in the depths of the house the vacuum cleaner stopped and heads and ears leaned toward the argument in the gun room.

Lavinia clenched her fists, she was becoming extremely angry. 'Surely I have a right to know, Josh.'

'I don't see why, you've never taken much interest in the business before. The estate has made money and you've been happy enough to spend it.'

Lavinia frowned. This simply wasn't fair. Josh had never bothered her with matters of business. Indeed he considered business matters a man's concern. He heartily disapproved of men that involved their wives in their financial affairs.

'Josh, why are you being so aggressive?'

Tears were coursing down his cheeks now. 'Because, Vinnie, I'm ashamed, ashamed that I've brought you to the brink of ruin, and it's easier to blame you than it is to blame myself.'

'Oh, Josh, Josh, why didn't you tell me, why didn't you share all this with me?' She fell into his arms. 'Oh, Josh, it'll be all right. For goodness sake look at the collateral we have – surely we can borrow on it.'

Doris the cleaner put her hand over her mouth to stifle a giggle. 'My. How the mighty fall,' she murmured to her colleagues, who nodded their heads in gleeful agreement.

Josh kissed the top of his wife's head. 'Vinnie, we have borrowed on it. We're stretched to the limit. The bank is holding us up – if they pull the rug, we'll go under.'

'Oh,' was all that Lavinia could say.

Doris pushed her sleeves higher up her arm. 'Well,' she said to her audience of village cleaners. 'Well, wait till the village get to hear about this,' she nodded her head. 'Mrs Dobbs at the Post Office will laugh her head off when she hears. She's always going on about the Elliots with their la-de-da ways.'

'Yes,' Josie Stevens chipped in, 'she's never really forgiven them for catching her Fred poaching pheasants off them.'

'And you ought to mention it to Marge Hartley _ they get all their bakery stuff from her. I bet they have an account with her. If they're broke she has a right to know,' Trish Gage offered helpfully.

Josh and Lavinia were back in the kitchen, thick black smoke was pouring out of the Aga. Lavinia had quite forgotten about the bread rolls. Burning her fingers she raked them out of the oven, put the soup to reheat and slotted two pieces of bread into the toaster. Josh was sitting with his head in his hands. She prized one hand away from him and softly kissed his cheek.

'Josh?' Her voice was very low, hardly above a whisper. 'I think Birmingham would suit me better than Coventry.'

He removed his other hand from his face. 'Vinnie, you goose,' he said. 'Oh, Vinnie, I love you so very, very much.'

CHAPTER FOURTEEN

'What a difference a month makes,' Lavinia said as she helped Josh move some of his papers from his cold bleak study into the brightly lit kitchen.

'What?'

'Well, about a month ago, when the girls were home, I remember you telling Zoë that there was no problem with Lloyds, and now, less than a month later, you're telling me that there's a real crisis.'

Jocelyn looked down at his shoes. 'I thought I'd explained about that, Vinnie.' He sighed. 'I'm sorry. I'm truly, very sorry.'

'But you must have known I'd find out,' she insisted. 'I mean, I would eventually have noticed that the heating wasn't on, in fact, you're damned lucky I didn't phone the plumber.'

'No, Vinnie. You're lucky. You'd have looked the fool when he told you we'd run out of oil.'

'Then I'd have phoned the oil company and ordered some more.'

Josh gave her a weak smile. 'And they'd have said that they were sorry, but as there was a large outstanding debt, they would be unable to supply us. They'd have said it ever so politely, of course, and they'd have used little phrases concerning company policy, and shareholder's interest.'

'Oh, Josh. Is that what happened?'

'You can't blame them, they do have a business to run.'

Lavinia swung round on him. 'Well, I do blame them. We've been customers, good customers for years – the least they could do is see us through a bad patch. What are we supposed to do? Freeze to death?'

Josh scraped a pile of bills out of his middle desk drawer; most were decorated with red stickers.

'Oh, Josh. So many?'

'It's not as bad as it looks. There's about three reminders and court warning notices to each bill.'

'Is that supposed to be a comfort?'

Josh reached over to the bookshelf and retrieved a blue box file. 'These are the more urgent ones,' he said.

They carried the papers through to the kitchen, along with a calculator and paper and pencils. Lavinia had insisted on knowing the whole situation, and she had offered to help Josh form a plan of action. Although Josh had long since exhausted any idea of finding a solution.

Lavinia scribbled some headings on pieces of paper. 'Right. On this pile we put urgent bills. On this – the ones that can wait a little while. And on this, the ones that can wait but we'd rather they didn't – local tradesmen and the like.' She smiled cheerfully. 'Then we'll put income here.' She drew a line down the middle of a piece of paper. 'And our outgoings there.'

Half an hour later a huge stack of paper wobbled on the urgent pile, three accounts lay on top of the ones that could wait but they'd rather they didn't, and nothing topped the non-urgent pile.

Lavinia made a pot of tea, she poured it, reseated herself, and pushed her reading glasses further up her nose. 'Right! Now income. And I suppose I'd better look at the bank statements as well.'

Josh ran his finger around the collar of his shirt; he looked at his watch. 'You know, it'll be dark soon. I ought to take Fen out for a run.'

'Josh, we have to start this thing. Go and get the bank statements.'

Josh went back into his study and returned a few minutes later with several folders of bank statements. He looked at his watch again. 'Poor old Fen will wonder what's happened to me,' he said, half to himself.

Lavinia tutted. 'Fen will have to wait for a few more minutes.' She knew that Josh was trying to avoid facing up to the reality of the situation and she was determined not to allow him to go on any longer.

'Yes. Yes of course. I was just worried that she might pee herself, that's all.'

'Steve's in the stable yard – get him to take her out.'

Josh looked at his watch again, 'No. No, she expects me to take her, you know. She'll be all right for a minute or two.'

'Good,' Lavinia said crisply. She glanced at the bank statements. 'But, Josh, look here, we've got lots in this account – thousands in fact.'

Despite the gloom of the situation Josh couldn't help smiling. 'No, darling, that's a minus, see? See the little line in front there?'

'Good God, Josh. What's our limit?'

Josh rubbed his temples with his hands. 'We passed that about nine months ago.'

'Oh.'

'I'm sorry, Vinnie. I know I should have told you, but I kept hoping that things would come right. Then I'd get another bad prediction and have to borrow a bit more, and the more in the red I became, the harder it was to tell you.'

'Well, we'll have to sell something to pay this lot off, won't we?'

'Sell? Sell? We can't just nibble away at the estate – we can't just sell a little bit here and a little bit there. Before we know it, they'll be none left.'

Lavinia looked around her. 'Josh, we've got loads of things we can sell. We've got one or two good pictures and there's the Bloomfields, you're always telling the twins how much they're worth. No one ever looks at them anyway.'

Josh's face had taken on a look of horror.

'Well, when was the last time you opened one of them? Besides, the insurance on them must cost a packet.'

Josh bit into his bottom lip wondering if he could find the words to explain that the household insurance expired months ago. He'd not had enough money to renew the policy.

He heaved himself up from the table and went into the library corridor. Vinnie was right, he couldn't remember the last time he'd looked at them. The books had belonged to his grandfather; he'd be loath to let them go. Even so, perhaps he wouldn't find them quite so fascinating now that the chips were really down. He ran his fingers along the twenty-four leather bound volumes and selected volume twenty-two. He may not look at them very often, but he knew which one featured Hulver Castle and its surrounding area. He took the book back to the kitchen and opened it on the kitchen table. It fell open on a lovely watercolour of Hulver village. He flicked the page over, there was another watercolour, this time of Hulver Church and then further on, Hulver Castle. All the paintings came from the Norwich School. He let his fingers wander over the pages.

Lavinia sat silently watching him.

Eventually, Josh said, 'If they were sold, they'd be broken up, so that the paintings could be sold off individually. There're several Ninhams amongst them, you know, and one's said to be by Cotman.'

'You don't know that they would be broken up, Josh. A book collector would more than likely buy them.

They're very rare – only what? One or two other sets ever produced? Hardly surprising when you consider all the illustrations are done by hand.'

'Three in total,' Josh said. 'And this is the only one still in private hands.' He looked down at his own hands as if to put a literal emphasis into the statement.

Lavinia took the volume from him and, resting it on her arm, she walked back along the library corridor and replaced it.

She came back into the kitchen. 'We'll think of something else,' she said cheerfully.

She pushed her glasses back again. 'OK. Now what

about our regular income?' She had her pencil poised above the paper.'

'Income? What sort of income, Vinnie?'

'Well, we must have an income. We don't live on fresh air, do we?'

'We've already had the income for this year. We've had all the wheat and barley money in, there's the sugar beet money to come, of course, but that's already spoken for – wages for the farm men, and then there's the lease hire on the harvester and the like. Nothing else is due now.'

'But there's the rent from Applegate Farm, isn't there?'

'Oh yes. Yes of course, but that's not due until Lady Day – it's paid in two tranches – Michaelmas and Lady Day.'

'When's Lady Day?'

'Twenty-fifth of March.'

'Oh God. Not till then?'

'And it's spoken for, the bank have already made me sign it away.'

'Oh. Well, what about the other rents?'

'What other rents?'

'The cottages, Mrs Jarvis's, and the Taylor's, and that little row of cottages over at Applegate Farm and — '

Jocelyn interrupted her. 'But, Vinnie, they don't

bring in any rent, darling. Some are tied cottages. Some are let to ex-farm workers or their widows, and others are on a peppercorn rent, fifty-pence a year or something.'

Lavinia smiled at this news. 'Well, that's it then. We'll charge them rent and we'll have this lot paid off in no time.' She made a movement with her right hand toward the pile of bills. The disturbance of the air caused the pile to topple and some of the papers floated down onto the kitchen floor; Fen sniffed at them excitedly.'

Josh made a noise somewhere between a laugh and a moan. 'Are you serious? I can't charge these people rent, Vinnie. Half of them were born in those cottages. They don't expect to have to pay rent. Besides it would be a drop in the ocean, it wouldn't begin to tackle that lot.' He too made a sweeping movement with his hand and yet more of the papers joined their companions on the floor.

'Well, let's see shall we? Now how much do you think Keeper's Cottage is worth?'

Josh shrugged his shoulders. 'How would I know?'

'Take a guess. Twenty? Thirty? Forty pounds?'

'A month?'

'No, a week'

'You're joking. Those people couldn't afford that sort of money.'

'Then those people won't have to pay. We live in a welfare state, remember?'

'You think the government will pay us to house our own people?'

'I don't see why not. The government would pay their rent if they lived anywhere else.'

'Vinnie, this is not a good idea – I know that it sounds good, but it is not. Why, the tenants would be up in arms.'

'Not if we handle it right. I could ask social services or the council or whoever deals with it, to send me some forms, and then we could go and help them fill them in, and we'll reassure them that we won't expect them to pay if they can't afford it.'

'And you'll have a revolution on you're hands.'

Lavinia threw her arms up in the air. 'OK. OK. You obviously have a better idea, so let's hear it?'

Josh sighed, 'I don't have a better idea. I just don't think your idea is a very good one, that's all.'

'Oh. Well, I've just thought of a better idea.' Lavinia's eyes flashed with anger, her cheeks were flushed and she practically spat the words out at him. 'I know. Let's do nothing. Let's not even try. We'll go bankrupt and whoever buys the estate can be the ones to ask the tenants for rent, because I assure you they will, they won't buy the place to run it as a charity.' Lavinia was shouting.

Mrs Jarvis, who had come in to cook the evening meal, was paused outside the door. She was nearly knocked over by Josh when he abruptly left the kitchen, shouting over his shoulder that he was going to take Fen for a walk and implying that his dog spoke a deal more sense than his wife.

'Not interrupting anything, am I?' Mrs Jarvis said rather meekly.

'Shit,' Lavinia murmured under her breath. 'Nothing at all, Mrs Jarvis – just let me move these papers out of your way.'

Lavinia scraped all the unpaid bills into the blue box file. She threw the pad of paper and the calculator in after them. 'There we are, all nice and clear for you now, Mrs Jarvis.'

'Where will you be eating tonight, Lady H? All the dining room's heaters are broke and them rooms are as cold as the grave.'

'Yes, I'm afraid the boiler's broken down again.'

'It's time you had a new one, Lady H. That boiler's as old as me, and I could keep a body a lot warmer than that does.' She gave a high-pitched cackle at her own joke. Her next statement left Lavinia in no doubt that she had overheard her and Jocelyn's conversation. 'You ought to try and live in my little cottage, Lady H, there's no central heating in that, you know. Why I'm surprised the council haven't made his Lordship pull it down. I mean, I know I don't pays no rent for it, and that's as well really, cause if I did, well I'd have to ask for it to be brought up to standard like, and that would cost a pretty penny and no mistake.'

Lavinia tipped Josh's cup of cold tea down the sink, and gave her cook a narrow eyed smile. 'We'll eat in the small dining room, Mrs Jarvis. I'll get Lord Hulver to light a fire in there.'

Lavinia pushed the box file onto the desk in Josh's cold office and hurried down the library corridor and up the stairs to her bedroom. She plugged in the electric fire, turned it on full, and perched on the bed in front of it rubbing her arms with her hands to try and get warm. 'Damn you, Josh,' she muttered. 'How could you have let things go this far?'

No sooner had the words left her mouth than she was overcome with guilt, and at that moment Josh entered the bedroom. He was carrying his customary tray of drinks.

'As Doris would say, it's as cold as charity out there, Lady H.'

'I'm sorry Josh,' she said, lifting her scotch from the tray.

He looked at her tenderly. 'What are you sorry for? It's me that's the devil of the piece. I should be asking you to forgive me, not the other way round.'

He nuzzled his head into her neck. ' And I was mistaken about the dog. I asked her for her ideas and all she could come up with was a rabbit chasing business. She did however offer her services as chief catcher and she promised to be managing director.'

Lavinia laughed, 'Oh, Josh, you fool.'

'That's better, I like it best when you laugh.' He drank some of his whiskey. 'Vinnie? Perhaps tomorrow you'd find out where we get the forms? To claim the rent, that is. And, Vinnie, perhaps when I see the tenants you'd come along and explain things to them? You're better at that sort of thing than I am.'

'Of course I will, my darling.'

'And, Vinnie, I've thought of a brilliant way of keeping ourselves warm.' He pushed her over onto the bed.

'Silly you,' she said. 'I thought of that ages ago.'

CHAPTER FIFTEEN

'Hello, darling.'

Lavinia was reluctant to admit that she couldn't tell the difference between her two sons on the telephone; a general 'Hello darling' was a safe bet. The boys became quite offended if she mistook one for the other. The twins were not identical but their voices sounded very alike over the airwaves.

'Mummy? Hi, how are you?'

'I'm fine, darling. How are you? How's school?'

'It's fine,' her son sighed, 'but Sebbie's being a bit of a pain.'

Good, that meant she must be talking to Quentin. 'And in what way is your brother being a pain?' she asked.

'He's been copying my project for C.E.'

'Oh, I see.'

Lavinia heard a scuffle as her younger son – younger by less than twenty minutes, snatched the telephone away from his brother. 'I have not.' Sebastian's voice resounded down the telephone. 'He's been copying mine.'

Another scuffle and Quentin came back on the line. 'That's a lie, Mummy. He took mine,' her elder son said.

Not for the first time Lavinia wondered if the nurse had got it right –if Quentin really was her first born son, destined to inherit Hulver and the title that went with it. She wondered how Sebastian would feel about that in later life, just twenty minutes making the difference between a fortune and a peerage, and an ordinary run of the mill Honorable. She smiled sadly; as things stood at the moment there was a good chance that the title would be the only thing left to inherit.

'Don't fight boys, please.'

As always, any form of reprimand made the boys bond together, as if they were suddenly one single unit.

'We're not,' chorused two reticent voices.

Lavinia smiled. 'Good, I'm glad to hear it.'

They talked for a while, mainly about the impending Common Entrance examination and both boys expressed a fear that their brother might gain a place at Edgeford School and that they themselves might not. Then the subject got around to what they would do in the rapidly approaching Christmas holiday. Lavinia neglected to tell them that their usual Christmas celebrations would change quite dramatically. For one thing there would be no New Year ski trip for the Elliot children. It had been the custom on previous years for all four of the children to join the Morgan Tour in the Alps, leaving the older Elliots free to enjoy the New Year shoot at Cameron House, home of Philip and Ailsa McTodd. This year there would be no ski trip and no shoot. Lavinia frowned as she replaced the receiver, she felt suddenly ineffectual. She desperately wanted to see her boys; put her arms around their thin pre-adolescent bodies and reassure herself that lack of money and position counted for nothing beside her beloved children. She had the sad feeling that the children themselves would mind more that she did.

Thinking of the boys made her smile. Bless them! They were so full of life, so full of love. Moments after she had replaced the receiver the telephone rang again.

'Lavinia? It's Brooke. Look, I went to see Hillary today. She's really in dire straights, you know. When I got there, there were these men all over the place, and do you know what they were doing? Taking Hillary's baby grand away, that's what!'

Lavinia really didn't see the significance, until Brooke, hardly pausing for breath, continued.

'She's having to sell it, you see. To pay for some ghastly insurance debt.'

Lavinia gave a rather halfhearted, 'Oh.'

'Well, don't you see? We can't let her do it – her piano's the only thing that keeps her sane. She'll be as mad as poor old George without it.'

'But I don't see what we can do, if she needs the money she — '

'We'll have to go to the auction and buy it back for her, then she can have it on permanent loan.'

'Brooke, I really don't think — '

'Oh, I know what you're going to say, all that garbage about the British pride, stiff upper lip, take what's coming, and all that nonsense. Well, sorry, but we simply have to do this thing. Hillary will just have to swallow her pride. You know, Lavinia. Sometimes one has to make things happen, not everything happens by itself.'

'It's not that, Brooke, it's just that – well,' she took a deep breath, 'I'm not very flush myself at the moment and— '

'And nothing! It can't be worth that much – it's donkey's years old.'

'Precisely. I think it is worth a lot, otherwise Hillary wouldn't be selling it, would she? In fact, I know it's quite valuable – it came from our Grandmother's house. George inherited it from her in the sixties.'

'Even so, it can't be beyond our reach if we chip in together and buy it between us. It's only a piano, for goodness sake.'

'Sorry, Brooke, but ... How is George anyway?'

'George? Oh yes, poor lamb, he's really, really crazy. Hillary is just a little short of being a saint to cope the way she does. You know what happened this morning? Well, as I said, the piano men were there and they had parked this big van thing in front of the barn, and George went out to them and started to apologize to them for the van being there. I'm afraid the van driver wasn't very kind, he kept calling George, Granddad. He said something like, "What you apologizing to me for, Granddad? It's my blooming van, and it's me that parked it there." And poor, dear, George couldn't understand it at all. He just carried on apologizing. And Hillary was in a dreadful state. She said it was like saying goodbye to a lifelong friend. I assume she meant the piano, not George.'

I felt the same way when I said goodbye to my mother's silver candlesticks and the little constable oil sketch, Lavinia thought bitterly; thinking of the things she and Josh had recently sent off to the auction house.

'It's only a possession, you know, Brooke. Times are hard. We've all had to part with things we feel sentimental about.'

Brooke was silent for a few moments.

'So you won't help Hillary, then?'

'Not won't, Brooke, I can't. I would if I could, you know I would, but truly, I can't help.'

Brooke's voice became quite sharp. 'Oh. I see. I understand.'

No you don't, thought Lavinia. You haven't got a clue. You're an American, you can't possibly know what it's like parting with things that have been in the family for generations, things that you have enjoyed, and things that your children should inherit and enjoy after you.

'Oh well,' said Brooke. 'I don't expect I shall see you now until after Christmas, but I'll see you in the New Year at the McTodds'?'

Lavinia hesitated. 'I . . . I don't think so, Brooke. I think we're going to give it a miss this year.'

'Give it a miss? But you always go. I thought we should take Hillary and George, making sure George doesn't shoot of course, but there's little danger of that, he's deteriorating so quickly. I doubt if he even remembers his shooting days. Don't be a spoil-sport – of course you must come.'

'It's difficult.'

'How is it difficult?'

'Well, it's a long drive and the children will all be home this New Year.'

'Why will they be home? Aren't they skiing? Don't they usually go on the Morgan ski trip?'

'Yes. Usually they do, but this year it's not possible. There are four of them, you know.'

Brooke sounded puzzled. 'There were four of them last year, Lavinia.'

Lavinia didn't reply.

'Right, well . . . ' said Brooke, not bothering to cancel the puzzlement in her voice. 'Change you mind and come. Bring your young with you. Ailsa won't mind. I'm taking our little ones, they'll all have a lovely time. After all, if Henry Junior and the twins are going to Edgeford together, it's time they got to know each other a little better.' Lavinia heard Brooke take a deep breath. 'And don't worry about the piano, I'll get Henry to buy it.' She hung up just as Henry walked into the room.

'Buy what?' He said.

'What?'

'You said you'd get Henry to buy something.'

'Oh yes, yes, it's Hillary. She's caught up in some sort of insurance scandal. I confess, I don't really understand the ins and outs of it, but she needs help, Henry – so I thought, being as you're such a thoroughly good all round egg, we could help her?'

Henry took his wife by the hand. 'Come and sit down, Brooke. I want to talk to you.' He led her over to the sofa.

'Brooke, my dear, we can't help Hillary. In fact, very soon, we won't be able to help ourselves.'

CHAPTER SIXTEEN

It was a grim prospect that greeted the Elliot children on their return that Christmas. Josh had the task of telling Zoë that her beloved pony Zeus and Tiggy's pony Bramble would have to be sold. He could, he said; no longer justify keeping animals that didn't pay their own way. As it was, he explained, the horses didn't get enough exercise whilst the girls were away at school – it wasn't fair on the animals.

Tiggy took the news well. Shrugging her shoulders, she said that Bramble deserved a more attentive mistress anyway. But Zoë became sullen and spat back at her father that Fen certainly didn't earn her keep and perhaps he should think about having the animal put to sleep. He would, she insisted, save a considerable sum of money on dog food. Whereupon Lavinia intervened, siding heavily with Josh and expressing a desire that Zoë adopt the same helpful attitude as her sister. Uttering feelings of hurt and victimization Zoë went off in the direction of the village, where she confided all her problems to her ever-willing listener, Steve Jarvis.

The rent rebate forms arrived from the Housing Benefit Office. Lavinia and Josh spent a weary day visiting the tenants; and both householders and landlord expressed dismay at the repairs that needed doing on the properties. Lavinia valiantly tried to explain that a little rent would enable the Elliots to invest money to improve the cottages. A logic that was totally lost on the tenants, who politely reminded their landlords that they had lived rent-free for many years and didn't see why they shouldn't continue to do so. One tenant, a retired farm worker, named Tom Firgreen, complained so bitterly that Josh almost lost his temper with him. 'Look, Tom,' he said. 'I agree. It would be nice to put in a new kitchen, and yes, replacement windows would be lovely, but the estate is really hard up at the moment, it simply can't run to such an expense.'

'Huh,' Tom replied. 'Well, I'll tell you what, Squire. I wish I were as 'ard up as you, I tell'e truth I do. Why, if I were as 'ard up as you, I'd be living off the fat of the land in 'Ulver Castle, and not in yon puny little hovel.'

Despite the injustice of the remark, Josh blushed.

'He's got a point, Vinnie,' he said afterwards. 'You've got to admit, he does have a point.'

But Lavinia simply set her mouth and refused to

agree or disagree. She had achieved what she had set out to do, and for the first time in many years the Hulver Estate would start to draw some rental income from its numerous cottages.

'The first thing we shall do, Josh, is buy a tank of oil,' she said. 'Do you know the last time we had heat in the house was mid November?'

'Yes, I know, Vinnie. You remind me most days.'

'Well, I feel the cold more than you, and the children really feel it. I'm convinced that the boys' prep school is overheated, that's why they get so many colds.'

'And how are you going to buy this tank of oil, Vinnie?'

'With the rent money, of course. Look, Mrs Hawkins has already agreed to pay twenty pounds a week, and Mr and Mrs Webber, they're a really sweet couple, aren't they, Josh? They've agreed to pay thirty pounds a week. Mind you, I think they know a good thing when they see one, both those cottages are worth a lot more. Still, it's a start.'

'You misunderstand me, Vinnie. I mean, how, exactly, are you going to turn the rent money into oil?'

'I'll pay the money into the bank, then pay off the oil bill, of course.'

'Don't let me shoot you down in flames, Vinnie. But any money you put into the bank will be swallowed up by the overdraft, and even if you did manage to let the oil company have it, they still wouldn't deliver any oil. You'd need to pay off their entire bill and produce the money in advance for the new lot of oil.'

Lavinia bit into her bottom lip, they were driving out of the village toward the castle.

'Let's go to Norwich,' she said.

'What, now?'

'Yes. Now.'

'Do you mind telling me, why?'

'To open a new bank account, of course.'

'Whatever for? We're servicing too many accounts as it is.'

'No, no. At a different bank – in my maiden name. We can use it as a sort of domestic account.'

Jocelyn frowned. 'Is that legal?'

'For God's sake, Josh. Does it really matter?'

'Well of course it damned well matters. We may be in deep shit, but at least it's legal shit.'

'I don't know if I agree with you there, Josh. But look, you won't be breaking the law, I will. So I'll go to prison, not you.'

'Vinnie, I think —'

'I don't care what you think, Josh. I really, truly no longer care. I'm cold, and I'm bloody-well fed up with pretending that I don't mind being cold.'

Josh, his face set, drove her to Norwich in stony silence.

The next day, a hand delivered note arrived. It was from Tom Firgreen; it listed all the things wrong with the cottage he lived in. It then went on to list all the improvements he had personally made. Finally it offered to take the property off the Elliots' hands for the princely sum of five thousand pounds.

Josh paced up and down the kitchen. 'The bloody cheek of the man, how dare he? That cottage is worth at least sixty thousand pounds.' Then, catching Lavinia's skeptical gaze, he amended his statement. 'Well, forty thousand, then. You know what? He must think we're stupid. He saw us coming, and decided that we were on our knees and would do anything to raise cash.'

'Well, we would, wouldn't we?'

'We won't trade our children's inheritance. That's one thing we won't do.'

'The candlesticks were our children's inheritance.'

'Hardly, they came from your family, not mine.'

'Jocelyn Elliot, you render me speechless,' Lavinia screamed. 'What's so very special about the Elliots? It's the Elliots who got into this stupid Lloyds thing – it's the Elliots that thought they could get something for nothing.'

'Lavinia, keep your voice down, the boys will hear us.'

'And why shouldn't the boys hear us, why

150

shouldn't the boys know that it's their father got us into this mess? Don't tell me you're ashamed of it, Josh?'

'That's not fair, Vinnie,' Josh was shouting too.

The boys were playing marbles in the library corridor. 'Oh, Lord,' Sebastian said. 'The parents are arguing again. That means they'll spend the afternoon in bed,' he rolled his eyes, 'making up.' He and his brother Quentin, collapsed into a heap, laughing.

The boys were only partly right. Their parents were driven from the bedroom by the cold, and in fact patched up their differences by spending a steamy half an hour in the little shower room that was heated by a single radiator running off the kitchen Aga.

Christmas was rapidly approaching. As always, the estate produced a bounteous fare: pheasant, goose and duck were all on the menu. The village ladies complained that the house was too cold to work in. Which gave Lavinia the opportunity to say that she agreed with them and, as it would probably be some time before the boiler could be fixed, it was perhaps better if they postponed their cleaning activities until the spring. The cleaners then decided that the house wasn't that cold; indeed, they insisted, it was better to be a little cold than too warm, it meant that they got more work done. No, Lavinia said with equal insistence, she wouldn't dream of them working in such conditions. They were to take a good long break. She apologized for being behind with their wages, she hadn't got around to going to the bank; she'd let them have what she owed them within the next few days, certainly before Christmas.

She told Doris that, as the girls were home from school, and as they had proved to be so helpful, she really didn't need her to come in every day, every other day would be fine. 'And expect me to do twice as much, when I do go in,' she muttered to the butcher, the baker and the people at the general store. 'If I were you I wouldn't let them have any more credit,' she confided. 'They're going bust, you know? I hear these things, not that I eavesdrops or anything, but you can't help but notice. His Lordship was on the phone last week, ringing round the garages, asking what they'd offer him for the Bentley. But he got no joy. I heard him telling Lady H, "There's not much market for old gas guzzlers like them," he said.'

Most of the tradesmen were of the same mind: Lord and Lady Hulver had been good to them over the years, they'd never owed them a penny before, and they were sure the bills would soon be settled. However, both the butcher and the general store, with much embarrassment, told Lavinia that they'd had to review their policies on credit. They'd made the same conditions for everyone. It wasn't as if they had heard any rumours – well, even if they had, they were people of the world and they didn't listen to idle gossip. All the same, they had made new rules. Lavinia said that she quite understood, and would they like her to settle her account then and there? The general stores said no, of course not, end of the month would do as always, only it was now the end of three months – but not to worry, the end of the month would still do. The butcher said, yes please, he would like Lavinia to settle his bill right then and there. It was only when she scavenged about in her handbag that she realized she'd forgotten her purse. Oh, that was all right, the butcher said, next time she was passing would be fine.

Despite their changed circumstances, Christmas turned out to be the best they could remember. They lit huge log fires in every room that had a fireplace _ even in the bedrooms, and the boys were put in charge of stoking them up. The halls were literally decked with boughs of Holly, and Christmas carols rang throughout the old house from top to bottom. Lavinia, with no staff to help her prepare the Christmas meals, began to wonder why Christmases past had seemed so complicated; it was as if her helpers had brought their own set of problems and confusions with them. On Christmas morning Steve Jarvis arrived, to make sure, he said, that they had enough firewood to tide them over. They weren't to misunderstand him, he said, he didn't want payment, it was just a goodwill gesture. Only Zoë noticed the roguish wink he gave her, and only Steve noticed her responsive giggle.

Ailsa McTodd telephoned on the evening of Christmas day. She begged the Elliots to join them for the New Year shoot – Philip was terribly depressed about the Lloyds thing. He needed cheering up – well, didn't they all? Brooke and Henry Osbourne-Pennington were coming. Clever Brooke had had an idea about how to make some money, they were all to get together and discuss it. She wouldn't take no for an answer, the Elliots just had to be there, all of them. Why didn't they bring that nice young man with them – Steve somebody or other? They could use his help over the weekend. They'd had to let a lot of their own staff go, and he was such a strong young man; he could maybe drive the Elliots up to Scotland?

CHAPTER SEVENTEEN

Steve willingly agreed to drive the family to Scotland.

'Fancy yourself do you, boy?' His mother had teased before he left.

'And why not?'

Betty Jarvis snorted. 'You're better than them any day of the week, and don't you forget it.' Betty's hours had been cut, so that now she only cooked for the Elliots on Fridays and Saturdays. She didn't hide her bitterness even from Lavinia. 'I expect you'd like me to do a bit of baking for you, Lady H. Help you out like, for the rest of the week, when you're trying to cook for yourself. Though it seems a bit of a shame to try and cook for yourself when you could be eating good, decent food properly prepared by me.'

Once Lavinia had challenged her. 'Are you saying my food's not good, Mrs Jarvis?'

Betty Jarvis had smiled. 'Phew. Not that, Madam.

155

But well, I've seen your fancy French recipes – not an once of goodness in them. And please don't think I'm being rude, Lady H, but you're not the most organized of people, are you? Not in the kitchen, that is.'

'My husband likes my cooking, Mrs Jarvis,' Lavinia said defensively.

Betty shook her head. 'Ah yes, always the gentleman, Lord Hulver. Always knows how to give a compliment, even if he has to tell a little white lie to give it.'

Lavinia vowed never to challenge her cook again.

Steve left early to go to the Castle; he wanted to clean the Range Rover and fill it with diesel.

Zoë was waiting for him. 'Need any help,' she asked, blushing to the roots of her hair.

'Ah. Miss Zoë,' he said cheerfully. 'What you offering to help with then?'

She became flustered. 'I thought you might like some help cleaning the car.'

He raised an eyebrow. 'I don't think Lord Hulver would quite approve of that, do you?'

'I don't care what he does, or does not approve of,' she replied.

'Well I do, Zoë girl. There've been too many redundancies on this estate for me to risk blotting my copybook. Now you wouldn't want me to get the sack, would you?'

'No,' she sighed.

'Tell you what though, Zoë girl,' he whispered. 'I could give you a nice soft job, to be done in private like. What'd you think?'

Her brow creased. 'What?'

He went around to the side of the car where she was standing, as he passed her he took her hand and brushed it on his crotch. 'Just hold this till it gets hard, will you?'

'What?' Zoë was now very red and flustered.

'Soft job. Get it? Hold this till it gets hard.'

Zoë snatched her hand away, and covered her mouth. 'Oh!'

'Just a joke, Zoë. No offence meant. But well, you are supposed to be my girlfriend, aren't you?'

She nodded.

'Well, that's what they do, boy and girl friends, you know.'

She bit her bottom lip and nodded. 'I do want to, Steve. It's just that, well, I —'

'A bit scared, are you?'

She nodded.

'Well, I'll let you decide when the time is right. Meanwhile, do remember that a chap does have needs and I can't wait for you forever.'

Panic clouded Zoë's face. 'Oh, no, Steve. I mean, I

don't expect you to wait. I . . . I do want to – really I do.'
'Good. But as I say, it wouldn't be fair on you not to tell you that I might be forced to look around. You know, I'm just a natural bloke, no more, no less.'

'Scotland. When we get to Scotland. I'll come to you – one afternoon, when I can get away. I will, I promise I will.'

Steve smiled. 'I can't wait,' he said. Whistling, he continued to clean the car.

The journey was long, arduous, and, apart from getting lost once or twice, uneventful.

Cameron House was much more of a castle than ever Hulver was. Built in 1745 of gray whinstone with red Ballochmyle sandstone dressings the baronial hall stood in a fertile valley at the head of the lock, surrounded by wooded hills. It had a turreted south front, but the first floor reception rooms all faced west and had stunning views over the water. A flight of steps ran up to the main entrance door, beyond which were the principal rooms. Above this door was carved a prominent and very decorative cartouche containing Ailsa's family coat of arms flanked by the mottoes Salve (welcome) and Pax intrantibus salus exeuntibus (peace to those who enter; safety for those that leave). A huge stable complex backed onto the house with twenty-five heated loose boxes surrounding a large sheltered brick-floored yard. Only two horses remained to benefit from such luxurious surroundings.

Steve was billeted with a dour Scot who spoke rarely and drank copiously. Ailsa McTodd greeted Josh's man with open arms and open legs, devouring him in private as if he were a long awaited feast, and ignoring him in public, as if he were a nasty piece of dirt picked up on someone's shoe and deposited on her nice clean carpet.

Everyone was there. Brooke and Henry Osbourne-Pennington had brought Hillary and George. Rupert, Lavinia's brother, and the sulky Rosemary, William Hunt the retired Major, and even the Henchforths had made the long journey from Sussex.

New Years Eve was spent eating and drinking too much, punctuated by depressing predictions of the future of Lloyds. Some said they'd sue the organization for mismanagement, others said they'd refuse to pay, and others simply accepted their fate. Of all the company, Philip was certainly the most pessimistic. He was very drunk, and several times, much to Ailsa's disgust, he burst into tears, sobbing that he didn't know what was to become of them all. George did not repeat his actions of the Pennington shoot, in fact he didn't seem to notice what was going on at all, but sat for hours with a benign smile on his face, tapping his fingers to imaginary music.

Half way through the evening Ailsa excused herself from her guests and went in search of Steve Jarvis. 'I want you to do something for me,' she said.

He smiled. He smiled even broader when she whispered her instructions in his ear.

'You won't let me down, will you, Steve?'

'What's in it for me?'

'Oh, I think I can assure you that you'll be amply rewarded.'

He smiled again. 'You're a real scheming cow, aren't you, Mrs McTodd?'

'That's what you like about me, isn't it, Steve? When it comes to schemers we're about on an even par, wouldn't you say?'

Steve pushed a none too clean hand inside Ailsa's cream silk blouse. She didn't pull away but pushed her body toward him and ran her painted nails down the zip of his jeans.

He nodded his head, still smiling.

'I see we understand each other perfectly,' she said. 'Oh, and there's a bicycle in one of the stables, it might be of some use to you.'

With that she withdrew her hand, pulled her blouse together, threw back her head and laughed. 'You're a star, Steve Jarvis,' she said. 'A bright, shining, bloody star.'

The next day, New Years Day, the day of the shoot,

was very cold. A heavy hoar frost had developed during the night, the sky was gray and misty, and the air was very still.

'Perhaps the sun will break through,' Josh said, as the men, guns broken over their arms, mounted the gun trailer.

'Perhaps,' agreed Philip gloomily.

Josh was nursing a hangover and knew that his friend's head must also be pounding. Philip had drunk far more than he the night before; Josh suspected that every step of the way jarred Philip's aching temples, and added to the weight of his depression.

At that moment, Ailsa came running from the house. 'Philip! Philip! Just a moment! My car's gone, it's been stolen!'

Phillip looked confused and almost frightened.

'Oh God, no,' he said. 'Whatever else can go wrong?'

The men decanted themselves from the cart and stood about, unable to decide what they should do.

Questions were fired back and forth. 'Are you sure you left it there? When did you last see it? Did you leave the keys in it?'

In the end there seemed little to be done, and it was decided that Ailsa should ring the police, whilst Philip and the other men got on with the shoot.

'What else can go wrong?' Philip sighed again.

Josh patted his arm. 'Well old chap, don't get me wrong, but at least you don't have children to worry about. I've got four of them still being educated. Zoë leaves school this year, but university isn't going to be any cheaper, and the twins will be moving from prep school to public school.'

'I wish we did have children,' Philip said mournfully. 'At least you have something worth fighting for.'

Josh gave a weak smile. It seemed everything he said to Philip was taken in a negative vein. Really, he thought. Why didn't Philip pull himself together?

'Look here, old chap. You've got to start looking on the bright side. This Lloyds thing is not the end of the world, you know. It'll all come right in the end. The names are getting themselves organized, we have a lot of ammunition, you know – you must join the action group. That's what the rest of us are doing – that's right, isn't it chaps?' He appealed to the other guns.

There was a general nodding and muttering of agreement.

'Josh is right,' Henry said. 'If we all stick together we can probably get some sort of compensation. You should take a note of what my wife says. "If things aren't happening by themselves, then you must give them a helping hand, and make them happen".' He spoke Brooke's words with force, almost with vehemence.

'It's all right for you and Josh,' Philip said miserably. 'You've got more behind you than me. I've over-speculated you see – sunk a lot of money into the business park. Now I can't let the units for love nor money. It's not my money, you see – the Lloyds guarantee is on the property and, as you know, the estate came from Ailsa's family, not mine.'

'Philip,' Henry said, he sounded rather irritated. 'You must stop all this doom and gloom. We're all in trouble, and yes, some more than others, but we don't spend the whole time moaning about it. Now, come on, man. Pull yourself together, let's enjoy the day.'

'Your wife's Mercedes hasn't just been stolen,' Philip said as if to justify his misery.

'My wife doesn't have a Mercedes,' Henry said. 'And if she had, I'd have sold it a long time ago.'

Philip lifted his sad face. 'That's the point, Henry. It's not mine to sell, it's Ailsa's'.

'Well you're married, aren't you? You know the form – what's yours is hers, and what's hers is yours.'

Tears were once again welling up in Philip's eyes. Henry and Josh exchanged uncomfortable glances. 'She got such a bad deal when she married me,' he said dolefully. 'I had nothing, you know, and then – when we didn't have any children . . . Every day she must regret marrying me.' He put his head in his hands.

Henry patted him on the shoulder. 'Has she ever said that, Philip? Has Ailsa ever expressed regret?'

Philip gave half a smile. 'No, she's never said as much, but she does get irritated with me these days.'

'Not surprising,' Josh murmured under his breath.

The sun never did break through; the air hung damp and heavy the whole day. White frost still lingered under the trees and hedgerows, but the shoot went well and the bag was large.

Ailsa contacted the police and a sergeant and a constable arrived from Oban to investigate. Whilst they were there a message came through to say that the car had been found, it had been burnt out, and was parked way up on the moor. Details were taken and questions asked, but the police held out little hope of catching the criminals. Joy riders, they said; it happens. 'They torch the car to destroy any clues, fingerprints and the like'. The sergeant explained.

The police drank the coffee that Ailsa offered, accompanied by a small dram that was acceptable even though they were on duty – purely to ward of the bitter highland mist, of course. Ailsa gave a performance worthy of an Oscar, cursing the perpetrators of the crime and vowing revenge if they were ever caught, and the police left, warmer but no wiser.

CHAPTER EIGHTEEN

At lunch, Brooke announced that she wanted to call what she termed an Extraordinary Meeting of Lloyds Ladies. She was rather pleased with herself for thinking of the name. The ladies freshened up and regrouped in the large first floor drawing room, a grand, but nevertheless cosy room, originally designed by Leiper in 1884. They arranged themselves around a huge roaring fire, many of them regretting the wine they had drunk with their lunch, as it made eyes heavy and robbed them of enthusiasm.

George sat at a small games table in the corner of the room, lining up chessmen as if playing with a toy fort. Lavinia afterwards told Josh that it was as if Hillary had a toddler tied to her – as if she had to find the child amusement, so that she and the other adults were free to enjoy an uninterrupted conversation.

'Right,' said Brooke. 'I thought we should all get together and decide on a plan to deal with this ghastly Lloyds problem.'

Lavinia and Hillary looked at each other.

Rosemary tutted and raised her eyes to the ceiling.

'Surely there's nothing we can do,' Ursula Henchforth said. All eyes turned to her. 'Well, I mean, the money will have to be paid, and somehow we, or rather our husbands', will have to pay it. We can't stop the debts from becoming due, can we?'

'No,' said Brooke, 'but it seems to me that we can at least stop moaning about it, and try and find some ways of both saving, and making, money.'

Everyone was staring at her in stunned silence. Lavinia was the first to speak. 'Brooke, we have been trying, you know – we've had no heating at Hulver for six weeks.'

'Through choice, or necessity?'

Lavinia shrugged her shoulders. 'Well, we ran out and the oil company won't let us have more until the bill's paid and — '

'That's not an economy, Lavinia, that's deprivation. Economies are what you choose, not what's inflicted on you because you're strapped for cash.'

'Oh.'

'What other economies have you made?'

Lavinia looked slightly embarrassed, she wished someone else would speak up. Brooke sounded quite aggressive.

'Well, I did try and die my own hair,' she said.

'It looks great, Lavinia. Well done. That's the sort of thing.'

'No. No, you don't understand. You see, I went and bought this stuff from Boots _ my hair was really showing the gray, or silver as Josh insists on calling it.' She paused, waiting for the others to appreciate Josh's sweet nature. No one said anything, but looked at her in an expectant sort of way. She smiled weakly and continued. 'Well, of course, I only half read the instructions. Josh always laughs at me for that, you know. He says that I only read the instructions if all else fails.' This time there was a polite titter amongst the company. 'Anyway, I was in such a hurry to get rid of the gray, I felt so dowdy. I didn't see that they supplied plastic-gloves. They were sort of fused onto the back of the instruction sheet. Even if I had noticed I probably wouldn't have used them. There were two bottles in the pack and I had to mix the contents together. Even after they were mixed, the stuff looked perfectly clear, quite watery in fact. Well, there I was, merrily pouring this liquid over my hair – do you know, it's amazing what you do with your hands? I know, because after about ten minutes, the clear liquid turned dark brown and it was everywhere, all over my hands and down my neck. I'd even managed to get it all over my nose – I must have scratched an itch, I suppose. I'd also got it on the waste bin, and on the taps, and of course, it was all over the tiled floor –

the bathroom I used doesn't have a carpet, thank God. I'd got it on my bathrobe, and I'd ruined a good white towel. It was even on my bra straps, everywhere – the stuff was everywhere. I had to soak my hands in household bleach to get them clean.'

Brooke was laughing. 'Was there any on your head, Lavinia?'

'Oh yes, most certainly. I know, because when the stuff had dried my hair was bright red! Well, not red exactly, more an amazing mahogany colour. It looked awful. How can I describe it? It was the colour of soggy beech leaves, and my hair felt like straw. So the next day, back I went to Boots, wearing a headscarf, of course, and I bought a darker colour. Back home I went through the whole process again, except this time, I did wear the gloves. But I still managed to get it everywhere, and, oh Lordy, this time my hair turned out to be almost black. I looked like a witch.'

'But I like it, Lavinia,' Brooke said.

'So do I,' agreed Hillary.

'No. No, you don't understand, it was such a mess that I had to throw myself on my hairdresser's mercy, and ask him to put it right.'

'Ah,' said Brooke, 'I see, but well done you, for trying.'

Lavinia nodded. 'Thanks, Brooke. Oh, and

another word of advice.'

'Yes?' Came several voices.

'Don't ever try and wax your own legs!'

Everyone laughed.

'Has anyone else any advice?' Brooke asked.

There was silence. 'Come on, we all have to get together and think of ways of making money.' She looked around at the dumbstruck faces. 'Don't look at me as if I just said a rude word, for God's sake. You English – you always act as if making money is obscene. Well, like it or not, we have to do something or we'll all go under. We can't just sit around and hope that things will come right _ we have to make them come right. Look at you, you must have some talents between you?'

The silence continued; the women looked at each other, each one waiting for another to put the American woman in her place.

'Well, what can you do, Lavinia? Apart from hairdressing, which I probably wouldn't advise, what can you do?'

Lavinia looked rather non-plussed. 'Nothing, well I did study fine art when I was young and I did work in a gallery for a short time, but — '

'Well, that won't pay the debts, will it? Ursula what about you?'

'I helped out at some stables when I was in my

teens, and of course, I did a stint as a chalet girl. Didn't everyone?'

Lady Osbourne-Pennington ran her fingers through her wild blond hair. 'In other words your career has been marriage?'

The women started to object.

Brooke held up her hand. 'No. No, you misunderstand me.'

'We've sold things,' Ursula suddenly said.

'We've all done that,' put in Rosemary.

'The trick there is to sell things that you're not going to miss.'

'Like what? Our husbands?' Rosemary said, causing the women to laugh again.

'Well, what is it we all have that most people do not have?'

'Lloyds losses?' Rosemary offered.

'Yes, okay. But why do we have Lloyds losses?'

'Because Smith Benson are rotten judges of the market?'

'No. No, we've all got losses because we are members, and we're all members because of what?'

Everyone looked extremely puzzled.

'For God's sake Brooke, spit it out, we're all too well lunched to play a quiz game,' Lavinia said.

'We have collateral.'

'Had collateral,' Hillary said, rather sadly.

'We still have it, we all live in lovely houses.'

'You're not suggesting we sell Hulver?' Lavinia said.

'No, not sell it – use it. Don't you see? I've been trying to point out your qualities, you're all what?'

Ailsa was looking confused. 'Why don't you cut the guessing game, Brooke, and just tell us?'

'Don't you see? You're all good wives, mothers and housekeepers and you all have a huge saleable asset.'

Lavinia frowned. 'What?'

'The family seat of course.'

'But I've already told you, we can't sell Hulver.'

'Not sell it, rent it.'

'Rent it! But where would we live?'

'No. No, bed and breakfast, you could all do bed and breakfast. Loads of Americans would pay the earth to stay at Hulver Castle.' Seeing Lavinia's face, Brooke began to laugh.

'What are you laughing at, Brooke?' said Lavinia indignantly.

'You. Your face! You look as if I've just suggested prostitution.'

'Yes. Well, you have. You've suggested that we sell our privacy, our family life. What's that if it isn't prostitution?'

Brooke did not reply, but continued. 'The other

big easily saleable asset that most of us have, is a shoot. Of course, our hardest job will be convincing the men.'

Lavinia shook her head. 'There is no way that anyone will persuade Josh to rent out the shooting.'

'Then you'd better explain to him that he'll go under if he doesn't.'

'What's the point? We'll all go under anyway.' Rosemary said.

'No. No. I won't. I personally intend to survive. And I'll make sure the Pennington estate survives for my children.'

Hillary, who had said very little, spoke now. 'I think Brooke is right,' she said. 'At least we could try. At least we'll go down fighting.'

'I don't know if I'd be much good at bed and breakfast,' Lavinia said, she looked at Brooke who was frowning at her. 'But I don't suppose there's anything to lose by trying,' she added.

'You'll be able to buy heating oil on the business.' Ursula said.

'Really?'

'Oh yes, and much of you own food as well.'

'Really?' Lavinia said again.

'And cleaners and house maintenance.'

'Really?' Lavinia said a third time.

CHAPTER NINETEEN

So it was all settled. By four o'clock, when the men returned from the shoot, the women were united, and an advertisement was written ready to place in *The Sunday Times*, *The Sunday Telegraph*, and *The Independent*.

Enthusiasm was born and nurtured. They would have a black and white brochure printed, everything would be in excellent taste, leaning toward the understated. They allocated each other jobs. Brooke would be in charge of bookings. Hillary would place advertisements in the newspapers. Ursula would contact cash-and-carry firms and negotiate special terms. Everyone was excited. 'I feel exhilarated,' Ailsa said. 'As if I'm no longer at the mercy of Lloyds.'

But Rosemary became sulky. She berated them, her hands on her hips. 'You're mad, all of you, quite, quite mad. If you think I'm going to become a skivvy for Lloyds, you've got another think coming! There is no way I'm prepared to wait on people. No. Rupert got us into this, and Rupert can damned well get us out of it. I'd rather go bankrupt than become a hotelier. Who the hell do you think I am?'

Brooke's eyes betrayed her anger, but her lips smiled. 'You don't seriously expect me to answer that, do you, Rosie?'

'And what is that supposed to mean?'

'It means, Rosie dear, that you probably don't want me to tell you that you're a none too bright, none too successful, ex-model, that married Rupert in order to get a meal ticket. And now that the poor man has a problem, instead of standing by him and helping him, you can only whinge and whine. You don't want me to tell you that, do you?' Brooke finished with a bright smile fixed to her face.

'How dare you?' Rosemary actually stamped her foot.

Lavinia's sharp intake of breath was audible. She covered the smile on her face with her hand, everyone knew that she'd been wanting to say similar words to her sister-in-law for months – years in fact.

Rosemary turned and flounced over to the door. 'I'm not staying here to be insulted,' she said.

It was pitch dark outside. Steve was cleaning Josh's gun when Zoë found him. He was in one of the loose boxes;

174

the heat was turned up high causing a warm, damp, fuggy atmosphere.

Zoë had run over from Cameron house. It was a distance of no more than two hundred yards, but her face was flushed, and she was out of breath.

Steve smiled at her. He was cleaning the gun barrel with a slow, deliberate, rather suggestive movement.

Eventually he put the gun to one side and went over to where she stood just inside the door. He moved up close to her, and brought his face within inches of hers.

'Zoë. Remember. I won't do anything you don't want me to do. If you think things are getting too hot, just tell me, and I'll stop whatever it is I'm doing. OK?'

She nodded, she was too short of breath to speak; the nearness of him was squeezing the life out of her.

He leaned over and kissed her very gently on the mouth, tenderly and slowly, no pressure, just his warm moist lips on her rather cool dry mouth. He held the kiss like that for a long time, just touching her, an hors d'oeuvre, a taste, a promise of things to come. She held her breath. He reached up his hand and ran his fingers gently around her face, and slowly down to the corners of her mouth, still not removing his lips from hers.

She felt weaker and weaker. The closer she leaned toward him the weaker she felt, as if he were somehow tapping her strength and robbing her; taking away all her freedom of choice, denuding her of her will. He put the very tip of his tongue into her mouth, letting it rest just short of her teeth; he didn't push or probe, but just held it there. Zoë felt as if she were drowning with desire. She snatched a breath and he pulled away from her.

'Let's sit down,' he said. 'Come over here.' He led her to a dark recess that was stacked with hay bales. He took out his penknife and cut the string on a couple of them, loosening the sweet smelling hay over the standing bales.

'Let's see how long we can touch and not move,' he said.

Zoë gave a nervous giggle. Steve resumed his position, lips to lips, but this time Zoë's tongue met his own, and moments later they were probing each other's mouths. He gently pulled away from her.

'I want to see your breasts,' he said. 'May I?'

Zoë was still unable to speak.

'I'll stop whenever you say,' he said.

She nodded her head. He started to undo the small pearly buttons on her blouse and eventually revealed a very plain white cotton bra. He didn't undo the bra, but slowly pushed his hand inside one cup and then the other, lifting her breasts free so that her bra formed a plateau supporting and lifting her high.

Her young breasts were large and firm, her nipples

small and pink. He kissed her neck and ran his tongue down from just under her chin to her breast and encircled first one hard nipple and then the other. He was pushing her back against a hay bale, her breathing was laboured, and her heart beat wildly.

'Relax,' he said. 'Trust me, I won't do anything you don't want me to do.'

She made a noise halfway between a groan and a cry.

'You've never been fucked, have you, Zoë?'

She shook her head.

'Do you know what a man looks like?'

Again she shook her head, but said, 'I saw my brothers' when they were little.'

He laughed. 'I can assure you that mine don't look anything like your little brothers'.' He took her hand. 'Do you want to feel?'

She nodded and he placed her hand on the bulge in the front of his trousers. Zoë gave a weak smile.

'Shall I show you?'

She nodded again.

He undid his belt and unzipped his fly; he was still covered with his underpants. Zoë was wide-eyed and shaking.

'Are you ready for this?' Steve said, and he laughed.

'Yes.' Her voice was very small, almost a whisper.

He pushed his pants aside and revealed himself. He laughed again. 'It won't bite, you know, you can touch it.' She put her hand forward and he guided it onto him and slipped his foreskin back with her fingers. 'There you see, not a bit like your little brother's willy, is it?'

She gave a funny breathless laugh. 'No,' she said.

'Right, having got that straight, this . . .' he rubbed her hand back and forth over his penis. 'This, really needs to go in there.' He ran his fingers down the zip of her jeans. 'Shall I fuck you, Zoë?'

She frowned, but whispered, 'Yes.'

'Don't look so worried – it can be fun. Or so I'm told.'

He led her deeper into the recess of the stable and peeled off all his clothes, the warm light from the main part of the room threw huge shadows up onto the walls. He stood amidst the hay, pushing his foreskin slowly back and forth, back and forth. 'Right, I'm ready. Now off with your gear. Let's see what you've got to offer me.'

Colour fused her cheeks, and her hands shook so much, that he had to help her. Soon she stood naked, except for a pair of snowy-white knickers; she looked down at her feet and shivered.

'You've left the best bit till last,' he said. He knelt down in front of her and smoothed the panties down over her knees. She stepped out of them as he gently kissed her firm inner thighs, then his tongue gently parted the flattened pubic hair.

'You're a pretty fit girl, Zoë,' he said. He led her over to the hay. 'Right, Zoë. Now look, see – I'm going to wear a rubber. We don't want to get you pregnant, do we?'

She gave a nervous giggle, 'No,' she said, 'otherwise you'd have to marry me.' Her voice sounded very small and very immature.

He paused for a fraction of a minute. 'That's right, I would, wouldn't I?' he smiled. 'Remember, Zoë. Whoever you go with, make sure they use a rubber, right? There's worse things than pregnancy you know.'

Zoë backed a little away from him. 'But there won't be anyone but you, Steve,' she whispered.

He laughed. 'Yeah. Well, just in case. You remember that, OK?'

He spat on his fingers and rubbed them between her legs. She was a well built, strong girl, her thighs and belly were smooth and firm, his hands were rough and callused, and for Zoë very exciting. She gave a little sigh as he pushed first one and then two fingers inside her. He rolled over on top of her and, holding himself aloft with one arm, he took his penis with the other and parted her labia, he then proceeded to stroke her with the very tip. She wriggled, she couldn't catch her breath; she was drunk with the sensation of him. She was so excited by him that she hardly felt him actually enter her, it certainly wasn't the painful experience that her friends had talked about.

He came quickly and apologized for his speed.

'That's all right,' she said embarrassed. 'Really, that's OK.' But in truth she had wanted it to go on forever. Never in her life had she experienced such an all-consuming sensation, and she wanted more.

He pulled out of her. She started to get up.

'No, no, my love. I may be your father's errand boy, but I'm a real gentleman as far as sex it concerned. No gentleman leaves a lady unsatisfied.'

He plucked a piece of hay from a nearby bale and placing it in his mouth he chewed it until it was soft and pliable. That done, he wrapped it around the first two fingers of his left hand. 'Lie back,' he commanded.

He pushed his thumb up into her vagina and, slowly at first; he rubbed his hand over her clitoris. He took her nipple into his mouth and he teased it between tongue and teeth, whilst his hay-wrapped fingers gained speed and rubbed expertly between her legs. Moments later Zoë began to moan, the words she said were completely indiscernible, the meaning however was perfectly clear. Zoë Elliot would be Steve Jarvis's slave for life. He would be the man she would forever fantasize about, he would be the one to compare with future lovers, and he would be the lover who would outshine the rest.

They dressed. Zoë was flushed and still extremely embarrassed. Steve bent over her and kissed her cheek.

'You know what, Zoë? That was a first for me.'

She blushed an even deeper shade of pink. 'You're my first, too,' she said shyly

'Oh,' he laughed. 'I didn't mean that you were my first woman. I meant that you were my first virgin.' He threw his head back and laughed. 'I hope you won't be my last though. Perhaps you could put in a good word for me with your sister?'

Although now fully dressed, Zoë felt completely naked, exposed, used, and really rather foolish. Her eyes filled with tears, she sniffed, turned, and ran from the stable.

'Hey, Zoë. It were a joke, that's all. I didn't mean anything by it.' Steve ran after her.

Half way across the yard she ran headlong into Ailsa, who was out looking for Philip.

CHAPTER TWENTY

Zoë was extremely flustered. Steve ran out from the loose box, but stopped dead when he saw Ailsa.

Ailsa had come into the yard in search of Philip. She was worried. He had reacted to the loss of her car in a severe and exaggerated manner.

'Why? Why?' He'd said. 'All this other trouble, and now the car, what else can life throw at us? Oh, Ailsa. I'm so, so sorry, it's all my fault. I should never have got involved with Lloyds. What with that and the business park – oh, God, what are we going to do?'

'It's not that bad,' she assured him. 'I was tired of the car anyway. The thieves have done us a favor. The car needed a lot of work doing on it, it would never have passed its MOT, and the insurance money we get will be far more than we could have got if we'd sold it. The cash will keep us going for a good while. In fact, I think the thieves have saved our bacon.'

'Ailsa. Ailsa, you are so brave. Always trying to look on the bright side of things. You've never blamed me, you know – you've every right to blame me, but you don't.' Philip's face had creased with pain and he was wiping the tears from his cheeks as he left the room.

Throwing her hands up in the air, Ailsa had let him go. Philip could be so weak; there were times that she despaired of him. But that had been over an hour ago and his guests were waiting to be entertained.

'Zoë? What are you doing here?' She looked from one young person to the other. 'Steve?' She fumed. "What have you two been up to?'

But of course, the answers to her questions were quite obvious. Ailsa took the scene in; then, without warning, she flew at Steve. 'How dare you? How dare you?'

He laughed at her, his breath forming clouds of condensation in the cold night air. 'Come, Mrs McTodd, not jealous, are you? Do you think I should save myself for you? Wait around until you've wined and dined your posh friends? Then come running when you need servicing? You know the score as well as I do. Stands to reason a bloke's not going to turn down a girl of his own age, and Zoë is, after all, my age.'

Ailsa began to utter another curse but her voice was lost in the sound of a single blast from a shotgun. It resounded around the yard, echoing in the corners, bouncing through the still night, a terrible sinister roar resounding through the air. An explosion that ricocheted from the old stone walls; a deafening noise that drowned out every other night sound. Then the stable yard was eerily still and very, very silent; nothing moved, nothing creaked, the air was stagnant with darkness, thick, black and suffocating. The three of them stood completely still holding their breath. Only their eyes betrayed the fear they felt; each nursed a wild, frightened, expression. Ailsa was the first to speak. 'What was that?' She said, her voice a croaky whisper.

Zoë's face had drained of all colour. Steve drew in a deep nosy breath. Ailsa put her fingers up to her mouth.

As if they were performing marionettes brought to life by the same hand, all of them moved in unison. They were suddenly all action. By instinct, Steve, followed by the two women, rushed over to one of the loose box doors. He flung it open and, rushing inside, found it empty. The door to the tack room beyond showed a brilliant bead of bright light around its edges. He threw his weight against the door but it wouldn't budge. He continued to push against it, the women looked on, the white look of dread on their faces. Steve eventually managed to open the door wide enough for his body to squeeze through. The sight that greeted him brought burning acid bile into his throat, he slapped his hand over his mouth, fearing that he might vomit. He backed away, breaking out into a cold dizzy sweat. Then he retched, his stomach heaved and his hands shook as his supper was deposited on the tack room floor, where it mingled with slimy chunks of Philip McTodd's, gray, shattered brain. He fought for his breath and his self-control, but his body would not obey him.

'Don't come in,' he snapped. 'For God's sake, don't come in.'

But it was too late. Zoë and Ailsa stood at the door, staring in horror at Philip's maimed earthly remains. Leaning on each other, they grabbed the door jam for support.

Then Zoë began to scream. She dug her nails into her cheeks, actually drawing blood, and she screamed and screamed, a high-pitched wail, which was soon accompanied by Ailsa's tearful but equally high-pitched sobs.

The gunshot and the screaming brought the rest of the party from the house. None of them wanted to look at poor Philip. Yet each one in turn, looked. It was as if they were compelled to look, an imperative need to see, a need to be convinced that this terrible thing had actually happened.

It was well past midnight before Philip's bloody remains were taken away, and well past three o'clock when the party finally dispersed to go to their beds. Statements had been taken, photographs snapped, and a minute search of the stables and loose boxes had been made. The only unusual thing to turn up had been Steven Jarvis's used condom. The police were already weaving a fantasy about Philip and a mystery lover. The local doctor had arrived and given both Ailsa and Zoë a sedative. The police, who respected the doctor's opinion, had then capitulated and said they would return on the morrow to take further statements from the party. Everyone was told that they were to remain at Cameron House until the police had satisfied themselves that their presence was no longer required. They were also advised to achieve the impossible, and not speculate or discuss the matter between themselves.

CHAPTER TWENTY-ONE

With his thumb and forefinger Josh massaged the bridge of his nose.

'God. What a bloody awful day,' he said.

'You can say that again,' Lavinia replied.

They were in one of Cameron House's guest bedrooms. The heating had gone off for the night and Lavinia shivered, she pulled the covers up around her shoulders. She pushed her head back into the pillow and stared at the ceiling. It was painted to look like blue sky and had little puffballs of clouds floating across it. Here and there a cupid flew, another sat on one of the clouds, and others were busy firing arrows into the air.

'I just can't believe it,' she said. 'It seems a lifetime ago since you left to go shooting this morning.' She snuggled up to him. 'Oh, Josh, what's happening to us? It's as if the world has gone completely mad.'

He kissed her cheek and tasted, but did not

register, the salt of her tears. Vinnie didn't know just how closely Josh echoed her sentiments; first poor old Jimmy Laughton and now Philip. What indeed was happening to them?

'I just can't believe that Philip has gone,' she continued. 'I expect him to bounce around a corner any minute and say, "Here I am! That fooled you all, didn't it?" Especially here in his house, it's as if he's still here, somewhere, only I can't quite place him.' She smiled sadly. 'Do you remember Philip in the old days, Josh? He used to be such fun, he was always the life and soul of the party. Do you remember when you and he went off to shoot some wild geese?'

Josh laughed at the memory. 'Yes, that time old Jock lent us his car? And Philip fell asleep in the back.' Josh's laughter was getting louder. 'And I was driving, and suddenly I came across this police roadblock – there'd been a burglary somewhere or other and . . . ' Josh was rocking backwards and forwards. 'And I shouted to Phillip, "Police! Police!" And he thought I said "Geese! Geese!" And he pokes this bloody great gun practically up some constable's nose.'

Josh was laughing so hard that tears were running down his cheeks and his ribs ached. His laughter suddenly died, but the tears did not.

'Oh, Vinnie. We were so young and carefree, so

very carefree.'

His chest heaved as the tears coursed down his cheeks. He cried like a child, resting his head on his wife's trembling breast. 'Vinnie, what's happening to us?' He felt and sounded utterly bewildered. She moped up his tears with a tissue; it was then that he realised that she too was crying.

She wiped her tears on the back of her hand. 'Josh, I just want to go home,' she sniffed. 'It won't seem so bad once we're home.'

Josh sighed.' I know, darling. I know. But we can't. We have to stay here until the police give us permission to leave.' He kissed her cheek again.

'You're allowed to say it now,' she said.

'Say what?'

'Old thing, because I want to be back in the past, too.'

'Oh, Vinnie.'

He felt immeasurably miserable, and yet both to his shame and his surprise he desired her. She felt the stirrings of his passion and turned to him, and very soon, although immersed in sadness, their bodies were contorting in a passionate frenzy; as if the action might ward off the devil that seemed to lurk in every corner of the McTodd's baronial Scottish mansion.

For three long days, the guests at Cameron house

moped around, drinking endless cups of tea, experiencing strange mood swings, and doing their best to comfort both Ailsa and the stunned and shocked Zoë.

It was during these three days that it was discovered that Philip's affairs were in a far greater mess than anyone had realized. His desk was crammed full of letters from his creditors, and amongst the papers was a warning from his bank saying that they had no other choice than to declare him bankrupt.

Ailsa spent a painful morning working her way through the bills and telephoning the firms concerned. She explained what had happened and persuaded them to give her more time. Why take a shilling in the pound, she reasoned, when her planned enterprises look set to pay the entire debt. The bank were not so easy to please, the local manager blamed his superiors in Oban, and the Oban manager told her it was up to the gray-suits in London. But by the end of the afternoon she had persuaded them to give her three month's grace. With determination, and a heavy heart, Ailsa faced the future.

CHAPTER TWENTY-TWO

On Thursday morning the female guests and their children left, taking George with them. The men would wait another day at Cameron House in order to see Philip laid in his final resting place.

Steve drove the Elliot women back to Hulver and Brooke took Hillary and George back to Glowers Boothby. The men would take the train home on Saturday.

Zoë sat hunched up in the back of the Range Rover, meeting and holding Steve's eyes for minutes at a time in the rear-view mirror. When they got back to Hulver, Steve rushed ahead. He lit fires and turned on lights before returning to the car to collect the luggage.

Lavinia was exhausted. She hadn't slept well since Philip had killed himself, and every bone in her body confirmed that fact. Steve Jarvis proved himself invaluable. Not only did he unpack the car, he even carried the women's cases up to their bedrooms. Zoë showed him where to put the things. Once in Zoë's room, he pushed the door closed with his foot, grabbed her to him and kissed her. It was the first time they had been together since that terrible night at Cameron House. 'I really was only joking,' he said.

She looked confused. 'What?'

'About Tiggy.'

Her frown deepened. 'Oh. Oh that.'

'I was only joking. You do know that, don't you?'

A tear slipped silently down her cheek. She sniffed. 'Steve. I love you,' she said, and colour suffused her cheeks. Then she began to sob. 'Oh, Steve, I can't bear it. I keep seeing his face – all gone, and that gray slime all over the saddles. It wasn't supposed to be like that, it ought to have been such a special night, the first time, and now it's all spoiled. All I can see is Philip's brains splattered all over the place.'

Zoë's vivid description brought the scene flooding back into his mind. He was ashamed of himself for vomiting that night. But there had been so much blood, so very much blood. Even now, days afterward, the thought of Philip's body unnerved him, making his stomach shake and threaten to disgorge its contents.

'You have to wipe it from your mind, Zoë. You have to stop yourself from thinking about it. I know it's hard. I've found it hard – but you have to. The minute it comes into you mind you have to think of something beautiful instead. Do you know what I think of, Zoë?'

She shook her head, tears were slowly trickling down her cheeks.

'You, of course, naked and beautiful – and I think of how much I want you and how much I love you.' He pushed his body closer to hers. 'Look, I can't stay here like this now.' He nodded toward the window. 'Leave the window open with the light on. I'll come to you tonight, later on, OK?'

She gave another tearful nod.

He heard a noise on the stairs, and he quickly pulled her bedroom door open. Lavinia had just reached the top step. Steve still kept his arm around Zoë. 'Thank goodness you've come, Lady Hulver. I was coming down to get you, but I didn't like leaving Miss Zoë on her own. I think the shock has finally hit her. She's very upset. I suppose she's let it all come out with me, because we were together, like, talking in the yard, when he was found, like. Mr McTodd, I mean.'

'Steve! I didn't realize Zoë was up here with you. Oh dear. I'm sorry you've had this . . . Oh dear, oh dear – and after you've had such a long drive as well. Come on, Zoë, my darling, let's go down to the kitchen. It's warm in there and the boys are starving. I bet you are too.' She put her arm around her daughter and guided her down the stairs. She glanced at Steve over her shoulder.

'It's only omelettes, Steve. But if you'd like to join us you'd be terribly welcome. You must be just as hungry and exhausted as the rest of us.'

Steve swaggered down the stairs after her. 'Thank you very much, Lady Hulver,' he said.

During supper, Steve entertained the twins with jokes and anecdotes. He even got Zoë to laugh and was described by her young brothers as, "really cool". Lavinia found herself telling Steve all about her proposed business ventures, although she didn't tell him the reason for her sudden enthusiasm to make money. She was doing it, she said, to relieve her boredom. Steve played footsy under the table with Zoë and declared that he never got bored.

'You'll have to get your boiler fixed before people come,' Steve said.

'We just need to buy oil,' Zoë said. Then covered her mouth with her hand as if to hide her slip of the tongue.

At ten, Steve went home, and Zoë told her mother that she was feeling much better, but thought she might take the Valium that Ailsa's doctor had prescribed. Her mother sanctioned her plan and explained that she also intended to take a sleeping pill. What they all needed, Lavinia said, was a good night's sleep in their own beds.

At twelve, Steve shinned up the drain pipe to

Zoë's bedroom, where he shared her single bed until almost four in the morning, justifying Zoë's breakfast declaration that, despite a night spent in her own bed, she was as tired as ever. He mother said that it was bound to take time, and that she should try and do the same that night and probably the next night as well. Eventually, she assured her daughter, she was bound to get a good night's sleep. Zoë smiled to herself, she doubted that her mother was right. Steve had already promised that he would return that night and she felt a night's sleep and a night spent with Steve did not blend well together.

Philip's funeral was held, in true McTodd tradition, on the following day. The only female to attend was Ailsa, Philip's widow; no other woman, except the deceased's wife, ever attended a male McTodd funeral. Quite when or why this tradition had started no one was sure. Some said it was started at the time of the battle of Culloden, when so many brave Scottish warriors were laid to their rest with only their brother soldiers to mourn. Others said it was to stop the laird's widow being embarrassed by her husband's mistresses and conquests. But whatever the original intent, the custom was still fiercely upheld by the clan. Ailsa, clad from head to toe in trailing widow's weeds, walked at the very rear of the mourners, who, as custom again decreed, were led by a lone piper, piping the McTodd Lament, a dreary, whiney, yet haunting melody. The same lone piper would stand at the head of the glen on every night of the following month playing his solitary lament to guide the soul of the Laird home to his forefathers.

The inquest was adjourned for two months, at which time the whole of the shooting party were expected to attend, with Ailsa, Zoë and Steve warned that they would be summoned to give evidence. Ailsa announced that a service of remembrance would be held in the family chapel in the late summer.

Zoë continued to see Steve Jarvis, taking unofficial exeats from school and meeting up with him either in Cambridge or Norwich. When she was home, he came at night to her room, and once, she went with him to his cottage when his mother was out shopping for the day. She had been appalled by the state of the Jarvis' living accommodation. Steve's bedroom, where they had spent most of the time, was clean and tidy, which was in stark contrast to the rest of the house, which was filthy, especially the kitchen. Zoë vowed that she would never eat another dish that Mrs Jarvis had prepared. She wished she could tell her mother of the state of her cook's quarters, but knew that she'd never have a valid reason for doing so.

CHAPTER TWENTY-THREE

Winter hurried headlong into spring. The shooting season ended, and Josh and Lavinia sold more of their possessions. Things that they no longer needed, or perhaps, things that they convinced themselves they no longer needed. They didn't, for instance, need the old rocking horse that stood in the castle nursery, although Lavinia knew she would regret its absence if ever blessed with grandchildren. They decided that they didn't really need Josh's collection of fine wine, most of which had been laid down by his father, and was now at its peak. Again they tried to sell the Bentley, but no one seemed to want it. The Elliot's lack of funds was apparent in the poor condition of the car's bodywork.

As planned, Brooke placed the advertisements for bed and breakfast in the newspapers and much to everyone's joy and surprise, they were answered with enthusiasm, and all the ladies were inundated with potential bookings.

Philip's inquest was held in a dreary courtroom in Oban, and in the event, the shooting party was informed that their presence would not be required. Only the actual witnesses were needed. Zoë took time off school and she, Steve, and Lavinia made the long journey north by train. Josh had offered to go with them, but there seemed little point.

The results of the hearing surprised no one. Philip had taken his own life whilst the balance of his mind was disturbed. The bank was strongly criticized for its handling of Philip's affairs, and the coroner expressed a hope that Philip's widow would be given due consideration and help in clearing up her late husband's debts. The company that had insured Philip's life sighed with relief at the verdict, as the policy did not cover his suicide. Although, as Ailsa later said, the final irony must be that it had been insurance worries that had driven him to his sad end.

The inquest over, the little party returned to Cameron House for lunch, and afterwards, when Lavinia had expressed concern regarding Hulver Castle's lack of heating oil, Ailsa explained how she had arranged to have her car stolen and burned.

Lavinia had at first been shocked. 'But that's a criminal act,' she exclaimed.

'The insurance market got us into this mess,' Ailsa

retorted, 'and I damned well think they should get us out of it.'

And to her own surprise Lavinia admitted that there was some logic in what Ailsa said.

'Get Steve to do the Bentley, Lavinia. He won't let you down. Give him a couple of hundred pounds. He'll do it for you – he did it for me. Come to think of it, I never did get around to paying him.' She smiled to herself. 'I must find him and make right with him.'

Steve at the time was bestowing his manly charms on Zoë, and Zoë in return was endeavoring to entertain him to the best of her naïve ability.

Ailsa took Lavinia aside. 'I have an idea,' she said. 'Leave Steve here with me for a couple of days. I need to get the house ready for Easter. I've three rooms let for three days, and there's so much to do. I've no staff now to speak of, and what with Phill . . . 'she sniffed. 'I'm sorry – I just can't seem to get my head around it. One minute I feel really sad and upset, and the next, I'm just plain, bloody angry with him. Sometimes I want to weep, and then at other times I want to shout at him and ask him how he could leave me like this. And that's the frustrating part, he can't hear me – I can't share my anger or my sorrow with him.' She frowned. 'I was never a good wife to him,' she murmured under her breath. Then she shook her head as if trying to dislodge the thought from her brain.

'If Steve will stay, then I'm sure — ' Lavinia began.

Ailsa sniffed. 'No. No, you don't understand. Just let me finish. You see what I thought is this, Steve stays here for the weekend and then he can go back to Norfolk on Monday – only I'll make sure that everyone thinks he went on Tuesday. I'll go into the train station on Tuesday morning and I'll cause a scene of some sort, and I'll explain that I've just put him on the train. I'll sprain my ankle or something and then I'll tell whoever helps me that I've just put him on the train. I'll even wave at him from the opposite platform. Someone is bound to wave back, they always do. Have you noticed that? If you're insistent enough and keep on waving, someone always thinks they recognize you. Anyway, Steve will really come home on Monday, so you must take the Bentley to Norwich and leave it there for Steve to dispose of. Then you must bus home and report the car as being stolen.'

Lavinia frowned. 'Bus home? Can't I take a taxi?'

'Don't be silly, the taxi driver will be able to recognize you.'

'But so will everyone else on the bus!'

'Not if you wear a disguise, a blond wig and dark glasses or something.'

'But I don't have a blond wig, and dark glasses will look stupid this time of year.'

'Lavinia? Are you being deliberately awkward?

Wear a headscarf, believe me, it won't occur to the peasants that Lady Hulver will be on the village bus.'

Lavinia had to admit that Ailsa was probably right.

The plan was hatched, and Ailsa took it upon herself to approach Steve with the proposition. He in turn readily agreed, perhaps knowing that the success of the exercise would put him in a very powerful position.

On Monday morning, Lavinia announced that she was going to take Fen for a walk. The statement was met with surprise and pleasure from Josh who immediately offered to go with her. His wife reminded him that the game-keeper was coming to see him. Josh was trying to accept the fact that next year the shoot would have to be let as a commercial proposition, a prospect that Lavinia knew both troubled and saddened him.

Once she was sure that Josh was safely tucked away in his study, Lavinia backed the Bentley out of the garage. She put Fen into the back of the big shiny car, and drove away. She stopped at a derelict barn on the edge of the estate, and gently, with soft and soothing words, she tied the black Labrador onto a piece of rusting farm machinery. She left a bowl of water at the dog's feet and promised her she would be back within the hour. Fen put her soft black head on one side as if she were trying to make sense of her mistress's strange behavior.

Avoiding the village and with a thumping heart, she maneuvered the big black car down a network of small country lanes; eventually she came to the city. She had chosen an out of the way car park, but one within easy reach of the bus station. As arranged, she parked the Bentley as far away from other cars as possible. She slipped the keys under the floor mat, and hurried off in the direction of the ladies lavatory, where she donned a headscarf and dark glasses. She glanced around, hoping she was not being observed. All the time her hands shook, her legs felt weak and her wretched heart pumped and rattled.

Less than an hour later she had retrieved Fen and was making her way over the fields back to Hulver Castle.

She was relieved to find no one at home. Josh had obviously gone out with the gamekeeper. She made herself coffee, and looked at her watch. She had arranged with Ailsa that she would discover the car missing at three-thirty. The coffee made her heart beat even faster and she was finding it hard to steady the cup to her lips. When Josh came in moments later he remarked on her white face and shaking hands.

'It's nothing,' she said. 'I went for a longer walk than I intended.'

'And you didn't eat breakfast today, did you?'

'I wasn't hungry.'

'Well, eat something now, your blood sugar's low, I

expect.'

'It'll spoil my lunch,' she said.

'You sound like your mother,' he laughed. 'Tell you what, we'll make a deal, I won't tell her if you don't.'

She thought that Josh seemed surprisingly jovial, considering he'd just told the keeper that the shoot was to be let. She tried to join in Josh's laughter, but her face seemed frozen, set, so that it wouldn't bend into a smile.

She gave a funny little cough. 'How did the keeper take the news?'

'What news?'

'About letting the shoot.'

'Ah. Oh well . . . you see, Vinnie. I've been thinking.'

Lavinia groaned. 'Oh, Josh. You haven't told him, have you?'

'Look, Vinnie. I'm just not convinced that it's the right move. I mean to say – having strangers tramping all over the estate – whatever would my father say?'

Lavinia's adrenaline level was now at an all time high, her face was a pasty white colour and the tips of her fingers tingled.

'Your father would say that it was a damned sight better renting out the shoot than selling the whole damned shooting match,' she yelled, her hands planted firmly on her hips. 'Josh, you're so unfair. You expect me to give up everything, and yet you won't give up even a little.'

'I didn't say I wouldn't give up the shoot – I only said that I felt we should talk about it a little more.'

'Talk then.' Lavinia was glaring at him.

'Well, it's just that I think there are other ways in which we can save money. If we get rid of Steve — '

Lavinia was seized with panic. 'No! No! We can't do that, we can't, we just can't.'

'And why not?'

'We just can't, that's all. Who would look after things, do the odd jobs and things, the firewood, and, and, and clean the cars and things like that.'

'Ah, well. You see that's just it. I've had a word with Toby, the keeper, and he'd be willing to take on that sort of thing and — '

'No. No, Josh. I just won't hear of it.'

'You won't, won't you? And don't I get a say in this? You keep on about what you've given up. What about me? Don't I get a choice?'

'I didn't get much of a choice, did I?'

'Choice about what?'

'Choice as to whether I'm warm or cold,' she shouted as she stormed from the room.

They ate lunch in complete silence, but afterwards, when they were drinking coffee, Josh put his hand out to her. 'Can't we be friends?' He said.

Lavinia was in a state of near panic, she looked at

her watch; there was still another two hours before she had agreed to report the car as being stolen and she was a jangle of nerves. 'Not if you sack Steve,' she said.

Josh shook his head. 'Gosh, you've certainly changed your mind. A few weeks ago Steve was the kiss of death. You were terrified that he had his eye on Zoë.'

'No, Josh. You. You were the one terrified of that, not me.'

'I'm sorry, Vinnie, but it was you, not me. I told you he was all right.'

Lavinia was in no mood to argue. 'OK, have it your own way. Let's just say that I've come around to your way of thinking, and I think that Steve Jarvis is an asset to the place, and that once we get the B and B's going, he'll be an even bigger asset.'

'But that's what I'm saying. Toby Elton will do all that Steve does, and more, and he'll do it in a lot less cocky way than young Steve Jarvis.'

Lavinia was near to tears. 'But that's what I'm saying.'

'What Vinnie? What are you saying? It seems to me that you are agreeing with me.'

'Oh, stop it, Josh. You're trying to confuse me,' she sobbed

Josh looked alarmed. 'There, there, darling. Don't take on so. I say, wrong time of the month is it?'

'Josh! That's such a typical male remark. No, it is not the wrong time of the month. I'm just, I'm just . . . Oh, Josh, I just don't want you to get rid of Steve, that's all.'

'But, Vinnie, I think — '

'I don't care what you think, Josh. I ask very little of you. I just ask that you don't let Steve go.'

Seeing and hearing how adamant she was Josh tried to lighten the mood. 'I say, Vinnie, not your lover, is he?' He laughed heartily.

'That, Josh, is not terribly funny.'

Josh shrugged his shoulders. 'No, I can see that by the look on your face.'

He put his arm around her, but she shrugged him off. 'Come on, old thing. Calm down.'

'Old thing? Calm down?'

'Just a term of affection,' he said.

'Oh men!' she said, and stormed off to her extremely cold bedroom and threw herself down on the bed and wept. She was so tired. She had slept little the night before, lying awake, feverishly planning how she would get the car out of the grounds. She pulled the duvet over her for warmth and very soon fell asleep, which is why she didn't hear the phone when Steve called to say he couldn't start the car.

CHAPTER TWENTY-FOUR

Josh went out into the yard. He had told Toby Elton to clean both the Range Rover and the Bentley. He'd decided that he would have a word with Toby and tell him to go easy on the indoor jobs. Lavinia would come around to his way of thinking; she just needed a little time. Women were like that; they could be led, but never pushed. Meanwhile Toby would be instructed to keep a low profile.

Toby had made a good job of the Range Rover, and Josh said as much.

'I'll do the Bentley now, Sir, shall I?'

'Good man. Lovely job, the old crate looks quite respectable with a bit of spit and polish, doesn't she? Yes please, Toby. Carry on with the mean machine, see if you can get her looking as good as this old girl.'

'Where is it?'

'The Bentley? In the garage, of course.'

'No, Sir.'

Josh smiled, 'What do you mean, no Sir?'

'The car's not there, Sir. Not in the garage.'

Josh wasn't worried, the man obviously hadn't

looked in the right place. He went with slight impatience over to the big garage and swung the doors open. He glanced over his shoulder, and then looked back into the garage as if he might have missed the car the first time round. He stood for a full five seconds, wondering where he could have left it. He put his hand on his brow to try and aid his memory. He glanced toward the house and back again to the garage, he must ask Lavinia.

After some searching, he found his wife in the bedroom fast asleep. He decided that there was no point in waking her, she was tired; that's why she was on such a short fuse, it was best to leave her to sleep it off. He pulled the covers up over her shoulder. Lavinia wouldn't know anything about it; she never drove the big car. In fact no one drove it very much, it was silly to cavort around the countryside in such a gas-guzzler, and it was the very devil to park. Not that he didn't trust his wife's driving; she was a good driver, for a woman, that is. No, the Bentley was a man's car, a rich man's status symbol.

He went down to his office and rang the police.

Steve had spent a steamy weekend with Ailsa. They had made love in almost every room of the house. They had even spent a very satisfying afternoon on the kitchen table, a ritual that had involved certain food stuffs being spread and devoured from the most surprising and imaginative of places. At night, Steve had lain on Philip's side of the bed, and had done things to Philip's wife that would have been beyond Philip's wildest dreams or fantasies. In Ailsa's opinion, Steve had achieved far more sexual prowess in two days than Philip had achieved in their entire marriage.

The police were quick to respond to Josh's call and, after statements were taken, a description of the car was issued. Within an hour of Josh reporting the car as missing, all local police stations and patrol cars were aware of the theft. Less than half-an-hour after that, Steve, who had been spotted by an observant constable trying to bump start the car on Munroe Hill, was arrested and taken to Norwich police station. At approximately the same time Josh made Lavinia a cup of tea, and informed her that the car had been stolen. She woke having gained little refreshment from her sleep, looked at her watch and in a voice filled with panic, announced that they should not inform the police for at least an hour.

'Too late for that, I've already done it. They're awfully nice chaps you know, our local bobbies. I told them what had happened to poor old Phillip, when he discovered Ailsa's car had been pinched.' He laughed. 'I had to promise them I wouldn't do the same. But I said to them, "don't look too hard, the insurance is worth more than the car is, and I've been trying to sell the wretched thing for months" Josh gave another hearty laugh. 'Funny though, isn't it? Ailsa's car being stolen, and now ours? I don't know what the world is coming to, I really don't.'

Lavinia agreed that it was indeed an odd coincidence, and took a long gulp of her tea.

'I say, darling, don't look so miserable. It's a blessing in disguise.' He walked around the room. 'The car must have gone sometime last night.' He chuckled. 'With any luck at all, it's miles away from here by now. Let's hope they never, ever, find it. It'll solve one or two of our immediate problems if they don't, won't it?'

He came over to the bed and stroked his wife's cheek. 'Vinnie. It's all right you know. Don't look like that.'

'Like what?' She whispered.

'Like the end of the world has come. Like you've just been sentenced to death. I'd no idea that you were so fond of the beastly thing.'

'I wasn't,' she said. But Josh didn't seem to have heard her.

'Oh, I admit it was a pretty car – lovely in fact. And the engine was as good as new. Spot of trouble with the starting motor, but that could soon have been put right. The body work though, now that was a different matter. That's why we couldn't sell it, you know. The body work was in a hell of a state. No, the thief has done us a real favor, let's hope he gets away with it, what?'

'Yes,' Lavinia agreed rather weakly.

CHAPTER TWENTY-FIVE

Lavinia was seeped in misery; she began to cry. Why, oh why, had she agreed to such a hare-brained scheme? When she really thought about it, she couldn't understand how she had got involved in such a stupid act. She'd have liked to blame Ailsa, but that wasn't Lavinia's style. No, it was definitely her own fault. She got up from the bed, and went into her dressing room, where she washed her face and brushed her hair. She stared at herself in the mirror, she felt suddenly old, her face seemed lined, and the slight indentations under her eyes looked like enormous black pits. Oh God, what had she come to? She went down to the kitchen, still the only warm room in the house. Josh was sitting at the table reading the newspaper. Lavinia slipped into the seat opposite him. She took a deep breath, she would have to tell him, of course, and he'd be horrified. She didn't think he'd even believe her. His image of her was about to be shattered.

The telephone rang. Josh leaned back, picked up the receiver and brought it to his ear.

'You have? That's wonderful . . . Yes, yes, of course . . . I agree, bit of a foolish choice . . Yes, every one's going to notice a Bentley . . . Yes . . . Mmm . . . Yes . . . When? . . . Where? . . . Norwich? . . . Good Lord . . . Hang on a minute. Who?'

Lavinia listened to the conversation with dread. She glanced down at the headline of the paper Josh had just discarded. LOCAL COUNCILLER IN INSURANCE SCAM, it read. Lavinia swallowed, her mouth suddenly felt extremely dry. Steve would tell them what had happened, and then they would come and arrest her. They would send her to prison; she knew they would. They were always hard on people of her class. She wouldn't survive in prison; she had signed her own death warrant. She tried to stop the tears from falling, but they came anyway. Josh was still talking.

'Yes, of course I know him, he works for me . . . Good, God . . . whatever next? . . . I can't see how he hoped to get away with it . . . Well I suggest you find out what his intentions were . . . Exactly, if he has found a buyer I'd very much like to hear about it. I've been trying to sell the damned thing for months . . . Yes, yes, of course . . . Yes . . . Thank you for letting me know. Goodbye.'

Josh replaced the receiver. 'Vinnie, can you believe

it? Steve Jarvis stole the car! Steve! I can hardly credit it. There you see, I was right about him all along. I knew he was a wrong 'un. I just knew it.' Josh got up and started to pace the kitchen. Lavinia thought she was going to be sick. She made a funny little noise and slumped back in her chair.

'I say, you look dreadful. Are you all right? Shock is it? Can I get you a drink? Brandy or something?'

Lavinia shook her head, tears were coursing down her cheeks. 'Oh Josh, I've been such a fool, I took the car to Norwich and — '

'When?'

'This morning I —'

'But why didn't you tell me?'

'Don't you see, I couldn't. I wanted to try and get some money for the heating oil, for when the B and B's start and — '

'Don't tell me, Vinnie. I think I know.'

'I know it was stupid. I was at my wits end and I couldn't think of any other way —'

'Were you going to pawn them, or sell them outright?'

'What?'

'Your bits of jewelry – I assume that's what you're talking about.'

'Josh I — '

213

But Josh carried on talking. 'Of course, I didn't tell you about the starting motor, did I? I've been meaning to get it done ... but – well, it's all money. Poor darling, then when you came to drive home the car wouldn't start. So you asked Steve to go and retrieve it for you, and then you were asleep when I discovered that the car had gone and – oh dear. So the poor chap got arrested for doing his job. Josh took her hand; he twisted the solitaire engagement ring around her finger. 'You didn't sell this, though?'

Lavinia's mind was racing ahead; she daren't trust herself to speak.

'What did you sell?' But he didn't wait for her to answer. 'Oh, Vinnie, that I have brought you to this,' he shook his head. 'Perhaps poor old Philip had the right idea.'

Lavinia gulped back her tears. 'Don't say that, Josh. Please don't ever say that.'

He patted her hand. 'I'd better ring the police – get poor old Steve out of the clink.'

He picked up the telephone. Lavinia watched his every movement, she studied the way his mouth moved and the way his kind, tired eyes looked at her as he spoke. She had never in all their married lives lied to him, and now deceit seemed to come so easily. Oh, Josh. What am I doing? What has this thing brought us to?

Josh replaced the receiver, he smiled at her, 'I said

I'd go and get him. I'm afraid the police are rather annoyed with me – they weren't exactly unpleasant, just not very helpful. Silly Steve is still refusing to talk to them. He's demanding a lawyer!' Josh shook his head. 'I expect he watches too many crime stories on the television.' Josh shook his head again. 'But even so, wouldn't you think he'd just say he was doing a job for you?'

Lavinia gulped, she was about to add to and compound the lie. 'I think that might be my fault. You see I didn't want you to ask what I was up to, and so I asked Steve not to tell you.' She gave a weak insincere laugh. 'I guess he's taken my request a little too far.'

'You didn't tell him why you were going to Norwich?' Josh sounded alarmed.

'Of course not – I simply said that I'd taken the car shopping, and that you would disapprove of me taking it to town. Which you would, wouldn't you?'

'Well, it's such a gas guzzler,' Josh said defensively.

He nodded, and then he frowned. 'But why, Vinnie? Why tell Steve that I wouldn't approve? He must have thought that it was damned odd? Anyway, I didn't think Steve was getting back until tomorrow?'

'Josh, why all these questions? You sound as if you don't believe me.'

'Nonsense, of course I believe you. It just that it doesn't make a whole lot of sense that's all.'

215

'Please, Josh. Can we leave it now? I'm sick and tired of the whole thing.'

'Okay, old thing. We'll let it drop.' But the frown stayed on his forehead.

'And, Josh? Please stop calling me "old thing".'

Josh was able to convince the police that his wife, unbeknown to him, had taken the car to Norwich and, after being unable to start it, had asked Steve to go and get it. The police accepted his explanation, but he felt they were extremely suspicious of him and he couldn't understand why. Josh himself was still very puzzled. Why had Vinnie left the car and come home? How did she get home? Why hadn't she told him at lunchtime? But then he remembered that he and Lavinia had quarreled at lunchtime, quarreled about Steve in fact. Steve did seem very loyal to Lavinia, he was not surprised that she championed him.

'Lady Hulver, has told me all about the arrangement,' Josh said, once he and Steve were well on their way back to Hulver. 'You should have told the police the truth, it would have explained everything.'

Steve gave a soft snort. 'You're joking?'

'No. No, I'm quite serious. By staying quiet they thought that you had something to hide. They thought you'd been up to some sort of monkey business. You should have told them that Lady Hulver had broken down and told you to collect the car for her. A simple phone call would have put the matter right straight away, and you wouldn't have ended up in a police cell.'

Steve nodded his head; he had one of his rare smiles on his lips. 'I was always told never to speak to the police unless I had a lawyer present,' he said.

'What nonsense! An honest man has nothing to lose by telling the truth.'

'No,' Steve said, 'I don't suppose an honest man does.' He turned his head toward the window, he had an even wider smile on his lips.

CHAPTER TWENTY-SIX

A few days later, Lavinia had a long talk to Brooke. Over the past few months the two had become close friends and confidantes. So it was quite natural for Lavinia to share her worries concerning the lack of heating in the castle.

'It's the one thing I can't gloss over. If the B and B's are cold, they won't be at all happy, no matter how good the rest of it is.'

'Then you must borrow the money for the oil,' her friend said.

Lavinia laughed. 'Borrow it from where?'

'The bank, of course, that's what they're there for.'

'Is it? Oh, but look, the bank have refused us money, they've done something, iced it or – ' She frowned, trying to remember the term that had been used.' No, no they've frozen our account – that's right, frozen it. If I didn't have this little account in my own name we wouldn't even be able to eat properly.'

'But that's the answer, don't you see. The bank has refused you and Josh because he's a Lloyds member. But not you, Lavinia Elliot, Lady Hulver.'

'Seabrook actually, I've got the account in my maiden name.'

'Better still, make an appointment with your bank manager, and tell him that you're starting a little business up on your own, and you need an overdraft facility.'

'Oh, fine. I expect he'll give me carte blanche to buy as much oil as I need,' Lavinia said with disbelief in her voice.

'No, no. First of all, make sure he knows who you are?'

'Who I am?'

'Yes. Mrs Josh Elliot. Lady Hulver of Hulver Castle, née Seabrook. Explain to him that this is your very own business venture, and therefore, you don't want to ask your husband for the money to finance it. Take a business plan and a cash flow with you, and our little brochure. Oh, and take a few photographs of the Castle to show him, they should go down well. Dress up to the nines, Lavinia. Put on every bit of gold you posses. Look rich at all costs – so that he thinks that if you make a muck of it, your rich husband will bail you out. I assume your account's at a different bank to Josh's?'

Lavinia said that it was.

'Insist on seeing the top man,' Brooke advised. 'Don't be fobbed off with some little minion.'

'Fine, but how do I produce a business plan?'

'You don't. You borrow mine.'

'Oh, I say, Brooke. That's frightfully good of you.'

'That's what friends are for.'

A few days after the conversation, Lavinia set off to Norwich to see her bank manager. She dressed in her smartest suit and, as advised by Brooke, wore every bit of flashy jewellery she possessed. She could, as Josh had suggested, always pawn it should her visit to the bank be unsuccessful.

She carried Josh's brief case, in which she had placed Brooke's carefully prepared business-plan, cash flow, and the other documents and photographs Brooke had advised.

Mr Sedley, the bank manager, was obviously impressed, both by Lavinia's smart business-like approach, and perhaps a little more so by her title. She presented her sceme in a matter-of-fact way, and more than once she indicated that should Mr Sedley's bank be either unwilling or unable to help, her husband's bankers would be only too happy to come to her aid. 'Only you see, I really do want to do this on my own. It would be too easy to ask my husband to finance me.'

Mr Sedley offered her coffee and beamed at her.

He gave a small cough. 'You'll forgive me for asking, Lady Hulver, but . . . er . . . um, why do you want to do it? I mean, why start a business? What I mean to say is, well – I've looked at this business plan and it all seems very sound, and the brochure looks extremely impressive. Hulver Castle looks magnificent, but, but – why?'

Lavinia gave him a glorious smile. 'Why? Why at my time of life do I want to work, when I could be playing the Lady of the Manor, tennis parties and bridge evenings and all that? To tell you the truth, Mr Sedley, I'm just plain bored with all that. Do you know, I see the same old crowd, the same dreary lot of faces, and have the same tedious conversations, day after day. I want new company, Mr Sedley. I want to give wonderful dinner parties. I want to make Hulver come alive again. I can't remember the last time we used the big dining room. My boys are about to start at Edgeford in September, and I'm bored now. Goodness knows how I'll fill my time when they're away at school full-time.' She neglected to mention that her boys were already away, full-time, at prep school. 'My friend Lady Osbourne-Pennington is going to do the same. Look, this is her house, here in the brochure. We have so many bookings between us, we're having to turn people away.'

Mr Sedley nodded his head. He was a tall, thin man with furtive eyes and narrow wet lips. 'I must say it seems a brilliant idea,' he said. 'I'm sure you will do extremely well. So, why have you come to see me? How can I help?'

'I'll need an overdraft facility.' She swallowed, she felt as if she were asking for a gift or begging for an interest-free loan. 'Just until I get started, that is. You see, I'm determined to do it all by myself. As I said, my husband, Lord Hulver, is happy to lend me the money, but I know he wouldn't take any interest payments, and I just want to do it all properly, on my own – prove myself. I'm sure that you, being a man of business, will understand?' She leaned forward and smiled at him; they were confidantes now.

'Oh yes, of course, my wife's the same. She's got herself a little job now that Kylie, that's our daughter, has started at the comprehensive school.'

'What a pretty name!' Lavinia exclaimed, and was rewarded by a narrow wet smile.

Mr Sedley ran his finger along the bottom figures of Brooke's cash flow. 'I see that you think your income will peak in August?'

Lavinia gulped, it had not occurred to her to study the wretched thing. So she smiled as if to say wasn't that obvious, and didn't the figures tell him all that he needed to know?

'Of course, peak holiday season. Although, you

know, I think September might also be a good month.' Mr Sedley observed.

Lavinia smiled again. Mr Sedley pointed to several more columns of figures. Eventually, he said. 'It looks as if the very most you'll ever need is five-thousand, but we'd better make it six, just to be on the safe side.' Lavinia swallowed. Warm house, here I come, she thought.

'We do of course charge an arrangement fee, usually half-a-percent.'

'Oh, yes, of course.'

'Now. Interest rates. What are you paying at the moment?'

'With the Estate bankers?' She asked.

He nodded.

Lavinia smiled. 'Really Mr Sedley you wouldn't expect me to tell – '

Mr Sedley pointed again to the cash flow. 'I can work it out from this,' he said.

'Yes of course,' she said weakly.

'Looks like what? One-and-a-quarter over base?' Lavinia, who didn't have the slightest idea what he was talking about, smiled. 'Clever you,' she said. 'I can see there's no chance of pulling the wool over your eyes.'

He gave her another damp slash of a smile and jotted a few things down in a small neat hand.

'Well, Lady Hulver, I can see no problem at all. I'll

get my secretary to draft a letter out to you, and I'll make sure that funds are made available to you right away.'

Lavinia got up to leave. ' Thank you so much,' she said warmly.

He shook her hand, but didn't let go of it immediately.

'Lady Hulver, it's been a pleasure.' He held up his fore finger. 'One more thing. I don't know if Lord Hulver has ever thought of changing his bankers? But we do, as you see, offer a very personal, friendly service.'

'Oh indeed,' Lavinia replied, trying to prise her hand away in the least offensive manner. 'I have certainly found you most helpful, and I look forward to introducing you to my husband. Perhaps you and your wife should come to dinner one evening?'

'Delighted, delighted, dear lady,' and for one ghastly minute Lavinia thought he was going to kiss her hand.

Lavinia went straight from the bank to the oil company. She paid them a cheque for fifteen hundred pounds and they promised to deliver a full load of oil first thing the next day, but they also made it clear to her that, in future, they would always want the money up front.

'Certainly,' she said as if that was the only way she would consider doing business with them.

She telephoned Brooke the minute she reached

the castle. She was light headed with her success.

'And so I said to Mr Sedley, that's the manager's name, I said, 'Oh yes, you really must come to dinner one evening!' The man was ecstatic. I thought he might wet himself. Of course, I forgot to tell him that it would cost him at least twenty-four pounds a head.'

'Lavinia! How very unkind of you, after all the help he's giving you? You might at least give him a discount. Twenty-three-fifty sounds about right.'

Brooke and Lavinia ended the conversation giggling like two naughty schoolgirls.

CHAPTER TWENTY-SEVEN

Steve hooked first one of Zoë's legs, and then the other, around his shoulders.

'Ouch, that hurts,' she hissed. 'My hamstrings are too tight.'

'Then we'd better stretch them a little,' he whispered.

'No, it really hurts.' She was no longer controlling her voice.

He bore into her; she began struggled. Shooting out her arm, she knocked the lamp off her bedside table, sending it crashing to the floor. They lay perfectly still, afraid that someone else in the house might have heard it. But it was well past midnight and Hulver Castle was cloaked in silence.

Zoë began to giggle. The Easter holidays had begun the day before; all the Elliot children had broken up from school, and the lovers were hungry for each other.

'That'll teach you. Now lie still,' Steve whispered, his amused grin showing up by the lamp, which although broken, still gave out a beam of light.

'No,' Zoë giggled back. 'It'll teach you to lie still.'

'What? Lie still, when I'm in a beautiful woman's bed? That's too much to ask of any bloke. Even a bloke with as much self-control as me.'

They didn't move for some moments more, with Zoë stifling her mirth, and Steve anxious to continue making love. But all was quiet.

From along the passage, Josh had heard the noise. It sounded to him like something being smashed, a window perhaps?

'What was that?' He hissed.

Lavinia rolled over, her eyes were locked in sleep, her eyelids heavy, her lower and upper eyelashes sealed together. 'Wha . . . What?'

'Did you hear a noise?'

'Noise? Wha . . . what noise? Go to sleep, darling, it's very late.' She turned back to her previous position.

Josh lay back on his pillow, straining his ears, alarmed at every creak. Soon he dozed off. But moments later he was awake again – had he heard another noise?

He got out of bed and slipped into his dressing gown; he ran his fingers through his hair. The alarm clock told him it was just gone one o'clock. He crept down the dark staircase stopping and listening every few steps. The house was eerily silent. Holding his breath, still in darkness, he negotiated the long library corridor, but at the kitchen door his nerve failed him and he switched on the light, deciding it was better to scare a burglar away than confront him.

He walked through the rest of the house flicking on the lights as he entered each room. His smile broadening as he went. What a fool he was, there was no one there. He checked that all the doors were locked, and for good measure checked them all again. He shook his head. He must be getting neurotic in his old age.

He put out the lights and retraced his steps up the wide staircase. He was about to extinguish the stair light when he heard a noise, something between a little cry and a moan. He crept stealthily along the passage and listened at Tiggy's door. He opened it just a crack, his daughter was sleeping soundly, her head turned toward the door, her lips slightly parted and her arm around her ancient teddy bear. He smiled; he would tease her about that in the morning. He went a few yards further on. Just as he reached his elder daughter's door he heard the noise again; he stopped in his tracks. A thousands thoughts crammed into his head, a thousand explanations, and even though the truth had hit him instantly, his panic plied him with other plausible answers. Perhaps she was watching a late night film or listening to the radio, he even suggested to himself that she might be doing yoga exercises, anything but what he knew to be the case. He swallowed, and hesitated. For one long moment he thought he might knock on the door and wait for her to answer. Then he heard a small male cry and anger rose in his throat like regurgitated acid. He flung the door open wide.

His daughter was sitting astride Steve Jarvis; her long blond hair was flying back and forth and Steve's knees rocked in harmony. For years he would remember what he'd said, and years later he would laugh about it; but not for very many long years. 'What the hell are you doing?' He said.

Zoë cried out; she slid off Steve leaving him naked on her bed. She struggled to her feet. Josh, who had never seen his daughter's grown-up body, stared at her with shame and amazement. She was so beautiful; the firm young breasts, the slim waist, the triangle of soft, downy, pubic hair.

Zoë tried to cover herself with her hands to ward off her parent's invasive stare. Steve didn't bother to cover himself, but propped himself up on his elbows. His face had lost all sign of mirth and his body had lost all sign of passion. The three of them were frozen in the moment. No one seemed to know what to do, or what to say.

Zoë spoke first, using a very traditional and quite

229

unsuitable phrase, she said, 'Daddy, it's not what you think!'

Her words galvanized him into speech. 'Good, because I think my odd-job man is fucking my daughter.'

Josh rarely swore, and Zoë could not recall ever having heard her father use such language. 'Oh,' she placed her hand over her lips, for a moment exposing her breasts, then quickly returned it.

'Zoë, cover yourself up. And you!' The word, you, could not have been spoken with greater derogation. 'Get dressed, and get out.'

Zoë struggled into her dressing gown. Steve pulled on his jeans and sweater. Josh noticed that he wasn't wearing any underpants and wondered if that was the norm or if he had left them somewhere in Zoë's bedroom. Steve went over to Zoë's window in order to leave.

'I think, Mr Jarvis. You'd better leave by the door.'

Josh practically frog-marched the boy to the side door, where Fen greeted them with excited tail wagging.

'I'll see you at nine o'clock tomorrow morning. You can hand in your keys and collect your P45.'

Steve tossed his head and shrugged his shoulders. He pushed his hands into the pockets of his jeans and walked away without a word or a backward glance.

Josh climbed wearily back up the stairs debating whether he should wake Lavinia or if it would be wiser to leave it until the morning. This time he gently tapped on Zoë's bedroom door, and walked in.

If he'd expected her to be full of remorse, he was disappointed. She was sitting on a small velvet bedroom chair, her feet and legs curled up under her. She looked as if she had been crying, her face was red and swollen, but nevertheless her look was one of defiance. Father and daughter met each other's eyes; his full of sorrow, hers showing no such weakness.

'Well?' He said.

'Well, what?'

'Zoë, you know what.'

'You had no right to just walk into my room like that,' she accused.

Josh almost laughed. She was trying to put him in the wrong. 'I'll do what I want, and I'll go where I please in my own house,' he said.

But Zoë was onto another theme. 'You can't sack him, you know.'

'Oh, can't I? You just watch me.'

'On what grounds?'

'You need to ask me that?'

'Yes, on what grounds? You can't sack him just because he fucked your daughter.'

'Zoë! Your language.' He was very glad that he hadn't woken Lavinia.

'Right, it's okay for you to say the F word, but not me.'

'It's not right for anyone to talk like that.' Josh said, his voice calmer.

'Well you did.'

'Yes, and with good reason.'

'Anyway, you can't sack Steve. I'm well past the age of consent, and I'd given him consent. If you try and sack him, he'll have you before a tribunal, and not only will you look pretty stupid, but you'll be cleaned-out as well.'

'It'll take a better man than Steve Jarvis to do that.'

'Well you can't sack him. That's all.'

Josh clenched his teeth. He had the awful feeling that Zoë was probably right. 'I can stop him seeing my daughter, and I can certainly keep him out of my house.'

'Come on, Daddy, get real.'

Josh, the most benign of men, wanted to take her by the shoulders and shake her, then suddenly his anger seemed to evaporate and be replaced by a profound sadness. 'Zoë, you're throwing yourself away you know. If you don't care about yourself, think of your mother.'

'Mummy really likes Steve,' she said.

'As an employee, Zoë, not as her daughter's boyfriend.'

'Husband,' Zoë corrected. 'We're getting married.' Steve would have been as surprised as Josh, had he heard the announcement.

Josh couldn't help but smile. 'Married? You and young Jarvis?'

Zoë suddenly looked shy and vulnerable. 'I love him, Daddy, I love him more than anyone else in the world.' Her face crumpled and she began to cry.

Josh was overcome with compassion. 'Come, come, Zoë. I was young once. It will pass. First love is very sweet, but the taste soon dulls and is forgotten. They'll be other – more suitable chaps. This feeling won't last. I promise you it will pass.'

Zoë sniffed and wiped the back of her hand over her nose and cheeks. 'Others?' She said, her voice loaded with sarcasm. 'Others? Spotty faced Harrow or Edgeford wets? Is that what you've got planned for me?'

'No. It's what you'll have planned for yourself in a few years. And just because a fellow's had a good education doesn't mean he's a wet. When you get to university you'll meet all sorts. You won't think twice about a country bumpkin like Steve Jarvis then.'

Josh had placed his arm around her shoulder, but she pulled away from him. 'I know you want me to marry some Hooray Henry, but I won't. We've progressed, you know. Arranged marriages are no longer the form. And I'm not going to university. I'm going to stay here and marry Steve.'

'Zoë. You're talking nonsense. You're not even eighteen – you can't think of getting married.'

'Mother was only twenty when she married you.'

'Yes, and, as you so logically point out, things have changed a lot since then. Where would you live, and what would you live on?'

'Steve works, doesn't he? And he works hard, which is a lot more than you can say about your Hooray Henrys.'

Josh shook his head. 'There are other people to consider, Zoë. What does Mrs Jarvis say about all this?'

'She doesn't know yet.'

Josh continued to shake his head. He said more to himself than to Zoë, 'I don't know what young Jarvis is thinking of, asking my daughter to marry him. He has nothing to offer – nothing.' Then he looked at Zoë. 'He insults you, you know. He can offer you nothing, yet he asks you to give up all this, to become his wife.'

Zoë stood up. 'No, Daddy. That's not fair – he didn't ask me. I asked him and he said – well, he said, he couldn't – because he was so poor and I was so rich.' She laughed. 'Little does he know, Daddy! Little does he know.' Zoë's face was still red and she seemed flustered.

'Whatever is going on?' Lavinia stood at Zoë's open bedroom door. She was yawning and her eyes were dull and heavy with sleep.

Josh shook his head and let out a great sigh, he turned and put his arm around his wife. 'Nothing, old thing. I'll tell you all about it in the morning.' He looked over his shoulder at Zoë. 'Get some sleep, Zoë. We'll talk about it tomorrow.'

Once back in his own bed he kissed his wife goodnight, assured her that there was nothing to worry about, and that he would tell her all about it as soon as he had had some sleep. He closed his own eyes and willed oblivion to smother him, but sleep came only in brief glimpses, and the vision of his daughter straddled across Steve Jarvis, haunted both his waking hours and his fitful snatches of slumber. At one time he cried softly, mourning the loss of his beautiful daughter, and hating Steve Jarvis for robbing her of her innocence.

CHAPTER TWENTY-EIGHT

At six-thirty Josh abandoned all attempts at sleep, made Lavinia tea, and returned with it to their bedroom, where, with as little emotion as possible, he told his wife all about the events of the previous night.

'And Zoë says that I can't sack him for breaking into my house and raping my daughter!' Josh proclaimed. 'Oh, Josh,' Lavinia sighed. 'Have you never heard of the saying, "Out of the mouths of babes and sucklings"?'

'What's that got to do with anything?'

'A lot. You're going at this all wrong. It makes you feel better to see Zoë as the innocent party. Steve obviously didn't break in, and by the sound of it, it was far from rape.'

Josh pulled himself up indignantly. 'Now you're taking his part!'

'Shush, keep your voice down – Zoë will hear you. We have to think and we have to think quickly. What time did you say Steve was to come?'

'Nine – I think. I can't quite remember.'

'Right. When he comes, tell him the meeting has been put off until eleven.'

'Why?'

'Because, it will give us time to consult our lawyer and find out exactly where we stand. I assume you don't owe the lawyer anything?'

Josh didn't answer; he just gave her a black look.

'Well, do you?'

'What?'

'Owe the lawyer?'

'No, of course I don't.' It was a lie, but the lawyer was his friend and would not let him down. 'I'm not as hopeless as you suppose.'

She reached out and patted his arm. 'Don't worry, it'll work out. We can handle this.' Then her eyes jolted wide open. 'Oh, my God. The B and B's start today, and they want dinner.' She leapt out of bed.

'They want dinner,' Josh said, 'but not for another twelve hours. Even you can't take that long cooking it!'

Lavinia stopped and looked at him. She was very still. Her voice was calm but held a threat. 'What do you mean? Even me, Josh?'

Josh looked flustered. 'Nothing – a joke, darling – just a joke.' She continued to look at him. 'I mean . . . well

. . . you don't like cooking, and you are rather slow at it. That's all right, of course. Good thing, in fact. The slower a dish cooks the better the flavor, don't you think?' His voice trailed away weakly.

Lavinia pursed her lips. 'Well, you'll be relieved to know that Mrs Jarvis is coming in to do the cooking. The guests won't have to endure one of my slow, flavorsome meals.' She was very angry, but then she said, ' Josh! You can't sack Steve. I need Mrs Jarvis to carry on here.' But another thought had already struck her; Steve had a hold over her concerning her attempted disposal of the Bentley.

'Huh,' Josh said. 'There are other Mrs Jarvises in the world – damned sight more efficient ones, too.'

'Yes, Josh, dear, I know. But we don't live in the wider world – we live in Hulver. Look, get dressed. When Steve comes, put the meeting off, just so that we can find out where we stand legally. I'll talk to Zoë and then we'll make a decision. And, Josh? Go easy on everybody, don't take it out on everyone else.'

Josh snorted.

'And, Josh. Don't forget we'll be eating dinner with the guests tonight. You must put your DJ on and play the perfect host.'

'Vinnie, I won't be any good at that, you know I —'

But Lavinia interrupted him. 'Josh, that's what they're paying for. A night in an English home with the

Lord and Lady of the Manor.'

'But, Vinnie?'

'Just do it, Josh.' She gave him an uncompromising look. 'For me?'

He nodded and went to dress.

Zoë was right. Josh had no good reason for sacking Steve. He could, of course, make him redundant, but then he couldn't take anyone else on in his place. Josh suggested several ways in which he might force Steve to leave, but his scenarios were either morally unacceptable or verged on the illegal. The best thing, Josh's lawyer said, was to offer the chap a few hundred pounds to clear the place of his presence. Josh didn't go into the reason why that was both unacceptable and impossible.

Zoë was far more repressed with her mother than she had been the night before with her father. Lavinia had given the whole matter a lot of thought and a plan had formed in her mind. On the face of things she would accept, even encourage the relationship, whilst at the same time she would do everything in her power to sabotage it.

Yes, she told Zoë, of course she could go on seeing Steve. And no, of course they wouldn't sack him. Her father had been shocked and angry the night before. He'd found it hard to accept the fact that she was no longer his little girl. She was a woman, a woman who preferred another man. But Lavinia asked for two promises in return for the acceptance of Steve as the man in her daughter's life. She must promise to finish her studies. If she and Steve really cared for each other, then their love would stand the test of time. She must also organise some form of contraception for herself. It would not be fair, she said, to trap Steve into fatherhood and marriage. If she and Steve were to be together, it must be a matter of choice on both sides. 'And one last thing, Zoë.' Lavinia said. 'You and Steve are not to satisfy your carnal lust within the confines of Hulver Castle.'

Zoë hugged her mother. 'You really are the bestest mother in the whole world,' she said.

Lavinia smiled sadly. In her heart she knew she was doing her daughter no favors. But, hopefully, one day Zoë would understand. One day she would be a mother herself. One day she would recognise a sense of duty. She would know that there was a right way, and a wrong way to live her life, and that Steve Jarvis belonged to the latter.

Josh went for a walk with Lavinia to discuss the lawyer's opinion in private, and she in turn repeated her interview with Zoë.

Josh was white with rage. 'You said what? You seem to be extremely practical, Lavinia. Carting her off to the family planning clinic, whilst I lie awake imagining Steve deflowering my daughter.'

'What do you object to, Jocelyn? The man, or the

act?'

'Both.' He snapped. 'I'm telling you, Vinnie, seeing that . . . that . . . rake with Zoë made me feel ill. She's barely more than a child.'

'I seem to remember that when I was Zoë's age, we were having the time of our lives.'

'That was different.'

'How was it different?'

'I was older. I'd been around a bit. Good God, Vinnie. I'd already been married. I knew you were the girl I wanted. Besides, our families both welcomed the match.'

'Yes,' she said. 'They did, didn't they?' And for the briefest of moments, Lavinia saw in her mind's eye the young fresh face of her brother's friend Robert: a boy she had never even kissed, but a boy who had played the lead role in her fantasies for years afterwards. But it wasn't passion that had attracted her to him; it was the very fact that he was of a different class. The excitement of a boy from a different part of town replaced passion; replaced love even. Kicking against convention was the thing that had appealed and excited her.

'Josh, calm down and listen to me. When I was eighteen and we met, I was . . .' She stopped talking.

'Was what?'

'Let me put it another way. You were not my first choice, Josh. You were my parent's first choice'

He gave her a puzzled look.

'You see, there was this boy. A friend of my brother's – he was a scholar at Edgeford. He was as poor as a church mouse, but extremely clever. His father was a butcher, I think. Anyway, he was obviously not the sort of chap my parents expected me to marry, and that's why I wanted him.'

'And?'

'And, I got over him. I met you, and I loved you in spite of my parent's approval. He – Robert – faded into the background.'

'You didn't sleep with him though.'

'Oh, Josh. Things were so different then, but I would have done if he'd asked me.'

'Vinnie!'

'Don't act so shocked. Don't you see? Zoë's attracted to Steve because she knows we'll disapprove. It will all come right, especially if we pretend that we do approve of him.'

'But I don't.'

'Josh, I know you don't, neither do I. But we have to be a bit clever, you know.'

'You've never slept with anyone else, have you, Vinnie?'

She threaded her arm through his. 'You know I haven't – you know I was a virgin when we met.'

'We've been together a long time,' he said.

'What are you saying? Have you had anyone else?'

He laughed, and squeezed her arm. 'You know what they say? Why go out for Cod when you've got Salmon at home?'

'Variety,' she said. 'Salmon every day would become a bore.'

'Not for me.'

'Well, Josh Elliot, you'll be pleased to know, that you are the only one that has done it for me. You know, got me there.' She raised her eyebrows as she said it.

He tutted. 'Vinnie, you have the strangest way of expressing yourself.' He put his arm around her shoulders.

'Turns you on though, doesn't it?'

'Vinnie!'

'Well, all I'm suggesting is that we play it a little cooler with this Steve and Zoë business. We'll appeal to the gentleman in him.'

'Huh!' Exclaimed Josh.

'Jocelyn, listen. We have the opportunity to set the ground rules. We have a chance to control how far things go. If we don't go along with it, Josh, we'll lose Zoë. This way, we can, if we're clever, limit the damage.'

'So we're not going to sack him?' Josh said miserably.

'No indeed. I'd much rather have him here, where

I can keep an eye on him.'

Josh nodded his head. 'Vinnie, I'm not sure if you're extremely clever or extremely foolish.' He thought for a moment. 'This fellow, your brother's friend, what's he do now?'

Lavinia hooked her arm through his. 'He's the president of a merchant bank.'

Josh nodded his head. 'Just as I thought,' he said. 'You're extremely silly. You certainly backed the wrong horse.'

'No, Josh. I didn't.'

CHAPTER TWENTY-NINE

Steve was amazed at his reprieve. He promised Josh faithfully that, in return for the privilege of taking Zoë out, he would always behave honorably toward her. He also promised that he would encourage her studies, and stand by her at all times. 'Lady Hulver and I have every faith that you will not let us down.' Josh said. 'We know you will protect and care for Zoë as we would ourselves.'

Steve replied that he was honored to be trusted. But his face held the look of a trapped animal.

'Yes,' Josh said, of course he could take Zoë to the disco. He knew that she was in safe hands, but please could Steve have her home by eleven? And when, later that evening, Steve had insisted she be home on time, Zoë had been furious, calling him a creep and a boot-licker.

For all the trust Josh had supposedly placed in Steve, he nevertheless fixed Zoë's bedroom window so that it wouldn't open more than six inches. He'd thought of pouring used tractor oil over the drainpipe, but Lavinia persuaded him that that was going too far.

The first lot of paying guests arrived at just gone four o'clock. Lavinia asked herself a dozen times why she was so nervous. Why should she be in such a state, just because someone was paying for the privilege of staying at Hulver?

She didn't hear the car draw up. She was in the kitchen with Mrs Jarvis, trying to convince her to serve the vegetables in individual dishes. 'But we always serves them in the big covered dishes, Lady H – them little fiddley side things don't hold enough to keep a knat alive.'

Lavinia smiled as sweetly as she could. Mrs Jarvis was being very difficult. 'I know, but tonight is different, Mrs Jarvis. Tonight I want you to use the side dishes. And, Mrs Jarvis, make sure the beef is really rare, won't you?'

Betty Jarvis turned her nose up. 'I will, Madam, but I don't know what them there guests of yours will think, the food not being cooked proper, like.'

'And the vegetables, Mrs Jarvis. Please make sure that you don't overcook them.'

Mrs Jarvis had just opened her mouth to reply, when they heard a voice coming from the hall, 'Coo-ee. Hello, hello, is anyone at home?'

The women in the kitchen looked at each other. Lavinia pulled a face and went into the library corridor where she came face to face with a tall lanky woman cradling a Pekinese and followed by a small rounded man with a handlebar mustache.

'Hello,' the woman said exuberantly. 'I'm Mrs Fitzgerald and this my husband, Mr Fitzgerald.' It seemed that titles were very important to Lavinia's first paying guests.

Lavinia held out her hand. How dare they just walk in, she thought. This is my home, how dare they? 'Hello. I'm Lavinia – Lavinia Elliot. I'm so sorry, I didn't hear the door bell.'

'Oh. Oh.' the woman peered beyond Lavinia as if expecting someone else. 'I didn't ring the bell.'

'That would explain why I didn't hear it,' said an irritated Lavinia.

The woman continued to look beyond Lavinia.

'Could you tell Lady Hulver that we're here, she is expecting us.' Her stature added to the feeling that she was both physically and mentally looking down on her host.

A hint of sweet triumph in her voice, Lavinia said, 'I am Lady Hulver.'

'Oh, my dear.' Mrs Fizgerald at last took the proffered hand, and once again introduced herself and her meek husband, and this time, she introduced the dog. 'And this is Fitzy. Say hello to Lady Hulver, Fitzy.'

The dog stuck out a small pink tongue and licked

the end of its nose.

'Fitzy, that is so rude,' his mistress said. 'But I know you don't mean to be rude, do you, Fitzy-Witzy?' She bent her head so that the dog might lick her cheek. 'That's right, give Mummy-wummy a kissy-wissy, there's a darling.' She kissed the top of his head. 'Isn't he sweet, Lady Hulver?'

'Very. But I didn't know you were bringing a dog, Mrs Fitzgerald. We don't actually take dogs.' Although Lavinia was furious, she was trying hard not to show it.

'But Fitzy isn't just a dog. He's our little boy, aren't you, Fitzy,' she gave the dog an affectionate hug.

'Where does Fitzy sleep?' Lavinia asked.

'Oh don't worry, Lady Hulver. He sleeps with us, on our bed.'

'But – ' Lavinia began to protest. The doorbell rang. She hesitated for a moment. 'Come through to the hall. I'll just answer the door and then I'll show you up to your room,' she said.

The doorbell heralded some more of her guests, a kind looking doctor and his wife who had driven up from London. 'Lady Hulver? Miles Green, and this is my wife, Liz. I do hope we're not too early? What a beautiful part of the world you live in, and what a wonderful house.'

The doctor's soothing words were balm to the wounds inflicted by Mrs Fitzgerald. For Lavinia, it was like

248

greeting old friends, and she visibly relaxed.

She showed both couples to two of her guestrooms. On the half landing they met Sebastian who was running a small car down the banister. 'Boy,' said Mrs Fitzgerald. 'Take my bag for me!' Seeing the chance for some fun, Sebastian grinned. 'Certainly, Madam,' he said, and took the bag from her.

Lavinia gave Dr Green and his wife the better of the two rooms, and promised she would have tea ready for them in the morning room. Sebastian deposited Mrs Fitzgerald's bag on the suitcase stand and stood to attention 'Will that be all, Marm?' He said. He turned the palm of his hand up to her as he spoke.

'Oh, yes. Yes, thank you, boy.' She fumbled in her bag and placed a ten pence piece in his upturned palm. He brought his hand up quite close to his eyes, and, as if he couldn't believe the smallness of the sum, he turned it over and over and studied it. Although Lavinia wanted to giggle, she nevertheless thought Sebastian was over the top.

'That will do, Sebbie,' she said.

Sebastian slipped the coin into his pocket but didn't move. He replaced his hand in its former position and stood very straight and still. Mrs Fitzgerald looked uncomfortable. Her husband came to her rescue with a fifty pence piece, which again Sebastian studied. Eventually he appeared satisfied, and pocketed the coin.

He said, 'Please let me know if there is anything else I can do to make your stay at Hulver Castle more comfortable.' He then gave a short bow. 'Sir, Madam.' He left the room, collapsing into laughter on the landing outside.

'Sebbie, you're a naughty boy.' Lavinia hissed, as she joined him outside the bedroom. But she could hardly keep a straight face as she spoke.

When she'd left them to unpack, it hadn't occurred to her that they wouldn't know where the morning room was. The problem was solved however; Dr Green rang the front door bell. Apologizing profusely, he explained that he didn't think it quite right to pry and so felt that was the best way to gain her attention.

The Fitzgeralds, as predicted, tried every door they came to in search of the morning room and ended up in the kitchen. Lavinia took them to the morning room to join the Greens for tea. As she left, she overheard Mrs Fitzgerald remark that she, Lavinia, was not all that she was cracked up to be; indeed she didn't believe she was a Lady at all. Everyone knew that proper aristocracy served afternoon tea in the afternoon room and morning coffee in the morning room.

Lavinia smiled. That would be something to tell Brooke and the others.

The last couple did not arrive until gone seven, by

which time both the Greens and the Fitzgeralds had consumed a plentiful amount of the Elliot's gin, and were ready to go into dinner. The new arrivals were a sweet couple, quite young, and extremely shy. Like the Greens, they also came from London. They hastily changed and joined Josh, Lavinia and the other guests in the dining room where Mrs Jarvis was serving dinner.

Lavinia thought that the first course of smoked salmon parcels was quite acceptable. The conversation was stinted, and at one point had degenerated to the use of power showers and jacuzzis. Mrs Fitzgerald had Fitzy on her knee throughout the entire meal, feeding him tidbits from her own plate, and talking to him as if he were a major contributor to the success of the evening. The entrée consisted of roast beef and Yorkshire pudding. She had expected Mrs Jarvis to serve it as she usually did on a carving board, ready for Josh to carve. But her cook had seen fit to carve it herself; not only that, but she had portioned it out on the plates, and added gravy and a dollop of horseradish sauce to each. To complete the course she had piled the individual half-moon vegetable dishes high with sloppy, overdone vegetables, and placed them on the plate on top of the meat and gravy.

'A dogs dinner if ever I saw one,' Josh remarked under his breath.

The beef was extremely well done, its edges were

251

dry and curled where Mrs Jarvis had carved it earlier and then placed it back in the oven to keep warm.

'This is very nice, isn't it Fitzt-Witzy? Your cook certainly knows how to cook food properly, none of this underdone Nouveau Cuisine business,' Mrs Fitzgerald remarked.

'No,' agreed Lavinia. 'Certainly none of that.'

She would, of course, kill the woman. That's what she told Josh as they got ready for bed.

'Which one? Mrs Jarvis or Mrs Fitzgerald?'

'Both, and Fitzy-Witzy as well.'

'Before you do' said Josh, running his hand down her thigh and back up again.

'Oh, Josh. No. Not tonight. I'm so tired and I have to be up early to cook breakfast.'

Josh rolled over onto his back. 'Bugger Lloyds,' he said, as he drifted into sleep.

'Josh, turn over, darling, you're snoring.'

'I'm not, I'm wide-awake.'

'You were snoring.'

He turned sulkily onto his side. 'No, I wasn't. I was wide-awake.' A few moments later he gave another snort.

CHAPTER THIRTY

Lavinia was deeply asleep when the alarm sounded at six-thirty. Josh turned onto his side and flung his arm over her, pushing his hips close up to her thigh. With a 'don't be silly Josh, there's no time for that, I have to get breakfast,' she struggled from the bed.

Josh propped his chin on his hand and elbow. 'I love you, Vinnie,' he said. He had said the same words every morning for twenty-two years.

Lavinia stopped in her tracks. 'Oh, Josh. I love you, too,' she knelt on the bed and leaned forward to kiss him. The neck of her nightdress hung lose and he could see her breasts. He reached up and cupped them in his hands.

'I want you,' he said.

'Oh, Josh.'

'When are these bloody people going? When do I get my wife back?'

'Monday morning,' she replied. 'Only the rest of

our little group are coming on Tuesday for a couple of days – to compare notes and such-like.'

Josh wrinkled his nose. 'What group? Whatever are you talking about?'

'Brooke, Ailsa and Hillary. Don't worry, they won't disturb you.'

'They will if they prevent me from having my conjugal rights!'

Lavinia stuck her tongue out at him. 'Aren't we being a wee bit selfish here?'

Josh lay back on his pillow and folded his arms across his chest.

'What are you doing?'

'I'm giving the matter careful thought,' he said.

She laughed. 'I must go, darling.'

She got up from the bed to go into the dressing room, but he caught hold of her and pulled her back. He put his arms around her and kissed the back of her neck. 'So when did you say your business advisers were leaving?'

'Thursday morning.'

'So do we have a date next week-end?'

'Well actually we've got more paying guests arriving on Friday afternoon.'

'Oh. And when do they leave?'

'Sunday morning.'

'And when are the next lot due?'

Lavinia thought for a moment. 'Wednesday – or Thursday, I think.'

Josh was counting on his fingers.

'What are you doing now?' Lavinia asked as she wriggled into her skirt.

'Just working things out. Now let me see if I've got it right? It's Saturday, Sunday, Monday, Sexday, Wednesday, Thursday, Sexday, Saturday, Sunday, Sexday, Sexday.'

'Oh, Josh, you idiot.' She laughed. 'I do love you.'

She brushed her hair and flicked it back over her shoulders. Josh watched her from the bed. His eyes followed her as she moved around the room with her unique grace.

'Zoë! Zoë! Come and help me, please. And tell Tiggy to get up. She can set the table ready for breakfast. Come on they'll be down in a minute.'

Zoë sighed and, with a sour face, helped her mother cook the mountain of eggs and bacon for the guest's breakfast and, unable to rouse her younger sister, she set the breakfast table in the small dinning room.

Mrs Fitzgerald was the first down, accompanied by her dog. Her first task was to exercise the animal. She took it onto the gravel drive in front of the castle and encouraged it to defecate.

On seeing this, Josh was enraged. He stormed into

the kitchen.

'Have you seen? Have you seen what that woman is doing with that stupid little lap-dog?' He exclaimed.

'How can I see?' Snapped Lavinia. 'I'm trying to cook breakfast.'

'It's shitting all over the front gravel!'

'Stop making such a fuss, Josh, you can easily clear it up.'

'Oh, I can, can I? I'm now the chief shit-shoveller around here, am I?'

'Keep your voice down, Josh, the guests will hear you.'

'It may have escaped your notice, but I live here!'

'Not for much longer, if we don't make some money,' Lavinia snapped back.

'I feel like a stranger in my own home.' Josh shouted as he slammed out of the kitchen.

He collected Fen from the gun room and left by the side door. Unfortunately, Mrs Fitzgerald also decided to take Fitz for a run down the side of the castle. On seeing each other the two dogs stood perfectly still. Josh, who could visualize what was about to happen, tried to call Fen to heel. But the dog had other things on her mind, her tail gave a half-wag, the hackles on her neck stood high and proud, she took a step forward, and again she wagged her tail.

'Fen! Fen! Come here girl. Good dog.'

The Pekinese's short legs trotted to Fen's back end. Fen stood quite still. The little dog reached up on his back legs and sniffed the bitch's rear quarters. Fitz's tail wagged and he gave an excited yelp.

Suddenly the Pekinese tried to mount the Labrador. This was too much for both Fen and her master. Josh made a grab for his dog. At the same time, Fen turned on her would-be suitor and snapped at him. Mrs Fitzgerald began to scream, which frightened both animals, and Josh received a nasty bite from his own dog and a lesser bite from his guest's dog.

'Damn and blast,' he said. 'Can't you keep your bloody dog under control?'

'Your dog tried to bite my Fitzy-Witzy.' Mrs Fitzgerald retorted. 'He's dangerous, you should have him muzzled.'

'It's a she,' Josh snapped. He grabbed the dog by her collar and literally dragged her back to the house, leaving Mrs Fitzgerald crooning over the Pekinese.

'Did the nasty black dog frighten you, darling? There, there, Mummy will find you some chocolate and make you better.'

Josh crashed into the kitchen and put his bleeding hand under the tap.

'Bloody dog bit me.'

'What dog?' Lavinia asked.

'Fen and that stupid fluffy object.'

Zoë began to laugh.

'I don't see what's so funny, Zoë. Look at this – I'm bleeding. That bloody dog tried to mount Fen, can you believe it?'

Lavinia laughed. 'Well his mistress is pretty pushy.'

'You seem to find it as funny as Zoë does.'

'Oh, Josh. Look, I'm sorry, are you badly hurt? Will you need a stitch?'

He blotted his hand on a tea towel. He studied the wound; it didn't look half as bad as it felt. 'I'll live,' he said.

'When are these bloody people leaving?'

'Monday morning – I told you.'

'I don't know why you said you'd accept dogs, Vinnie.'

'I didn't. You know I didn't. She just turned up with it.'

'Well you should warn people before they come that they can't bring pets with them.'

Lavinia didn't bother to argue. 'Yes dear,' she said. 'That's a good idea.'

The door to the kitchen opened and Mrs Fitzgerald put her head around it. 'Ah, there you are Lord Hulver. Not too bad a scratch, I hope?'

Josh snorted.

'I'm so sorry, although quite why I should be sorry I don't know, but I'm afraid your dog has had a little accident in the hall.'

Josh frowned. 'Accident? What sort of accident?'

'A little puddle, I'm afraid.'

'What was Fen doing in the hall?'

'That was my fault I'm afraid. I let him out you see – it's not right for a dog to be cooped up in that little room all day.'

'Fen's a bitch,' Josh scowled. 'Not a dog.'

'Whatever, it's not right. So I let him out, and I gave him some of Fitzy-Witzy's liver, and a little chocolate. Fitzy-Witzy loves chocolate.'

'You shouldn't have done that,' Josh said.

'Oh nonsense, Lord Hulver. Fitzy-Witzy didn't mind a bit, he just wants to be friends.'

'I think he was looking for a little more than friendship.'

Lavinia shot Josh a warning look.

'Two breeds so different from each other, don't really make good bed fellows.' Josh said, and this time Zoë was the one to give Josh a threatening look.

Mrs Fitzgerald put her hand over her mouth and giggled. 'Oh, Lord Hulver, you make it all sound so, well . . . so rude! Naughty Fitzy, he's quite a boy, isn't he?'

'Saints preserve us,' said Josh. 'I'd better go and get

my dog.' He was now standing very close to Mrs Fitgerald. 'Fen piddled because she doesn't like other dogs here. She was marking her territory, that's what bitches do.' He almost spat the words at her.

He left to clean up the mess. Lavinia gave an insincere laugh. 'Don't mind my husband, Mrs Fitzgerald. It's just his way, he's an old softy really.'

'Don't worry, Lady Hulver, he's just the way I expected a real-live Lord to be, sort of gruff and in command. A no nonsense sort of fellow – chases the village girls as well, I expect. It's all very exciting. Very pagan and baronial, isn't it?'

'Is it?' Said Lavinia. 'Yes,' she sighed. 'I suppose it is.'

CHAPTER THIRTY-ONE

'I'm sorry, Mrs Jarvis, it really will not do.' Thus Lavinia spoke to her cook when she arrived to prepare dinner on Saturday evening. 'Good plain English food, as you call it, is fine for the family, but it just isn't what our guests expect. Let's have something with a little flair and imagination.'

Lavinia was exhausted, she had been on her feet all day; first cooking breakfast, then making beds and tidying the house, and now she was trying to organize the dinner.

'I suppose you'll be wanting me to cook some of you fancy French dishes next?' Mrs Jarvis said, her face without even the hint of a smile. 'Although what good honest folk can see in anything that comes from the frogs, is hard to tell.' She was chopping carrots into beefy wedges.

'No. No. Not like that, Mrs Jarvis. Like this, in thin delicate slices,' Lavinia pushed her hair away from her eyes as she took the knife out of Betty Jarvis's hand. 'Oh, I might as well do it myself.'

'That's good,' said Mrs Jarvis, pursing her lips and looking rather triumphant. 'Only it being Easter Sunday tomorrow, I shan't be able to help you out, see?'

Lavinia felt weak at the knees, she clenched her teeth. 'That's perfectly all right, Mrs Jarvis. Zoë and Tiggy are here to help. In fact,' she said maliciously. 'I was going to give you the night off anyway.'

If anything, the dinner party went off better than the night before. Mrs Fitzgerald held forth about the correct diet for a dog and told Josh, in no uncertain terms, that she felt Fen was neglected, almost to the verge of ill-treatment. The young couple spoke hardly at all, but held hands all through dinner and excused themselves as soon as the meal was over, saying they were tired and needed an early night.

'I'll bet you anything that they're not married,' Josh said. He was helping Lavinia wash and dry the coffee cups, Mrs Jarvis having left for home as soon as the dessert was served. 'No married couple would hold hands all evening and then feign tiredness and want an early night.'

'You would.'

He kissed her. 'Yes, I suppose I would. In fact I do, only I'm not feigning. I am tired and now it's late, and I'm desperate for my bed.'

'You go up darling, I'll finish here. I just want to check the breakfast table. I got the girls to set it in the small dining room ready for morning. Good idea, don't you think? We could keep that dining room just for breakfast, and use one of the other two for dinners. That way I need never really clear the table in there.'

'You miss the point, Vinnie. I want you to come to bed with me.'

'But Josh, it's so late, and there are so many people in the house.'

Josh stood back from her; he looked puzzled. 'The house has been full to bursting before, and it's never put you off. In fact I seem to remember that the twins were conceived when — '

'We won't go into all that now, Josh. Let's just finish this and get to bed.'

'All right,' Josh said lightheartedly. 'I can take rejection.'

'Josh, I'm not rejecting you. I'm just tired, can't you show some understanding?'

'Vinnie, I was joking.'

She gave him the merest twitch of a smile. 'I'll be up in a minute.'

But when she got into bed, Josh made it perfectly clear that he expected her to be sexy and loving, but she simply didn't have the energy. Why couldn't he see that?

Why was he so insensitive to her needs? Why couldn't he just cuddle her until she fell into a well-deserved sleep? She turned with her back toward him, but he snuggled up to her and she could feel that he was hard and ready to make love. She turned over so that she was facing him, her knees curled up to her chest so that she wouldn't be able to feel his passion. She closed her eyes, but she could not sleep. She was silently seething, silently cursing Josh and all mankind for not understanding a woman's frailties.

She woke before the alarm clock sounded and lay in the darkened room gathering her thoughts. Josh was lying on his back gently snoring. She felt guilty. She had always lived by the rule that one should never go to sleep on a quarrel. Well, they hadn't really quarrelled, had they? She had just been angry with him, that's all, and now she regretted her anger. She punched the button on the top of the clock and disconnected the alarm. She had fifteen minutes before she need get up. She could make it up to him. She snuggled close to him, and kissed him under his chin. He put his arm around her. 'Morning, old thing. You feeling a bit better?' He kissed the top of her head. ' I love you, Vinnie.'

She reached out for him; he was hard. 'Darling,' she said. 'Have you been like that all night?'

'Very nearly, I woke at four wanting you like crazy, but I daren't risk your wrath so I did the gentlemanly thing and let you sleep.'

'I'm not asleep now,' she said.

He kissed the top of her head again. 'Don't go away, I've got to pee.' He staggered into the bathroom.

He was gone for what seemed like ages. Lavinia glanced at the illuminated clock; five minutes of the precious fifteen had already passed.

Josh got back into bed, 'Sorry it took me so long, it doesn't work very well when it's stiff.'

Try as she might, she could not relax, she watched the seconds tick by. Josh was sweating profusely, and twice he asked her if she was all right. She tried to make little noises, imitating the sort of noises she made when they made love, but she simply wasn't aware of the sounds she usually made, and she ending up by making strange little grunts, grunts that alarmed Josh and, very soon, he became anxious too. Eventually he lay back on his pillow. He was red and panting, 'I'm sorry, Vinnie. I can't seem to make it. I think I'll save it till later,' he said. 'You all right?'

Lavinia leaped from the bed. 'I'm sorry, Josh. I have to go.'

He sat up. 'Was it all right for you, Vinnie?'

'Darling it was wonderful,' she lied.

Josh pulled the pillow up behind his head, and watched Lavinia through the open dressing room door. 'The shape of things to come,' he murmured.

'What's that, darling?'

'Nothing, nothing at all.'

After Lavinia had gone down the stairs, he started to masturbate, seemed to think better of it, got out of bed, dressed, and went to help Lavinia with the breakfast.

Breakfast went much smoother than the day before, there were no contretemps with the Fitzgerald's dog and the dishes were cleared in record time. At ten-thirty Josh went up to change. When he returned to the kitchen, Lavinia was peeling potatoes in the kitchen sink.

'Not ready yet? Come on darling, you'll be late.'

She looked puzzled. 'For what?'

'Church, Vinnie. It's Easter Day.'

'Oh. Oh, yes. Of course – Josh, I don't think I can come – I've got tonight's dinner to prepare and I've got the beds to do.'

Josh looked annoyed. 'But it's Easter Day, Vinnie. We always go to Church on Easter Day.'

'What we always do is no longer relevant, Josh. We cut our cloth to suit our needs now.' She bit into her bottom lip. Part of her felt that she was letting Josh down and neglecting her duty. But another part of her recognized the fact that her duties had subtly changed. It was her duty to put Hulver to rights now.

'Very well, I'll round up the children and we'll go without you.' He sounded very angry. He shook his head.

'You know, Vinnie. This B and B idea was a nonstarter from the very beginning.'

He left the kitchen, and a few moments later, she heard the car drive away. She didn't mean to cry but her bottom lip trembled and, very soon, she was unable to see the potato she was peeling. She felt alone and used. She flopped down at the kitchen table, put her head in her arms and wept. She couldn't remember anytime in her life when she had felt so tired and alone. It was too much; it was all too much.

When Josh returned two hours later, he was in a much better mood. He'd been to drinks with Major Hunt and he presented Lavinia with a little bunch of primroses from the Major's garden. 'Happy Easter, darling,' he said.

'Happy Easter,' she replied. 'I'm sorry about this morning.'

He kissed the end of her nose. 'So am I.'

Dinner that night was a nightmare. Lavinia found it hard to be attentive and polite at the dinner table and head cook and bottle washer in the kitchen, all at the same time. At one point she went into the kitchen to find the twins devouring bowls of cornflakes. It was then that she remembered that she had provided for the guests but not for her own family. Later she returned to the kitchen to make coffee, and found the boys up to their elbows in soapsuds washing the dirty dishes.

'What darlings you are,' she said, not having the heart to point out that the crockery needed rinsing, and anyway, was far from clean.

'That's all right, Ma,' said Quentin. 'We're trying to earn a few brownie points so that we can cash them in to watch the midnight movie.'

Lavinia didn't even ask what movie was showing but willingly agreed. At which point the boys decided that they had done quite enough chores and they abruptly left the kitchen, leaving their mother both bemused and frustrated.

'You know,' Lavinia said to her husband as she waved goodbye to the last of her paying guests. 'The sad thing is, that we had two perfectly nice couples to stay, and one simply ghastly couple, and I'll soon forget the nice ones, but I shall always remember the awful Fitgeralds.'

Josh agreed with her. He sighed, 'God, what a bloody awful weekend,. What a bloody awful Easter. The whole thing has worn me to a frazzle.'

Lavinia gave him a tight-lipped smile. She would have liked Josh to acknowledge her lion's share of the work, but she didn't insist. In her pocket were the fruits of her labour. She was amazed at the amount she had earned in three days, suddenly the effort seemed very worth while.'

'Pay up all right, did they?'

As soon as they were out of sight Lavinia produced two cheques and a bundle of cash from her pocket, Josh stared at it in disbelief, 'Good Lord Vinnie, how much have you got there?'

'A little over a thousand pounds,' she said proudly.

He took the money out of her hand and studied it. 'Goodness me, it's money for old rope, isn't it?

She took the money away from him and smiled. 'That's right, darling. But let's not forget who's the chief rope-maker around here.' Feeling rather pleased with herself she stuffed the money back into her pocket and returned to the house.

When they entered the kitchen, Tiggy and Zoë were arguing whether Tiggy's silk blouse was green or blue.

'It's turquoise,' Lavinia said in a no-nonsense voice. 'Now, I'm glad you're all together, because I want to explain a few things to you.'

Josh backed toward the door.

'Don't go, Josh. This concerns you, most of all.'

Josh stood still.

'From now on, I'm going to do the cooking. Whilst you, Josh, will eat with the guests in the dining room.'

'That doesn't seem right, Vinnie.'

She gave him a rather indulgent smile. 'All right, you do the cooking and I'll entertain the guests.'

'Point taken,' he said.

'And Zoë and I will wait on table during the holidays, and the boys can help with the washing up,' Tiggy said.

'Count me out,' said Zoë.

Lavinia gave her elder daughter a sideways glance.

'OK, I'll do it for half of the week, but I must be allowed to see Steve afterwards.'

Lavinia still kept her eyes on Zoë.

Zoë flopped down into a chair. 'Oh, all right. I'll do it, no conditions. I'll just do it.' She added something under her breath regarding slave labour, but everyone ignored the remark.

Lavinia pulled her body up straight. 'Thank you,' she said. 'If we all pull together we can make a real success of it.'

None of the family replied; an air of gloom seemed to have settled upon them all.

CHAPTER THIRTY-TWO

'Ailsa, how are you?'

Lavinia's guest shrugged her shoulders. 'Oh, you know. All right I suppose.' She stopped speaking and thought for a moment. 'I just can't get used to things without him – Philip, I mean. He was a good husband.' She shook her head. 'I know he drank too much, and he . . . well, he had his faults, but he really was a good man. I just can't get used to him not being there. It's all the practical things, locking the doors at night and that sort of thing. I didn't realise that he he did so much for me. I go about in a daze most of the time, not really thinking about where I am, or what I'm doing. It's sort of surreal, as if I'm living outside myself — a spectator watching myself go through the motions of living.'

'Give it time,' Lavinia said. 'It's still very early days. Why, it's less than six months.'

Josh was waiting to speak to Lavinia whilst this

exchange was going on. He touched his wife's arm. 'Can I have a word, old thing?'

'Would you excuse us just a moment, Ailsa?'

He had an open letter in his hand. 'You may need to protect me, Ailsa,' he said. He gave a nervous laugh.

'She's going to be furious with me.'

He handed his wife the letter. She quickly skimmed through it. She handed it back to him. 'So? What's that to do with me?'

The letter was from a Lloyds action group, inviting Josh to attend a meeting the following week.

'Nothing, only we were meant to go to Edgeford on the same day. The boys are supposed to meet the rest of the new intake and we were meant to be doing the jolly-parent bit.'

'Oh, Josh!'

'I'll ring the school and try and fix another date.'

'You can't do that. The whole point of the afternoon is for them to meet the other boys, and for us to meet the other parents. Why don't you ring your silly little action group and get that date altered?'

'I can't do that. It's a really important meeting.'

'And your children aren't important?' She shook her head. 'There's no point in going to Edgeford anyway. There's no-way that we'll afford the fees.' Lavinia's voice was raised.

'My boys *will* go to Edgeford. Education is the last thing we'll sacrifice.'

'We don't have a choice, Josh. Be sensible. We simply don't have a choice. We can't afford it.'

Ailsa coughed and moved a little away.

Josh pushed the letter roughly into his pocket; he turned abruptly on his heels and, as a parting shot, he called to Ailsa. 'Thank your lucky stars that you haven't any children, Ailsa.' He yanked the door open. 'I'll be in to lunch at one.'

Lavinia gave a shy little laugh. 'Sorry about that, I — ' But when she looked up, she saw that her friend was crying.

'Ailsa, I'm sorry, what is it?'

Ailsa sniffed. 'Everyone keeps telling me how lucky I am not to have children. Everyone assumes I should be grateful for being childless. Doesn't anyone understand? Our infertility was the greatest tragedy of our marriage.'

'Ailsa, I'm . . . Oh dear, I don't know what to say. We — and everyone else, always assumed that you . . . well, that you didn't want to be . . . I mean, I had no idea. I'm so sorry. You never ever said . . . I mean, you've never sort of mentioned that you and Philip were . . . well you always gave the impression that . . . '

'The impression that I preferred to flirt than to

273

nurture?'

'Well . . . Yes.'

'I used to flirt to punish him, you know. I blamed him for our not having children, and now I miss him so much.' More tears trickled down her cheeks.

'Was it Philip's? I mean, was it his fault?'

'I don't know. We never went to a doctor. We never even talked about it between ourselves. I think we went on the principal that as long as we didn't face up to it, then it wasn't true. Do you understand what I mean?'

Lavinia nodded.

'The thing is, I think at the end of the day it was probably my fault. You see, I was never very faithful to Philip and I never got pregnant.'

'Oh?' Although not surprised, Lavinia was embarrassed by Ailsa's revelation.

'Funny how all these things dawn on you when it's way too late, isn't it?'

Lavinia was relieved when Brooke entered the room. 'I just met Josh, he's in a foul mood.'

'I'm cross with him because he's going to a Lloyds action group meeting next Thursday, when we're meant to be taking the boys to Edgeford School.'

'Tell me about it! Henry told me the same thing yesterday. So it looks like it's just you and me left to fly the Elliot-Pennington flag.'

'Josh should come,' Lavinia insisted. 'I can't see how we can possibly send the boys to Edgeford. He should come, and he should jolly well explain it to the boys. It's unfair to build their hopes up in this way.'

'You talk like Henry. He's told me that if he doesn't get the Lloyds thing sorted there won't be any money left for little Henry's school fees. So I've had to agree to go on my own. Come with me Lavinia. It will be fun. We can flirt outrageously with all the masters.' She turned to Ailsa. 'You want to thank your lucky stars that you haven't got children to educate, Ailsa.'

Ailsa caught Lavinia's eye. 'Yes indeed,' she smiled. 'You'll never know how lucky I feel right now.'

Much to their surprise, Rosemary, Lavinia's sister-in-law turned up for the meeting. Hillary was also there. Her daughter had offered to sit with her father for the day, and so Hillary had a rare day of freedom.

Each woman related their first weekend's business ventures. Lavinia told them how Mrs Jarvis had served a meal said to contain good, old-fashioned, English cooking; and how, when Lavinia had complained, Mrs Jarvis had taken the night off. She then told her friends about Mrs Fitzgerald and Fen the Labrador. Brooke was taking notes and she wrote down that they must be sure to explain the situation concerning dogs in their brochure.

When Rosemary was asked how many B and B's

she had entertained, she said that several people had inquired, but obviously she had been unable to take anyone as she had been invited to Cheltenham races. No one would expect her to miss a day at the races, would they? Besides, she said, Rupert was exaggerating their financial crisis. He'd told her that they might well lose their house. She may not be too well up on business matters, but even she knew that it could never come to that. She then went on to tell the group that she thought they were all quite mad. She ended her speech by stating that nothing on earth would persuade her to become a skivvy for the sake of Lloyds.

Hillary had had an exhausting weekend. George had been quite unsettled having strangers in the house, and although Hillary had explained that the doors must be kept locked at all times, one of her guests had inadvertently left the back door open. Hillary had given George tea at four, but had not realized that he was missing until she had looked for him at seven. 'He spends hours by himself, just tapping his fingers and humming,' she said. 'To tell you the truth, I was just relieved that he wasn't being demanding, and I was able to get on and prepare the evening meal. Then, at about seven, I thought I'd get him a drink and tidy him up a bit. But he was nowhere to be found. I looked everywhere, and when the guests came down for dinner, they looked as well. Eventually, I called the police, and they sent a team out searching. The guests were very sweet – they all went to the pub for supper. At about midnight the police called the search off. They said that they would arrange for the river to be dragged the next day. I had the most awful night, I can tell you. Then at six the next morning, a farmer went out into his field, and found him. He'd dug himself in, you know, like they did in the war. He must have made the hole with his bare hands, his fingers were filthy and bleeding, and his nails were chipped and broken and impacted with dirt.'

'Hillary! Was he all right?'

Hillary gave a weary nod. 'Oh yes, they took him to hospital for a check-up. The doctor gave me a bit of a telling off for letting him out on his own, but he was all right.'

'Cheek,' said Lavinia. 'It's all very well for them to talk.'

Hillary gave a weak smile. 'They said that I should put him in a home.'

'They have a point, Hillary,' Brooke said.

'Oh, I know, but we can't afford it, we really can't. All his pension goes on repaying the bank for his Lloyds losses, and we have no capital. Except the house of course, but I couldn't sell. Well, I suppose I could, but Lloyds would have first claim on the money.'

'Does it have to be a private home, surely there

must be an N H S one around here?'

Hillary shook her head. 'There is, but the waiting list is very long and the theory is that as long as I'm around, I can look after him. And the home is not particularly wonderful. Anyway, all's well that ends well. George is back safe and sound and my guest's were all right about it. I couldn't charge them, of course.'

'What!' Exclaimed Brooke. 'Why ever not?'

'Well, what with all the bother, and not cooking them supper, and all that. I must say they were very nice about it all, and they insisted on giving me ten pounds towards the washing.'

'What?' Brooke said again.

'Ten pounds, they gave me ten pounds. I couldn't have charged them, they were already getting a bit aggressive about George. They gave me such a lecture, said I ought to put him in a home and they said other, quite unkind, things. They were worse than the doctor at the hospital.'

'But, they were the ones that let George out of the house.'

'I don't actually know that. I mean it's just possible that, with all the panic about getting their meal ready and things, well . . . I suppose it could have been me.'

'Oh, Hillary, you're so nice,' Ailsa said. 'I'd have blamed everyone else. I certainly wouldn't have considered myself capable of making a mistake.'

Ailsa's house party had gone well, although she was surprised to find two of her visitors looking around her own bedroom and her own private sitting room. When confronted, they had explained that they were just having a little look around. The wife, whom Ailsa amusingly described as a thin, pale-faced woman with mean lips and puffy eyes, told her that she just couldn't resist a little nose. She wanted, she said, "to see how the other half lived".

'So what did you say?' Brooke asked.

'Nothing, but I spat in her soup the next evening.'

Everyone laughed, except Rosemary, who said she thought that Ailsa was disgusting.

' I *am* only joking,' Ailsa said.

But Rosemary continued to scowl at her.

Brooke wrote down a suggestion that locks should be fitted to the doors of any room where guests would not be welcome. When she had finished writing, she gave a little cough and asked if anyone else thought that they had worded the advertisement badly.

'In what way?' Hillary asked. 'We all got lots of replies.'

'Maybe it was something I said on the telephone then, I don't know.' She wrinkled her brow.

'What?' Said Lavinia.

'Yes, do tell us,' agreed Hillary.

'Well, as you know I had two couples and this single guy, he'd be about thirty or thirty-five, I think. Did I tell you that Henry was away on Saturday night? He had to go and see his brother. Perhaps if he had been there then it wouldn't have happened.'

'What? Oh, do tell.'

'Well I took some drinks in before dinner, and he, the single guy, was on his own, I think he was Arab or Middle Eastern.' She frowned. 'Or he could have been Indian, I suppose. Anyway he said to me, "What time do the girls arrive?" he was rubbing his hands together. I told him that I didn't know what he was talking about, and he more or less implied that the advertisement had said that I could supply him with anything he needed! I thought at first that he was joking. I told him that we were clean out of girls, and he'd have to make do with me. Then I realized that he was serious. I was jolly relieved when the others came and joined us for drinks.'

Lavinia put her hand across her mouth and laughed. Ailsa asked how much he was willing to pay. Hillary asked if he was nasty; had he taken no for an answer? It was generally agreed that locks should be fitted to all bedrooms as soon as possible to avoid anything untoward happening in the future.

CHAPTER THIRTY-THREE

But Brooke had not been quite honest with her friends; at least, she had not told them the whole story. Henry had only gone to visit his brother because she and he had argued. Henry had, that morning, told her that there was no point in either of them attending the open day at Edgeford School, because Henry couldn't find enough money to pay the school fees. Henry junior would have to take his chance at the state school. It would, her husband assured her, 'do him no harm and might even do him a little good'. Brooke had envisaged her son, the Honorable Henry Osbourne-Pennington, attending a comprehensive complex; she had imagined the teasing, the verbal abuse and had even pictured him being beaten by the sons of Henry's farm laborers.

'How much?' the little dark Arab had asked.

The sum had slipped from her tongue as if it had been lurking there in advance. 'Three hundred – cash of course.' It had all been so easy.

'Of course,' he repeated.

So, when she had finished tidying the dining room and had put out all the lights, she made her way, first to her own room, where she undressed and slipped into blue silk pajamas and then along the wide upstairs passage to her guest's room.

'You'll use a condom?' Were the first words she spoke.

'I'm clean,' he said.

'I'm sure you are, but how do you know that I am?' she replied.

'Four hundred, no rubber, and you stay all night,' he said.

'Four hundred, with condom, and I'll stay until six tomorrow morning.'

'You drive a hard bargain, Lady Osbourne-Pennington.'

'Is there any other sort?'

And that had been that, she had spent the night with the Arab. She had not found him particularly sexy, although he had been extremely demanding. She would have liked to have told Henry about him. 'He was just like a frustrated buck rabbit' she would have said. He was at it all night long and entered her from every angle. She really hadn't minded. In fact she had felt rather noble doing it, knowing that every thrust brought her a little closer to paying her son's school fees. That's how she had thought about it and she had remained cool and completely detached. At six, the man had duly counted the money into her hands; she had left the room and placed the money in the envelope that contained Henry junior's school uniform list. She had then gone to her bathroom, where she had washed her hair and had lain in the bath for well over an hour. She didn't feel in the least bit guilty. It was, she told herself, a means to an end. Her guest slept through breakfast and lunch and left in the late afternoon cheerfully paying his bed and breakfast bill, again in cash.

'I will send my friends? Yes?' He said, before he left.

'Do,' Brooke replied, 'and tell them to ask for my special room service.'

He nodded. 'Special room service! Yes. I like that, Lady Osbourne-Pennington.'

Henry returned later that day and told her that he'd had a long chat with his brother. He had agreed to go back into the family firm until the Lloyds situation become more stable. It would mean living away, of course. He would live in his brother's basement flat during the week and come home to Pennington at the weekends. It would be all right, he assured her. In fact, time spent apart during the week would make the times together more fun, wouldn't they?

Henry apologized for his loss of temper the previous day, but said that he hoped that he had at least made her see sense. With him working in the city, and she taking paying guests they might just about scrape through, but an expensive school for Henry junior was out of the question. She became very angry then. What was the point of them both working so hard if their beloved son had to be deprived of his education? She was prepared to work hard, prostitute herself if necessary, so long as their child went to Edgeford.

So when, at the Lloyds ladies meeting, Lavinia asked if she thought they should change the advertisement Brooke said, 'No, let it run.' She had, she said, handled the situation well. She felt it had been a one off and she was sure that they wouldn't get any more problems. But in her heart she hoped that the Arab gentleman would send many of his rich friends to lie with an English Lady. It could be the solution to all her problems.

CHAPTER THIRTY-FOUR

The following Thursday three very excited boys were wedged into the back of Brooke's car and driven to Edgeford School.

Josh had gone with Henry to the meeting in London and, as planned, Brooke and Lavinia had agreed to team up on the school visit. They arrived at the Great Hall with time to spare but found difficulty in parking the car. As a consequence, the Headmaster, Charles Ferguson, was almost five minutes into his welcome speech when they actually got into the building.

Afterwards Brooke and Lavinia agreed that the headmaster was a very handsome, very charming man. His wife Helen well deserved her name, for she was very beautiful.

'It's easy to be attractive when you've no worries,' Lavinia commented to her friend. 'They're obviously a charmed couple, they have the world at their feet.'

'What was all that about titled ladies?' Brooke asked.

Lavinia made a face. 'I haven't a clue, some private joke I think – well that was what he said, wasn't it, but I don't know – you don't think she was poking fun at us, do you?'

'What was it she said? "We're such awful snobs here at Edgeford, we like to have few titled ladies amongst the parents in the school" was that it? And did you see the mischievous look she gave her husband?'

'He pinched her bottom.'

'What?'

'The head, Charles Ferguson, he pinched her bottom when she said that titled lady bit, didn't you notice?'

'No, but they obviously found it very funny.'

'Well, he did say it was just a private joke they had between them, so I expect we'd better take it on face value.'

'As long as the joke wasn't at our expense. I say, you don't think they know, do you?'

'Know what?'

'About Lloyds. About us and Lloyds, that is?'

'I don't see how they can know we're involved. In any case, as long as we pay the school fees, it's none of their business.'

Lavinia sighed. 'I don't know that we can pay the fees, Brooke. Josh did take out insurance toward the boys schooling when they were born, but it only covers about half of it. I don't know how we can find the rest. I try to talk to Josh about it and he simply won't listen, he's blinkered, he can't see to left nor right. As far as he's concerned the boys are coming here, and that is that. He hasn't thought where the money will come from.'

The women were sitting in the quad; the day was bright and sunny. The boys had been taken on a conducted tour of the various boarding houses.

'Well, Henry has told me that he can't find the fees for Henry junior, but I'm determined that he should come here and, if necessary, I'll pay for it myself.'

'But, it's what? Four-and-a-half-thousand a term or something like that. How can we possibly make that sort of money from B and B?'

Brooke looked at her shoes. 'We'll diversify, we can do wedding receptions, and special dinners, and offer other things as well. You told me yourself that you took a thousand pounds in a weekend.'

'But that wasn't profit. I have all the expenses to cover and I'll have a huge tax bill to pay.'

'Suppose there was a way that you could earn tax-free money?'

'How?'

Brooke confessed then. She said it was a tremendous relief to tell someone.

Lavinia swallowed. She could hardly believe what Brooke was telling her. At first she wanted to laugh, it seemed both bizarre and ridiculous. She did not feel comfortable listening to Brooke's confession. Yet Brooke spoke as if her money making venture was quite normal. Indeed at one point, she said that they must consider selling anything that was saleable. Lavinia crossed her legs, a subconscious act, displaying the fact that, for her, some things could never have a price.

'But what does Henry think?'

'I couldn't begin to tell Henry. What is it you say? What the eyes cannot see, the heart doesn't grieve about?'

'But what if he found out?'

'I think he'd be rather proud of me. Anyway, knowing Henry's sexual appetite, it would probably turn him on.'

Lavinia panicked, she certainly didn't want to know about Henry's lustful feelings. 'I tried to make some illegal money,' she blurted. Her confession was more of a ploy to stop Brooke from going into greater details.

So Lavinia told her about fixing to have the car stolen, and how she had imagined herself rotting away in Holloway women's prison, or another similar establishment.

Brooke laughed. 'But the Bentley! For Gods sake, it's hardly inconspicuous is it?'

Each woman thought the other's crime the worse. Although Brooke pointed out that her crime wasn't actually illegal, whereas Lavinia, had she been caught, might well have ended up in prison.

'Are you sure about that? Prostitution is illegal. I'm sure it is.'

'Soliciting and running a brothel is, as is living off immoral earnings, but a little arrangement between me and a guest is quite legal. I checked.'

'Who on earth with? Not your solicitor?'

'Of course not, I looked it up in the library.'

Lavinia thought for a moment. 'Brooke, I couldn't, I just couldn't, I'd feel —'

But then the boys returned and she was unable to finish her sentence.

Josh and Henry returned from London with an air of gloom, the meeting had gone well, but the cost of any legal action made the venture out of the question. Both Josh and Henry agreed that to risk money trying to recover what they had already lost was both impractical and unwise. The two couples had dinner in the kitchen: none of the children joined them. The three boys ate in front of the television and Zoë and Tiggy had gone to the cinema in Norwich.

'So,' said Henry. 'Will the twins be going to Edgeford?'

'I don't think so,' said Lavinia.

'Of course,' said Josh at the same time.

The discussion that followed was almost an

argument, with Brooke and Josh both insisting that Edgeford was the only school suitable for their sons, whilst Henry and Lavinia explained that such a high profile school was out of the question.

'But, where will you send them?' Brooke asked. 'You can't be thinking of sending them to a state school.'

'A private day school perhaps,' Lavinia suggested. 'We've insurance enough to cover a day school.'

'And where is this wonderful day school?'

'I don't know, there must be one.'

'Well there isn't,' Josh snapped. 'All my family have gone to Edgeford, and my sons will go too.' He laughed then, as if embarrassed by his own zeal. 'If the twins were identical, we could send one, one term, and the other, the next,' he joked.

Everyone laughed except Lavinia who, fixing Brooke with her eyes, said in a determined way. 'And how do you intend to raise the money for the school fees, Josh? Perhaps we women could set up in business, a little sideline. Perhaps you'd like us to become high-class prostitutes? Yes, that should bring the money rolling in, shouldn't it?'

'I say, Vinnie old girl, have you been drinking?' He looked terribly embarrassed.

'Sounds like a good plan to me,' said Henry. 'I'd like to book myself in, Lavinia. If that's all right?' He was laughing heartily.

Josh was red in the face. 'I say, Henry. I don't quite like the way this conversation is heading.'

'A joke, Josh, the women are teasing us. Can't you see that?'

'Right. Yes, well, I didn't for one minute think they were serious, but it's hardly the sort of thing one expects a lady to say, now is it?'

'Josh, you're such a prude,' exclaimed Brooke.

'That sort of talk's all right in the club, Lady Brooke, but it's hardly the sort of thing to be said at a chap's dinner table.'

'Calm down, Josh.' Lavinia said. 'Nothing was meant by it.'

Josh was still very red in the face; he didn't answer his wife

Brooke smiled broadly at both Josh and her husband. 'As long as you realise that we women won't be beaten. You don't know what we're capable of.' She laughed. 'In fact, my dears, you have no idea. We'll find the school fees, you concentrate keeping the roof above our heads.'

'I'll drink to that,' Josh said, raising his glass.

Lavinia surveyed the rest of the company. She would have liked to have read their minds. What exactly were they thinking? What were they feeling? What would Henry say if he knew about Brooke's exploits?

CHAPTER THIRTY-FIVE

The bed and breakfast guests came in thick and fast, Brooke and Lavinia were rushed off their feet, as was Hillary. Ailsa, living in such a remote place was not as busy. In any case her farming interests were taking up most of her life. The vast areas of pasture and rough grazing attached to Cameron House carried an enormous head of sheep, and Ailsa was entirely at the mercy of the three shepherds that ran the flock. None of these hardy Scots had been paid for three months, and whilst their complaints were justified, they were made in a halfhearted way, so that Ailsa took their discontent as only half serious.

Meanwhile the children of Hulver sat exams. The twins took common entrance and Zoë sat her A levels. She had done very little work and even less revision. She announced that she didn't feel that she had done very well. She added that, as she had no intention of going to university, her results didn't matter very much anyway.

When asked what she would do instead, she told her worried parents that she would marry Steve.

So when Ailsa telephoned to say that two of her three shepherds had been offered and accepted jobs on a neighboring estate, it was a natural solution for the Elliots to offer Steve Jarvis's service at least until the end of the summer.

Zoë swore her undying love for Steve as she kissed him goodbye at the station. 'I'll come and see you soon,' she promised.

'Better clear it with your Ma and Mrs McTodd first,' he advised.

'Don't worry, I can handle them,' she said confidently. She pushed her body up close to his, not caring that people were staring at them. 'I love you, Steve. I love you, so, so very much.'

'Ditto,' Steve replied, not very sincerely.

Ailsa met him from the train and drove him back to Cameron House. She showed him the shepherd's recently vacated cottage, then took him into Cameron House, where she had a meal ready and waiting for him.

'You know I can't pay you?' she said.

'Oh, I think you can.' He gave her one of his rare smiles. He really was a remarkably handsome man.

She laughed. 'I mean money – you fool. I can't pay you any money.'

'Then we must come to some other arrangement.'

His bag was on the floor near to the kitchen door. He got up from the table, picked up the bag and headed for the main staircase.

'Where are you going?'

'To find my room.'

'But I've given you a cottage.'

'I know. I'll take that as my wages, and now I'll find my room.'

Ailsa looked dumbfounded. She followed behind him as he mounted the stairs. He walked boldly into Ailsa's bedroom, and opened the wardrobe. It was still full of Philip's things. He scraped the heavy tweed suits to one side, and hung his own clothes in place of them. He pressed his hand into the mattress on the bed as if feeling it for spring and comfort.

'This is where I'll be sleeping, but you're welcome to join me.' He gave her a handsome, rather crooked, smile.

'But —'

'Take it or leave it, I may not offer twice.'

She smiled. She was inexplicably attracted to him.

'I'll take it,' she said. 'For the time being, that is.'

'I thought you would. I don't disappoint.'

'I know.'

Steve's shepherding skills were minimal. But under the guidance of the one remaining shepherd, and with his self-acknowledged gypsy blood giving him confidence with any animal, by the end of the first week he was as competent a shepherd as he was a lover; neither the sheep nor Ailsa had any cause to complain. He worked long hours. In his spare time he renovated the old shepherd's cottage, called it Shepherd's Purse, and placed it with a holiday cottage letting agency. Bookings rolled in at a pleasing rate and Ailsa was so enthusiastic that she persuaded him to begin work on another cottage, and very soon was to be found by his side helping in the renovations.

As time went by they became more than lovers. A friendship emerged. Ailsa began to talk openly to him about her late husband. 'You know, I can't remember what Philip looked like.' She was painting a wall in the cottage, holiday guests were due the next day and there was a rush to get it ready.

'That's a good sign,' Steve said. 'Don't worry – you'll remember him again soon. It's nature's way of healing.'

'I can't quite define what I feel about him anymore. I mean, I feel a feeling, an emotion, but it's fleeting, and when it is with me I can't quite put a name to it.'

'I know that feeling,' he said, thinking of Zoë. 'You're lucky it's not with you all the time.'

When he'd first put down roots at Cameron House he'd gone home at the end of every month, to visit his mother, he said. But he'd barely spoken to his parent. It was Zoë he sought out, Zoë he talked to, and Zoë he lay with.

Zoë's plans for their future were both romantic and impractical. She had woven a dream, a fairy tale. They would live together in undeniable poverty, but Zoë's ideas of poverty were based on the Elliot's present lack of funds. She was, despite their proclaimed embarrassment, well clothed and well fed.

'Do you know what I earn, Zoë?'

She shook her head.

'Then I'll tell you, my basic wage is a hundred and fifty a week, before the tax man has his cut, that is.'

'But that's loads.'

'Is it Zoë? How much did that jacket you're wearing cost?'

She shrugged. 'Not much, Daddy bought it for me, but that was ages ago. We're really poor now, after this insurance thing.'

'Yeh, sure. I wish I was as poor as your family, Zoë. I really do.'

After the first couple of months Steve's visits south dwindled. Zoë was beginning to irritate him, her ideas were so out of touch with reality. It was quite obvious that her parents would never agree to their marriage. He was fond of Zoë, but he was fonder of the wealth and position a marriage to her might mean. He wanted an assurance of wealth and security before he embarked on such a plan. Besides, Ailsa was gradually winning his loyalties. Zoë was young and pretty and potentially rich, and part of him loved her. Ailsa was twenty years older than he, she was exciting and very, very sexy, and she had a sort of honesty about her. She saw him for exactly what he was, he needed to put on no acts; he needed no pretence. He was sure that he could never love Ailsa, he wondered if he could ever really like her. It was something else, a deep-seated respect combined with mutual admiration. Ailsa always seemed to be one step ahead of him. She calculated things, always weighing up where things would lead and what she could gain from them. Her affair with Steve was just one such calculation. But didn't Steve also calculate? Weren't they in some ways an ideal pair? A long-term future with Ailsa was out of the question, of course. She was rich enough, despite her protestations that the bank could take everything away from her in one foul swoop. But Steve had no illusions; he knew that, although she welcomed his hands on her body, her wealth and her lifestyle were completely out of bounds to him.

His romance with Zoë had paled; it had been fun when he was sneaking in and out of the castle, cocking a snook at his elders and betters. But once the Elliots found out and approved, the excitement waned. It was as if the parent's acceptance of him had robbed the daughter of her attraction – all the fun had drained away. Besides, Zoë had become so clingy. She'd get upset if he so much as looked at another girl. She'd have a fit if she knew about Ailsa. Zoë was filled with such naïve innocence and she wasn't at all adventurous. If only she could be a bit more like Ailsa McTodd; now there was one funky lady. She may be getting on a bit, her body maybe mature and past the first flush of youth, but she knew how to please a man, and that was a talent that counted for quite a lot. Zoë was always on about getting married and settling down, perhaps in a little cottage on the Hulver estate. Who the hell wanted to settle down, at Hulver or anywhere else? Not Steve Jarvis, he had bigger dreams than that. On and on Zoë nagged. When should they announce their engagement? Wouldn't it be better to start a baby right away, then her parents would have to agree to them being together. Really the girl was off her head, she didn't know the first thing about how to go on.

When Steve cut out his visits south, Zoë made a hundred excuses for him and, eventually unable to bear it any longer, she planned a reunion. She announced that she would go to Scotland and she would bring her lover home. She said that she thought that he had spent far too long helping Ailsa. She insisted that it was time he came back to Hulver and claimed her as his own. She explained it all to Brooke when they were waiting for Lavinia to return from a shopping trip.

'You see, Brooke. Steve and I have something very special between us, a bond that's unbreakable. I love him so much. You can have no idea how much I love him. If only Mummy and Daddy would try and get to know him properly, they'd like him, I know they would. He's so – well, he's so, so . . . Mr Darcy.'

'Mr Darcy?' Brooke's eyebrows were raised.

'Yes, you know, Pride and Prejudice.'

'Ah, yes, Jane Austin. So your Steve Jarvis is like Mr Darcy? Only?'

'Only what?'

'Mr Darcy, without the education or the estate?'

'That's just typical. You're all the same, I thought you'd be different,' she had tears in her eyes. 'You only think of money. You're like my parents, they want me to marry some Alexander or, or, Rupert or, or...'

'Jocelyn?' Brooke asked helpfully.

'Precisely,' Zoë snapped.

When told of Zoë's plans, Lavinia raised no objection. She discussed the matter with Josh, and told him that from her brief chats to Ailsa she had a good idea of the mistress's and shepherd's relationship. Both parents were in no doubt that Zoë would come home broken-hearted. 'Why don't you surprise him?' Lavinia advised. 'Don't tell him you're coming, he'll be so thrilled to see you.'

In the second week of June, Zoë, having finished her exams, took the train to Scotland, and arrived, unannounced, at Cameron house in the middle of a sultry summer's afternoon. Steve had been up early that morning, moving a large flock of Scottish Black Faced sheep from one part of the estate to another. Ailsa and two bright-eyed border collies had helped him. They had arrived back at the house hungry and thirsty at two o'clock. A letter from Ailsa's bank manager was waiting for her. She eyed it cautiously, tossed it to one side and suggested they had a beer.

Steve picked up the letter and turned it over in his hands. 'Aren't you going to open it? It'll be about the cash flow I did for you.'

'It might be telling me they're going to pull the rug,' she said. 'I'll open it later.'

Steve ripped the envelope open.

'Steve, that's private.'

He ran his hand down her back, and pushed it through her legs, grabbing her crotch with his strong fingers.

'Nothing you've got's private,' he said.

She pulled away from him and snatched the envelope out of his hand. She smoothed out the letter and read it. A slow smile spread over her face. The letter was short and concise; it stated that the bank had reviewed her loan facilities. They were impressed with her cash flow, and they wished her luck with the holiday cottage venture. They were cheered to see that her flock had almost doubled its income from the previous year. She handed the letter over to Steve; he read it and grinned.

They made love then, right there in the kitchen, with Ailsa bent forward over the back of a kitchen chair, and Steve rutting her from behind. Steve then staggered down to the cellar and retrieved a bottle of very good burgundy, which they consumed in bed between spasms of laughter, and acrobatic bouts of lovemaking.

They were still in bed and a little drunk when the ringing of the doorbell announced Zoë's arrival.

At first Ailsa was very much at pains to conceal her relationship with Steve, but as the day worn on, and Ailsa noted Zoë's claim on her lover, she became more and more possessive of him. She even indicated that she and Steve had spent the afternoon in bed.

'Take no notice of her,' Steve said later that night as he lay by Zoë's side. 'She's been trying to get my trousers off since the day I arrived.'

'She talks as if she's succeeded,' Zoë said.

He smiled. 'She may have, but as long as there's plenty left for you, you can't complain, now can you?'

Very much later that night, he was to utter the same taunting words to Ailsa.

The next day Zoë once more said the words that Steve dreaded. 'I want to have your baby, Steve.'

Steve laughed, but she was adamant.

'Don't you see, they'll have to let us marry if I'm pregnant?'

'And what if they don't?'

'I'm eighteen, they can't stop me.'

'They can cut you off without a penny.'

'They won't.'

'I wouldn't like to bet on that. In fact your father more or less told me as much not so very long ago.'

'Is that all I mean to you? Money?'

'No, but you'd be pretty miserable without it.'

She cried. 'No. No, it's you I want. We don't need money.'

'If I were to marry you, Zoë, love. It would be clean and above board, and with your parent's blessing.'

'Then we'll never marry,' she sobbed.

'So be it,' he said in a matter-of-fact way.

'Then I'll get pregnant anyway.'

'Not by me, you won't.'

Zoë went back to the south that afternoon. When she arrived home, she announced that she had changed her mind about her life. She only hoped that her A level results would be good enough to allow her to go to university.

CHAPTER THIRTY-SIX

The last week in June seemed to mark a turning point in everyone's life. Lloyds worked three years in arrears and the losses for1990 were no longer vague estimates but hard cruel facts, payments had to be made by 31st August 1993 and somehow the money had to be found.

Henry, working in London, did not receive the dreaded envelope, but Brooke recognized it for what it was, and she opened it in his absence. Her business was thriving. Her paying guests paid well, so much so, that she lived a life of quiet luxury, employing not only a good cook and housekeeper, but a butler as well. But her real profit lay in the string of men who visited Pennington, diplomats and foreign businessmen, all willing to pay whatever price she asked. They would identify themselves by saying that they were single gentlemen wishing to spend a night or two, and they sincerely hoped she would be able to provide them with decent room service.

But despite her newfound wealth she blanched when she saw the amount that Henry would have to find. She was sitting in the morning room when the telephone rang and a well spoken male voice identifying himself only as James asked if she had any vacancies for that very night. He was, he said, booking the room for his boss who was a man of some influence. They would, of course, need two rooms, but only his superior required room service, and he sincerely hoped that the service would be as special as he had been led to believe. As his employer was very much in the public eye, absolute discretion was paramount. Brooke glanced down at the letter still in her hand, a smile played on her lips. 'It can be as discreet and as special as you want it to be,' she said. 'But it will not come cheap, and the payment must be in cash.' 'I think I understand,' the man replied.

After she had replaced the receiver, she glanced at her booking book and noted that she already had a single gentleman due that evening, in brackets after his name she had written 'wants room service'. 'Well for sure I can't do both,' she said aloud. 'Mr Kirby will have to try elsewhere.'

She dialed the contact number she had taken for him. It turned out to be a barrister's chambers in Lincoln's Inn, and the clerk said that he had made the booking himself. Mr Kirby was to appear in the Norwich Crown Court the following day.

'But he's asked for room service,' Brooke said.

'Is there a problem with that?'

'I'm not sure I can manage it. But I do have a friend who lives not far away. She's closer to Norwich than I am. Lady Lavinia Elliot, of Hulver Castle. I'm sure he'll be very comfortable with her.'

The clerk sighed, he sounded bored. 'I'll tell Mr Kirby as soon as he gets in,' he said.

Meanwhile, at Hulver Castle, Josh and Lavinia were pondering over their own agent's letter.

'I have a little money,' Lavinia said. 'But I'd sort of earmarked it for the boys' school fees.'

Josh covered her hand with his own. 'No. No, I'll go and see the bank. We've done pretty well. Bamford won't let me down, I'm sure he won't. I pay enough for the guarantee.'

'But I thought you'd already topped the guarantee.'

Josh let out a deep breath. 'I have, in theory. But don't worry. I'll think of something.'

He went into his office carrying the letter.

Moments later Brooke rang, and explained that she was passing the barrister on to Hulver. 'The only thing is, he's has asked for room service.'

'For what? Oh, oh yes! Your special room service! Forget it Brooke – I couldn't. I just couldn't.'

'For five hundred pounds?'

'How much?'

'Five hundred. Well, it's normally anything from two upward, but I've found you can more or less name your price.'

'Two hundred?'

'Well, you can push him up, I'm sure you can. You have to assess each individual and charge accordingly. And you get the B and B money on top of that.'

'Wow. No wonder your business is thriving. But listen, Brooke. I couldn't, I really, really couldn't.' She gave a shy little laugh. 'How would I explain it to Josh for a start? He does expect me to be in his bed at night.'

'Well you'll just have to tell Mr Kirby that room service isn't available.'

'Will he accept that?'

'I'm sure he will. He'll have to, won't he?'

'Will he want dinner?'

'I expect so. He was expecting a long night and will need some nourishment.' Brooke giggled.

Lavinia laughed too. 'You know, Brooke. I can't believe the sort of conversations that I have with you! I'll take him as a paying guest, but I couldn't possibly . . . you know . . do it. You know . . . *it*.'

'Lavinia, you're such a prude. I'm going to do *it* and I shall make a very good profit to boot.'

'Each to his own,' Lavinia replied. 'Each to his

own.' She hung up.

Josh came through to the kitchen. 'I've just phoned my agent. It looks like Lloyds are getting a scheme together to help us. I'm going up to London this afternoon to see him. He can't see me until six, so I'll probably stay the night with Henry.

CHAPTER THIRTY-SEVEN

Lavinia tidied her hair as she made her way to answer the door. Alexander Kirby greeted her with a broad smile.

'Have I come to the right place? I had a message from Lady Osbourne-Pennington.'

'It's dinner, bed and breakfast only,' Lavinia blurted. Best to tell him what he could and could not expect right away, before any misunderstandings could arise.

He frowned. 'Yes, yes. Right. Good,' he said. He cleared his throat. 'Well? Can I come in?'

Lavinia drew in a deep breath, but she didn't move to let him pass. She wanted to be perfectly sure that he understood her terms of business. 'So that's acceptable, is it? Dinner, bed and breakfast, only?'

'Perfectly,' he said. His face held a puzzled expression.

She moved to one side to let him pass. Then she showed him up to one of the double guestrooms. Still she was afraid that he hadn't understood her. 'I'm sorry that I don't offer the same sort of service that Lady Pennington offers,' she said. 'You do understand, don't you?'

He still wore a puzzled face and looked around the room. She had given him what she considered to be one of her best rooms. She thought it might compensate for his sexual disappointment.

'But this looks perfect,' he said. He opened the bathroom door and glanced inside. 'Absolutely perfect.' He smiled at her. He was a very handsome man. 'It's all lovely. I may never want to leave.'

His smile disconcerted her and she blushed. 'And you'd like dinner? Just dinner?' She added.

'And breakfast, of course,' he said.

'Oh yes, that goes without saying. I just wanted to make it clear that ... well ... that I didn't offer the same facilities as Lady Brooke.'

'Then Pennington must be a very grand house indeed,' he replied.

'Oh, it is. It is. Dinner at seven-thirty then?'

'That's fine. But ... well, I know you've made it clear that you only do dinner but I wondered if––'

She interrupted him. 'Oh no, I couldn't possibly. Really I couldn't.'

'Not even if I pay the same price? As dinner, I mean.'

She was perspiring profusely. 'I'm sorry?'

'I have a lot of reading to do, and I had a rather protracted business lunch today. I really don't want a big meal – a light supper would suit me so much better. I'm quite prepared to pay for the full works, though.' He blinked; his eyes were wide apart and very blue. She thought he looked honest and uncomplicated.

Relief shrouded Lavinia's face. 'Oh yes.' She exhaled loudly. 'I've no one else in tonight. In fact, I'm on my own – my husband has gone to London. You can eat with me if you like? Just a scratch meal in the kitchen.' She frowned, why did she have to tell him that Josh was away? As soon as the words had left her mouth she instantly regretted them. It was as if she felt a need to advertise her own confusion and vulnerability.

He smiled; he certainly was a good-looking man. He was, she guessed, probably in his mid forties, he had dark hair grizzled with gray at the temples. His face looked slightly tanned, he had a straight nose, a square chin, and even, white teeth. He was not quite as tall as Josh, but he was broad and muscular. He was clean-shaven, and his hands were white and smooth. His suit spoke of Saville Row and his shoes were polished to a high shine.

She explained to him where he could find the kitchen, and invited him to join her there in half an hour.

Lavinia went down and opened a bottle of cheap red wine intending to add a little of it to a spaghetti

310

Bolognese she was preparing. She poured some of the thin red liquid into a glass, telling herself that a sip of wine would calm her nerves, but she found she was taking large gulps of it. The letter Josh had received that morning stood propped on the kitchen dresser. She could hardly bear to look at it. She took it down from the shelf and pushed it under her tablemat.

Alexander Kirby joined her at precisely seven-thirty. He had shed his city suit and was now dressed in casual slacks and an open necked shirt. He complimented her on the castle, on her food, and even on the well-behaved Fen. He was utterly charming and she could see that he was probably very good at his job. Certainly had she been on a jury she would have been swayed by his charm alone. They sipped their way through the first bottle of wine, and she opened another. This time of a better quality; apologizing for the first, and explaining that she had intended it for cooking, but had somehow managed to start drinking it.

He told her about the case he was on; he was defending a man accused of drug smuggling. Apparently his client had been caught red-handed whilst driving a vanload of cannabis through Norwich. There had been so much hash in the van, he told her, that the police driver that had driven it to the pound was overcome by fumes and needed hospital treatment. They both laughed at the mental picture the scene conjured up.

'Is he guilty?' Lavinia asked.

'Undoubtedly.'

'And you're defending him?'

'Defending him, not judging him. No doubt you think he should be locked up and the key thrown away?' 'I have teenage children,' Lavinia said as if to explain her disapproval.

Alexander Kirby nodded. 'This lad is little more than a teenager, he's the product of a one parent family.' He waved his hand around Lavinia's kitchen. 'He has had to survive by his wits, and when someone offered him a lot of money, a lot of money for him, that is, he grasped the opportunity with both hands and never thought to consider the consequences.'

'There are jobs,' Lavinia said indignantly.

'Sure there are, but he doesn't come from a work orientated family. He was both silly, and shortsighted to drive that van, but you'd have to be a hardhearted woman not to give him another chance. And you know, silly though it might sound, this just might give him a chance. There'll be experts around to help him, if I can keep him out of jail'

'I'm not hardhearted,' she said indignantly. 'As I said, I have four teenage children.'

'Right. And do you think that sending my client

312

to prison for a few years will save your children?'

'It's a start,' she said, once again with indignation.

'Not for him it isn't. He'll go in a petty criminal, and come out a serious convict. And for every young lad like my client there are a dozen more to take his place, so your kids still won't be safe. No, it's the big boys, the people that hired him, that need to be caught and punished.'

'And I suppose you'd defend the big boys, as you call them?'

'Hardly. I only do legal aid work, the big boys can afford a better barrister than I will ever be.'

Lavinia was suddenly very interested. 'Why? Why only do legal aid?' She smiled and remembering the well-cut suit he had arrived in, she added, 'It must pay jolly well.'

He smiled back at her. 'Oh that's another story.' He glanced at his watch. 'Good Lord, it's almost eleven o'clock. I really do have work to do. I'm afraid I've drunk rather too much of your excellent wine.' She noticed that his speech was slightly slurred.

He got up and gave her a slight bow. 'I haven't enjoyed an evening so much in a long time. I must make an effort to stay with Lady Brooke sometime. If you're second best, she must be quite a girl. I'm only sad that it has to end here.' He took her hand, gave it a gentle kiss and left the kitchen.

Lavinia stood for some moments frozen to the spot, the touch of his lips on her hand had disquieted her. She had spent the best part of the evening wondering what it would be like making love with him. He was a good twenty years younger than Josh; he would be vigorous and vital, he would be new and exciting. Josh had been her only lover; she had no one to compare him with.

She drained her glass of the rest of the wine and packed the dishwasher. She cleared the tablemats from the table and, in doing so, revealed the hateful letter. She turned it over in her hands. Still holding on to it, she opened the back door and let Fen out for a last run. The dog was gone for ages, but Lavinia seemed unaware of the time she took. She stood, as if in a daze, playing the envelope over her lips, as if trying to make an important decision, and yet her thoughts were of nothing in particular. Fen eventually returned to her, she settled the dog down for the night, put out all the lights and, still holding the letter, she climbed the stairs to bed.

CHAPTER THIRTY-EIGHT

Lavinia, like her guest, had drunk a little too much wine. She almost overbalanced when she removed her tights. She put the letter down on her bedside table; from where it greeted her when she returned from the bathroom, having enjoyed a long, hot, but not very sobering shower.

She slipped into a pair of cream silk pajamas and got into bed. She turned over and tried to sleep, but the thought of the Lloyds losses invaded her brain and robbed her of her slumber. Eventually she sat up and flicked on the bedside light. It was twelve-fifteen. She propped herself up on her pillows. The answer was easy. Why did she think she was so special? If Brooke could do it, why couldn't she? She had only to walk along the passage – would it be so very wrong? Alexander Kirby was a very attractive man, that made it easier, but did that make it any less wrong? She flopped back onto the pillow; she wasn't going to sleep anyway. And she was doing it for Josh, for the children, and for Hulver. It wasn't as if she were an innocent little virgin, was it? May be she was being selfish in not doing it? Her fuddled brain tried to work out the pros and cons. She got out of bed and went as far as her bedroom door. She shook her head, pushed the door firmly closed, turned, and got back into bed. She snuggled down into the duvet, but did not turn off the light. She lay and stared up at the four-poster's canopy.

She looked at the clock again; it was twelve-thirty. Once more she got out of bed. This time she left her room and made her way along the passage to Alexander Kirby's room. She stood for some moments outside the door; twice she turned and almost went back to her own room. Eventually, her breath short, she tapped on the door and waited. A few moments later she tapped again, this time she didn't wait, but entered. He was fast asleep. Lavinia closed her eyes, she could turn back now; he was so soundly asleep, he'd never know that she had been in his room. She looked down on her sleeping guest; he really was a very handsome man. 'Down to the very last shirt button,' she said aloud as she slowly undid her pajama top, slipped out of the bottoms, and climbed into the double bed beside him.

'What? What is it?' Alexander turned toward her. He suddenly sat bolt upright. 'What the devil —?'

Lavinia's lips were extremely dry, she moistened

them with her tongue. 'I changed my mind,' she said.

'Changed your mind?'

'About room service.'

The bathroom door was open and the light had been left on; she saw the glint of his teeth as he smiled in the soft reflected light.

'Room service? Room service?' He said, and laughed. It was a low chuckle of a laugh. He nodded his head. 'I'm not a man ever to pass on room service.'

He slid down the bed next to her, she was lying on her back. He put one hand around her waist. 'God,' he said. 'My God, I've died and gone to Heaven.'

She gave a nervous little laugh; her heart was thumping so loudly, it seemed as if it were making the whole of her body tremble. She could still leave if she wanted to, couldn't she? She could still back out, the harm wasn't yet done, was it?

He was wearing old-fashioned striped pajamas, which were soon deposited on the floor beside the bed.

She put out her arm and touched the bare skin of his shoulder. He felt hot, as if his flesh was on fire. He snuggled into her neck, his breath seemed to scorch her skin.

'You felt it too,' he said. 'The chemistry. I thought it might just be me.'

She didn't know what he was talking about, or did

317

she? Was she there because of Josh, or because of herself? Was she using Josh as an excuse to satiate her own fantasies and desires?

He kissed her shoulders, her arms, her elbows. 'Let me see your back. Turn with your back toward me,' he said. 'I have a thing about backs. I love women's backs.'

She turned onto her side and he began to kiss her back, starting at the top near her neck, kissing and caressing, placing a kiss, a caress, on every one of her vertebrae. Then working his way down around her shoulder blades, massaging, nipping, kissing and stroking. Down her spine to her thighs, he played his tongue over the backs of her knees. He threw the covers back, and lay beside her. The length of him against her own glowing flesh made her yearn for him. He was so strong and firm, and in control. Was that it? Had she always been in control with Josh, was she the one that dictated when and how? She rather thought she was. She loved making love, she always had, from the very first. But she had known no other than Josh. Now here was a different man, a different experience. But she wasn't like Brooke, was she? Brooke loved sex, she made no secret of it. It made her feel superior and in control. Lavinia had always been in control, but not now, not with this new man.

He was sucking her toes and turning her over. He worked his way back up the front of her body, kissing her inner thigh, his tongue seeking and caressing her navel, his soft lips sucking her nipples and then, at last, his mouth seeking out her clitoris.

Lavinia was no longer capable of logical thought. With Josh she had always tried to think and act in a way that would please him. Now she sought only to please herself and it pleased her to kiss his chest, his lips, his belly, it pleased her to bend her body above him so that his penis rubbed between her breasts. She had always loved making love with Josh; from the very first she loved the intimacy, loved the sight of his male body. Even before she had grown to love him, she had desired the act itself. But now with this new man there was a new dimension added, passion and lust were too slight a phase to describe what she was feeling. She knew that if he didn't enter her again, and again, she would die for the need of him, and she could wait no longer. She pushed him back on the bed, and forced herself down on him working her body back and forward as if her life depended on it. She came quickly, long before he, yet still she craved for more. Spluttering and panting, her breasts rubbing his chest, her thighs holding his hips, they reached a crescendo of satisfaction together. She slumped forward onto his chest, their breath and sweat mingled together.

They lay entwined, her on top of him, for a long time, until he took her chin in his hands and, bringing her head up toward him, he kissed her. He rolled her over onto her back, and kissed her again. 'There's no question about it, I really have died and gone to Heaven,' he said.

He kissed her again, and she felt his flaccid penis begin to harden again against her thigh, a sensation that awoke her newfound passion. She pushed her tongue into his mouth, she explored his teeth, his tongue, his inner lips; nothing had ever felt so intimate, so sensual, before. And then he was inside her again, sending her soaring to new heights of passion, new depths of need.

They made love for hours, as if neither of them could satiate their desires. At some point, in the early hours of the morning, they decided they were hot and sticky and they climbed into the shower together. But the sight of their naked bodies in the full light brought with it more desire and they made love again, with Lavinia bent over the bath and Alexander's knees rubbing against the tiles on the bathroom floor. Then it was back once more to the bedroom and their wet shinny bodies once more devouring each other in total harmony.

CHAPTER THIRTY-NINE

Lavinia stretched out in the bed. Her mind had not yet slipped into gear and her head ached. It was dark in the room, but the single shaft of sunlight that pierced the blackness through the crack in the curtains was very bright. She opened her eyes wide, and blinked. She spent some moments studying the dust motes that floated in the sunbeam. Despite her headache, she felt ridiculously happy, but couldn't quite recall why she should feel so elated. She smiled. 'Jesus wants you for a Sunbeam,' she said aloud. She pushed her hand above her head, expecting to feel the heavy carved wood of her own four-poster, and Josh lying beside her. But the bedhead was soft and velvety, the elation of a few moments before drained away from her like water from a bath; she bent her body as if trying to catch hold of her happiness and keep it for just a little longer.

She jumped from the bed and, as she did so, a slow

trickle of semen ran down her inner thigh, she put her hand between her legs and stood frozen to the spot. The man, the barrister, where was he? For Christ sake, where was he? Her fingers were slimy and sticky. 'Who was he?' She said aloud. 'Who the hell was he?' She staggered back toward the wall, leaned against it, then gently collapsed to her knees. 'Oh, God. What have I done?' She said. She put her hand up to her mouth, trying desperately to gather her thoughts. Her hand smelled strongly of him. She began to cry as a thousand thoughts crowded her brain. She thought of Josh, would he ever forgive her? But she had done it for him, hadn't she? Somehow it would have been all right if she hadn't enjoyed it. But that was the trouble, she had loved every minute of it, she had wanted it to last forever, she had felt a passion that she didn't know she was capable of. She couldn't get enough of the dark stranger that had shared her bed. And that's what he was, a stranger. She knew nothing about him; and yet she felt as if she'd waited all her life for him. But the fact was, she didn't know him, he could be anybody. He might not be a barrister at all, he could be a criminal, an axe murderer. She laughed at her thoughts. She wondered if he was married, if he did this sort of thing often; she supposed he probably did, seeing that he'd asked Brooke for her special room service. Then it hit her, he probably slept around, he probably carried all sorts of diseases. Her mouth was completely dry and her heart began to pound. 'Oh shit,' she said. 'Shit. Shit. Shit.' She was still curled up in a crumpled heap on the bedroom floor. From somewhere in the castle she heard Fen bark. She pulled herself to her feet, walked slowly over to the window and opened the curtains; she had no idea what the time was. Sunshine flooded the room. On the pillow, next to the one on which she had woken, lay a note.

Dear Vinnie, she read, (had she told him her nickname, the name only Josh and her very close friends used, or had he made it up himself?) *I couldn't bear to wake you, you looked so beautiful and so peaceful. I am due in court at ten and I am already late. I have left a cheque for the B & B on the dressing table. Phone me at my chambers any time, please, the number is at the top of the page. Vinnie, about last night, it was a night I shall remember all my life. I will be in touch.* He'd signed it simply, Alex.

She crumpled the note up in her hand, thought better of it, and smoothed it out again. There was nagging sick feeling in the pit of her stomach. 'Oh Josh,' she said and her eyes filled with tears. She grabbed a towel from the bathroom, pulled it roughly around her and made her way to her own room. The house was eerily quiet, even Fen had stopped barking. From her bedside clock she saw that it was almost ten o'clock. How could she have slept so late?

She hesitated, she desperately wanted to shower, but knew that she must let Fen out before she had an accident. Without bothering to wash or even clean her teeth she pulled on a pair of slacks and a tee shirt. She wore no bra and her nipples teased against the soft cotton of the shirt; the arousal made her think of Alex Kirby. This was ridiculous, how could she still want Alex Kirby's touch when she was riddled with guilt concerning Josh and, at the same time, terrified that she had contracted some deadly sexual disease? 'Oh sweet Jesus, this can't be happening to me,' she said. Tears welled up in her eyes.

Fen had not held out, a large puddle soaked into the gun room doormat.

'Oh Fen,' she said.

The dog, her head held low, her ears flat against her head, got out of her basket and gave two very halfhearted wags of her tail. She came over to Lavinia and cowered at her feet. The dog rolled over on her back, the flesh fell away from her face and the whites of her eyes were just visible.

'Oh, Fen, you fool! I'm not cross – it's my fault. I've left you far too long.' She stroked the dog's stomach. 'Your stupid old Missis has been up to no good, Fen. She spent last night fucking another man. Now there's a good old Anglo Saxon word – fucking. Your Master wouldn't like me to use that word, Fen, but I can't think of a better one, can you?'

The dog's tail began to thump against the quarry-tiled floor; she licked Lavinia's hand. Lavinia stopped stroking the dog, she pushed her hands up beneath her tea shirt and held onto her breasts. 'What the hell am I going to do, Fen? I'm absolutely terrified that I might have caught Aids and yet I want to do it all again.' She pushed one of her hands down between her legs. 'Now, in fact. I want Alexander Kirby again, right now.'

CHAPTER FORTY

'Brooke? It's Lavinia.'

'Hi! Wow, have I got something to tell you.' And before Lavinia could so much as mention her worries. Brooke launched into a description of the night before spent at the mercy of her Parliamentary customer.

'A thousand pounds, Lavinia! Imagine that? Bonked silly by one of her majesty's ministers, and he had a penis on him the size of the Empire State Building. He shot off a pint at a time. I thought I'd run out of condoms. And he was getting on, sixty odd if he was a day. Mind you, it wasn't without risk, the old sod nearly split me in two with his appendage. Let me assure you, size does matter.' She laughed. 'It was quite an experience, it really was. I can see why MP's have a reputation for screwing around, it's obviously in their make-up – they need a lot of sex. I'll have to ask Henry to be gentle with me when he gets home on Friday.' She laughed again. 'He's always panting for it, poor lamb, so it's not as if I can avoid it. I only hope I can sit down by then!' She laughed yet again. She was euphoric with her success. 'But tell me, how was Mr Kirby? Was he the answer to a maiden's prayer? I hope your changed you mind, and I hope you charged him well, but you're such a prude Lavinia – I don't suppose you did?'

'I did,' Lavinia replied, her voice barely above a whisper.

'You did! Wow, how much? Or perhaps I shouldn't ask?'

'I didn't charge him.'

'What?'

'It's worse than that.'

'What could be worse than that? For God's sake, Lavinia, you're hopeless.'

'I didn't ask him to wear any protection.' Saying it aloud to her friend made her feel sick.

'Protection? Oh, a condom, you mean. Oh, God, Lavinia. Might you be pregnant?'

'No, no, I was sterilized after the twins were born. I'm worried about disease and stuff like that.' There, she had said it, and it didn't seem too bad now that it was out in the open. Brooke would tell her that there was nothing to worry about

'Oh, my God.' Brooke was silent for a moment. Then she said, 'Look, Lavinia, the chances of that one man being infected with anything are so remote that —'

Lavinia interrupted her. 'He sleeps around, that's obvious.'

'It's not obvious at all, you can't possibly surmise

that.'

'He sleeps around,' Lavinia said firmly.

'Is that what he told you?'

'He didn't need to, he's skilled at it. He was ... well, let's just say he had a degree in it, probably a PhD as well.'

'So did my MP but —'

'You're telling me that your MP doesn't sleep around?'

Brooke was silent for a moment, eventually she said, 'I see your point. Well, what are we going to do?'

'We? It's me that's going to die of a hideous disease.'

'I think you're getting carried away, Lavinia. People don't die of Syphilis or Gonorrhea. It's embarrassing, but it's not fatal.'

'Aids is fatal,' Lavinia said, and once more tears threatened to fall.

She heard Brooke take a sharp breath.

'We must go to your GP and get you tested. I'll come with you. Don't worry.'

'My GP! Oh yes, sure, he only happens to be a close family friend.'

'But he can't tell anyone.'

'That doesn't matter. He'd know – I can't possibly go to him.'

'Then we'll go privately. Look, I'll throw on a few clothes, and I'll be over to you within the hour. Don't worry, Vinnie. We'll sort this out.'

'You called me, Vinnie?'

'So? It's your name isn't it?'

'Josh calls me Vinnie,' she said rather weakly. She was frowning.

'If you'd rather I didn't?'

'No. No, I like it. It's a name reserved for Josh and very special friends,' she said, and once again she pushed her hand down between her legs and thought of Alexander Kirby.

True to her word, Brooke arrived at the castle a little before twelve-thirty. 'God, Lavinia. I can't believe you've been this stupid, you're all the time lecturing Zoë on contraception and Aids and things, and then you go and do it yourself!' She shook her head. 'Right. Let's get on with it. Where's your 'phone book?'

They looked under every heading they could think of, starting under A for Aids and working their way through to V for Venereal Diseases. But they could find no relevant reference at all. It was almost two o'clock when Brooke suggested that they should at least telephone the receptionist at the doctor's surgery, and ask whom they should contact.

'I can't,' Lavinia said. 'The receptionist will recognize my voice. She'll know it is me for sure.'

'Then I shall do it.' Brooke picked up the

telephone and dialed the number, it was some moments before it was answered.

'Hello, yes,' she said with confidence. She then went on to say that she had a friend that had recently had unprotected sex, and her friend was worried about possibly being infected with the Aids virus. She then spent, what seemed to Lavinia, an age, listening to the reply, with Brooke contributing a very few short words to the conversation. 'Yes . . . Yes, I see . . . Right . . . OK.'

Brooke was smiling when she eventually put the receiver down. 'Well, she obviously didn't believe it was my friend!'

'What did she say?' Lavinia's face was white, her hands shook, she remembered that she hadn't eaten anything that day. She put the kettle on the Aga, and dumped a biscuit barrel on the table.

'Well it's under —' Brooke began drawing the telephone directory toward her, but the telephone rang before she could finish her sentence.

It was Josh, he was catching the three o'clock train, he'd see her later, and he loved her. Lavinia had bare-ly replaced the receiver before it rang again. It was Alexander Kirby, would she come to Norwich that after-noon? He'd be out of court by three-thirty; the case was bound to be adjourned, could she meet him? He needed to talk to her.

Lavinia's white face was suddenly suffused with colour; she was flustered. 'No,' she said, she had other arrangements; she couldn't possibly meet him. In that case, could he book into the castle for the night? 'No,' she said, rather abruptly, she was fully booked. Tomorrow night then? He had to see her again – he just had to.

'I'm booked for the whole week,' she said and smashed the phone down onto its cradle.

'Turning business away?' Brooke said.

'No,' Lavinia lied. 'I am fully booked.' She stared at Brooke, mentally blaming her for her present predicament. If Brooke hadn't suggested sex for profit, she wouldn't be in this mess.

As if she'd read her friend's mind, Brooke raised an eyebrow. 'Right. Back to the matter in hand.' She consulted the few notes that she had scribbled whilst talking to the doctor's receptionist.

She began to flick through the telephone directory. 'It's under GUM: genito-urinary medicine or STD: sexually transmitted diseases. She says that you can have the test with your GP, but then it will have to be entered into your medical records. If you go to the clinic it will be strictly confidential.' Brooke was dialing a number as she spoke. The call was answered immediately.

'I have a friend,' began Brooke. The person on the other end of the line spoke at length.

'No really, it's not. It's my friend.' Brooke listened again. 'Well no, she's right here beside me. For goodness sake . . . Okay. Here she is.'

Brooke handed the receiver over to Lavinia, who, after listening for the shortest of time asked three questions and gave three answers. Where and when could she have the test? What did it involve? And when would she get the results? In return she told the woman that she was forty-four, married, and that she'd had unprotected sex the night before. She jotted some information down on the same piece of paper that Brooke had scribbled on, and hung up.

'I have to go to Norwich,' she said. 'They'll see me this afternoon.'

'I'll drive you?' Brooke offered.

Lavinia showered and dressed and, still without nourishment, the two women set off for Norwich.

The GUM clinic turned out to be a drab dungeon of a place situated next to the boiler room of the city hospital. The receptionist, who looked terribly young, asked her name and address. When she hesitated, she told Lavinia that she could use a number instead and she passed a blue card over the counter with 114456 written on it. She and Brooke were then directed through into a dull, square, waiting room, the walls of which were covered with posters, advising the reader not to share needles and always to use a condom, recommending a stronger condom for anal sex with plenty of water-based lubricant to help prevent it splitting. Brooke whispered to Lavinia that she wondered if the splitting referred to the anus or the condom.

Lavinia felt numb. Whatever was she, Lady Lavinia Elliot, doing here in this sordid little room? She got up to leave. Brooke grabbed her arm. 'Where are you going?' She hissed

'I'm leaving. I'll go private. I shouldn't be here.'

Brooke cast her eyes around the room, she sighed. 'I know a good gynaecologist in Harley Street.'

Lavinia flopped back down on her chair. 'And he'll probably know me, or Josh,' she said.

A girl entered the room, she was wearing a very short leather skirt, her peroxided hair showed very dark roots and she was chewing gum. She was not much older than Zoë. No sooner had the girl sat down than a woman in a white coat entered. 'Tracy? Doctor will see you now.'

Tracy got up and followed the woman. She walked with an exaggerated swagger, she turned as she reached the door, and blew a big pink bubble in Brooke's direction.

The white-coated woman returned almost immediately. She looked expectantly at Brooke. 'Number 114456? Our counsellor can see you now.'

Lavinia was led through a large room with curtained cubicles, and then into a very small room no bigger than a walk-in cupboard. Here she was introduced to a middle-aged woman who told Lavinia that her name was Jane.

Jane did not ask why Lavinia was there, but launched into a list of the services they were able to offer. She reminded Lavinia that she, or her partner, could have the virus and look perfectly healthy. That many people did not know that they were HIV positive, and that the only way to be sure was to have a test. She then went on the tell Lavinia that if she had the test and was found positive it might bar her from getting life insurance and that she might not be able to get a visa for certain countries. By the time she had finished the tears that had lurked on the outer edges of Lavinia eyes were in full flow, and she poured out the fact that her husband was away from home and she had been foolishly indiscreet.

A blood test would be taken and Lavinia could telephone the next day quoting her allocated number to know the result. She might then be invited back to the clinic to consult with another counsellor. She was also warned that a single negative test would not be enough to rely on, it could take up to three months, and occasionally longer, for the HIV antibodies to show up in the blood. So even if the test was negative, she was advised to go back and have a repeat test in three months time. The counsellor also offered to test her for other, sexually transmitted diseases.

'I might as well have the works.' Lavinia said, her voice was remote and dull.

It was gone four o'clock when Brooke and Lavinia emerged into the daylight. Brooke suggested tea in the hospital canteen, but Lavinia wanted to get as far away from the place as possible. They agreed to go to Jarrold's department store for refreshment.

Back at the clinic, Jane brought Lavinia's bloods and swabs through to the reception area. 'Pop these down to the lab on your way to tea, will you, Janet?'

The young receptionist took the polythene bag containing the samples from the older woman; she twirled it round in her fingers.

'Be careful with that,' Jane said. 'It's probably infectious.'

Janet read the number aloud. 'Huh! 114456, my foot. You know who that was, don't you? That was Lady Elliot, from Hulver. My Dad used to work for Lord Hulver, a right stuck up toff he is as well. Sacked my dad for taking a gallon or two of petrol, he did.' She smiled. 'Everything comes to them that waits,' she said. She went off in the direction of the path lab, deliberately swinging the samples in order to alarm Jane. 'Wait 'till my dad hears about this,' she said under her breath, as soon as she was sure Jane was out of earshot.

CHAPTER FORTY-ONE

Lavinia had slept badly, what snatches of slumber she had enjoyed brought dreams of desolation with them. Josh had arrived home and evaded all her questions concerning his visit to Lloyds; she hadn't wanted to face him anyway and had said she was tired and had gone to bed before him, where she feigned sleep in order to avoid any intimacy. But Josh had other ideas.

'Are you awake?'

She lay quite still and breathed loudly.

He shook her none too gently. 'I say, darling. Are you awake?'

Still she did not respond.

He placed his leg over the top of hers; it was hot and heavy. He snuggled up close to her. 'Vinnie? Are you awake?'

He heaved himself on top of her, she could feel his erection sandwiched between their abdomens. She wondered how Brooke coped with Henry at the weekends.

Josh was rocking back and forth on top of her.

'Vinnie, darling. Wake up,' he said.

Lavinia tried to roll over and dislodge her husband. 'Josh, I'm tired,' she murmured.

'I won't be long.' He sounded like a little boy pleading with his nurse. 'I promise I won't be long.'

'Josh, for God's sake, I'm tired,' she snapped. She couldn't let Josh make love to her, he might catch Aids from her.

'But I want you, Vinnie. Feel me, feel how hard I am for you.'

'For Christ sake, Josh, let me get some sleep.' She wriggled out from under him and turned her back to him.

'Sorry, Vinnie,' he said. 'I just missed you last night, that's all.'

'Why do you call me that stupid name?' She spat.

'What? Vinnie? I always have,' he said, he sounded bewildered. 'I'm sorry. Have I done something wrong?'

Tears filled her eyes. 'No. No, Josh. I'm sorry – it's me. I'm tired. I don't sleep when you're not here.' You certainly didn't last night a little voice in the back of her head said. She turned back toward him. 'I'm sorry, Josh. It's me, not you.'

'I'm glad you don't sleep without me, Vinnie. I

want you to need me always.'

He snuggled up to her and soon she realized that he had fallen asleep, and for a second guilty night Lavinia Elliot gave most of the hours of darkness over to thoughts of Alexander Kirby.

Josh woke her at eight with a cup of tea. 'Feeling better, darling?'

She smiled at him, avoiding his eyes, certain that he could read the guilt that was written on her face. 'I'm fine – I was tired, that's all. I need a few days off. We've no B & B's until Saturday and Mrs Jarvis will be in to cook, so I should be able to catch up on some sleep.'

Josh shook his head. 'Oh dear, then I think perhaps I've boobed. A fellow rang up and asked for a room for tonight, and I agreed.'

Lavinia became immediately irritated. 'Then you can damn well ring and put him off. I need a few days rest, Josh. I need to gather my thoughts and recuperate.' She didn't add that she needed to face her own mortality. 'Don't you understand? Surely I deserve a few days off? You must ring him back and say you've made a mistake.'

Josh looked down at his boots. 'Can't do that, old thing.'

'And why not?'

'Forgot to take his number.'

Lavinia plopped back on the pillow and groaned.

'Don't worry, old thing, I'll cook dinner.'

'Oh, no, Josh. You didn't promise him dinner? And please, please, please, stop old thinging me.'

He nodded. 'Not a problem, Vinnie. I'll pop to M & S and get something tasty.'

'You can't do that.'

'Why not? Damned good stuff from there, Mrs Marks is a bloody good cook and Mrs Spencer makes some delicious puddings.' He laughed, but Lavinia refused to join in.

'Shit,' Lavinia said.

'Well, I'll clear up afterwards and you can get to bed early.' He smiled rather sheepishly. 'And I promise I won't wake you up when I come to bed.'

She leaned over and buried her head in his shoulder; she didn't want him to see the guilt that was clouding her eyes.

Lavinia had been told to ring the clinic at any time after twelve. She rang at five past, only to be told by Jane, that the results weren't back from the lab, and could she ring again in half-an-hour. It was a long half-hour; thirty minutes in which Lavinia convinced herself of the worse possible result; why else was it taking so long?

She could hardly speak when she was told that her tests were all clear. The relief flooded her body like ink on blotting paper. 'Thank you,' she said. 'Oh, thank you.'

Jane warned her that she could still develop the antibodies and advised her to come back in three months time. Lavinia promised she would, but how on earth was she going to avoid making love with Josh in the mean time? She rang Brooke and told her the news. Brooke advised her to go out and buy some condoms for Josh. 'Tell Josh you've developed a rash, an allergy or something, and you've been advised to use them until it clears up.'

'But he'll guess.'

'Why would he? He trusts you doesn't he?'

'Yes,' agreed Lavinia miserably. 'That's the trouble.'

'Lavinia? Tell me? Have you ever slept with anyone besides Josh?'

'No, have you?'

Brooke made a joke of it. 'Well actually, I've never slept with Josh at all.'

'I mean Henry – I mean up until you . . . well, started to . . . well, you know, before you . . . er . . . I mean.'

'Oh, Vinnie, you do have a problem with calling a spade, a spade, don't you? What you mean is, before I did it for money, did I do it for pleasure? Sure I did, but not after I married Henry. We promised each other . . . well, with children, things are a little different, aren't they?'

'You mean Henry knew and didn't mind.'

'You really don't know Henry do you?'

'I've known Henry for over twenty years,' she said indignantly.

'And he never made a pass at you? Shame on him.'

'Of course, he didn't.'

'Oh no, of course. Over here Henry is the perfect gentleman, the perfect English Lord. But I met Henry in America, he was wild then – we did a lot of stuff together, Henry and I.'

'Henry?'

'You really don't get it do you? In a nutshell I had a lot of sex and Henry enjoyed what I did. I used to tell him about it. It turned him on, it still does.'

'You mean you'll tell him, about the ... about, well ... about the other men? And all that?'

'No. Well, I might do, but I shall tell him it's just a story, or maybe I'll tell him that it happened a long time ago in New York. It will excite him no end.'

'Oh.' Lavinia put her hand up to her mouth. Why couldn't she be as casual about sex as Brooke.

'How will you explain?' Lavinia dropped her voice. 'About taking money for it?'

Brooke laughed. 'Have you heard the joke about the two women who lived in an identical pair of semi-detached houses? Well, both had husbands working at the same factory and both had children of the same ages, and yet one couple had a much higher standard of living than

341

the other couple. On investigation, it turned out that the well off wife went up to London each Saturday to ply her trade. After some consideration, the less well off wife decided to do the same. Anyway, she returned on the following Sunday morning with Three hundred pounds and fifty-pence in her pocket. She was jubilant. 'Which mean bugger gave you the fifty pence?' her husband asked.

'All of them,' the wife replied.' Brooke paused, waiting for Lavinia to laugh.

But for Lavinia, it was a bit too close to her recent unprofitable sexual exploit, and she was unable to raise even a smile. 'That doesn't sound quite nice,' she said.

'Mercy on us! Is this the same woman that visits Aids clinics?'

Lavinia pursed her lips. 'I must go. Josh has booked in a B and B. I must get myself organized.'

At four Josh went off with Fen for her evening walk. Before he left, Lavinia put her arms around him and pushed her head into his neck. If she herself were infected that was one thing, but she couldn't let it spread to Josh. She couldn't bear to look at him whilst she lied. 'Josh? Will you walk as far as the village, and buy some Durex at the chemist?'

Josh pushed her away from him. 'What on earth for? I say, not Zoë?'

Lavinia was red and flustered, 'No, no. Us.' She

pushed her head back into his neck. 'Don't you remember when we were courting? It would be fun to pretend it was like that again.'

'I hate the bloody things,' he said.

'It would turn me on,' she said.

'Come on, Vinnie, since when did you need anything to turn you on? You've always been hot ever since I met you. Christ you were always so hungry for it you'd hardly give me time to open the packet. Don't you remember? By God, you were a hot one.' He laughed. 'You still are, unless, of course, you're tired.'

She felt desperate. 'Please, Josh. Humour me, please?'

He shook his head and laughed, he pushed her up against the kitchen wall. 'You sound pretty hot now,' he said.

Fen barked and jumped up and down at her master's sudden movements.

'All right, Fen,' he said. 'I'll take you for a walk.' He turned to Lavinia. 'I'll see to you when I get back.'

'The Durex, Josh?'

He shook his head again and laughed. 'Oh, yes, I can just imagine it. Lord Hulver buying Italian Postcards! It would be all around the village that I had a mistress.' Still laughing, he took Fen out into the home meadow.

Seconds later the doorbell rang.

'Oh shit,' she said. She made her way down the library corridor and across the marble hall to the front door.

Alexander Kirby was leaning on the carved door jam. At that moment Lavinia knew what the saying to have *one's breath taken away,* meant. She literally couldn't breathe, let alone speak. He was undeniably handsome, and she wondered if she had mentioned that point to Brooke.

'Vinnie,' he whispered. He ran his tongue around his lips, a sensual action full of meaning.

She stepped to one side to let him pass. Her breath was still short, and what little she could muster was meanly given.

'Alex, my, um.' She swallowed. 'My husband has just taken the dog for a walk.' She snatched a gulp of air. 'Same room?' He said.

'Didn't realize it was you,' she said, her words running together and making little sense.

He followed her up the stairs to the same guestroom.

'This is stupid,' the words whirled around in her brain. 'This is stupid, Josh will be home in a minute.' 'Not for at least half-an-hour, possibly an hour,' the little voice said. 'After all that business with the Aids Clinic,' her common sense said. But then the destructive little voice cut in and overruled her common sense. 'This is the one man you can make love to. If you've got Aids, so has he,' it said.

She walked into the room ahead of him.

He threw his bag on the bed.

She went over to the door and closed it. She turned the key in the lock and stood with her back leaning against it.

Their eyes were fused together.

He unzipped his fly.

She pulled up her skirt and stepped out of her panties.

And then he was in her, right there, standing up against the door, her legs curled around his back. He was grunting with the weight of her and she was crying out with the thrill of him.

'This is wicked,' her mind said. 'This is wonderful,' the little voice said. 'Take it, whilst you can, it won't always be on offer.' 'But this is wrong.' 'So repent tomorrow.' She felt sick with anxiety and yet her need of him shut everything else out.

'I can't get enough of you.' Alex said. They were calm again.

'It's wrong, Alex,' she said.

He put a hand up to her cheek. 'It's right, Vinnie. Don't you see, you know it's right, you knew it long before I did. Why else did you come to me the other night.'

'You wouldn't believe me if I told you,' she said.

But his reply was lost in his kisses, for he already wanted her again.

Lavinia said very little at dinner that night. They ate in the small dining room and because they had only the one guest, both Lavinia and Josh ate with him. Josh didn't seem to notice Lavinia's discomfort, or her silence. He commented once or twice that she wasn't eating very much, but apart from that, he made no other observation. He was highly entertained by the barrister in their midst. Lavinia felt apart, an alien in her own home. The two men were so friendly toward each other and it confused her. They had a mutual interest that bound them together, and yet that was the very thing that should render them apart and make the pair of them enemies. She was afraid to meet either of their eyes, afraid that her face would betray her.

At ten, Josh insisted that Lavinia went up to bed explaining to Alex that he had been away on Wednesday night and Lavinia had had very little sleep. This time she did look for Alex's reaction and was greeted with a tender yet passionate glance. She bade them goodnight and went to her bathroom to bathe.

She had been in bed for over an hour when Josh joined her.

'Are you awake?'

Of course she was awake. Didn't he know that her

heart was thumping, and her loins were aching, didn't he know that her lover was in the house, wanting her just as much as she wanted him? Alex filled her consciousness, and restricted her breathing. He had become the very atmosphere that settled around her. How could Josh not know this? Was it not obvious?

She gave him a sleepy grunt. 'Yes, I'm still awake, just.'

'Sorry I've been so long, Alex helped me wash up and then we had a nightcap. Damned fine chap that, pleasure to have him in the house.'

'Yes,' agreed Lavinia, her voiced sounded so weak it was almost inaudible.

Josh pushed his hand under her nightgown. 'Seeing as you're awake?'

'Josh, it's late.'

He nuzzled into her neck. 'Just a quickie?'

'Josh, I can't.'

'Oh, wrong time of the month is it? Never bothered you before?'

She grasped the excuse. 'I know darling, but I'm heavy this time.'

'Oh, oh I see. Then how about?' he moved up the bed a little and put her hand on his penis.

'Josh? Go to sleep.'

Josh turned over and pulled the covers up over his

shoulders. Fifteen minutes later he was softly snoring.

Lavinia couldn't sleep. She tossed and turned. She snuggled up against Josh's back and kissed him. 'I'm sorry, Josh,' she whispered. 'I'm so, so sorry.'

She heard the clock downstairs strike twelve, then one. Eventually she slipped out of bed and made her way along to the one occupied guest room.

'I thought you were never coming,' Alex said.
'But you knew that I would, didn't you?' She replied with a tremor in her voice as she slipped into bed beside him.

CHAPTER FORTY-TWO

'Where were you last night?'

'What?'

Lavinia was dressing in the dressing room. She had returned to Josh in the early hours of the morning. He'd been fast asleep, and she had been sure that he was unaware of her brief absence. She turned her face away from him. It was easier to lie when he couldn't see her eyes.

'Last night, where were you? I woke up and you weren't here – you weren't in the bathroom either.'

'Oh, then?' She looked down at the floor. 'I woke and I couldn't get back to sleep, so I went downstairs and I read for a little while.' A sick feeling swept through her stomach; an disquiet that she was beginning to recognize as a 'lying-to-Josh' syndrome.

Josh came over to her; he put his arm around her and kissed her cheek. 'You should have woken me up,' he chuckled. 'I could have given you a little of my sleeping stick, you know it always gives you a good night.'

'Don't be crude, Josh.' She was tight lipped. She didn't seem to be able to define her emotions; she felt guilt, and irritation, and love, for him all at the same time, but in varying quantities.

'Are you still cross at me for taking the B and B? He's a jolly nice chap, isn't he? He wasn't any trouble, and we do need the money.'

'*We* need the money, Josh? No, Josh, you need the money, and you don't care how hard I have to work to get it.'

'We, Vinnie. It's our home we're talking about, the children's home, their inheritance.'

'Why do you call me that?'

'What?'

'Vinnie, it's such a silly name. Lavinia is much nicer.'

Josh stood quite still, his head on one side as if he were studying her. She felt uncomfortable with his eyes on her. She felt that he must be able to read her, as if her unfaithfulness was written into every angle of her body.

'What's wrong, darling? What's troubling you?'

She felt that she might cry. The words she uttered in reply were meant to reassure him, and yet they snapped out of her like a firecracker. 'Nothing's wrong. I'd be all right if you just left me alone.'

He didn't say anymore, but the look on his face

told her that the words had hurt him as much as any physical blow.

'Josh, Josh darling, I'm sorry. I'm tired that's all, just tired. I need a few days off. Do you know that from this Friday, the season will be well and truly underway? We're fully booked for weeks to come. I just find it hard to face. The children on holiday from school, very little help in the house, and thousands of B and Bs.' She gave him a weak smile. 'It's all rather hard to cope with.'

Josh visibly relaxed; he rubbed his hands together. 'Never mind, my darling. Think of the money, it couldn't come at a better time with the Lloyds payment due.'

Lavinia tightened her lips. 'You don't have to do the work,' she said softly, and another tiny seed of resentment was sown somewhere deep inside her.

Toward the end of breakfast, Josh left to take Fen for a walk, leaving Lavinia and Alex alone.

'He's a good sort, your husband,' Alex said.

'I don't wish to discuss my husband, certainly not with you, and certainly not behind his back.'

Alex nodded his head. 'I see.' He nodded again. 'Making love behind his back is all right, is it?'

'No, it's not all right. That's why you must never come here again.'

He smiled as if he understood. 'I see.' He paused and frowned. 'Well, to tell you the truth, I don't see, and I would very much welcome an explanation.' He sounded sad. 'You see, Vinnie. I can't just leave it at that. I can't just walk away and leave you.' He grabbed her hand; she snatched it back from him. 'I've fallen for you, Vinnie. We've stumbled on something too precious to throw away. We were made for each other – I know it, and you know it.'

'Don't be ridiculous. You know nothing about me – you have no idea. And I don't know you.'

'Then give it a chance, try getting to know me. And you're wrong – I do know you. I know you're the sweetest, loveliest woman that ever walked the earth.'

She laughed, but the laugh was not quite sincere.

'You know nothing, Alex, nothing at all.'

'Then give me a chance,' he spoke in earnest.

The telephone rang, it was another booking for the coming weekend, but all Lavinia's guest rooms were already fully booked. She was about to turn it down when the Lloyds debt popped back into her brain. She could move Tiggy's things into Zoë's room and rent out Tiggy's room. It was a mammoth task, but she could do it. She took the booking.

'I have to get on,' she said. 'I've a busy weekend ahead.'

He was gazing at her, his coffee cup poised halfway to his lips. 'Why do you do it? The hotel lark?' He maneuvered his coffee cup in a circular motion indicating the room. 'You have so much here, what use do you have for more?'

She told him then. 'Ever heard of Lloyds?' she said. She poured out the whole sad tale. How much the estate meant to Jocelyn, and how he was determined not to part with one square inch of it. How Josh insisted that his boys went to Edgeford, and how hard she was working to help maintain the way of life they had come to expect.

Alexander Kirby laughed.

'What's funny?'

'You are. For God's sake. Sell a cottage or two, you won't miss them. Or sell off a few acres of land. You must have a neighbor just dying to get his hands on a bordering field.'

'Josh won't hear of it. He says that once you start nibbling away at the Estate, in no time it'll be gone, and then there won't be enough land to support the house.'

'So he'd rather have his wife working night and day instead?'

'That's not fair, it's my choice,' she snapped.

'What's you choice?' Josh said. He'd returned without either of them noticing.

'The wall paper,' Lavinia quickly replied holding Alexander's eyes with her own.

Josh put his arm around her. 'It certainly is.

Wonderful taste my wife has, haven't you, my darling?'

'I couldn't agree with you more,' Alex said, his eyes still firmly fixed on hers.

CHAPTER FORTY-THREE

Alex paid his bill and left. But not before Lavinia told him very firmly that he must never come to Hulver again. If he really were fond of her, then he would be kind and leave her alone.

By ten o'clock, she had cleared Tiggy's room and made it ready for her weekend guests. Josh spent the morning in his study. He had an appointment in the afternoon with a prospective shoot tenant and he was busy preparing maps and making lists.

At eleven the telephone rang. It was Alex; he wanted her to meet him for lunch.

'I can't, Alex – this is leading nowhere. It's best to leave things as they are. It was fun, but it can't go on, someone will get hurt.'

'Then I shall come to you,' he said.

'I won't take your booking.'

'I shall come anyway. Josh will give me a room, he

won't turn good money away.' His voice held a note of sarcasm.

'That's not fair.'

'I want to see you, Vinnie. And if I have to be unfair in order to do it, then so be it.'

'Alex I——'

'The Cat and Fiddle? It's near the central car park in Norwich.'

'I know where it is.'

'Then you'll be there?'

'Alex, I can't.'

'You'll be there,' he said with authority.

'I can't,' she said again, but he had already hung up.

'Who was on the phone?' Josh said a few moments later when he came into the kitchen.

'Oh . . . er . . .' her brain sought for an answer, but why didn't she just tell him the truth? 'It was Brooke, she wants me to meet her in Norwich for lunch.'

'Her treat?'

'I expect so, she's always very generous.'

'Hmm, I don't know how she and Henry do it. They seem to glide over the top of this Lloyds business.'

'Yes. Yes, they do.' Lavinia said absently.

'So are you going?'

'Going?'

'To lunch with Brooke.'

'Of course, I never pass up the opportunity of a free lunch.'

'There's no such thing as a free lunch,' Josh said, and laughed. He kissed her on the forehead. 'Have a nice time, darling. I'm glad you're feeling better.'

But she wasn't feeling better; in fact she was feeling quite ill. An illness that had drained her of all her will power, and had taken away any control she had ever had over her life. Yet had both infused her with energy and at the same time, rendered her listless and unfulfilled.

Perhaps she really was ill? She took her temperature, it was quite normal, but she didn't feel well. She swallowed, she had no sign of a sore throat, and yet her breath was short, her appetite had disappeared and her thoughts were no longer her own. Whatever was the matter with her? She could not put her thoughts in order. Alex Kirby was dominating her life. And then it hit her like a bolt of lightening. She was in love. The feeling was exhilarating and suffocating, it was painful and destructive, it was unpleasant and humiliating, and she wanted to be rid of it. But the choice wasn't hers. She was in love, and no matter how uncomfortable the condition, she could not disregard it. It was in charge of her, not she of it. Lavinia stared at her reflection in the mirror with a kind of wonder; she had so often craved to be in love. So often had she desired to experience that emotion and now it was hers, and she was afraid that the power of it might destroy her.

She reached the Cat and Fiddle long before Alex.

He came bustling in, carrying a brief case and a large bundle of papers.

'I thought that you had taken me at my word, and weren't coming,' she said.

'I knew you'd come,' he replied.

Yes, she thought. Because I am in love with you, you have complete control over my actions.

The Cat and Fiddle was an up-market wine bar. It sported scrubbed pine tables and a middle class clientele. Alex ordered a carafe of dry white wine and a seafood platter to share between them. They talked of nothing; the weather, the traffic, the quality of the wine, each, it seemed, reluctant to broach the subject of the situation in which their hearts had placed them.

But eventually Alex said. 'So, Vinnie, you sleep around a lot, do you? I'm just one of many, am I?'

'No. No, I don't. No. No, you're not,' she was indignant.

'But you came to my bed, not once, but twice.'

'The first time . . . ' and then she told him. Told him about Brooke and her room service, and how she had thought he'd expected it of her. She explained all about their financial problems and the boy's school fees.

'So I owe you some money?' he said mildly, and smiled at her. 'My clerk asked for room service. He knew I had a lot of work to do and he thought I'd like food served in my room. Lucky day for me that he did, wasn't it?'

They had drunk a whole carafe of wine and had started a second. The more she drank the more she talked. She told him about the GUM clinic and how afraid she'd been that she had contracted Aids.

'Why didn't you ask me?' He said. 'I left you my 'phone number.'

'And what would you have said?' She looked at him coolly.

'I'd have told you that the last woman I slept with, was my wife.'

'Oh.' Lavinia swallowed, for now a new emotion swept through her, a powerful invasive force named jealousy.

'And I'd have also told you, that was well over three years ago.'

'Oh,' she said again. But the bitter army of jealous soldiers wouldn't retreat.

'I'd have also offered to come with you to the clinic, and had a test myself. Dear lady, you would not have contracted anything from me. It seems, however, that I might possibly have caught something from you?'

'No. Oh no,' she said, putting her head in her hands.

'And if you'd have told me that your husband was willing for you to prostitute yourself in order to save his precious estate, I'd have smashed his face in – as my client so eloquently said to the Judge this morning.'

'That's so unfair. Josh didn't know. Doesn't know.' She shook her head and gave him a hard look. 'Must never, ever, know.'

She shook her head again as if trying to mark an end to the subject. 'How long have you been divorced?' It was a fact that was suddenly very important to her.

'I'm not, we don't love together, and we don't live together.'

'I see.'

'Do you?'

'No, I don't.' And she laughed at his perception.

'We were at law school together, we married a week after our finals, neither of us realized that we were both headed in different directions. Professionally she went her way, corporate law and all that. She's quite a high flyer is Sarah. And I went my way, legal aid cases, working for the underdog and the like. Eventually the same happened to our marriage, neither of us stood still, we both went in different directions.'

He laughed.

'What's funny?'

'The fact that you can sum a marriage up in the space of a few sentences.'

'Why are you still married?'

He took her hand. 'Because, up until now, I hadn't found any reason not to be. But what's more to the point. Why are you still with Josh?'

'Because I love him,' she said simply, without having to give his question any thought.

He threw his head back and laughed. 'Huh! You're his property, Vinnie. He'd rather see you worn out and wasted, than part with a centimeter of his precious land.'

'That's unfair,' she said. But the little seed of resentment that had been planted earlier in the day germinated and took root.

'Let's go to a hotel,' he said. He signalled for the bill.

'Alex, I can't, I've got guests arriving tonight. I have to go home. They might arrive early, before I get back.'

'Then Josh will cope. I'll make sure you're home by six.'

She felt suddenly lightheaded. Yes, Josh could cope, and why shouldn't he? Didn't she deserve a little freedom, a little fun?

They took a room at the Maid's Head. The excess

of wine made it all so easy.

Afterwards, as they lay together, they talked.

'Will you come and see me in London?' He said. 'I have a very nice house, comfortable and convenient for chambers. You could come and stay overnight with me.'

The effect of the wine was wearing off, leaving a dull thick headache in its wake. What on earth was she doing? 'I can't. There's Josh . . . well, it wouldn't be right. I can't, Alex.' She tried to pull away from him. 'I shouldn't be here now, it's not right.'

He held onto her. 'Why are you doubting this? You know this is good, Vinnie. You know what this is. It's right for both of us.'

'I'm married, for God's sake! You know this isn't really right. You're a barrister, you should know that this is . . . well it's —'

'What? What is it, Vinnie?'

'It's sordid,' she stopped pulling away from him, he had his arm firmly around her; she gave in and snuggled into his shoulder. 'Being unfaithful to Josh, he's – he's a wonderful man. I love him. You met him, Alex – he doesn't deserve this.'

'But you came to me, Vinnie. *You* came to *me*.'

'I know, but it wasn't for . . . Well, it was because . . . I mean the money thing. I know I was wrong, but Brooke sort of persuaded me that I could do it, and . . . and

. . . '

Alex nodded his head. 'I see, my dear. It's all right to do it for money, that's not harming Josh. But to do it for love, or lust if you prefer, isn't on?'

'No.' She shrugged. 'Well, yes. I suppose so.'

'Poor Josh, whichever way you look at it, he loses doesn't he?' Alex said.

'I don't understand.' She felt close to tears. What was happening to her, she was like a child. This man could lead her wherever he wanted, and she was bound to follow.

'If you do it for money, you'll lose all your respect for him, and if you do it for lust, he'll lose your love.'

'I don't follow,' she said.

But Alex didn't seem to hear her. 'He's lost you already, though, hasn't he? He lost you the moment you decided to come to my bedroom door.'

'I love Josh,' she said very firmly.

'You think you do, Vinnie, but you don't.'

CHAPTER FORTY-FOUR

She was still feeling lightheaded when she reached the castle. Josh was waiting for her. 'Where the hell have you been?' He grumbled.

A leaf of resentment appeared on the seedling. She pushed her fingers through her hair, and made her way toward the kitchen.

'The guests were here an hour ago, I had to greet them!' He sounded outraged. 'I was worried sick about you.'

'I had things to talk to Brooke about.'

'I know,' he said, his voiced raised. 'I phoned her.'

Lavinia stopped dead in her tracks. 'You did?'

'Yes. She said to tell you that she's found the recipe you wanted, and she'd like you to phone her as soon as you get in, only don't – the guests will be down wanting drinks in a minute.'

'I'll ring her later.'

Lavinia offered up a silent prayer. Thank you, Brooke. You must have twigged awfully quickly.

Lavinia cooked dinner. As was her custom, she did not join the guests at their meal but left Josh to do the entertaining. It was easier for her to cook and serve and wash the dishes without the distraction of conversation. Josh seemed perfectly relaxed and at ease in the dining room, and although it had been Lavinia's choice that he should play the host, and she her chosen role, nevertheless she felt bitter and resentful. The words that Alex had said over lunch came back to haunt her. She was nothing more than a servant to him.

After the guests had been served with cheese, Josh came into the kitchen.

'Can I help?' He said. 'I'll do coffee if you like?'

'I can manage.' Her tone was less than charitable.

Josh nodded as if he understood. 'Well, leave the clearing up, old thing, I'll do it later. You look tired, why don't you go up to bed?'

'Why do you say I'm tired?' She snapped.

'Well, you did say that you didn't sleep last —'

She wasn't listening to him but had launched into a tirade. 'I mean, why should I be tired, for God's sake? I've only cooked a five course dinner and waited on nine people hand and foot, whilst all you've done is pour Beaujolais down your bloody throat.'

'Claret, actually,' Josh said weakly.

'Whatever,' she snapped.

'Darling, what's wrong?'

She caught the troubled expression on his face and was filled with remorse. Tears pricked at the corners of her eyes. 'Oh, Josh. I'm sorry. I didn't mean anything. You're right, I'm tired, very tired. I didn't have a good night.' Then she thought of Alex Kirby, and she bit into her bottom lip. A strange logic told her that Josh ought not to be made to clear the dinner things when the reason for her exhaustion was the illicit bedding of her lover.

'Here,' she said, handing him the coffee tray. 'Take this through to the drawing room, will you? I'll just clear the kitchen. Then, yes, I'll go up, if you don't mind. Why don't you give the guests a brandy on the house?'

He kissed her forehead as he took the tray from her. 'I'll see you later, my darling. Leave the dining room, I'll clear it after they've gone to bed.'

She nodded and smiled. She cleaned the kitchen and then went through and cleared the dining room. Her conscience would not allow her to leave it to Josh.

It was just gone ten when she reached her bedroom. She suddenly remembered that she hadn't returned Brooke's call. She dialed the Pennington number. Brooke's very proper butler answered. Madam had already gone to bed, he said, but she had left a message should Lady Hulver telephone. The message was simply that Lady Pennington had several important diplomats staying at the

Manor, and therefore, Lady Pennington was having an early night. Lady Pennington would return Lady Hulver's call the following day.

No sooner had Lavinia replaced the receiver than the telephone rang. It was Alex. 'I just rang to say good-night,' he said.

Lavinia was alarmed.

'What if Josh had answered?'

He laughed. 'Then I'd have asked to speak to you, and I'd have booked a room.'

'You can't come here again, Alex.'

'Then you must come here.'

'I can't, Alex, this thing must go no further.'

'I can't let you go, Vinnie.'

'I'm not yours – it's not a question of keeping me or letting me go. We had sex, that's all. Just sex. It was wrong of us – we're both married. I can't risk hurting Josh. It was a fling —' The words were tumbling out; said quickly enough, she might just be convinced by them.

'No. No, Vinnie, you're wrong, and what's more, you know you're wrong. I love you Vinnie.' He said the last sentence very softly so that she was hardly sure that she'd heard him.

'It's flying in the face of God,' she whispered.

'God?' He said. 'Vinnie, what we've found is blessed – it's the stuff of sunsets and magic shows.'

'It's lust, and it's destructive and it's extremely selfish,' she replied. 'I'm going to put the phone down now, and you must never contact me again.'

'You know I can't do that.'

Lavinia gently replaced the receiver. She went into the bathroom and she showered, she sprayed herself with her favorite perfume, she wriggled into a back silk nightdress. It was time to make amends for her actions; it was time to rebuild her intimacy with Josh. She believed all Alex had told her, and she was confident that she was not harboring some dreadful disease as the result of her liaison with him. She lit several candles in the bedroom, and she opened a bottle of sensual massage oil and placed it on her bedside table. She dabbed some of the oil on her fingers and began to massage it into her thighs, her belly, her breasts. The hall clock struck eleven. She pushed her fingers between her legs, but instead of enjoying thoughts of Josh, she began to enjoy thoughts of Alex Kirby. Her fingers reenacted his touch, her body ached for him and she yielded to the memory of his lovemaking. She was hot and panting. She ripped off the black nightgown and lay glowing and hungry for him. She turned on her stomach and pushed herself into the mattress. Then onto her side pushing a pillow between her legs, grabbing it between her thighs. Where was Josh? He was passing up on an opportunity; what did it matter that Alex was in her thoughts, as long as Josh was in her bed? The clock stuck twelve. Lavinia raised her hips up and down. Where was the man?

At one, Lavinia wriggled back into the nightgown and was about to get out of bed and go in search of Josh, when he appeared. She thumped back onto her pillow and drew her knees up.

'Where have you been? I've been waiting for you,' she accused

Josh staggered a little. He didn't go into the dressing room but peeled his clothes off in the bedroom, supporting himself by the corner of the four-poster bed as he did so.

'Been talking to those American fellows – hit the port a bit heavy, I'm afraid.'

He sighed and flopped into bed naked beside her.

'God, I'm tired! Bloody hard work this B and B lark, what?'

'Yes. Bloody hard work,' Lavinia agreed sarcastically.

'All right for you,' he said. 'You don't have to sit and entertain them like I do – you just scrape a meal together and leave the hard work to me.' He laughed, and Lavinia didn't know if he was joking or not. She chose to believe that he wasn't; it almost justified her infidelity with Alex.

'Josh, you haven't cleaned your teeth.'

A loud snore was his only reply.

CHAPTER FORTY-FIVE

Lavinia rang her friend at nine the next morning. The butler answered and told her that Lady Osbourne-Pennington was busy with the police. He would, however, tell her that Lady Hulver had telephoned and no doubt her ladyship would call her back.

Lavinia was alarmed. 'What's wrong?' She demanded, but the butler was giving nothing away.

It was over two hours later that Brooke returned her call. She was distraught. 'Oh, Vinnie, we've been burgled.'

It appeared that the well-known diplomat wasn't well known at all, not when the police looked into it. No one had ever heard of him. He'd told Brooke that he was the governor of some remote Caribbean island and she'd had no reason to disbelieve him. Several paintings had been taken, along with much of the family silver, and other antique trinkets.

'The police say that he must have had at least one accomplice waiting outside, until the house was asleep, and then he must have let them in,' Brooke wailed. 'I could hardly tell the police that I was fucking the boss, whilst the assistant stole the goodies, could I?' But Brooke's main gripe seemed to be that the men had left without paying for their accommodation, nor the exorbitant fee the so-called diplomat had offered for the privilege of bedding her.

'I woke up in the guest room and he'd gone. The nerve of the man! He must have had a real laugh at my expense.'

Lavinia listened patiently, offering suitable words of comfort.

'The police even wanted to know how much insurance cover we have. I almost think that they think we've arranged to have the goods stolen ourselves.'

'Stranger things have happened,' Lavinia said, remembering her own failed attempt at insurance fraud. 'What does Henry have to say?'

'I haven't told him yet – I can't get hold of him. He's out of the office, and won't be back until later. He's coming home tonight anyway, so he can deal with Mr Plod, and his accusations, when he gets home.'

'They didn't actually accuse you?'

'Not in so many words, but it was obvious what they were thinking.'

'But you didn't, I mean, you haven't?'

'No, Vinnie, I haven't. And if I had, I'd make a much better job of it than they did. I wouldn't steal an easily recognizable family portrait for a start.'

'Of course,' agreed Lavinia, but she wasn't entirely convinced. She had discovered that Brooke had a very determined streak. Brooke believed that most ends justified most means. Indeed, she often said that if you wanted something to happen, then it was up to you to make it happen.

'Anyway, where were you yesterday? At the clinic I suppose?'

'Right,' said Lavinia.

'I don't mind covering for you, but you might let me know beforehand. Josh was really, really cross, you know?'

'I know, but I think I deserve a little time off occasionally, don't you?'

'Careful, Vinnie, you're beginning to sound quite radical.'

Lavinia was quiet for some moments.

'Lavinia? Are you still there?'

'Yes. Yes, I'm here. But, Brooke, what are we doing? Has it ever occurred to you? Is it really worth it?'

'Of course it's worth it. How can you question it? What we're doing will save our husband's estates, and that in turn will save our marriages. What would happen to

372

Josh and Henry if they were the ones responsible for losing six hundred years of land ownership? Ask yourself about their mental stability. You can't seriously imagine them as sad little men living in a converted farmhouse on the edges of the land they once owned, can you? It would kill them both – psychologically, that is. And what about the boys? They've been brought up to expect that one day they'll inherit, what would happen to the relationship between them and their fathers' if they suddenly lost it all?'

'You sound like I used to, Brooke.' There was a hint of sadness in her voice.

'We'll see it through, Vinnie. It will all seem like a bad dream in a year or two.'

'But you're prostituting yourself, Brooke.'

'So are you.'

'I didn't get paid. Besides, I'll never do it again.'

'I'm not talking about your barrister friend. I'm talking about you slogging away making beds and cooking dinners.'

'At least it's respectable.'

'Look, Lavinia. We each have a task to do, and you shouldn't criticize me just because I choose to do it differently to you. I personally think that cleaning other peoples toilets is a much more demeaning way of making money than opening your legs for them.'

'I don't clean other peoples toilets.'

'No? Who does then?'

'Well obviously I clean the rooms and the bathrooms when people leave but —'

'I rest my case,' Brooke said, and Lavinia was immediately reminded of Alex.

'Anyway, are you coming here for the meeting next week or are we coming to you?' Brooke asked. 'It's probably best you come here. I have at least got staff to help cope if Hillary brings George. I'll ask Hillary and George to stay the night, it will give her a break.'

'But what if you're —'

'I won't be, I'm not at it every night you know?'

'I know, but —'

'Okay, that's settled then. I'll ring Hillary and let her know. Will Josh come with you?'

'I don't know, I don't expect so. The children will be home from school and we don't like leaving them on their own, we like one of us to be here.'

'Then why don't you all come and stay over for the night?'

'We can't, Brooke. I've got a full house. I'll need to be back in time to cook dinner.'

'And you don't call that prostitution?'

'No, I don't,' Lavinia said, as she gently replaced the receiver.

CHAPTER FORTY-SIX

Only Lavinia, Brooke and Hillary were at the women's monthly meeting, apart from George, who sat in the corner of the room humming his usual tuneless, repetitive chant. He had deteriorated a good deal in the past months and Hillary admitted that she was at her wits end. Her daughter, a sweet and caring girl, had announced that she was no longer capable of looking after her father; the responsibility had become too much, even for her. George would wonder away at a whim, he had no idea of his surroundings and no idea of his own identity; his wife and his children were total strangers to him, and he greeted his grandchildren with nothing more than a benign curiosity. Thus Hillary's brief respites had been taken away from her. She looked tired and drawn; her financial worries weighed heavily upon her. On the plus side, her bed and breakfast business was thriving, she had been inspected by the tourist board and given a high accolade, and paying guests flocked to her door. If only she didn't have George to worry about her life would be so pleasant and so simple.

Brooke glanced at the empty shell that she used to know as Lavinia's cousin George, and she shuddered, she was almost driven to tears by the sight of him. What if it were Henry, she thought, what would she do if it were Henry?

As if to voice her thoughts Lavinia spoke up. 'How are you coping, Hillary?' She said.

Brooke could see that Hillary was near to breaking point and she knew that Lavinia was thinking the same. She covered Hillary's hand with her own. 'Hillary, the time has come to let George go.' She smiled. 'Let's face it, darling – he's gone already. He's gone to a place where none of us can reach him.'

Hillary smiled in George's direction. 'Oh, I know. I know.' She frowned. 'But he has nowhere to go, we can't afford to put him in a home.'

'But in that case, surely the Government will pay?'

'Not if our assets total more than sixteen thousand.'

'But they don't, do they? You owe Lloyds, as much, if not more than you own!'

'Yes, but I have the house and if I sell it, Lloyds will take the lot. It's a ridiculous situation. Once I lose the house then the government will pay his keep. And as long as I have the house, I can earn money, but once that goes, both my ability to earn, and my home will be gone.'

'We'll think of something,' Brooke said. She shook her head and murmured in Lavinia's ear, 'It really is time she let George go.'

Lavinia swung her head toward her friend. 'What?'

Brooke smiled, shook her head, and then changed the subject

Lavinia set off back to Hulver at just gone four o'clock. It had been a productive meeting despite George's many childish interruptions. Back at Pennington the two remaining women picked at food in the kitchen, whilst Hillary spoon-fed George with pieces of bread broken up and soaked in tomato soup.

'Come on, Georgie. Eat up, there's a good boy,' Hillary coaxed.

Brooke looked on with an expressive mix of revulsion and compassion. 'You have to let him go, Hillary, you can't go on like this.'

Hillary laughed. 'Dear, Brooke, I appreciate your concern, really I do. But as I've already told you, I don't have a choice – don't you understand? I have no choice, there is nowhere for George to go. I have to look after him. Besides,' she said, 'I'm his wife, it's my job to look after him.'

'But if he knew what he was doing to you, he'd be so upset – he couldn't bear it. I know that Henry would rather die than let me do for him what you have to do for George.'

'Then I pray it will never come to it,' Hillary said softly.

'But there has to be an answer, Hillary. You know, when there isn't an obvious solution you have to make one of your own.'

'And what's *that* supposed to mean?'

Brooke shrugged her shoulders.

Hillary smiled gently. 'I know you always say that, Brooke. But I really don't know how anyone could make this particular problem come right.' She was turned toward Brooke and not George, and she failed to notice that he was spitting the soup-soggy bread out of his mouth as fast as she shovelled it in.

That night George took a long time to settle; he prowled the corridors opening doors and gently closing them again.

'I think he's looking for his memory,' Hillary said sadly.

'Well, he won't find it here,' Brooke replied.

Eventually Hillary persuaded George to go to bed. She sat by his side talking to him until he was asleep, just as a mother would calm a frightened, insecure, child.

Once George was asleep Brooke persuaded her friend to drink a nightcap before joining George in the luxurious twin bedded room. But all the time she was away from her husband Hillary fretted. She was, she said, afraid that George might get up and wander again.

Brooke woke with a start; something had disturbed her. She lay listening to the sounds of the sleeping house and was dozing again when she detected another unfamiliar noise. The opening and shutting of cupboard doors, perhaps? Was she being burgled again? She propped herself up on her elbows. The burglary last week had been a disaster in more ways than one. Henry had returned home and announced that he had not paid the insurance premium for the second year running. It had, he said, seemed like a safe risk: Pennington Manor had never been burgled before.

'That's the thing about insurance, madam,' the detective investigating the incident had said. 'It's really one big gamble, isn't it?'

'Right,' Brooke had agreed, wondering if the man had any idea on just how large a gamble Henry had placed in that particular market.

Things hadn't changed from the previous week; the contents of Pennington Manor were still not insured. She heard a door closing below and then the scrap of a chair on a wooden floor.

She got out of bed and slipped into her dressing gown. The door to Hillary and George's bedroom was open wide; she glanced inside. Hillary was sleeping soundly. She was lying on her back and exhaled with a soft whistle. George's bed was empty.

Brooke sighed. 'Oh, George,' she said. 'If only you were capable of knowing what you're doing to her.'

Bravely now, sure of herself, she descended the stairs. Working her way in the direction of the noise, she made her way toward the kitchen.

George was sitting in the center of the room, the refrigerator door was open, and the old man sat surrounded by broken packets of food. A bottle of milk lay on its side the contents spilling across the floor and soaking into the leg of George's pajamas. He had managed to open a fruit yogurt and was intent on scooping the pink goo into his mouth with his fingers.

When she entered the kitchen George looked up at his hostess and smiled. Brooke shook her head and smiled back. 'Oh dear, Georgie-porgie, whatever are we going to do with you?' She began to pack the undamaged items back into the fridge. She was talking to him all the time. 'I don't know how Hillary copes with you,' she said. 'You know, George, I told Hillary today that it's really time she let you go.' She bent down close to him. The thought, the idea, came into her mind very slowly, like a gentle wave caressing the seashore. But soon the first wave – the first thought, was replaced by a bigger, better, stronger thought.

George put his head on one side. He looked as if he understood her. 'You don't know what I'm talking about, do you?'

George put his head on the other side and frowned a little, as if he was concentrating very hard on what she was saying.

Brooke stopped cleaning up the kitchen and thought for a moment. The idea that had started as such a little, idle, thing had grown in her mind.

'George, dear, I really do think, for Hillary's sake, we must let you go.' She glanced up at the kitchen clock. It was almost two am. She picked up her car keys and, at the same time, she slipped her feet into an old pair of Henry's shoes that had found their way to the back door. She moved closer to her guest. 'Come on, Georgie. Let's go for a ride?' She held out her hand and the old man took it. She opened the back door and led him out across the courtyard to her car, and eased him into the passenger seat. 'I'm sorry about this, George, but if things aren't right, then it's up to us to put them right, and it's not right that you should rob Hillary of her strength and her sanity.'

They drove for miles; first west then south, then they took a track that led deep into the Thetford forest. At times George nodded off. At other times, he was wide-awake, and hummed his tuneless song. At three-thirty Brooke pulled off the track. She went round to the passenger door and offered George her hand. He held onto her like a child.

'Come on, Georgie, we're going to play hide and seek.'

George nodded his head as if he understood perfectly. He had a sweet serene smile upon his face. The moon shone brightly, but the path was treacherous. Brooke always carried a torch in the glove compartment of her car. She flicked it on. She didn't want to let the car out of her sight, there were so many paths crossing and re-crossing she was afraid that she too might get lost.

'That would be funny, wouldn't it, George. If I was to get lost as well.'

George smiled, but his eyes were as vacant as ever.

She went a short distance down the path arriving at a small clearing.

'Now, George, I want you to wait here.' She sat him down under a tree. She had found a packet of mints in the glove pocket, and she gave them to him. 'Here you are, Georgie, they're for you.' He took the mints like a child given a precious reward. She turned and walked a little way up the path, changed her mind, and went back to him.

'I'm sorry, George. But it really is best that Hillary

let you go. If you were capable of understanding, then I just know that you would agree.' She bent over him and gently kissed the top of his head. 'Goodbye, Georgie,' she said, and with tears streaming down her face, she made her way back to the car. She got into the driving seat, turned, gave him one last look, started the engine, and drove away. Her last sight of George was in the rearview mirror, sitting under the tree in the bright moonlight, tapping his fingers on his pajama clad knee, and humming his very own tune.

It took her over two hours to get home; she got lost on the forest tracks and went miles out of her way. It was daylight when she pulled into the yard. She crept into the house via the back door, leaving it wide open. The housekeeper would discover it when she reported for work at seven. She picked her way over the yogurts, the milk, and the cartons of food and made her way back up to her room. Checking on Hillary, she noted that she still lay, her head pushed back in the pillow, fast asleep.

'Sleep well, Hillary,' she whispered as she passed the door. 'I know I've done the right thing, both for you, and for George.'

CHAPTER FORTY-SEVEN

News of George's disappearance reached Hulver early, well before eight o'clock. Hillary was distraught; she blamed herself. She had slept too deeply; at home George usually woke her several times a night. He would have been disorientated in a strange house, she should never have agreed to stay overnight.

The police had told her not to worry; they were sure that they would soon find him. The nights were warm; he couldn't have gone far. A search party was organized. It was ordered to cover the surrounding ten miles, an old infirm man like Gorge couldn't have got much further than that. Only Brooke knew that their search was in the wrong area and not nearly wide enough.

'He's probably dead,' Quentin observed.

'Quen, don't be so awful! Of course cousin George isn't dead. He's lost, that's all. They'll find him,' Lavinia said.

Quentin shrugged. 'I bet he is, though. He was as nutty as a fruit cake, he didn't know his left from his right.'

'Quen's right, Mummy,' Sebastian chipped in. 'He was absolutely bonkers. If he wandered off he'd never find the way home.'

'Sebbie, don't be so cruel. You really shouldn't talk this way boys – what if cousin Hillary should hear you?'

The boys looked at her. 'Is it cruel to say the truth, Mummy?'

'Sometimes it is,' Lavinia replied. 'Sometimes the truth can be so painful that it's best left unsaid.' A vision of Alex Kirby's naked perspiring body came into her mind.

All day the search for George went on; Josh and the boys went over to Pennington to help. Even Zoë and Tiggy joined in. For the children, it was an adventure. For Hillary it was a nightmare. Lavinia stayed at Hulver and catered for her bed and breakfast guests.

The following day the search was widened and a broadcast was made on the local television and radio news. The local papers appealed for anyone who might have seen George to come forward. But no one reported seeing him.

A week dragged by, and then a second. Hillary went back to Glowers Boothby and was comforted both by her family and by the guests that came to stay with her. Life was easier without George, but it was surprisingly lonely, even the shell of the man had been some company. It was the constant stream of paying guest that kept Hillary from despair.

A month passed, and then two. It seemed that George had disappeared off the face of the earth. There were a couple of sightings reported, one in Manchester and the other in Bognor Regis, but the police didn't take either of them seriously.

Meanwhile the Lloyds ladies continued in their own individual ways, making what money they could. As summer faded into autumn, so did any hope of ever finding George alive.

Life settled to a comfortable, predictable pace. Hillary put all her energies into her business and although the huge debt George owed the bank did not recede; at least it was no longer growing at its previously alarming rate. George's insurers told her that after seven years, should George or his body not be found before, then Hillary would be paid a handsome chunk of money on his life insurance policy. Hillary knew that once the seven years had passed her money troubles would be over, the bank would be recompensed for the loan they had given against the Lloyds losses, and she would at last rid herself of what she thought of as a huge millstone around her neck.

Zoë spent the summer mourning the loss of her love. She was often sulky and unapproachable, and sometimes Lavinia heard her sobbing in the early hours of the morning. But she would take none of the comfort her family offered.

CHAPTER FORTY-EIGHT

Alex Kirby continued to visit Lavinia at the Castle. Twice she had refused to take a booking from him, but both times he had got a friend to book him in under a false name. Lavinia made a few feeble attempts to call a halt to the relationship but it was like trying to stop halfway through a free-fall parachute jump; there was no going back, no starting again.

As the months went by, the affair was no longer confined to Hulver. Lavinia met him as often as she could in either Norwich or London, depending on where he was working and how easily Lavinia could get away. She was becoming obsessed with him, she began to plan her life around their meetings and, as a result of her obsession, the core of her marriage to Josh was slowly being eaten away and her loyalties were shifting. Alex seemed to have the first call on both her love and her life.

The family rooms at Hulver were by far the grandest; Josh and Lavinia's was particularly fine. It had a fifteenth century oak four-poster bed and heavy tapestry drapes and hangings. It made sense to change their own rooms into guest quarters. So by the autumn, all of the family rooms had been taken over as guestrooms and the Elliots had moved up to the draughty rooms tucked under the eaves at the very top of the house, the rooms originally designated for the serving classes. Josh minded more than Lavinia, and he minded more for his boys than he did for himself. He was forever telling Lavinia how, when he was a young boy, the room they were now sleeping in, was once used by a maid or a cook he remembered from his childhood. His father, he said, was probably turning over in his grave at their loss of status.

'Then sell something, and we'll stop the B and B's and move back into our old rooms,' Lavinia suggested.

'Can't do that, old thing. Once you start whittling away at the estate it's the beginning of the end.'

But even that amount of communication was becoming rare. Their lives ran parallel but rarely interwove, if they did happen to touch, then the meeting was often abrupt and hurtful.

The shooting season would soon be upon them and with it would come strangers, tramping over the land that Josh loved so well. He'd have to stay at the castle and listen to shots fired at the birds he had so carefully reared and nurtured.

The meetings Josh had had with the shoot tenant had not gone at all smoothly. The tenant's demands seemed to Josh to become more outrageous as time went on. First of all he demanded that he bring in his own keeper; which meant that Josh had only been able to offer Toby Elton, his own keeper, part-time work, doing the odd jobs that Steve used to do, and controlling vermin around the estate. Toby had verbally added fuel to Josh's unease by constantly criticizing the new keeper's actions; they were breeding too many birds; the release pens weren't clean enough; and Toby thought some of the young pheasant polts looked as if they were going down with gape. Josh huffed and puffed and complained bitterly, his moans directed mainly to Lavinia; but as Lavinia reminded him, he had taken the man's money and used it to settle part of his Lloyds debt, so his influence on the shoot was minimal.

Then the tenant complained that Fen, Josh's dog, was out of control. She was, he said, running wild and he'd appreciate it if Josh kept her out of the woods; she disturbed the birds, he said. Josh retorted that Fen was as well trained a gun dog as his city friend was likely to meet, but the words had scarcely left his mouth when Fen, much to Josh's embarrassment, trotted up to him carrying a bedraggled hen pheasant in her mouth.

Josh talked constantly of the shoot. He was continually moaning about the way it was being run, and Lavinia repeated his discontent to Alex, who gained first hand experience of Josh's gripes whenever he stayed at Hulver.

'I don't believe your husband,' Alex whispered to her as he slowly drove his passion into her. 'He has you in his bed every night, lays next to you – he can be inside you whenever he wants.' He took a deep breath and pushed his body down into her with strength and force. 'All this,' he said, running his hands over her breasts and belly. 'And all he can think about is shooting a few feathered birds. The man needs treatment, for he's certainly quite insane.'

'That's not fair,' she whispered, her breath failing her. 'It's not the shoot he's moaning about, it's the loss of his way of life.'

'If I had you, I'd want no other way of life.'

She wrapped her legs around his waist and swayed gently back and forth. 'You do have me.' She rolled him over so that she was sitting astride him.

'I was thinking of something a little more permanent,' he said.

She pressed down on him, making him catch his breath. 'Be glad of what you've got Alexander,' she said. 'Remember, some of my friends would make you pay for it.' She giggled then. She was in love with him and could say what she liked to him.

He swung her over onto her back, and bore into her almost violently. 'I want you, Vinnie – not just the sex thing – I want you body and soul. I love you, and I know you love me.'

'I don't love you,' she replied. How could she explain what she felt, this extreme love, this obsession, was being in love, and not loving, how could she define the two? How could she make him understand that she was in love with him, but that she loved Josh? She hardly understood it herself, so how could she explain it to him?

'Oh yes you do,' Alex confidently replied.

She and Josh still made love, but rarely, and then deep in the night under the cloak of darkness; a function, satisfying a need, nothing more. They still said the same words, but the emphasis was different. The action was hurried, mechanical, rehearsed. Josh became withdrawn. His walks with Fen lasted longer. There were no evening drinks followed by pre-dinner sex. No early morning romps before the house woke up. With a heavy heart Lavinia realized that her husband had grown suddenly old. But it was more than that. He stayed up late, he drank too much, and often he didn't join her in bed at all, but slept fully clothed on the sofa in his study.

Lavinia was tired. She became thin, and yet she had never looked or felt more beautiful. She still moved with her cat-like grace but a new sensual dimension had been added. When the children were home from school she had little time for them, her only joy was found in the companionship of her lover. Alex Kirby meant freedom, freedom from all the domestic worry; freedom from the debts that still lay waiting to be paid; freedom to be sexually adventurous and uninhibited.

But Alex's intentions were becoming more and more serious. 'Come and live with me. I love you. I need you.'

She laughed at him. 'But I could never leave Josh, you know that. What's wrong with things as they are? Why do you have to complicate matters?'

'It's not enough.'

'It's all I have. I can give no more.'

'You're just an object to Josh, a possession, his brood-mare and his chatelaine.'

'I'm his wife.'

'And what are you to me?'

'I'm your lover.'

'You use me to get back at Josh.'

'Hardly, that would only work if he knew about it.'

'And he doesn't?'

'Of course he doesn't.' But in her heart she knew that Josh at some deep level must know that she was punishing him. He may not know how or where or why even, but he must know, because that's what she was doing, punishing him. He certainly didn't know that she had Alex, but he must know that she had grown distant from him. Josh was not a man capable of deep thought; he would recognize the symptoms but not the cause. Josh just sat back and watched in confusion as the gap between them widened.

'I love you, Vinnie,' Alex said.

Lavinia looked hard into her lover's eyes. 'I think I'm in love with you' she whispered in response. Surely that was true. Alex was everything that Josh wasn't, he was emotional and perceptive, he valued her for herself, not as an appendage to his wealth. Alex made her feel worthy. But what did she know about love? All her life she had waited to fall in love, defined being in love as a separate entity to loving, and she had had to analyse her feelings, afraid that she might miss the vital signs. Yet despite her searching she had never really known when love had begun. She always knew when she wasn't in love; it was easier for her to recognize the negative than the positive.

'What does Josh think about it? He must know that he's losing you.'

'I don't know. Josh never tells me what he feels, he keeps his emotions to himself.'

But Alex knew more of Josh's thoughts and emotions than even Lavinia. For it was to Alex that Josh

393

had confided, late one night, after too much wine and far too much port.

'Lloyds has mentally castrated me,' he said. 'Castrated me, and changed my position in Vinnie's life. When we were first married, she didn't have to earn her bread. I was the breadwinner, the provider. Now she's providing for me. In my day, women didn't work at all, let alone become the chief breadwinner. And the surprising thing is, she's so good at it.' He smiled. 'But then, she has never failed to surprise me. I remember when we were first together, she was such a prim little thing and yet – ' he broke off as if regretting his words, and Alex knew that his hesitation was due to the fact that Josh wasn't about to tell a paying guest about his wife's surprising passion. But Alex didn't need to be told, he knew firsthand.

'And yet?' Alex prompted.

Josh smiled. 'And yet, even then, she surprised me with her capabilities.' He took another sip of his port. 'She's a wonderful wife, and a wonderful mother,' he said. 'I don't deserve her.'

Alex flinched; he hated to hear Josh praising Lavinia, yet he never tired of hearing about her. Josh was drunk he could almost see the alcoholic haze that surrounded his host.

'Poor you,' Josh said. 'No wife and no children, I ought to be counting my blessings, ought I not?'

Alex didn't answer.

'You know, I do believe that if the twins hadn't been boys, Vinnie would have insisted on trying again, and again, until she'd given me an heir.'

'And would you have let her?'

'Let her? Oh, right. Yes, well, you obviously don't know my wife. If she'd decided she was having another child, then she'd have damned well gone ahead and had one. I'd have very little say in the matter.'

Alex laughed, but he knew his face lacked mirth. Josh's conversation was stirring up a jealousy that he hadn't realised he was capable of.

He wanted Lavinia away, before Josh confided his deeper feelings to her. Josh admired and respected Lavinia, but she seemed totally unaware of that fact, yet it was the main cause of the rift between them. A rift between husband and wife suited him. Many a lawyer's living had been made from such things.

'But it does take two – to, well, to tango, as they say.'

Josh laughed heartily then. 'You don't know Vinnie. Could you resist her? Could you say no to her? She's about your age, could you turn her down?'

Alex swallowed, but again, didn't answer.

'No, well,' Josh said. 'I certainly have never been able to say no to her, nor would I want to, nor will I ever want to.'

Alex made a grab for his port, but knocked it over, spilling the ruby liquid over the fine white linen cloth. Josh jumped to his feet and mopped it up with a napkin.

'Don't worry, old chap.' He immediately corrected himself. 'I mustn't say that – old chap, I mean. Vinnie tells me it's my attempt at running away from the present – you know escaping into the past.'

'And, is it?'

'Yes. Vinnie's always right. It's one of her annoying habits. If you knew her, you'd know what I mean.'

Alex reran the conversation in his head a second time, then a third time. He turned to Lavinia.

'Leave him, Vinnie. We'll set up home together.'

'I can't Alex, you wouldn't understand, but I can't.'

'Can't leave Josh or can't bear not to be Lady Lavinia Elliot?'

'I don't know,' she answered truthfully.

CHAPTER FORTY-NINE

'I'm tired, Vinnie, can't you put your light out?'

Josh turned over so that he was facing her. Lavinia was trying to varnish her nails. She had not had a moment to herself all day. Her lack of time was due both to the demands of her paying guests and to the fact that she had spent the afternoon in Alex's bed. He had rented a small flat in Norwich, and his close proximity to Hulver made him hard to resist.

'Please put the light out, Vinnie.'

'But I'm doing my nails.'

Josh wrinkled his nose. 'God, I wondered what that disgusting smell was. Can't you do it somewhere else?' Lavinia screwed the top back on the bottle, practically threw it on the bedside table and snapped off the light.

She lay awake long into the night seething with resentment and feeling fully justified in having a lover.

After all, her husband gave her scant understanding.

There were no bathrooms on the attic floor of Hulver Castle. The Elliots played, what the twins laughingly called musical bathrooms; that is to say, they used whichever bathroom was not occupied by paying guests. On the following evening, Vinnie was to be found in Tiggy's old bathroom. She had filled the bath to the brim, and was lying up to her neck in the soft silky water, attempting to remove the badly applied nail vanish of the night before. She screwed round and glanced at her watch, which she'd left on the edge of the basin. She had a little over an hour before she must begin to cook dinner. She smiled to herself, she had done well; cooking a five-course dinner meant nothing to her now; a year ago she would have shook in fear at the prospect. Her cooking reputation had become quite renowned – she no longer felt at the mercy of Mrs Jarvis. Although she was always quite pleased at the thought of a night off, she rarely took one. She felt her cook didn't do the meal justice and on the two nights a week that Mrs Jarvis came in, Lavinia would usually end up preparing the dinner with Mrs Jarvis acting as an assistant.

Josh interrupted her thoughts. He burst into the bathroom, clutching his toothbrush. 'God, I hate not having our own bathroom,' he said.

Lavinia dabbed some more acetone onto the wad of cotton wool.

'God, what's that awful smell?' He was staring down at her. 'Lord, are you still on that game?'

'What do you want me to do?' Lavinia snapped.

'Move into another bathroom? Perhaps you'd like me to move into another bedroom? I might as well. I would, but they're all full of bloody paying guests. You've no right to complain. I'm doing my best, Josh, trying to pay off your bloody stupid Lloyds gambling debts.' She dabbed more acetone onto the cotton wool and rubbed vigorously at the few remaining streaks of varnish.

Josh stormed out of the bathroom without cleaning his teeth.

After a while, Lavinia slowly climbed out of the bath and dried herself. She tucked a big towel around her, cleaned the bath, tidied the bathroom, picked up her discarded clothes and made her way up to the attic room that she and Josh now called their own.

He was sitting on the bed staring into space.

'We have to talk, Josh,' she said.

He didn't answer her, except with a nod of his head.

'There's something I must tell you,' she said. He nodded his head again.

He knows, she thought. Oh, God, he already knows. Suddenly she felt resentful again. After all, some of the blame for her infidelity had to be laid at Josh's feet. If it weren't for Josh, then she would never have met Alexander Kirby.

'We don't make love any more, Josh,' she began.

He nodded; he looked immeasurably sad.

'That is to say, not like we used to,' she continued. 'If we make love at all, it's as if by accident, in the middle of the night, as if it's a secret thing, only to be done under the cover of darkness. We never have nice sexy afternoons like we used to, and we never talk. That is to say, we never talk of love, only of pain.' She screwed up her eyes; she had paved the way, now she would tell him. 'There's something I have to tell you, Josh, I'm —' she heard him sniff and her eyes sprang open. Josh, his head in his hands, was crying.

She went to him. She couldn't ever remember her husband shedding tears, not like this. He'd wept with joy when his sons had been born, and she supposed he'd cried over the death of his first wife and son; but that had been before her time. The towel fell from her body, she put her arms around his neck. He brushed the hair away from her face and looked at her. The tears were gently coursing down his careworn cheeks.

He sniffed again. 'Don't you see, Vinnie? I'm ashamed, ashamed that I can't look after you anymore, ashamed that you have to work, have to cook and clean for people. You are so beautiful, Vinnie. I love you so much. You know I still can't believe that you married me.' He smiled through his tears. 'I used to wonder if you'd married me for this – the money and the title. He gave a sad little laugh. 'A bit Jane Austin of me, I know. But I could never believe my luck. You were everything, young and beautiful and sexy, and you've been a wonderful wife and mother. And now you're even prepared to work like this for me – for our family. You're too good to be true, Vinnie. I love you so much,' he sniffed. 'Basically I'm ashamed, I don't deserve you and I can't return what you're doing for me. I can't reciprocate. I feel humbled by you. I don't deserve the incredible loyalty you have for me. You never complain you just keep on, keeping on.' He gave her a small sad smile as he took her hand. 'I can't tell you how much I appreciate you, nor put into words the depth of respect and admiration I have for you.'

How could she tell him now? How could she not love him? What was Alex to her? This was the life she had chosen, this was the man she had chosen, for better or worse, for richer for – 'Oh, Josh, why didn't you say all this before? I love you so much. You know I do.' And then she was in his arms, and Josh, still almost fully clothed, was making love to her, and she was enjoying the smell of him, the mixture of tweed and gun oil. The old, familiar, secure smell; the smell that reminded her of all the goodness and all the love they had shared together.

'You haven't even undressed,' she laughed, as they

lay on their backs basking in the aftermath of lovemaking.

'I was in a hurry,' he said. 'Vinnie, what were you going to say?'

'Let's not talk about it now,' she said the words hurriedly.

'We must. We must get everything out in the open. We're drifting apart, Vinnie, and I can't bear it. I meant what I said, I'm ashamed of what I've brought you to, and sometimes I feel I can hardly look at you because of it. I want to make things right between us. What can I do, Vinnie? What can I do?'

She put her hand on his cheek. 'Don't be ashamed, Josh. Help me, that's all I ask. Be by my side. We're in this together, you know.'

So that evening, Josh Elliot, peer of the realm, opted to join his wife in the kitchen rather than his guests in the dining room. He donned his dinner jacket and waited on table, and afterwards he tied one of Lavinia's aprons around his waist and washed the dishes, and later still, whilst Lavinia finished setting the breakfast table, he polished the silver. And at eleven, after he had let Fen out for her last run of the day, he climbed the steep attic stair and he made love to his wife, almost, but not quite, like the old days.

The following morning Lavinia woke with a start, she had been dreaming. She dreamt that she was training to be a welder, but she'd forgotten to wear eye protection, so that she was welding with her eyes tightly closed. The welds she made were crude and very obvious. She wondered if the dream was an interpretation of the way that she was trying to hold her life together. She knew she must seek to protect herself and not stagger forward hoping she could make things right by instinct alone.

Later that morning, Lavinia phoned Alex. She was quite adamant; she would never see him again. She was concentrating on her marriage, she knew where she wanted to be, and it was a blessed relief. Alex could have no part in her life. The conversation turned into an argument, and bitter recriminations bantered back and forth. Alex's parting shot, 'Let me know if you or Josh are short of money, and I'll pay to fuck you. Although on second thoughts, I don't know whether you'd be worth it.' Hurt both himself, and Lavinia, more than either of them would care to admit.

In the early afternoon, Lavinia grasped the opportunity bathe, she wanted to review her thoughts and try and find some order in her life. So it was Josh who answered Alex Kirby's call.

'Is Vinnie available?' Alex asked.

Josh frowned, Vinnie? His wife's pet name on the barrister's lips sounded familiar and yet obscene. 'I'll see if I can find her, or can I take a message? About a room is it?'

Alex was a man whose tools of trade, were words. 'Yes. Yes, I spoke to her this morning. But I wasn't sure of my plans, and I wanted to tell her that I was sorry.'

'Right you are, I'll tell her. Nice to hear from you.'

Josh, with puzzled frown, replaced the receiver.

He climbed the stairs and tapped on the bathroom door. 'Vinnie? That fellow, the barrister – Kirby, just phoned, said to give you a message.'

'Yes?' Lavinia said from behind the door, she wiped her nose with the back of her hand, despite all her efforts, tears had been shed in her sanctuary. 'What did he say?' It was difficult for her to make her voice sound normal.

'Says to say that he's sorry, something about messing you around with his B and B arrangements.'

'Oh,' she said, her voice high pitched and squeaky.

'Funny,' Josh said. ' He called you Vinnie.'

'Must have heard you call me that.'

'Yes, I expect so. That would be it,' and reverting to the past, he added, 'Yes, that would be it, old thing.' He turned and walked to the top of the stairs, where he paused as if deep in thought. Then he went back to the bathroom door and tapped again.

'Vinnie?'

'Yes?'

'I didn't like it. Him calling you Vinnie.'

'No?'

'No. It seemed over-familiar, somehow.'

Lavinia, who'd got out of the bath and wrapped a towel around her, sank down to the floor, and leaned against the door. 'No,' she whispered to herself. 'The trouble is, Josh, I do like it. I like it very much.'

'What did you say?'

'Nothing. I'll be down in a minute.'

'No rush, old thing. I'll make some tea shall I?'

'Yes, Josh. Make some tea, I'll be with you soon.'

CHAPTER FIFTY

October brought with it days of golden sunshine. The twins were well settled at Edgeford School and Zoë went off to Warwick. Her A levels results were as good as her parents had hoped, and far better than Zoë deserved.

Philip's memorial service was to be held on the second Saturday of the month and Zoë had asked that she might join her parents on the journey north. The family were gathered in the hall and about to leave Hulver when Hillary telephoned to say that a man walking his dog in the Thetford Forest, had found George's body.

'The police couldn't understand how he had got so far. They think that someone might have given him a lift. You'd have thought they'd have come forward if they saw the appeal, wouldn't you?'

Lavinia looked at her watch, they would miss the train if they didn't leave soon.

'It always is a man out walking his dog, isn't it?'

Hillary was saying. 'I didn't understand why he hadn't been found before, but the police said that the undergrowth probably hid him from view, and now that it's dying back a bit, you know ... He wasn't far from the path apparently. He was just sitting under a tree – I expect he sat down to hum his tune.' Hillary laughed, but then Lavinia heard her voice break. 'I'm all right,' Hillary assured her. 'I'm relieved really, relieved that it's all over. It's just — '

'Just what?'

'The police. It's probably my imagination, but they almost seem to be suspicious, they kept on saying that they couldn't understand how he had got so far away. They said that there would have to be a post-mortem to make sure that he died from natural causes. You don't think —'

'You're imagining things, Hillary. It's all routine.'

'Yes, I expect you're right. I must ring Brooke now and tell her the news. I know she was dreadfully upset at the time George went missing. I know she didn't say a lot, but I think she may have felt that she was partly responsible. George disappearing from her house and all that.'

'Hillary, I don't think Brooke will be there. I think she'll have left to go to Philip's memorial service.'

'Oh gracious, I'd forgotten it was today. I did write to Ailsa and explain that I didn't feel I could go. It's just as well really, as things have turned out.'

The family had to drive to the station at break

neck speed to catch the train north, after Hillary had finally said goodbye.

The service was to be held at six in the evening, in the little chapel on the McTodd's Estate. It would be dark by then and Ailsa decreed that the chapel should be lit only by candlelight. Philip had so loved the Christmas candle-lit service. Afterwards a reception would be held at Cameron House. Ailsa had offered friends and acquaintances overnight accommodation, distributing her guests between the house and the holiday cottages.

'That's why she's chosen October,' Brooke remarked to Henry. 'She didn't want the service to interfere with her holiday lets.'

'Very wise of her,' Henry replied dryly.

Most of the local hotels were fully booked. It seemed that Philip had far more friends and well-wishers than Ailsa, or he, could have realised.

The Elliot's train was late, and they went straight to the chapel, having no time to call at the house first. The first sight of Philip's widow caused a stir even amongst the most unobservant of the congregation.

Zoë blanched, Lavinia looked as if she might laugh, but Josh was far more verbal. 'Good God,' he said, at the sight of the heavily pregnant Ailsa. 'So Philip managed it, after all!'

'Hardly,' hissed Lavinia, 'he's been dead ten

months.'

Josh seemed to think on this for a while; he frowned. 'Oh. Oh, I see,' he whispered back. But the frown remained on his face. He thought for a moment more. 'Then how can she be? You know . . . In the family way?'

Lavinia looked at Zoë in order to share the joke of Josh's naïve attitude. But Zoë looked as if she might faint, she was very white and her whole body was shaking.

There were to be more surprises in store for the women of the Elliot family before the evening was over. The candlelit service was strangely beautiful. The shock of Philip's death had passed, and the memories of the man were therefore no longer clouded by the tragedy, but were more in the nature of a celebration of his life. A hymn was sung and prayers were said. A boyhood friend talked about Philip's early life; a university friend talked about Philip the undergraduate, and finally Ailsa dragged her ungainly body up the steps to the ornate wooden pulpit.

She rested her hands on her protruding abdomen and gave a small cough to clear her throat. The congregation was mesmerized.

'Every one here has one thing in common,' she began. 'We all knew – ' she cleared her throat again, she seemed extremely nervous. 'We all knew and respected Philip McTodd. I was married to Philip for twenty years,' she said and she smiled. 'Philip was, as you will all know, twenty years older than me.' She smiled again. 'I will correct that, I promised myself that I would be totally honest.' She cleared her throat again. 'Philip was almost seventeen years older than me.' Several people laughed. The congregation was warming to her.

'Our marriage was not always blissfully happy – indeed it was often quite turbulent. But in the main, I think in our own way, we understood each other. We had no illusions about each other's characters, and I think we were happy.' The congregation stirred, some looked down at their feet, there was an air of shared embarrassment.

'This is not the time, nor the place,' Josh muttered under his breath.

'You're probably all thinking that this isn't the time nor the place to comment on our marriage.' Ailsa went on as if she had heard Josh's muttered sentiments.

More eyes looked down at the floor.

'But, our marriage was a big part of Philip's life, and it would be neglectful of me not to mention it, and it would be unforgivable of me not to be honest about it. We've heard all about Philip's childhood, and his early adult life. And now I want to praise Philip the husband. Philip was a good man, a tolerant man, and a good and caring husband. The only real mistake he ever made was to take his own life. Thus robbing those that knew him, and those that loved him. He was a man that had a lot to give

410

and a lot more living to do.'

Several people cleared their throats; it was as if Ailsa had been expected not to mention the nature of his death.

'I liked being married to Philip,' she went on. 'My experience with Philip has certainly not turned me against marriage – quite the contrary. He was a good and generous husband, and I know he would give his blessing to my newfound happiness. As you know, Philip and I were not blessed with children, but he would have been a wonderful father.' She bit into her bottom lip and then coughed. 'But so kind and generous a man as he was, he would rejoice at my impending motherhood. Knowing that, I hope that you, as his friends, will not judge me too harshly.' A tear trickled from the corner of Ailsa's eye. The chapel was completely silent; the candlelight threw huge silent shadows on the wall. Ailsa looked misty and almost saintly in the soft glow, a Madonna framed by shadows. Seconds ticked by, it was as if there was a collective holding of breath

'Here, here,' Josh said loudly into the silence. Lavinia shot him a black look.

Someone at the back of the chapel began to clap, and very slowly sporadic clapping broke out. Somebody laughed and several people shook their heads.

Ailsa had a sheaf of notes in front of her, she

sorted through them, waiting for the congregation to settle, but it didn't. People were whispering to each other, shuffling feet, flicking through hymnbooks.

Ailsa coughed, some of the congregation became attentive again. Most did not.

'Thank you,' she said. She gathered up the bundle of unread notes and, head held high, she descended from the pulpit. She nodded toward the lone piper, who, pushing the bagpipes securely under his arm, began to play the McTodd's dreary Lament.

Lavinia was indignant, how could she? Philip was hardly cold in his grave and Ailsa was obviously having fun with someone else. It was obscene. Poor Philip, how could Ailsa do this? As for trying to win the support of Philip's friends, now that really was off key. She glanced around her. To her left she caught the eye of Steve Jarvis who doffed an imaginary cap to her. She quickly looked away to her right. Her features froze. Alexander Kirby was staring straight at her. It had been almost six weeks since she had set eyes on him. Five weeks and four days to be precise – and on the subject of Alex Kirby, Lavinia was always most precise.

The piper was still wading his way through the whining, eerie tune.

'What's wrong? You look as if you've seen a ghost,' Josh whispered.

She forced herself to smile. 'No. No, it's Mr Kirby, you remember? He's been to stay with us. Several times in fact, do you remember him?' And at the thought of him her stomach felt as if it was somersaulting.

Josh leaned forward to take a look. Alex was still looking in their direction. Josh put his hand up and mouthed, 'Hello'.

CHAPTER FIFTY-ONE

The ground floor rooms of Cameron House were a seething mass of people. If Ailsa had offended anyone it didn't seem to prevent the guests from taking a full measure of her hospitality. Josh and Henry had found themselves a large scotch, and were ensconced in the library, exchanging stories of the horrors of having an alien shoot on their lands.

Lavinia searched desperately for Alex. She had to speak to him, although she had no idea know what she was going to say. Then suddenly he was there by her side.

'Ailsa's quite a woman. Does she do room service, as well?'

'I don't know,' Lavinia snapped.

Alex raised his glass to her.

'I didn't know that you knew Philip,' Lavinia said, her voice almost an accusation.

'I didn't. My wife was his adviser, for the Business

414

Park.'

'Well, she didn't advise him very well, did she?' Came Lavinia's bitter reply.

'She's over there, why don't you tell her that yourself.' He took her elbow. 'Come on, come and meet my wife.'

He said the word wife in a slow deliberate manner.

'You wife!' There was a hint of incredulity in her voice. How could he introduce her to his wife? Didn't he understand the way she felt about him?

'Yes, my wife,' he repeated, as he guided her across the room. And then under his breath he said, ' For God's sake, Vinnie. You're looking at me as if I've been unfaithful to you. It was a business transaction, wasn't it? Remember? Don't go and confuse what we had as anything more than that. It wasn't a love affair or anything, was it? Don't let what we had get confused with love. Come to think of it, I never did pay you, did I? On the other hand you never rendered me a bill. Perhaps you'd like to send me one?'

'Don't be silly, Alex. You know full well what was involved.' He voice was sharp, too sharp, and too full of panic and concern. His words had stung her. What a stupid woman I am, she thought. I can't still be in love with this man, can I? I can't be. I love Josh. I've always loved Josh. How could I ever have confused being *in* love with

415

loving? Being *in love* is such a poor substitute to loving. The whole thing was a figment of my imagination. I don't even know Alex, but I do know Josh, and I love him. I've always loved him, we've been together now for so long. We have a shared history – Alex was just a passing phase.

'Sarah, I'd like you to meet Lady Hulver.'

She was taller than Lavinia, tall and elegant. Lavinia knew that Alex was just turned forty, Sarah Kirby looked older, but Lavinia might have judged her age by the sophistication of her clothes. The Chanel suit, the blond hair swept up in a perfect French pleat, the hand-made leather shoes.

Sarah gave Lavinia a wide, insincere smile, and a weak handshake. 'So you're the titled lady that tends to my husband's every need when he's away from home?'

Alex raised his eyebrows, and Lavinia blushed.

'I must go and find my husband,' Lavinia said. 'It's nice to have met you, Mrs Kirby.'

'Wells. I never took Alex's name when we married.'

Alex raised his eyebrows again.

Lavinia pushed her way through the crowd; she was hot. She needed to think. She made her way out to the stable yard via the side door. Alex followed her. He didn't speak but took her hand and led her into the nearest loose box. Lavinia was relieved that it was not the one in which

416

Philip had killed himself.

Once inside the straw packed box he said. 'I know you love me, and I know you want me.'

She looked rather sad. 'We can't always have what we want.'

'In this case you're wrong,' he said, slipping out of his jacket.

She was lost, completely lost, all her resolutions melted away in his smile, all her plans faded at his touch.

Several stables beyond, naked and satiated, Steve Jarvis lay beside an equally naked Zoë.

'It's yours, isn't it?'

'So she says.'

'But it is, isn't it, Steve? I knew, you know. When I came up in the summer, I knew you and her were ... well, you know.'

'Then it's not a surprise to you, is it?' He said cockily.

'I don't understand, Steve. Why, why did you?'

'Fuck her? Or get her pregnant?'

'Both,' Zoë said tight-lipped.

'I fucked her because you weren't here, and I got her pregnant, because ... well, to tell you the truth, I didn't think a woman of her age could get pregnant. I mean, she's nearly fifty.'

'She's forty-three. Mummy told me.'

'Oh, Mummy told you, did she? Then it must be true.' He mimicked Zoë's accent.

'Are you going to marry her?'

'She wants me to.'

'Do you love her?'

'No, but I like her pretty well. We understand each other. We're two of a kind.'

'Do you love me, Steve?'

He ruffled her hair. 'Of course I do, Zoë, and I'll prove it to you.' He was back between her legs proving something he didn't understand, in the only way he knew how.

CHAPTER FIFTY-TWO

The lovely bright autumn wound down into a harsh winter. The cold north wind lashed at the castle walls, the ground was rock hard and some of the pipes froze. The frost and snow turned to rain; a bitter horizontal deluge, bringing with it a chill that penetrated the most insulated of clothing. Lavinia had not given Alex up; it was as she was no longer master of her own actions. Her love affair with Alex seemed to run parallel with the winter weather; the colder and harsher the frost; the closer Lavinia grew to Alex. She was out of control and so deeply entrenched in her lover that she thought of little else.

'Dashed glad I'm not shooting today,' Josh remarked, watching the beaters gather at the end of the park. 'If the birds fly at all, they'll be low ones not worth bothering with.'

Lavinia agreed with him, not sure if he really was glad, or if bravado was his way of dealing with disappointment.

'What are you doing today?'

'Nothing,' she looked away from him. 'I might go to Norwich, being as we've got no B and B's in.' Go to Norwich, where Alex would bed her and make her forget all the drudgery that now seemed to fill her life.

Josh stared out of the window again at the small gathering of men. The rain was soaking through their tweed coats. The game cart pulled up, followed by a covered trailer and the men scrambled inside.

'Bloody fools,' said Josh. 'What the hell do they think they're doing out there on a day like this. If I was them, I'd call the day off, it's a waste of everyone's time.'

'I've never known you call off a day's shooting,' Lavinia said.

'Well, I would on a day like this,' Josh retorted. 'I've never known a shoot day this rough. They know nothing about the job, bloody townies.'

Lavinia smiled. The shooting tenants had proved to be even worse than Josh had anticipated. Lavinia hoped that Josh wasn't going to discuss his shooting gripes again.

Her hopes were dashed.

'It's as if it's a matter of personal pride with them. They seem to think they must slaughter every living bird on the estate. If the bag's not huge they complain. They can't just take the day as it comes and enjoy the countryside.'

Lavinia gave a tight smile, she had heard this so

many times before.

'You know we had an agreement on how many birds they were allowed to rear and release? It's obvious that they're not sticking to it. In fact they've exceeded the limit several times over. I shouldn't think Henry has had to rear any birds at Pennington this year. I should think we've raised more than enough to stock both estates.'

'Probably,' Lavinia said absently. She was stirring soup, watching the way the wooden spoon cut through the thick broth and thinking of Alex and the new underwear that she was wearing, and how the black lace would contrast against her pale skin. She hoped it would excite him.

'You listening, Vinnie?'

'Of course, darling.'

'The tenant farmers are up in arms again, wanting compensation for the winter barley.'

'What?'

'There are so many birds, they're literally grazing off the young corn.'

'Oh, I see.'

There was a rap at the back door. The wind almost whipped the heavy oak door out of Lavinia's hands when she opened it. A red-haired boy stood under the torrent of rain, he wore a oilskin which was shiny and plastered to the outline of his body by the wind. Lavinia recognized him as one of the three keepers now employed by the shoot syndicate.

'Beg your pardon, Marm.' The boy touched his cap. 'Only the boss says, would Lord Hulver like to join the shoot. We're two guns short, so boss say he'd be welcome if he'd like to, come shooting, that is.' His words tripped over each other.

Lavinia smiled; the boy looked intolerably young and vulnerable, with the rain dripping from his hair onto his ginger eyebrows and on down to his chin.

'Come in, he's right here, you can ask him yourself.'

She ushered the keeper into the warm kitchen, but Josh, who had overheard the boy, was already on his way to the gun room, and Fen was jumping around the kitchen in a state of high excitement.

'I thought only mad men went out shooting on days like this?' She whispered as she helped him on with his coat.

'Normally,' he said, 'wild horses wouldn't drag me out on a day like this, but I want to see what's going on – see what these chaps are up to.'

She stretched up and kissed him on his cheek. 'I expect you'll go back to the pub and eat with them?'

Josh turned his mouth down at the corners and shrugged his shoulders. 'I may do. Why?'

422

'Only, if you're not going to be here, I might have a snack in Norwich, and then take in that movie.'

'What movie?'

'I don't remember the name, but it was one you said you really weren't bothered about. So if I'm not here when you get back, you'll know where I'll be.' She said the words too quickly, looking down at the floor as she spoke.

'Now you must go,' she said. 'They'll all be waiting for you.'

She watched as he climbed into the keeper's Land Rover and sped off to the group of men at the far end of the park. She pulled the soup off the Aga and closed the lid. She covered the saucepan with a tea towel and stood it to one side to cool. She turned her back and leaned against the Aga rail. She closed her eyes and ran her hands over her body, imagining that it was Alex's hands, caressing her. She was to meet him for lunch at one, and then she had the whole afternoon to spend with him, and hopefully, most of the evening as well. The thought of him diluted over eight or so hours took her breath away.

The shoot conditions were abysmal; the rain came down in sheets. Few birds flew, despite the heavy concentration. Josh plodded on with the rest of the guns over the brown plough. The sticky mud clung to his boots, making the effort of walking exhausting. The guns stood at their pegs for what seemed like hours before the cry went up. But despite the cry, no birds were to be seen. Then came another cry, and another. An ashen-faced beater appeared at the edge of the wood, he scrambled and fell over the plough until he finally reached the line of guns. He ignored the syndicate boss and made his way straight over to Josh.

'Sir, your Lordship, it's John Keen. He just keeled over, sir! He's as dead as a doorpost, Sir,' he flicked his fingers. 'Gone, just like that.'

Josh knew John Keen well. He had been a beater on the Hulver estate for over sixty years; he was a large man with a ruddy unhealthy complexion.

'What the hell's the matter now?' David Walsh the syndicate boss cursed.

'Seems like one of the beaters has passed away,' Josh replied. 'I'll go and check it out.'

He scrambled up the steep plough, trying to keep up with the frightened beater, who led Josh on through the wood and out the other side. The rain lashed down unmercifully, soaking through the seams of his waterproof coat and invading the warm tweed of his under jacket.

Sure enough, the body of John Keen was lying on the edge of the wood, surrounded by a group of beaters, some of whom had respectfully removed their caps despite the torrent of rain.

Josh bent over the old man and felt for a pulse,

there was none.

'Dead before he hit the ground,' one of the beaters informed Josh.

David Walsh appeared from the wood.

'What is it now?' His face was dark with anger.

The group of beaters parted to let him near the body. The rain was at last abating. David Walsh touched the dead beater with the toe of his boot.

'He's definitely dead,' Josh said.

'Roll him under the hedge,' David said. 'We'll deal with it at the end of the day.'

'We can't do that!' Josh exclaimed.

David caught hold of Josh's arm. 'Look, I've got a lot of money at stake here, do you know how much those chaps are paying for the day?'

'No,' said Josh. 'I don't.'

'Too much to let this spoil it.' He touched John Keen again with his muddy boot 'Look – the man's dead, he'll be just as dead at four o'clock.'

He nodded to the beaters. 'You all want a day's pay, don't you? It would be a shame to call the day off, wouldn't it? Look, the weather's brightening up now.' Everyone looked up, gray clouds still raced across the sky and the wind was howling in the trees.

The beater who had fetched Josh agreed, he turned to Josh. 'The gentleman's right, Sir. We ought to carry on, out of respect for the dead.'

'Afraid you'll lose your day's pay? What?' Josh said. He pinched the bridge of his nose with his thumb and forefinger.

The beater, looking extremely distressed, shook his head. 'We need the money, Sir.'

'Look, you lot carry on. I'll do whatever has to be done,' Josh said. He didn't wait for a reply but made his way down the side of the wood and toward Hulver, where he informed the relevant authorities.

Moving John Keen proved to be difficult. Even the Land Rover could not be made to negotiate the steep muddy field, and in the end a tractor and trailer had to be pressed into service to bear the body back to the village.

Once this was achieved, Josh made his way to the cottage that John Keen shared with his wife Edna. All the way to John Keen's widow he rehearsed what he would say to her. He was worried that she would be offended that the shoot had carried on, and was quite prepared to wax lyrical about it being what the dead man would have wanted.

In the event his kind words were not needed.

'Silly old sod,' she said, on hearing the news. 'I told him not to go today. It's as cold as charity it is. It serves the silly old sod right! Always did think more of the shooting than he did of me.'

With those few chosen words she shut the door in Josh's face; and Josh suspected that she went back to watch her afternoon television program, although he had no way of knowing for sure.

Josh trudged his weary way back to Hulver Castle with Fen at his heels, it was well past four o'clock. Vinnie was out, as he had known she would be. He found the saucepan of soup she had left and warmed some of it through. After he had devoured two large portions, he took a large scotch and the daily paper through to the drawing room and, with Fen at his feet, he dozed fitfully until well past eleven o'clock, when Lavinia, looking flushed and rumpled, appeared.

CHAPTER FIFTY-THREE

Lavinia was sitting by the ornamental pond, Josh by her side. The year had flown and it was September again. The boys had just gone back to school, and Zoë had returned to Warwick early in order to prepare for her final year. Lavinia watched the goldfish swimming in slow lazy circles. The Roman pavilion at the end of the garden threw a sharp reflection in the murky green waters of the pool. There was not a breath of air, the sun was hot and it reddened their faces as it shone down on them. It was four o'clock in the afternoon; Josh was nursing a mug of tea.

The order of life in the Elliot household had changed. Three years ago, a dainty tea tray, loaded with little cakes and sandwiches would have been taken out to the garden; and the family would have talked for perhaps an hour or more together. A game of tennis or croquet might have been played before dinner. Now only paying guests were served tea with any sort of formal grace. Today, afternoon tea for the Elliots consisted of a tea bag swished in a kitchen mug, squeezed out, and topped up with milk from the bottle. The dainty sandwiches of yesteryear had made way for a biscuit, served, as likely as not, from the cellophane packet in which it had been purchased.

Lavinia was writing the menu for the evening meal. She looked at her watch; in ten minutes she must go in, set the table, and begin to cook dinner. 'How do you spell en croûte Josh? Does it have a grave or an acute accent?'

'It doesn't have either – there's a circonflex on the u,' Josh replied, his eyes fixed far away on the horizon.

'Oh,' she said, and continued to write.

She'd got her bed and breakfast chores down to a fine art. She did it almost automatically, just as she almost automatically made love with Josh and almost automatically walked out of the castle, drove to Norwich and fell into the arms of her lover. It was a routine, a way of life. She didn't have time to feel guilty. She tried not to think too carefully about what she was doing. It happened, that's all there was to it, life went on.

The air was very still; a pair of blackbirds' squabbled over the garden wall. A pheasant barked in the woods. To all intents and purposes it was the most perfect English autumn afternoon, spent in a perfect English garden. But the garden was not so perfect as it had been three years before. The Castle gardeners had long since been made redundant. Josh had announced that he would do the gardening himself, but his efforts were hardly noticeable. The twins sat astride the motor mower in the school holidays and kept the main areas of grass neat, but the flowerbeds were wild and overgrown. Lavinia had declared, quite honestly, that she liked the wild romantic look of the place. But it depressed Josh to see his well-ordered grounds fall into neglect.

Josh was staring into the distance. 'Do you remember, Vinnie? About a thousand years ago, before Lloyds crashed and before this B and B lark?'

Before Alex Kirby, she thought. 'Yes,' she said, 'I remember.'

'Will it ever be that way again, do you think?'

She stared with him into the distance; so much had happened, their lives had changed beyond recognition.

'No,' she said. 'We're not the same people. I really don't think things can ever be the same.'

'No. No,' he said. 'I was afraid you might say that.'

She stood up, and reached over to take his empty mug, kissing the top of his head as she did so. 'Things might,' she said hesitantly. 'Just might, be better.'

He grabbed her hand and held it close to his lips. 'Vinnie, dear Vinnie, I wish I could believe you.'

She gave him a weak smile, and kissed the top of

his head again.

Josh was still staring ahead. 'I think it's time I sold my Bloomfields, Vinnie. They're worth a fair old bit. They'd pay for a couple of terms school fees. Maybe we could take some time off – have a rest from the B and B's?'

She noticed that he said his Bloomfields, not theirs, and she felt the divide between them widen a little more.

'There's no need,' she said. 'Things are all right – we manage, let's leave things as they are.' She sincerely meant her words. She wanted no change in her life. She didn't want Josh to give up his precious books. She thrived on her sacrifices and justified her actions by his lack of sacrifices. She had Alex, he had the Bloomfiels; in her mind it seemed like a fair trade.

'I've had them valued,' he said. 'Sotherby's say they're worth about twenty grand, and there's a Cotman amongst the watercolours, not a very inspiring one, but it might well fetch five or more.'

'A Cotman? But it couldn't be realised unless the books were broken up, and that's the very thing you dread.'

'Bloody books are a worry anyway. What if a B and B helped himself to one of them? You remember what happened to poor old Henry?'

'No Josh, I won't hear of it, it goes against everything you've always said. You've always valued those

431

books.'

'But we could sell the Cotman. We'd never miss it, we didn't even know we had it. It needn't even be sent to auction. There's a private buyer willing to give me five grand for it, and Sotherby's say that they think they could push him even higher.'

'No, Josh, we manage. Keep the books and the Cotman, I know how much you value them.'

She kissed his head a third time and walked away from him toward the house.

'I don't value the books as much as I value you, Vinnie,' he said. But she carried on walking. She either hadn't heard or hadn't cared to hear.

CHAPTER FIFTY-FOUR

Lavinia couldn't believe how quickly the years had flown. Her boys now nearing their sixteenth birthdays had grown into tall, handsome, independent youths. It seemed only yesterday that they were innocent little boys. Tiggy was taking a gap year and was travelling the world, sending her worried parents postcards from exotic, exciting places; whilst Zoë struggled her way through university.

Lavinia worried most about her elder daughter; she seemed forever discontented, forever searching for an elusive ideal. Zoë's college days had not been particularly happy; her relationships had been even less so. She spent her time searching for another Steve Jarvis, but she was too young and inexperienced to appreciate the uniqueness of any individual; and so she drifted from one unhappy love affair to another. And when she returned home to Hulver, she found herself demoted to an attic bedroom and her parents too busy to talk to her. Worst than that, she was pressed into service and, as she muttered to Tiggy, she felt as if she were a latter-day Cinderella.

The boys and Tiggy didn't seem to mind; indeed they seemed to thrive on it, whilst Zoë made no effort to hide the fact that she was sick and tired of talk that included phases like 'family effort' and 'pulling together'.

Then one day she met Christopher, he was articulate and charming and his family were extremely respectable. But Zoë misinterpreted his slick tongue for intelligence and his lazy attitude for good breeding. Here was a love that would gain her back her parent's approval. Christopher was just the sort of young man her parents would approve of. Very soon her letters home included accounts of her new partner, and her parents rejoiced.

They admitted to each other that they had both been very worried about her. But here was evidence that Zoë had finally forgotten Steve Jarvis and had at last found a suitable boy of her own class.

So that's it, Lavinia thought, they don't need me anymore. The realization was both exhilarating and depressing. Only Josh needed her, or did he? Once the Lloyds thing came to an end would he still need her? Or had her hard work depleted their relationship beyond repair? The charmed life they used to live had completely disappeared, what had they left?

The Committee of Lloyds had spent months

working on an acceptable settlement; she knew an offer would soon be made. Over a year ago at the end of ninety-three, Lloyds had offered to settle, but the names could not find the funds. Only thirty-eight percent of names had been willing to accept, and so the offer had been withdrawn. If a new more affordable offer were made, how would Josh find the money to pay? Would he sell something? The Bloomfield's Norfolk wouldn't be enough, even if they contained a dozen Cotmans. The lease to Applegate farm perhaps? Or would he borrow and expect her to work for the rest of her life to pay off the debt?

Alex was scathing about Lloyds. 'Things haven't changed, Vinnie. The business was always corrupt. Do you know how it started? A ship would be late getting into port, and the worried owner would try and get colleagues to insure against its non-arrival. Now these colleagues would have lookouts down the channel, and they would let the insurer know that the ship was safe, so the owner would pay over his money, ignorant that the insurer was gambling on a safe bet. Let me tell you, Vinnie, nothing has changed since those days. The insurer will always win over the insured.'

'But Josh was the insurer.'

'No, Vinnie, Josh was shouldering the insurer, the the ship went down. Lloyds didn't lose, their backers lost.'

435

Vinnie frowned. 'I don't understand.'

'You're not supposed to understand, that's the point. That's why the Gooda Walker action group have just won judgment.'

'What?'

'Not Josh's syndicate, so it's not Josh's victory. There are plenty more corrupt syndicates though.'

Alex always seemed to know and understand exactly what was going on. He was always terribly insulting about Lloyds and about the rich men and women that gambled on it. Now Alex was trying to explain to her that soon there would be another, better, offer and there would be the chance of a final settlement, and Lavinia wondered if that would be the point at which Josh would, finally, no longer need her. Would that be the point that she would be free?

CHAPTER FIFTY-FIVE

'So he came to the castle one morning and he said, "Sorry Lord 'Ulver, but me dad won't be able to dig anymore ditches for yer".' Josh was trying hard to put on a broad country accent. "I'm sorry to learn that," I said. "Why is that?" – I was frantically wondering if I'd remembered to pay his last bill. "Ee carn't because 'ee be dead," Albert's son said.'

Everybody laughed. Henry laughed so much that he had tears in his eyes.

'That wasn't the best of it,' Josh said. 'After he'd gone, young Quentin, who had not missed a word of the conversation, pipes up, "Gosh, Daddy, you were a bit slow there, why didn't you offer to buy the digger, you might have got it really cheap".'

The room burst into another peal of laughter.

Lavinia scraped her chair back from the table. She'd heard the tale many, many times before, she was pretty sure Alex had probably heard it before as well. She grabbed a pile of plates and took them through to the kitchen; she caught Alex's eyes as she left the room. Really it was too bad of Alex to come, how could he? How could he sit at dinner with her husband and make ordinary polite conversation? He needn't think that she was going to creep down the corridor to his bed; but even as the thought entered her head, she knew that she would. Why had he come? It was too bad; he'd only seen her the day before yesterday. Was his appetite for her so insatiable?

It irritated Lavinia that her husband and her lover seemed to get on so well. She knew they liked each other; was that a good, or a bad, sign? Did it mean that they were two of a kind with the same thoughts and the same tastes? Whatever it was, she did not feel comfortable about the two men talking together; she felt excluded somehow, almost as if they were having a joke at her expense.

Brooke came through to the kitchen carrying more plates. Alex was Lavinia's only paying guest that night and, as Henry and Brooke had come over, she had agreed to join them all for dinner.

'So, who is he?' Brooke said.

'Who is who?' Lavinia was noisily packing the dishwasher.

'The Adonis, the Greek God, the barrister. Boy has he got the hots for you!'

'Oh him? Actually Brooke, he's my lover.' Even as the words left her mouth, Lavinia couldn't imagine why she was saying them. To have a joke at the men's expense perhaps.

Brooke laughed. 'No. Who is he really? He's quite a dish, and I dare say you could have him for the asking.'

Lavinia stopped what she was doing and faced Brooke. She looked extremely angry. 'He's my lover. I've been seeing him on and off for two and a half years. He's taken the trouble to get a divorce from his estranged wife, and he spends a lot of his time trying to persuade me to go and live with him. So thank you for observing that I could have him, but the news is, that I have had him, many times, and in a variety of interesting positions.' Her voice was clipped and sharp.

Brooke was standing with her hands on her hips, her mouth was literally wide open.

'I can't believe that the shock of my revelation, has rendered you speechless, Brooke?'

'But he's so, so . . . er.'

'Handsome?'

'Young and sexy,' Brooke said.

'And Josh isn't?' Lavinia asked.

Brooke smiled. 'Josh is, well . . . Josh is a sweetie-pie.'

Lavinia sat down heavily on one of the kitchen

chairs. 'I know, that's why I can't hurt him.' She had tears in her eyes.

Brooke looked alarmed. 'Good God, Vinnie. You're serious, aren't you?' She also sat down. She looked as if she were searching for a solution. 'Look, Lavinia. Remember, if Josh doesn't know, he can't get hurt, can he? You're mad having him here though. I can't think how it is that Josh hasn't noticed the way – Alec is his name?'

'Alex.'

'Alex looks at you, I mean, he practically undresses you with one glance.'

'He's not supposed to come here. He books himself in. He waits until he knows I'll be out of the house, then he rings Josh and books a room. It gives him a buzz. Anyway you're a fine one to talk, you have your lovers in the house all the time.'

'Clients, not lovers.'

'What's the difference?'

'Money. The difference is money, Vinnie dear. They tinker with my body not my soul.'

'And how do you know it's not the same with me and Alex?'

Brooke laughed. 'He looks like a very exciting man. I must give him my number.'

Lavinia was overcome with jealousy. Leave him alone, he's mine, she wanted to say, but she held her tongue.

Brooke was watching her closely. 'Your face has just answered your own question, my friend. Now for God's sake get him out of Josh's house.'

Lavinia shrugged her shoulders. 'Maybe I was too young when I married Josh – he's nearly twenty years older than me, you know. Maybe he's a bit of a father figure to me. I'm grown up now, maybe I need someone more my own age.'

'Oh, Jesus wept!' Cried Brooke. 'You can at least be honest with me, Vinnie, I'm a woman of the world, remember? Okay, so you fancy this man – this Alec — '

"Alex,' Lavinia murmured.

'You and he want to fuck,' Brooke went on as if she hadn't heard. 'That, my dear Lavinia, is lust. Spare me all the psychological melodrama – it's lust, Vinnie, pure and simple. Nothing more. And you should remember that.'

When they returned to the dining room, the men were discussing the various fortunes and failings of their friends and acquaintances.

'And dear old Bill Hunt, he's a retired army major,' Josh explained for the benefit of Alex Kirby. 'He's lost everything. He lives in a mobile home, at the bottom of his daughter's garden. He used to have such a pretty little cottage. He misses his garden, I know that, but he doesn't

441

complain – he makes the very best of things. He says he's used to living in confined spaces and says he enjoys being near his grandchildren.'

'And there's Lavinia's brother,' Brooke said.

Alex, of course, knew all about Lavinia's brother, and about nearly everyone else they were talking about.

'Yes. Yes,' said Josh. 'Poor old Rupert, he was hit, really, really badly – lost everything, he went into hardship, you know. Lloyds took everything he had, even his wages, and they allocate him a few thousand a year to live on. His wife left him, you know – what – about a year ago?' He looked over to Lavinia for conformation. 'He's well rid of her, of course, but she was a pretty little filly,' he leaned over and squeezed Lavinia's knee. 'I mean to say, that's one form of entertainment that comes free, isn't it?'

Lavinia pushed his hand away rather roughly, and Alex winked at her.

'And there's been far bigger tragedies than that,' Josh went on. 'There was this chap I knew. I was at school with him, he killed himself.'

'Who was that?' Henry asked.

'Chap named James Laughton.'

'Ah yes, hung himself, didn't he?' Henry said.

'You knew him?' Josh sounded surprised.

'No, not him, but I know his brother-in-law Andrew. He married Laughton's sister Vicky. I know the press had a field day blaming Lloyds for his suicide, but according to Andrew the poor chap had other problems. He was a rageing poofta you know? His boyfriend had walked out on him, and apparently, the PM brought out the fact that he was HIV positive, although it's debatable whether he knew that at the time. He was a man of the cloth you know? Funny . . . you'd think that his religion would prevent him from taking his own life, wouldn't you?'

'His religion didn't stop him indulging in homosexual exploits, did it?' Josh said.

'No. No, that's true, poor bloody fool,' Henry said.

'Then there was Philip McTodd. You knew him didn't you Alex?' Josh continued.

'My ex-wife knew him. She acted for him when he formed the Business Park.'

'Ah, yes. Well his widow, Ailsa, has shacked up with our old odd job man.' Josh said.

'He's half her age. I'm amazed that the woman can stand the pace,' Henry butted in.

'I think they're happy,' Lavinia said rather wistfully.

'Well young Steve needn't invite me up to the New Year Shoot. Can you imagine?' Josh said.

'Yes,' said Lavinia. 'I can.'

Everyone looked at her. She got up. 'I'll make some more coffee, shall I?' She said.

CHAPTER FIFTY-SIX

Lavinia bustled into the kitchen. The short February day had left a light fall of snow on the ground and the evening was bitterly cold. Tiggy and Josh sat at the kitchen table, knives and forks poised, about to dig into the duck casserole that Lavinia had made to feed her family. Tiggy had been sick, cut her travels, and come home to recover. The Elliots were hosts to just two paying guests that night; an elderly pernickety couple, who'd fussed about everything.

Lavinia snatched the duck from under their noses. 'Bloody woman doesn't like fish,' she said by way of explanation.

'But — ' Josh began to protest.

'You can have the fish instead.'

Tiggy began to laugh. 'Two minutes later, Ma, and I'd have wolfed the lot.'

'I'm glad you find it funny, Antigone. I was really

looking forward to that,' Josh grumbled.

Don't moan, Josh.' Lavinia was annoyed, how dare he sit and complain? She slid the duck off the kitchen crockery and onto the dinner service plates, sprinkled the meat with chopped parsley and sailed into the dining room.

When she got back to the kitchen the telephone was ringing; neither Josh nor Tiggy made any move to answer it. Lavinia glared at them and snatched the receiver up to her ear.

'Darling! Where are you? . . . Yes I know that, I mean that it doesn't sound as if you're in a call box.' Lavinia's face was flushed with pleasure. She covered the receiver with her hand. 'It's Zoë,' she confided to Josh and Tiggy.

Zoë was still speaking, and Lavinia listened to her daughter for some time. Then she said, 'Of course, darling. That would be lovely. We'll expect you about six tomorrow then, shall we?'

Lavinia replaced the receiver. 'Let me have a word,' Tiggy said.

'Too late.'

'Oh, Ma!'

'You should have answered the phone.' Lavinia said.

Tiggy flopped down in the chair. 'This place gets

445

worse. First your food is snatched from under your nose and then you're not even allowed to speak to your own sister.'

'Don't sulk, Tiggy. Go and clear the table and ask them if they'd prefer their cheese or their dessert next.'

'And now I'm a waitress,' Tiggy said scraping her chair back from the table and moving ungraciously into the small dining room. 'I'm supposed to be convalescing, you know.'

Lavinia caught Josh's eye and they smiled at each other.

'Zoë's coming home for the weekend and she's bringing her young man with her.' Lavinia put her hand out toward Josh; he took it and squeezed it.

'You know I began to think that Zoë would never get over Steve Jarvis.' Lavinia said. 'I could have killed Mrs Jarvis at Christmas, going on about Steve and Ailsa getting married.'

'Well after the baby was born I suppose he felt he had to marry her,' Josh said.

'How little you know,' Lavinia said. 'Ailsa makes all the decisions.'

Josh patted Lavinia's hand. 'Well, we should be jolly thankful that she did then, at least it's solved Zoë's problems.'

Lavinia looked doubtful. 'I'm not so sure about

that.'

'What do you mean?'

'Oh, I don't know. Zoë was so besotted with him. I just don't think women get over men that easily, especially as Steve was her first love. It's the love you can't have that digs the deepest, and lasts the longest,' she said wistfully.

'But she's bringing a chap home?'

'Yes, but—— '

'What's his father do?'

'Josh, I don't know. But I think Zoë has made it perfectly clear that he's the sort of chap we'll approve of.'

'Is he at university with Zoë?'

'I assume so, that's what Zoë implied.'

Josh let out a deep breath. 'Phew, what a relief – thank God she's seen sense. I have to admit, Vinnie, that there have been times when even I've almost lost faith in Zoë. Well, perhaps I'm putting it a little on the strong side. I never actually thought she'd end up with the likes of Steve Jarvis. I always knew she'd sort herself out. She's been with this chap, what – six months? I always had faith in her really. That's your trouble, Vinnie. You had too little faith in her. Zoë is a sensible girl, I knew she'd never let us down.'

Tiggy had returned to the kitchen. 'They don't want cheese, or pudding, Ma,' she bent over and kissed her father on the cheek. 'Which means we get a crème caramel each, Pa.'

'Do they want coffee?'

'She wants Earl Grey tea and he wants decaf coffee.'

Lavinia sighed. 'Why can't they have the same?' She said to no one in particular, putting the kettle on the Aga.

'So what are you talking about? Not the handsome Christopher?' Tiggy said.

'You've met him?' Lavinia sat down at the table.

'At Christmas, at that party Zoë and I went to.'

'You didn't say.'

'Oh, Ma, why should I?'

'If Zoë's got a young man— '

'Oh, Ma, please. He's just a chap that Zoë knew.'

'But she's known him for ages – and she's bringing him home – her letters are always full of him.'

'So? Personally, I think he's a bit of a prat.'

'What does that mean?' her father asked.

'You know the sort, all mouth and trousers.'

'What?'

'He's all talk. All show. You know what I mean. He's not a patch on Steve.'

'Oh well, if we're using Steve Jarvis as a yardstick.'

'Steve was okay. You said yourself he's saving Ailsa

from certain ruin.'

'He's doing a good job at Cameron House, but he's hardly a suitable husband for Ailsa.'

'Well, Mrs Jarvis says that they are really happy together. She showed me some pictures of the little boy, he's awfully cute.'

'Oh? Has she forgiven Steve for not inviting her to the wedding?'

'I wouldn't go that far,' Tiggy said. 'But she's as proud as punch of her grandson.'

The kettle boiled and Lavinia got up, made the tea and the coffee, and took it through to her guests. When she returned she asked Tiggy to tell her all she knew about Zoë's boyfriend.

'Oh, I don't know much, but you'll see what I mean when you meet him. He's a sort of . . . Well, he's a bit of a wide boy.'

'Wide boy?' Lavinia repeated.

'Well, he's . . . Well, for instance, he's not at university, at least not anymore. He dropped out, but he hasn't told his parents, so they carry on paying for his flat, and sending him an allowance. He thinks it's funny.' Tiggy covered her mouth with her hand. 'Please don't tell Zoë that I told you.'

Josh and Lavinia spoke at the same time. 'Why not?' Said Josh. 'Of course not,' said Lavinia.

Tiggy shook her head. 'You two, you never have the same thoughts, do you?'

Lavinia stared into the distance. It was true what Tiggy said, they didn't think the same anymore. Her relationship with Josh had altered; the contact points had shifted. They had settled into a routine, they worked together with a routine, automatic, motion; they talked together avoiding controversy and they even made love together in a set, rhythmic, non-challenging pattern. Their criticism of each other was rarely voiced, how could it be? The house was always full of strangers; their marriage had become a superficial showpiece of pleasantries. She turned and looked at Josh, thinking that they lived at opposite ends of the same spectrum.

Josh's voice jolted her back to the conversation.

'So what do his parents do?'

Tiggy smiled. 'Oh, Daddy.'

'Well, I need to know that this . . . what did you say his name was?'

'Chris.'

'This, Chris – Christopher, is all right.'

'Suitable, you mean Daddy?'

'All right – suitable, then.'

'I think his father is something in the city, a stock broker or something.'

'They're a load of crooks,' Josh said.

Tiggy ignored him. 'And I think his mother has married again and lives in London. I'm not sure about that, but you must ask Zoë, not me.'

'That's enough, Josh,' Lavinia said. 'Will you help me clear the table?'

'But, I was only – '

'Tiggy's right, we must ask Zoë.'

Josh heaved himself up from the table. 'Come on then. Let's get cleared up, I'm exhausted.'

'You must be.' Lavinia said sarcastically. But Josh didn't hear the sarcasm in her voice.

CHAPTER FIFTY-SEVEN

Lavinia went to a great deal of trouble preparing a guest room for Zoë's boyfriend. For once they had no paying guests, but it was difficult for Lavinia to get out of the habit of being constantly on guard, and even when all her tasks were completed, she fidgeted about the house making sure that everything was in order.

The only time she felt really relaxed was in Alex's bed and that was where she found herself that afternoon. She had become adept, if not at lying, then certainly at being economical with the truth. She had things to do in Norwich, that was what she'd told Josh, and was now bent over her lover, kissing, caressing, touching. She reasoned with herself that she had not told a lie, she was doing things that she needed to do. And should Josh ask, as he often did, 'Successful day in Norwich, darling?' She would assure him that she had done everything that she had needed to be done.

She left Norwich at four and made her way back to Hulver. The roads were still quite snowy and she drove cautiously.

She had set the table and prepared the meal earlier in the day; Mrs Jarvis would be in later and she would clear and wash up. Josh and Tiggy were nowhere to be found and she assumed correctly that Tiggy had accompanied her father in taking Fen for a walk. She checked the dining room again and the guest room she had prepared for Christopher Goodland. Finding everything just as it should be she bathed and retired to her attic bedroom. It was cold up there, the heating on the upper floor proved to be inefficient because of the vast amount of roof above the rooms. She slipped into her bed for warmth, and soon she dozed.

The crunch of car tyres on gravel awoke her. She staggered to the window in time to see Zoë alight from a small red sports car. Unaware that she was watching, the boy squeezed Zoë's bottom. Lavinia experienced a strange unaccountable feeling of indignation. After all, Zoë was still very young, but then young people were different these days. She knew that Zoë and Steve had been intimate, but even so . . .

By the time she had dressed and gone downstairs Josh had welcomed his daughter and her friend, and he was pouring drinks for them both in the library. A roaring fire burned in the hearth. The curtains were open and the light from the window reflected on the snow outside.

Lavinia had not been in the room for five minutes when she decided that she didn't like the boy, and from the look on Josh's face, she gathered that for once he was of the same mind. Christopher Goodland had his arm around Zoë's shoulder, then her waist, and then her hips. He ran his fingers through her hair, at one point he even stuck a long pink tongue into her ear, causing Zoë to laugh and jokingly reprimand him. Lavinia gave Josh a warning look, it was better that he didn't voice his thoughts.

The telephone rang; a booking was taken. Josh made an excuse for the interruption. He's embarrassed, Lavinia thought. He's ashamed that we have to make money.

There was no disputing the fact that Christopher was a handsome boy, he was reasonably tall, and had fair hair and blue eyes. He was well spoken and extremely well dressed. He sported a Rolex watch, which he absently played with whenever his hands were not caressing Zoë. He accepted a large scotch, which he drank very quickly; he then politely asked if he might have another.

'Where are we sleeping, Ma?' Zoë asked. She gave her mother an almost defiant look.

'I've put Christopher in the red room,' Lavinia said pointedly.

'Come on,' Zoë said to Christopher, she didn't take her eyes off her mother, 'we're in the red room, I'll show you where it is.' She laid great emphasis on the word we.

Josh spoke: 'I think your mother assumed that you would sleep in your own room, Zoë.'

Zoë flicked her long blond hair back over her shoulder. 'Oh, sorry, Ma. I should have made it clear what our sleeping arrangements are.' She grabbed Christopher's hand and made her way toward the door, kissing her mother's cheek as she passed.

'No, Zoë!' Josh's voiced boomed through the room. 'We can't allow this. I'm sorry, but I don't want you to share a room.'

Zoë shrugged her shoulders. 'Okay,' she said.

'Then we'll have to go to a hotel for the night.'

'Zoë!' Her mother said.

'It's the way things are, Ma.' Zoë hesitated for a moment. 'We were going to wait and tell you the good news over dinner, but . . . ' she smiled at her lover and took a deep breath. 'Well, you see, we have some wonderful news.'

Josh and Lavinia looked at each other.

'You're going to be grandparents! Isn't that wonderful?' Zoë's face belied her words.

A smile could not have been found between them.

'I'll show Chris where we'll be sleeping, shall I?'

She didn't wait for a reply but led him from the room.

Lavinia felt numb, her stomach contracted and she felt physically sick. How could Zoë be pregnant? She was little more than a child herself. How could the pair of them take such an important step so lightly? Lavinia's palms were damp with sweat. Josh looked completely shocked. She was rather afraid that he might pick Christopher up by his shirt collar and render him unconscious. Zoë pregnant? That surely wasn't possible; Lavinia was far too young to be a grandparent. Old biddies like Mrs Jarvis became grandparents, not sexually active upper class women like her. It was a joke; it had to be. Zoë could never cope with a baby. Zoë was a child, and that was the trouble, she was playing at being grown-up. But she surely hadn't taken grown-up responsibilities on board.

The conversation at dinner was extremely stilted; it was as if they were playing some kind of team game; a game where no one wanted the responsibility of kicking the ball over the white line of controversy.

'So what does your father do?' Josh asked.

'Zoë said you'd ask me that.' He winked at Zoë. 'He's in the city.' No further information was offered.

Josh was dribbling the conversational ball dangerously close to the penalty area.

'And what do you do, Chris? How do you earn a living?'

'I work for Her Majesty's Government,' he said. 'At least they're the people that pay me.' Both he and Zoë began to giggle.

'What?'

'Oh, Daddy, he's on the dole,' Zoë said.

'Oh.' Josh's footwork was becoming clumsy. 'But how can you keep a wife and child on the, the . . . er . . . dole?'

'Wife? Good Lord! Marriage? Now that would be a wheeze, wouldn't it? So how much is it worth, to make an honest woman of her? What's your best offer? How much is her dowry? Or are you going to play the dictatorial father and put a shotgun to my temple.'

Zoë was beginning to look uncomfortable. 'But . . . we are going to get married, Chris, aren't we? You said we would, didn't you? Now we're having a baby, we must, mustn't we?'

She's afraid of him, Lavinia thought. She's afraid that he doesn't love her; this baby is a trap. Oh, Zoë, you silly, silly, girl.

Tiggy raised her eyebrows at her mother. Josh was beginning to huff and puff, he was running full pelt toward the ball, not caring if he scored a goal, or earned a penalty.

Christopher Goodland was still speaking. 'You see, Josh – you don't mind if I call you Josh, do you? I have a problem. Basically, I'm over qualified, I can't get work.'

At the mention of his Christian name Josh had gone scarlet. 'You can't get work?' He spluttered, his eyebrows were disappearing into his hairline. He began to tap his fingers on the table top.

'No, I just can't. I mean, well – there are jobs, of course there are, but not *my* sort of job. I mean, what do you expect me to do? Wait on table?'

'Why not?' Josh spat. 'I do.'

Christopher held up his hand. 'Ah, yes, Josh. I was meaning to have a word with you about that. It's my mother, you see, she really wouldn't approve of me fraternizing with hoteliers and–– '

'Hoteliers!' Josh spluttered.

'Please, Chris. That's enough,' said Zoë. She had an edge of panic in her voice.

'Oh, no, Zoë, let the boy finish. I'm very interested in what he has to say,' said Josh.

'My father wouldn't mind so much, he'd think it was a right lark,' Chris continued. 'Only I have to admit my mother is a snob, no other word for it, she's a snob.' He looked around the table, a self-satisfied smile upon his face. 'She'd have a fit if she knew what Zoë's parents really did for a living.'

Zoë's face held a look of embarrassment, mingled with panic. 'Chris? That's enough, Daddy doesn't appreciate your little joke.'

Too late! Poor Josh. It was a foolish move. His long years of experience had not taught him to hold his tongue.

' I may look a fool, but I'm not as stupid as you may think I am.'

Christopher's face still held an amused smile.

'Zoë's parents, as you call them, work hard, they work hard to give their children the best possible start in life, whilst you – you are an unemployed, cocky, n'er-do-well,   and   I'll   ..-. I'll — '

'Come on, Josh, loosen up, you do take things to heart. I was only joking,' Christopher said glibly. 'Surely you're capable a having a bit of a laugh? Surely you know I was only joking?'

Josh pushed his chair back from the table, threw his napkin down as if he were throwing down a gauntlet, and stormed out of the room. He did not return, but took Fen out into the bitter February air. The rest of the meal was eaten in almost complete silence. When Lavinia eventually climbed the two flights of stairs to her bedroom Josh was already in bed, his head was pushed deep into the pillow; the duvet was pulled tightly around his shoulders, and he was soundly asleep.

CHAPTER FIFTY-EIGHT

Lavinia hadn't slept at all well; she had lain awake deep into the night. Months ago, when Zoë had first told her about Christopher, she had rejoiced. She had thought that at last Zoë was settled, but now she feared for her daughter; something was wrong, very wrong. But Zoë was no longer a child, she was a woman and well able to make her own decisions, well able to choose her own friends and to plot her own life. But there was more to it than that, another dimension had been added. Lavinia's child was going to have a child of her own; it was as if Zoë's physical condition somehow altered Lavinia's state of mind. As if a pending grandchild ought to be the catalyst that must make Lavinia settle down; stop her from being in love with Alex. Now was the time for her to enter a new phase in her life. Now she must become staid and respectable. Whoever heard of a grandmother licking champagne from her lover's navel. Whoever heard of a grandmother straddling her lover in the front seat of a car on the edge of Thetford Forest? Or buying extravagant, sexy underwear? Or covering herself in massage oil? What grandmother fornicated the way she did? Now, now must be the time that she embarked on a new, decent way of life. But she didn't want to give Alex up, she was in love with him; and that was another thing – what sort of grandmother fell in love? What sort of grandmother experienced this crushing, painful, destructive emotion; yet carried on feeding her desires?

Zoë and Christopher went back to Warwick the following day, without saying goodbye to Josh.

'You don't like him, do you, Mummy?' Zoë asked her mother at breakfast before Christopher was down.

'It's you who have to like him, not me,' Lavinia replied.

Zoë pouted her lips and repeated the words Steve had said to her. 'I like him well enough.'

'Liking isn't love, Zoë.'

Her daughter looked down at the floor.

'Zoë, please think carefully about what you're doing, it's not too late, you know. Make sure this is the right man, before you commit your whole life to him.'

Wasn't that what she had done? She'd known that Josh was the right man when she'd first met him, and that knowledge had carried her through the whole of her married life. So why was she doubting it now?

'I'm in love with him,' Zoë said without conviction.

'Falling in love with someone and loving them for the rest of your life are not necessarily the same thing.'

'I don't understand.'

Lavinia looked pained. 'Neither did I, not for a long time.'

But Christopher joined them before Lavinia had time to say more.

Three days later, Josh and Lavinia received a scribbled note from Zoë thanking them for the visit, and announcing that, not only was she giving up her place at university but she was to marry Christopher. It would be a simple wedding, she said, with the child due in the summer they were desperately short of money; could Josh and Lavinia see their way clear to send them a cheque?

Josh spent days ranting and raving, he was determined that Christopher Goodland would have nothing of his. Lavinia wrote a loving note to her daughter telling her how much she loved her and hoped she and her husband would visit them again soon. She enclosed a fifty-pound note. She received no reply and no thanks. Six weeks later Zoë wrote again. Poor Christopher was still unable to get work although he was trying desperately hard; the electricity was about to be cut off, could Lavinia possibly help? They had no date set for the wedding yet, everything was so expensive, even the simplest of ceremonies would cost a fortune. So of course Lavinia sent them yet more money on that, and many more occasions.

Countless times she tried to explain to Josh what she thought their elder daughter was suffering. 'You know, Josh. Zoë was shattered when Steve married Ailsa. That week-end, the week-end of Philip's memorial service, when she saw that Ailsa was pregnant, I thought her heart would break.'

'Huh, now there's a young man who has ideas above his station, if ever there was one,' was Josh's ungracious reply.

'Give me Steve Jarvis over Christopher Goodland, any day of the week,' Lavinia retorted.

'They're both ne'er-do-wells,' Josh snapped back and left the room puffing and blowing.

Lavinia sighed. Josh wasn't even prepared to listen. But Alex listened, he listened and he advised, he poured soothing words on her troubled thoughts and he lovingly supported her in all she did.

Lavinia worked hard, she worked very hard; she had not a moment to spare, but moments could be stolen to see Alex Kirby. She had the dreadful conviction that her time with him was only borrowed, that one day she might well have to pay a price. It was as if a giant deficit was building up against her, and one day a knock would come on the door, and the collector of such things would be there with his demand. And she knew that should that day come, she would have no way of paying her debt. Alex was her sanity, her salvation, he listened to her pain, he rejoiced in her victories, and he understood her problems. It was he she confided in regarding Zoë. She used him as a sounding board; she practiced her own reactions on him. To her he was her sense of reason and he was becoming a greater part of her life than she had ever imagined possible.

Another shoot season ran its course, but although the actual season had come to an end the complaints did not. The keepers, for now there were five of them, spent the summer months building huge release pens in the woods and fussing over the tiny pheasant chicks. Chicks that soon grew into polts and grazed the tenant farmer's crops, leading to more complaints for Josh to follow up and sort out.

Life became a long list of strange, bizarre experiences – a pattern that seemed out of touch with the smooth order of their previous lives. A pattern that Lavinia felt sure would end in sorrow. She began to approach each day with a sense of foreboding, feeling that every hour she lived brought her closer to the time of reckoning.

CHAPTER FIFTY-NINE

Easter brought with it the start of another busy season of paying guests and Lavinia's life was set in a predictable pattern. She cooked, she cleaned, she entertained her guests and she juggled her finances, she ate and she slept. Once a month she had her hair done, twice a week she saw Alex Kirby; more, if her commitments allowed. She sympathized with Josh, and she tried to agree with his principles, but principles wear thin when sleep is short. And Alex was forever undermining her resolve, he didn't exactly condemn Josh for his beliefs; but he told Lavinia that his attitude was, and forever would be, different to Josh's. 'If you were my wife you would come before any property or inheritance.' He told her and said it with both force and conviction.

Josh was forever apologizing for the hard work she undertook, and justifying it with statements such as –

'I just want my children to inherit what is rightfully theirs. That can't be wrong, can it?' But his sweet words didn't make her any less tired or better tempered.

When she was with Josh she agreed with him, and when she was with Alex her loyalties shifted to his side. She felt frightened and lacking both in direction and control, her indecision and confusion began to wear her down. She confided her feelings to Brooke, who was completely devoid of understanding.

'Oh, Vinnie. You make such a big deal out of things, all this nonsense about loving and being in love. What you and Alex have has nothing to do with love – you're in lust with him, nothing more than that. Why make it so hard for yourself? You seem to think that if you were in love with him it would somehow justify the whole affair. But you should understand that you have lust between you, not love. It's escapism – nothing more than that.'

'And Josh?' Vinnie replied. 'What do Josh and I have?'

'Marriage – children – a history, that's what. All this stupid talk of love and loving, it's in your crotch, Vinnie, not your heart.'

The Lloyds crisis was talked about everywhere, the news papers were full of it. It seemed to Lavinia that everyday brought some new tragedy. Action groups were formed, lawyers employed and court cases were pending. Josh relied on Henry for advice, and Henry in turn relied on his city connections. A huge amount of paper from the Lloyds agent arrived by every post; communications that Josh pushed to one side, often not even bothering to open the envelope.

Josh refused to talk about Zoë and, for Lavinia, Zoë became another one of her secrets, a person she could no longer share with her husband, a shame not unlike the shame of Alex. If ever she tried to talk to Josh about their daughter, he would tell her that he would discuss Zoë just as soon as the girl came to her senses and had nothing more to do with Christopher Goodland.

'But, Josh, she's going to have a baby. I can't just turn my back on her.'

'You must do as you will, Vinnie. But don't expect me to do the same.'

Then came a rebuke that stung Lavinia and wounded her deeply. She wrote to Zoë telling her that she would go to Warwick and care for her when the baby was born. Zoë replied almost by return of post. They were once again desperately short of money; could Lavinia send them some? As for Lavinia's planned visit, Chris had decided that the child should have nothing to do with its maternal grandparents, and the message from him was that Lavinia would not be welcome in his home.

She showed the letter to Josh, who refused even to read, let alone discuss it. In the end, she showed it to Alex who soothed her and advised her not to send money but to go to Zoë unannounced.

But Lavinia was busy. Time passed; she was inundated with guests wanting B and B, the school fees were due again and so were the year's losses. She wrote back to Zoë enclosing a cheque, telling her to take care, and reassuring her that she would always be there if she were needed. The words, even as she wrote them, looked weak and feeble, but what more could she do?

The year sped past. By the end of the summer, Lavinia had gathered enough money for the autumn school fees, and Josh had taken out a loan to cover his losses.

A letter came from Zoë telling them that she had given birth to their first grandchild. She didn't even mention the sex of the child.

'Something's wrong, Josh, I know it is. I must go to her.'

'The only thing that's wrong is that nincompoop she's married to.'

'I don't think she is, Josh. Married, I mean.'

'I don't want to talk about Zoë,' Josh said sharply. 'You know I don't want to talk about her.'

So Lavinia talked to Alex, of course she did, and

Alex begged to be allowed to drive her to Warwick. Lavinia was overcome with relief and gratitude and she gratefully accepted his offer.

The week after the children went back to school, Lavinia announced that she was going to visit Zoë.

'Fine,' said Josh. 'But don't expect me to come with you.'

'I don't,' Lavinia said.

The journey to Warwick took over three hours.

The September sun heated the car and lifted their spirits. They stopped for a long lazy lunch and they talked and laughed like any other normal couple, they were relaxed and in love.

'Alex, it's wonderful to be with you.' Lavinia said at one point. 'I feel as if I'm a naughty child, playing truant from school.'

'It could be like this always,' he replied.

'It could, but we both know that it wouldn't be. It never is. Life never goes the way it's planned.'

He pulled her to him. 'You are such a pessimist, Vinnie Elliot. It could be good, if only you'd let go. What's the saying? Seize the day? If only you'd stop feeling responsible for the world, and be kind to yourself for once.'

'And am I being kind to myself by being in love with you?' She asked. 'It seems to me, that love brings its own special brand of pain.'

He looked at her tenderly. 'Vinnie, give us a chance?'

She turned away from him and laughed. 'Come on, I want to see my grandchild.'

He grabbed her arm. 'Vinnie?'

'No, Alex, it can't be.'

'Can't be what?'

'Forever.'

'You'll change your mind,' he said, smiling. 'After all, not many grannies get offers as good as this.'

She wrinkled her nose and laughed, the grandmother name did not sit well with her.

They reached the address on Zoë's letter at four in the afternoon. A thin, grimy faced girl, answered the door. There was a fusty unclean smell emanating from the tacky first-floor flat. 'No,' the girl told Lavinia; Zoë didn't live there; she just had her mail delivered there. Chris, Zoë's boyfriend, didn't want any of Zoë's family arriving at their door unannounced.

Lavinia, as quick-witted as ever, looked thoughtful for a moment.

'Oh dear,' she said. 'Now I don't quite know what to do. You see, Lavinia, Zoë's mother, is a friend of mine, and Zoë wrote to say she needed some money and, as I was coming to Warwick, I said I'd drop it in.'

'That's okay. You can leave it here. I'll give Chris a

bell and he'll come and collect it.'

Lavinia hesitated.

'It's all right, I'm not going to pinch it.' The girl looked indignant.

Lavinia hesitated a little longer. 'Do you have an envelope?' She asked.

The girl sighed, went back into the flat and appeared again with a crumpled white envelope. 'Will this do?'

Lavinia, put two twenty pound notes inside, wrote Zoë's name on the front and handed it to the girl.

'Ta,' the girl said, and immediately shut the door.

Lavinia went back to Alex, they maneuvered the car so they had a good view of the girl's flat and they settled down to wait. They didn't have to wait long. Within moments Chris appeared around the corner of the block of flats, he was on foot. This was not the Christopher she remembered from Hulver; she barely recognized him. He was unkempt, thin, and as Alex later said, a pathetic excuse of a man. They watched as the girl handed him the envelope, which he immediately opened. Lavinia could almost hear the derisive comment when he realized there was only forty pounds inside.

Chris walked back in the direction he had come. As planned, Alex hopped out of the car and followed him. Chris walked to the corner of the street, across a small concrete square dotted with a few park benches covered in graffiti, along a short street, and arrived at another block of flats similar to the one the girl had inhabited.

Chris bolted up the open steps to the first floor landing and pushed a door open. Alex hovered below, sheltered from sight by the overhanging balcony that ran the length of the first floor. Chris didn't close the door behind him, and Alex could clearly hear most of what was being said.

'I told you to write and ask your mother for some money. Look! Twenty bloody quid, what do you call that?'

Alex knew that Lavinia had left forty. Her wondered if the girl had helped herself, or if Chris had taken half of it.

'I can't specify how much she's to send, can I?'

Alex had never spoken to Zoë but guessed that it must be she who spoke.

'Get on the bloody phone to her, and bloody-well tell her you need some more.'

'I can't do that, Chris, my parents have given us enough, they work hard for their money.'

Alex heard a crack and knew exactly what it was even before he heard Zoë cry out. Zoë's cry was echoed by the thin insistent wail of a baby. He bolted up the stairs two at a time and barged into the flat.

'What the hell?' Chris said as Alex flung himself

into the room. Chris's hand was poised to deliver another blow. The baby was crying inconsolably.

'Police,' Alex said. He seized his wallet from his inner pocket and flashed his squash club membership card, instantly replacing it before Chris had a chance to register what it was.

'I don't believe it,' Chris said. 'Look, I'm clean, and if you want to search this place you'll need a warrant.'

Zoë was holding the side of her head, her face was red, and she was sniffing back tears.

Alex glanced around the room. The whole place was filthy, piles of baby cloths, unwashed bottles, dirty plates and mugs littered the floor; a large bluebottle fly buzzed around the room. A pram in the corner contained the howling child.

'I'd want danger money to search this place,' Alex quipped.

'Then, what do you want?'

'I was passing,' Alex said. 'I heard the young lady cry out. I thought something might be wrong.'

'Well, there is nothing wrong, so you can go on your way.'

Alex turned to Zoë. 'Is that right, Miss?'

Zoë looked tired and frightened, dark rings edged her dull eyes and her hair was lank and unwashed. 'That's right, there's nothing wrong,' she whispered.

'Are you sure?' Alex said gently.

'Of course she's bloody sure, she said so, didn't she?'

'Fine,' Alex said. He took a piece of paper from his pocket and wrote a number on it. He handed it to Zoë. 'Contact that number if you need any help,' he said.

Zoë glanced at what he had written; it was the number for Hulver Castle. Her mouth fell open and several tears slipped from her eyes.

Chris snatched the paper out of her hand and handed it back to Alex. 'She doesn't need any help,' he said. 'She has me if she needs any help.'

'Can't she speak for herself?'

'Get out,' Chris said. 'I know my rights – you've no business to be here. Now piss off.'

Alex held up his hand and backed toward the door. When he reached it he pointed his index finger at the man. 'Lay off, Goodland,' he nodded toward Zoë, ' otherwise you'll have me to deal with. OK?'

CHAPTER SIXTY

Alex returned to the car, and without saying a word to Lavinia he moved it so that they had a good view of the flat where Zoë and Chris lived.

'What is it?' Lavinia kept asking. 'Did you see her? Is she all right? Did you see the baby? Alex, speak to me.'

He switched off the engine, turned to her and held both her hands. Then he told her what had happened.

'So I wrote your phone number down on a piece of paper and gave it to Zoë, just so that she would know that I was from you and – Vinnie, if you could have seen the look on her face. She looked like a scared rabbit. Poor kid, she's very frightened, she looks all in.'

'I must go to her.' Lavinia made a move to leave the car.

'No, wait, he'll go out in a while.'

'How do you know?'

'He has a habit, and it needs to be fed, and he has

your money in his pocket.'

Lavinia wrinkled her nose. 'Habit?' She put her hand up to her mouth. 'Surely you don't mean drugs? How do you know?'

He patted her hand. 'I know, Vinnie. Believe me, I know. Half my clients have problems of that sort.'

'Then, why do you . . .' She sighed and started again. 'You've never told me Alex, why do you?'

'Represent them?'

'Yes.'

'It's a long story, but basically — ' he sucked in his lower lip. 'I had a brother who got himself in a bit of a fix. I was only a kid then. He couldn't afford a decent lawyer and he ended up with a court appointed representative. Needless to say he was sent away on remand.'

'And?' Asked Lavinia.

'And he killed himself. He couldn't handle it – being in prison – he couldn't stand it.'

'Oh, so you think representing the likes of Christopher Goodland will put things right? A one man campaign will rid the country of evil?'

'I'm a good lawyer, Vinnie. At least with me, they get a chance. At least I do my best. Everyone deserves a chance, Goodland isn't a dealer, Vinnie, he's a victim.'

Lavinia wanted to disagree with him; men that took drugs and preyed on innocent girls like Zoë didn't deserve a chance.

Before she could say more, they saw Christopher leave the flat, slamming the door as he went. The door bounced back from the door jam leaving it standing half-open. He looked neither left nor right, but put his head down, crossed the road in front of the car, and continued on his way.

They waited no more than a few seconds. Lavinia scrambled out of the car and, with Alex by her side, they made their way up to the flat.

'I'll wait here,' Alex stated as they reached the door. 'Just in case our hero returns.'

Lavinia pushed the door open and went in. 'Zoë? Zoë?' She called softly. She went through to the main living area. Zoë was hunched up on the settee, she was quietly sobbing; her once beautiful blond hair hung like a greasy shroud over her face. She was dressed in a grubby black tracksuit, and her feet were bare. She had put on weight and looked ungainly and not very clean.

Lavinia went over and sat down on the sofa beside her. Zoë didn't seem at all surprised. It was as if she'd expected her to arrive. Lavinia put her arm around her shoulders and the girl just fell onto her mother's breast and wept.

'I always knew you'd come,' she sobbed. 'I always knew you would.'

'Did you, darling?' That's' more than I knew, she thought. I wouldn't be here now if it wasn't for Alex.

'Mummy, I'm so sorry. I've acted so stupidly. I thought it was all going to be such fun, with him, Chris, I mean. But it's awful Mummy. It's awful. He —'

'Shush, darling, it's going to be all right. I'm here now, I'll take care of you.'

'Can I come home, Mummy? Please can I come home?'

'Of course you can.'

'Now, I mean. Now — before he comes back, please?'

A piteous little wail went up from the pram in the corner. Lavinia smiled. 'You can both come home,' she said, turning her head toward the sound.

'Who was the man? Is he really a policeman?'

Lavinia bit her bottom lip. 'Alex? He's a friend, just a friend. He's a lawyer, a barrister, and he offered to help me.'

Four hours later, Lavinia, Zoë and the baby, were safely delivered back to Hulver.

CHAPTER SIXTY-ONE

'But you wouldn't even talk to me about Zoë,' Lavinia retorted. 'I mentioned it to Mr Kirby the last time he stayed with us, and he said that if I needed any help I was to go to him and so — '

Josh interrupted her. 'How much did he charge? Really, Vinnie, I do think you should have consulted me first.'

'That's just the point, Josh. You wouldn't let me consult you.'

'I know, I know,' Josh shook his head and put his hand to his brow. 'I'm not blaming you but . . . well how much did he charge?'

'He did it as a favour.'

'What? What does he want in return?'

Lavinia blushed. 'Nothing. He said that he

considered himself a friend of the family.'

'Those boys don't do anything for nothing.'

'Josh, that's so unfair. He's a good man – he does most of his work on legal aid.'

'Isn't he a very good lawyer, then?'

Lavinia was indignant. 'He's very good – he just believes that everyone should have the very best legal representation.'

'You seem to know an awful lot about him.'

Lavinia blushed again; she turned her head away. 'I drove to Warwick and back with him, we had a lot of time to talk.'

'Oh. Oh, I see,' Josh said. He rubbed his temples with his fingers. 'I think I'll take Fen out for a walk.'

'Good idea,' said Lavinia. 'Why don't you take Zoë and your granddaughter with you?'

Josh wrinkled his nose. 'No, I think I'll just take Fen. You know, it's a bit awkward.'

Zoë had been home for two days and Josh had hardly spoken to her. He had seemed enchanted by the baby but had kept his distance from Zoë.

'Josh, you must talk to her. You can't go on like this – you must forgive her.'

Josh sat down heavily at the kitchen table. Lavinia thought he looked as if he were about to cry. 'Josh, what is it?'

'Don't you see? It's not a question of me forgiving her? I don't know how she'll ever forgive me. I hated it when she was with young Steve, and although I didn't like the Goodland boy, at least I felt that he was from a better class, more suitable for her. Yet Steve Jarvis has turned out to be both resourceful, and hard working – he's really pulled Ailsa's place into shape, whilst this other lad, whom I should have approved of, has turned out to be an absolute cad.'

Lavinia cradled his head in her arms. 'Josh. Josh, darling.'

'I'm a bit of a fool, aren't I, Vinnie? I always seem to get it wrong with the women in my life. I risk losing them because I'm too stupid to tell them how I really feel.'

Lavinia stared ahead of her. 'It's not your fault, Josh.' She was thinking of Alex.

'Oh it is. It is.'

'I tell you, it's not.'

Zoë came into the kitchen.

'What's, not what?'

She was looking much better, her hair was freshly washed and she was wearing decent clothes, the black circles under her eyes had faded and she had a spring in her step. In her arms she cradled a golden-haired, rosy-faced baby.

'You're father's blaming himself for not rescuing

you sooner.'

'Oh, Daddy!' She sat the baby in his lap and flung her arms around him. Standing the other side of him to Lavinia, she kissed the top of his head.

Josh smiled. 'Three women dancing attention on me, now that's three more than I deserve.'

CHAPTER SIXTY-TWO

'She can be awfully old fashioned,' Zoë said.

'Whatever do you mean?' Asked Alex.

It was Sunday morning. Lavinia and Josh had gone to Church. Alex had called at the castle. He said he was there to make sure Zoë and the baby were all right. Zoë was making him coffee in the kitchen, the baby was asleep in a crib in the corner of the room.

'Well, she's forgotten what it's like to be young.'

'Has she?'

'You wouldn't understand either,' Zoë said.

'Because I'm old?' He looked amused.

'I don't mean that. It's just that things have changed since you were my age. Everyone does drugs these days – everyone.'

'Do you?'

'Of course not, but I'm not like everybody else, am I?'

'You're not?'

'No, I'm different. I was talking about your average young person. What I'm trying to say is that Mummy is awfully judgmental. About Chris, that is. He's all right, really. He just hasn't grown up.'

'Not a very good omen for fatherhood.'

'Exactly, but it doesn't mean that he's all bad, does it?'

'Will you see him again?'

'I don't know. Daddy says he'll kill him if he comes here.'

'And your mother – what does she say?'

'She says that I'm old enough to make my own mind up.'

'And have you?'

Zoë laughed. 'Chris is a parasite. I don't think I'll ever see him again.'

'So what's the problem?'

'There isn't one. It's just that when the parents tell me I can't do a thing I automatically want to do it. Do you understand?'

'Oh yes. I'd feel the same way.'

'You see, there was a chap here once, he worked

for Daddy and I was terribly fond of him, and they didn't want me to see him, and so they sent him away.'

'They couldn't have sent him away if he hadn't wanted to go.'

Zoë frowned. 'He wanted to be with me, he – '

'What are you doing here?' Lavinia snapped as she entered the kitchen.

'I came to see how Zoë was. I — '

'She's fine,' Lavinia cut in before he could finish his sentence.

Zoë turned her back to make the coffee.

'How dare you come here?' Lavinia hissed under her breath. 'You're not a friend of the family.'

Alex smiled his confident lawyer smile. 'I thought that was my cover story,' he hissed back.

Zoë turned and looked from one to the other. 'Coffee? Mr Kirby,' she said.

'Mr Kirby's just leaving,' Lavinia said.

'Yes please, I'd love some,' Alex said at the same time.

'I see,' Zoë said. 'Actually, I don't see.' She held her hands up in front of her. 'However, I've got enough problems of my own so I'll leave you guys to it, shall I?' She backed out of the kitchen. 'Is it all right if I phone Tiggy? It's cheap-rate on Sundays.'

Tiggy was in Australia. Instead of one gap year,

Tiggy had decided to take two.

'Don't talk for too long, it's still expensive,' Lavinia said, not taking her eyes off Alex.

'I'm sorry,' Alex said as soon as Zoë had gone. 'I shouldn't have come. I just needed to see you, Vinnie. I want to be close to you.'

Lavinia looked close to tears. 'Please, Alex, you make it all so hard for me. You shouldn't be here, you don't belong in this part of my life.'

'But that's the point, Lavinia. I want to be part of all your life. Why won't you give me a chance? You deserve a better life than the one Josh is giving you.'

'You can't possibly know what sort of life Josh gives me, anymore than you can know what I do, or do not, deserve.'

Alex shook his head. 'You're quick, Vinnie. You know what? You'd have made a damned good lawyer.'

She laughed then. 'Oh, Alex, just go.'

'Tuesday?' He said as he reached the door.

She nodded. 'Tuesday,' she replied.

She poured herself some coffee. She couldn't go on like this. Why had it all become so complicated? In the early days it had seemed so easy, now she was being asked to make choices. Josh or Alex? Why couldn't she have both?

Her life was running away with her, she was late

for everything, everything except Alex. She always got to Alex on time. She'd been late for Church that morning. She knelt at her prayers and whispered, 'Sorry, God. Sorry I'm late, only I had to cook breakfast before I left.' She was reminded of the custom of putting a handful of wool in a shepherd's coffin so that the Lord knew his scanty attendance at Church was due to the demands of his profession. Perhaps someone would think to put a frying pan in her coffin.

Zoë came back into the kitchen. 'You don't like him, do you Mummy?'

'Who?'

'Mr Kirby. You don't like him, do you?'

'I do. He's all right, he's a good . . . good lawyer, I think. But your father doesn't like him to be here.'

'Daddy likes him.'

'Does he?' Lavinia looked weary.

'Yes, he does. So what have you got against him?'

'Nothing, Zoë. Leave it, will you?'

'That's so unfair, you judge people before you even know them, Alex is all right.'

'Alex?'

'It's okay. He told me to call him Alex.'

'I see.'

'You've got a bee in your bonnet about him. You always judge people before they've had a chance. You did the same with Steve. He's turned out okay and now you're doing it again, you're pre-judging Alex.'

'Zoë, I am not. You don't understand.'

'Too right I don't. You practically threw him out just now, and he only called to see if I was all right. You're so mean to him and he won't hear a word said against you.'

'Really.'

'So I think you should jolly well calm down, and stop judging people before you really know them.'

Lavinia took a gulp of her coffee. Life was getting very complicated; she was too tired to cope with this sort of thing.

'You're probably right, Zoë. Alex Kirby is probably a very nice man.'

'Well, he rescued me, didn't he?'

'No, Zoë, I rescued you. He came along for the ride. He was very supportive on that day and I think he's probably an excellent lawyer. But that's all he is to us, a lawyer, not a friend.' She pulled herself up from the table. 'I still have the beds to make, I must get on.' She fled from the kitchen and along the library passage. How dare Alex come into her home like this, how dare he invade her family life?

CHAPTER SIXTY-THREE

Brooke was excited. She had a booking, an important booking; she knew she could make a lot of money and there was nothing that Brooke liked more than making money. It had become an addiction with her.

Brooke's staff were well paid, and well trained. If they knew the true nature of her business they were discreet enough not to discuss it either between themselves or outside the house.

At six o'clock the butler announced that her visitors had arrived and Brooke greeted a manservant, who introduced himself as Abdul, and his master, whom he introduced as The Sheik. No other name or title was given.

Abdul explained that the Sheik did not speak English and therefore Abdul would be translating for him. He also informed Brooke that his Master would like to avail himself of her special room service straight away.

'Sorry,' Brooke said, 'room service doesn't begin until after nine o'clock, but I'd be glad to arrange it for you then.'

Abdul translated this to his master. The Sheik was dark skinned, very tall and very, very fat. He had fat jowls that shook as he spoke, and his hooked nose was squashed flat to his fleshy cheeks, making his breathing noisy. His eyes were buried in two narrow slits cut deep into his puffy face. He was dressed in traditional Arab garb and his large belly protruded in front of him. The manservant was a much more imposing man, he was tall and swarthy, his features were defined and handsome, he was fit and muscular.

Brooke surveyed the two men; she wished their roles were reversed, the servant was a younger and altogether more attractive proposition. She smiled to herself noting the expanse of gold that blanked out one of the Sheik's front teeth and covered each of his chubby fingers from the knuckle to the first joint. I can do this, she thought, I can do this very well, but it will cost him, it will cost him dearly.

At dinner, Abdul rewarded the waiting-staff with a crisp ten-pound note for every dish they brought to the table. Brooke looked on with veiled amusement. This will cost him a great deal, she thought again. The Sheik never took his eyes off her, but watched her with a crooked, rather lecherous grin. Occasionally he spoke to Abdul in Arabic.

'What's he saying?' Brooke asked.

Abdul laughed and said something to his master. The Sheik nodded his head as if to give permission for Abdul to tell her.

'The Sheik says you have very small breasts, like that of a girl child.'

Brooke gave an uncomfortable laugh.

The Sheik spoke again.

'The Sheiks says to tell you that he very much like deflowering girl children, so you will do okay.'

'Good,' Brooke said. She shuddered, the Sheik sounded not quite nice. I only hope he can afford me, she thought.

'The Sheik would like room service at ten o'clock sharp,' Abdul informed her.

At nine-thirty Brooke excused herself from the table and went up to her dressing room from where she telephoned Henry. She marveled at herself for being able to have a rational ordinary chat before earning her money lying on her back under a huge Arab Sheik. She shuddered again, what would it be like? And how much dare she charge? She acknowledged to herself that paid sex gave her a thrill, it made her feel powerful and in control.

Henry said that he was tired and was going to have

an early night. Brooke in return told her husband that she was about to do the same.

At ten, dressed in a flowing red caftan, Brooke made her way to the Sheik's bedroom. Although over the past couple of years she had slept with many men, most of them from the Middle East, but she had never encountered anyone quite like the Sheik. Certainly she had never made love with anyone as fat, and all the others had had a good command of the English language; nor had any of them admitted to liking young girls. But she put that aside. It should, she told herself, be both an easy and profitable night, a nice addition to the nest egg she was building without Henry's knowledge. She was determined to safeguard herself and her children against Henry's bankruptcy.

She tapped on the guest room door and was greeted by Abdul who was dressed in an elaborate, gold encrusted, robe. He ushered her inside the room locking the door behind her: an action that gave her a flicker of unease. The sight that greeted her left her open-mouthed. The Sheik was standing in the middle of the room, his feet planted firmly on a square red cloth. The great mountain of a man was totally naked. His body was smooth and completely hairless. Around him were several bowls of highly scented oils and the whole room was illuminated by dozens of candles.

Brooke gulped, she couldn't take her eyes off him, he had gold rings piecing his nipples, a heavy gold chain looped around his waist, and his penis, which stood large and erect, was also pierced with gold studs and rings.

'You are a little early,' Abdul said. 'That pleases the Sheik. As you see, he is almost ready for you, he will not keep you waiting for long.'

Abdul went over to his master and, dipping his fingers into the oils, he anointed his body. Starting at the shoulders and then massaging his chest, his buttocks, and finally his very, very engorged penis.

'Come,' Abdul said. 'Now I must prepare you, Lady Osbourne-Pennington.'

Brooke held up her hands. 'I don't think so, Abdul. I think it's time to leave the Sheik to it.'

Abdul smiled at her in a patronizing way. 'But you do not understand. I am the bodyguard. I do not leave my Master at any time.'

'That wasn't the deal,' Brooke said. She was beginning to sweat.

The Sheik said something to Abdul.

'His most revered Majesty says, what is the problem? Perhaps you would like to talk money, Lady Osbourne-Pennington?' He exchanged a few more words with the Sheik.

'The Sheik, he say, he would like to see your girl

493

body first, and then he make you an offer.' Abdul waved his arms toward the Sheik. 'You can see what a fine man the Sheik is. You are a very lucky woman.'

Brooke gulped; she was both frightened and excited.

'I'm not a camel, he can't look me up and down, prod me with a stick, and decide how much I'm worth. I have a price, and if the Sheik doesn't like it, then I'll leave.' She turned toward the door.

The Sheik said something in Arabic, and Abdul replied at great length.

Then, turning to Brooke, Abdul said, 'The Sheik says, how much?'

Brooke took a deep breath. 'Two thousand.'

'Two thousand?'

'Correct,' Brooke said.

'One thousand.'

Brooke turned as if to leave. The Sheik said something.

'OK,' Abdul said. 'Two thousand.'

'Cash, now, before you begin. And it's an extra five hundred if you want to watch – and make sure your boss wears one of these,' she handed him a packet of condoms. 'And make sure those ridiculous rings don't rip the rubber.'

'They won't,' Abdul replied. 'But they will give

you much pleasure.'

'I'm not looking for pleasure,' Brooke said. 'I'm looking for hard cash.'

'Maybe you will have both,' Abdul said, fixing her clear blue eyes with his muddy brown stare.

He took a silk wallet out of a drawer, counted out two thousand pounds in crisp fifty-pound notes, and placed them in her palm. She noted that the wallet still contained at least as much again.

'And the five hundred?' She said.

'I think we both know that you should be satisfied with what I have given you. Come, it is time to begin.'

Brooke bit into her bottom lip. Two thousand pounds wasn't to be sniffed at. She plunged the money into the pocket of her caftan.

The Sheik was still standing on the red cloth, he was holding his penis close to his fat stomach and he was running his thumb round and around the end. Brooke noted that his face held the same lecherous grin as it had throughout dinner.

Abdul took the hem of her caftan and pulled it up over her head. She stood naked, but she was not in the least bit embarrassed. She had a job to do, a job she had trained for years ago in New York, a job that had introduced her to Henry, Lord of the Pennington Estates. Seduction was her job; it was a craft she was familiar with, and a task that she did well.

The servant placed three pillows high on the bottom edge of the bed and, leading her by the hand, he gently laid her back over them so that her hips were in the air and her head was resting on the bed below. She couldn't see what the Sheik or his servant was doing. She waited quietly, a shudder of excitement went through her; she smiled and recognized again how much selling sex excited her. It always had, she was far more likely to get satisfaction from selling, even to the roughest of men, than ever she got from giving to the gentle Henry.

Suddenly, without warning, she felt a warm gush of water swell over her pubic area. My God, she thought, he's washing me – he must think that I'm not clean. She almost laughed aloud. Then she felt the tug of a razor as Abdul began to remove her pubic hair. She began to struggle. 'Keep still,' Abdul warned, 'I do not want to cut you.'

He wiped the blade of the razor on a cloth, and when Brooke saw that it resembled an old fashioned cut-throat, she lay very still indeed.

Abdul then took oil and anointed the whole of her body. It was warm and sweet smelling. Brooke relaxed; she breathed in the pungent fragrance and gave herself over to the expert sensual massage. Abdul's strong hands kneaded her buttocks, caressed her breasts and stroked her thighs, bringing her to such a height of arousal that she almost begged to be entered.

Abdul parted her legs and massaged her labia, then, at last, the Sheik moved from the red cloth and loomed over her at the bottom of the bed. She was sweating; tiny drops of perspiration trickled down her neck. She could see the Sheik's huge belly, but not his penis, which he lay along the length of her parted labia. He kept very still, she could feel his penis gently throbbing, she lifted her hips toward it, wanting more than anything for it to be inside her. The Sheik said something to Abdul. Abdul laughed and climbed onto the bed, sitting just beyond her head with a leg either side of her. She was not surprised to see that beneath the robe he too was naked. He leaned forward and placed a hand on each breast. He nodded to the Sheik and the Sheik in turn began to push his penis into her. The adornments on his penis made him feel huge, but Brooke wanted all that he had. She curled her legs around his wide girth and tried to maneuver him deeper into her, she wanted to be filled to bursting. She was breathing hard. She swung her head to the left and saw that she was facing Abdul's excited erection. Without a moment's hesitation, she took him in her mouth and sucked like a baby at the breast. His thighs squeezed her shoulders as he shook and convulsed with pleasure.

At the other end of her body, the Sheik, his hands

firmly on her hips, rocked back and forth. His vast weight added to his thrust, sending wave after wave of excitement through the Lady of Pennington Manor. To Brooke it seemed to go on forever, and yet still she craved for more, a desire that was not denied her.

She did not leave the Sheik's room until eight o'clock the following morning, and she had not closed her eyes for one single moment of the ten hours that she had been there. All parties felt that they had both given and received excellent value for money.

The Sheik and his man ate breakfast in their rooms. Before they left, the Sheik took Brooke's hand and, planting the lightest of kisses on it, he told her in perfect English that he had had a very enjoyable stay and that he hoped to return again the following month. He would, he said, like to introduce her to one or two of his favorite sons.

CHAPTER SIXTY-FOUR

On Friday evening Brooke greeted Henry with her usual American charm and warmth. They had dinner together and discussed plans for the following evening when Josh and Lavinia were coming to dinner.

'I thought Lavinia couldn't get away because of the B and B lark. Has she got some help at last?'

'No, not exactly, I told you, Zoë's home and she's going to hold the fort.'

Henry nodded. Brooke thought that he seemed suddenly old; she frowned. Men took loss of money so close to the heart.

'Good, good, I do need to talk to Josh about this new Equitas deal – he won't understand a word of it. I know it will be a huge relief to him, well, to both of them. I don't think Lavinia has been quite as successful as you with her money-making projects.'

'Some of us have what it takes,' she said. There was

not the slightest hint of either sadness or embarrassment in her voice.

They finished their meal. Brooke gave instructions to the butler regarding the plans for the following day and they retired to bed.

Brooke was sure of one thing, she did not want to make love with Henry, not that night – perhaps not any night. She did not understand what had brought her to this point. Her night with the Arabs had changed her. Perhaps she had always felt this way. If she were going to have sex, then she wanted payment in return. Perhaps with Henry the same deal had always existed? Henry had wealth and property, even a title; it seemed like a fair exchange. Now his money was being swept away, and with it had gone the excitement. He had a huge amount of money to find in order to finally settle his underwriting account. Perhaps the trade was no longer a good one.

She switched off her bedside light and turned her back toward her husband. The bed rocked as he got in beside her. She had undressed in the bathroom and put her silk pajamas on. Her lack of body hair made her feel ridiculously naked.

Henry put his hand on her back and moved it up and around her shoulders, she pulled the top of the duvet tighter around her neck. She heard Henry sigh as he turned over so that they were lying back to back.

In the early hours of the morning, Henry snuggled up to her and slipped his hand down beyond the elastic of her pajamas. He sat up abruptly, and flicked on the bedside light. 'What the devil?'

Brooke had been in a deep sleep; her eyes snapped open as the light assaulted her eyelids.

'Henry? Henry, what's the matter?'

Henry had pushed the bedclothes back, and he was now tugging at her pajama bottoms.

'Brooke, Brooke, what have you done?'

She tried in vain to pull her pants up. 'Oh . . . er . . . I thought . . . ' She shrugged her shoulders and then she laughed. 'Well, you know, Henry. Variety is the spice of life, isn't it?'

'Good, God, you look . . . well, you look naked, you look — '

She kissed him on the cheek; she had regained some of her self-control.

He had his leg over hers; she could feel his hardness on her thigh. Her pajamas were down around her knees; something in the arrangement of her clothes made her feel sordid and dirty. She tugged at the silk material with her right hand. With her left hand she tried to push Henry away from her. But he was immovable; he pressed onto her, rocking back and forth with his hips.

She was seized with an inexplicable panic. 'Henry,

I'm tired. Please, I'm so very, very tired.' But in fact she was wide awake, her mind was spinning. Not only did she not want Henry to make love to her, the thought of it actually repelled her. What had happened to her? Business or pleasure? The words hung about her brain and refused to go away.

Henry was very excited. 'So how am I supposed to find the right place with no fluffy stuff to guide me in?' He was sliding on top of her.

'Not tonight, Henry, please. Not tonight. Tomorrow. I'm tired – we'll make love tomorrow.'

'Okay,' Henry said. 'We'll do it tomorrow, but just let me have a little practice now.

'No!' There was true panic in her voice. 'No, Henry! No!'

He slid away from her, the light blazed in her eyes.

'What's the matter, Brooke?'

'Nothing, nothing, it's late, much too late. I have a lot to do tomorrow.'

Henry flopped back onto the pillow and Brooke felt that she was back totally in control. 'Sweet man,' she said. 'I do love you.' And as she said it, she knew that she did love him. Business or pleasure; the phrase popped back into her head. Last night was meant to have been business, but it had given her pleasure, far more pleasure than Henry ever had. Perhaps it had been that way for a long time –

she just hadn't realized it.

'Don't spoil it, Henry, I'll be rested tomorrow.' She would too. She'd work out exactly what her feelings of this moment meant. She'd sort her head out, she'd find the reason and then the answer, but for now she really was too tired.

Henry was staring up at the ceiling. 'Why'd you shave your fanny?'

She laughed. 'I'm an American remember? An American fanny is an English bottom.'

Henry wasn't laughing, he pushed his hand roughly between her legs. 'Here, just here,' he said gruffly. 'Why'd you shave?'

'I thought it might excite you – make you think you were with a young virgin.'

'That, Brooke, my dear wife, is an obscene thought and, by the way, I doubt you were ever a young girl, let alone a virgin.'

He thumped the pillow with his fist and turned his back toward her. Within ten minutes he was asleep.

Brooke lay in the darkness; sleep completely evaded her. Something had happened; something had changed. When? Was it the moment when, instead of paying all the special room service monies into the school account, she had salted some of it away for her own particular rainy day?

CHAPTER SIXTY-FIVE

Josh and Lavinia arrived at Pennington early. Brooke was still upstairs getting ready. Neither she nor Henry had mentioned the incident of the night. They had been polite to each other, but no more than that. Despite Brooke's resolutions, she had not thought through her difficulties with Henry. She just clung to the vain hope that it would work itself out, forgetting for once her favorite saying, that one had to make things happen, as they would not often happen by themselves.

Henry immediately took Josh off to his study in order to explain the details of the Lloyds settlement offer. Eventually Brooke joined Lavinia in the drawing room.

'This must be a record,' Brooke said. 'I've never known you guys to be early before.'

'Oh, I know, we should have done the polite thing and waited outside in the car, but it was so very cold out there. We figured that we knew you well enough to risk a black mark.'

'Black mark? Ah, you English are so proper. We Americans are much more down to earth and, frankly, much more honest. Why are you early, anyway?'

Lavinia laughed. 'It was Zoë. She more or less threw us out. We've got two couples in tonight and Zoë is cooking for them. She's been hard at it all afternoon and she was determined to do everything herself and refused to let me help. It's her way of thanking us.'

'Thanking you? For what?'

'Oh, you know. Having her back home, rescuing her, accepting her and the baby – it's very complex.'

'That's what I mean about the English, why can't she just say 'thank you' like any straight-talking American?'

'Because, Brooke, actions speak louder than words,' Lavinia laughed.

Josh and Henry joined them. Josh was quite literally scratching his head. 'I'll be ruled by you, Henry. If you say it's all right to sign, then I shall sign.'

'Yes, but how will you raise the funds to settle?'

'Oh, I've already spoken to Bamford about that.'

'Bamford?'

'My bank manager. You met him. Let me see now, it was the last year that the shoot was in hand.' He looked at Lavinia. 'When was that? Must have been, let me see? It was the same year that poor old Philip topped himself –

ninety-three? No, must have been ninety-two. It seems longer than that – a lifetime ago.'

Henry tapped Josh on the arm. 'You really miss the shoot, don't you, Josh? Never mind. If the names accept the settlement offer, in a year or two things will be back to normal.'

'I don't think anything will ever be normal again,' Lavinia said.

Henry knocked back the scotch he was drinking. 'What do you mean, Lavinia?' He laughed, but his eyes didn't laugh with him. He helped himself to another scotch, waving the decanter around in a gesture that offered it to the others, but their glasses were still full.

'Normal? I mean it can't be, can it? You can't go back, only forward. When all this started we didn't have a grandchild and — '

'You're surely not blaming Lloyds for the advent of Zoë's child?'

'Well it had something to do with it. If I'd had time for her – been around for her more, she might never have got herself into trouble. She never recovered from seeing Philip – you know, after he'd killed himself. And that's one thing you can lay at Lloyd's door, Philip's suicide.'

'I disagree,' retorted Henry. 'The industrial park was in trouble long before the Lloyds thing cropped up.

Philip was a bad businessman, that's all there is to it. Young Jarvis seems to have pulled the estate around, and he had Philip's debts to cope with into the bargain. If an uneducated man like Jarvis can do it, so could Philip.'

'Did you see the full page spread in The Times on Sunday about their holiday cottages?' Brooke hastily added. Henry and Lavinia were sounding rather heated. Henry was drinking too much.

'I can't think what Ailsa's thinking of, marrying a man old enough to be her son,' Brooke said.

'Don't you mean, young enough?' Josh asked.

'I can see the attraction,' Lavinia said. Everyone looked at her. 'What? Well, I can. After poor old Philip, Steve must have been a breath of fresh air.'

'And every woman likes a breath of fresh hair I expect,' Henry said, deliberately adding an H. He topped his glass up again.

'I think dinner is probably ready,' Brooke said.

No one made a move.

'So Bamford will see you through, will he?'

'Provided it's not too far over the top, yes.'

'But how will you pay it off?'

'Well, we'll still do the B and B's of course and — '

'You won't sell anything then?'

'Lord no, not if I can help it.'

Lavinia listened to the men talking and, for a brief

moment, she was back with Alex, and he was saying how he thought Josh undervalued her.

'The first thing I'll do if they reach an agreement will be to get the shoot back.' Josh rubbed his hands together. 'That'll be the day, hey, Henry? Back at Hulver for a good day's shooting, what?'

'But if we continue to let the shoot we could cut down on the Bed and . . . ' Lavinia's voice died away, no one was listening to her. Josh was relating his latest clash with the shooting syndicate. Henry was knocking back his third, or was it his fourth, scotch and glaring at Brooke, and Brooke was saying that she thought they should all go through to dinner.

Dinner was spent in more or less the same vein as the pre-dinner drinks. Henry was still drinking heavily and Josh couldn't stop talking about the antics of his shoot tenants.

Henry topped up everyone's wineglasses. He staggered a little as he made his way back to the head of the table; he was trying to put the cork back in the bottle. 'Look at that,' he said. 'I knew I could do it, given the opportunity. Look, I got it back in the hole and there's no hair around it to guide me.'

Even Josh stopped talking.

'Henry, please! You're drunk,' Brooke said. There was disgust in her voice.

'What? What is it?' Henry said.

'Henry,' Brooke said gently. 'You've had rather too much to drink. Sit down darling, you're making a fool of yourself.'

Lavinia tried to laugh. The room had become suddenly silent, but the sound of her effort died in her throat.

'Fool of myself, am I?' Henry said, his voice had lost its raucous edge. 'Fool? Yes that's me. A fool.' He sat down heavily. 'I am a fool, and I play the fool, whilst my wife rushes around making enough money for the ship to keep afloat, and what use am I to her? She's even paying for the bloody wine I get drunk on.'

The room was deathly silent.

Brooke scraped her chair back from the table. 'Come on – let's open up the ball room and dance. We have something to celebrate. We'll put some tapes on and we'll . . . '

Henry was sitting with his head propped in his hands, he turned to Josh, Brooke was still standing. 'Do you ever take the bookings, Josh. For the B and B's?' he didn't wait for an answer. 'I took one today, they wanted room service, they said. Does Lavinia do room service? If so, I think I'll come and stay at Hulver. I don't get much service here you see, despite the fact that I can get a cork in a bottle without hair around the hole to guide me in.'

Brooke sat down again. 'Henry? You're drunk, darling. You don't know what you're talking about.'

'Oh, I think I do, Brooke. The gentleman was most specific.'

Lavinia stood. 'I think it's time we went,' she said.

'But —' said Josh, gulping down the remaining wine in his glass.

'I definitely think we should go now,' Lavinia said. Within a few minutes Josh and Lavinia were driving back to Hulver.

'What was that all about? You'd think that Brooke was selling her body rather than catering to her B and B's.'

'Better to sell it than give it away,' Lavinia said flippantly.

'It depends who you give it to,' Josh joked back.

'Yes I suppose it does,' Lavinia said, thinking of Alex.

CHAPTER SIXTY-SIX

'I did it for us! If you can't see that, then you're mad.'

'You can't bear to have me touch you, can you?'

'Henry that's — '

'That's what? Not true? You shudder whenever I come near you.'

'That is not true, Henry.'

'Then why haven't we made love?'

'Probably because you're too bloody drunk.'

'The drunk and the prostitute, what a wonderful couple we make.' Henry was shouting.

'Keep your voice down Henry, the staff will hear.'

'The staff already know, my dear. Where do you think I got my information from?'

'What? You've been questioning my staff?'

'Your staff?'

'I took them on and I pay their wages.'

Henry had an almost cruel look on his face. 'And

I expect this is your house, is it?'

'Well I pay for its bloody upkeep.'

'Hardly, my dear, your charms may be wonderful, but not quite wonderful enough to run this place.'

'My charms, as you call them, are worth two thousand a night!'

'What? In that case, I can't afford you.'

Henry put his hand up to his brow. 'Did you say two thousand a night? A night? Are you sure?'

She nodded.

'So, how much? How much have you – have you scraped together?'

'I've been paying Henry junior's school fees.'

'And?'

'Well I've paid the staff of course and I've saved a bit.'

'How much?'

'How much what?

'How much have you got stashed away?'

'About a hundred thousand.'

'Good, God. You know, that might easily do it!'

'Do it?'

'Pay the settlement, get us clear of Lloyds.'

'No, Henry, that's my money. I earned that money.'

'But you're my wife.'

'Am I, Henry?'

'Yes, I'm afraid you are. That was the deal – remember? What I have, you share, what you have, I share. Only I haven't shared my body with anyone else.'

'I didn't share my body, Henry. I sold it. There's a world of difference.'

'There is, isn't there? And to be honest I don't like either option.'

Their arguments and discussions went on day and night. Henry didn't go into work the following Monday but took time off from the city. Brooke turned clients away, and still they could reach no compromise, no middle ground. Brooke insisted that she still loved Henry but no longer wanted an intimate relationship with him. Henry was the reverse. He said that he loved what he thought she was, not what she'd become, but he still very much wanted a physical relationship with her.

'Disease?' He shouted one day, 'What about disease? You could catch something, and give it to me or the children.'

'Well I haven't. I'm very careful. For God's sake, Henry, I know what I'm doing.'

'I can't bear it. I can't bear the thought of them touching you, their body parts coming into contact with you.'

'Men! What is your problem, Henry? Having sex doesn't use anything up. It doesn't take anything away,

513

there's always plenty left.'

'But there isn't, is there? You don't want to make love with me anymore. It should be me not wanting to make love with you, not the other way round.'

'I love you,' she said simply. 'Okay, I admit I've got a problem. I don't know – it's like the difference between, business and pleasure. I love you and the sex thing is like–'

'A job?'

'Yes. Yes, that's it. It's a kind of job, that's just what it is, and you know in your heart of hearts, that I value you above anyone.'

'But you don't feel anything for these men. Yet you happily go to bed with them but you can't bear me to touch you. Why can't you just pretend that I'm one of your customers?' He took a twenty-pound note out of his pocket. 'Here you are, does this help? Pretend that I'm paying you.'

'Henry, you're acting in a ridiculous manner.'

'Who else does this? Does Lavinia? Ailsa? How about poor old Hillary? Come to think of it, Hillary would probably be grateful for a bit of attention.'

'That's a horrid thing to say.'

'Well, answer me.'

'I'm the only one. Lavinia did it once, but didn't use any protection and frightened herself to death.'

It was obviously not the answer he had expected.

514

'What? Does Josh know?'

'Of course not. Henry, you won't say anything, will you? It only happened once and it was a mistake for her.'

'I'd expect Josh to tell me if the boot were on the other foot.'

'Henry, promise me you won't say anything?'

'Promise? Promise? What do promises mean? You promised me a few things once.'

'What things?'

'Something about promising to keep you only unto me for as long as we both shall live.'

'For God's sake, Henry. A load of religious mumbo-jumbo. I suppose you'd be happier if I'd found a man and had an affair with him, rather than made a bit of money to save your inheritance?'

'As a matter of fact, I would. At least it would show that you had a heart.'

The arguments continued. Brooke felt misunderstood. Hadn't she sacrificed herself for the sake of her husband?

'Just tell me that you didn't enjoy it, that's all I want to know. Tell me that it gave you no pleasure.'

'Henry, for God's sake. Of course I didn't enjoy it. It was a job, that's all — just a way of making money.' But that was a lie, and at least she recognized it as a lie.

Brooke Osbourne-Pennington lived in a beautiful house, she had staff looking after her, and she could afford almost anything she wanted. She had a title, a handsome sociable husband, and she had what she now acknowledged as a bizarre and exciting sex life. Not all her clients had been exciting. Indeed a good percentage had been boring and tedious, but these men were forgotten. Her Arab Sheik and his manservant had quite literally rubbed all the other memories away. But why couldn't Henry just leave it alone, why did he have to go on about it so?

'Were they good at it?'

'Who? Good at what?'

'Your men? Were they good at sex?'

A shiver went through her. She thought of Abdul; she could practically taste him in her mouth, she remembered her scented body next to his thigh. She took too long to answer.

'Of course they weren't good at it. If they were they wouldn't need to pay for it, would they?'

'What if I did that, what if I sold my body? Or what if, to make money, I sold child pornography or something like that?'

'Then you would be breaking the law, and that's different. I haven't done anything that's illegal.'

'Okay, so what if I sold my body – became a male

rostitute?'

'With women or with men?'

'Both – either – what the hell. Where would you raw the line, Brooke?'

'But you're not queer or anything and –'

'Maybe I'd get to like it? Maybe I'd find it a urn-on and wouldn't want you anymore. Is that what's appened, Brooke. Is that the case? Your clients have urned you on, and you don't want me anymore because ney are more exciting? Well if it's excitement you want –'

He took her by the wrists and dragged her toward ne wide staircase. He pulled her up the stairs one at a time, ne struggled and she fought. She tried to pull away from im; he was hurting her wrists. She was half standing and alf-kneeling, her knees were burned on the edges of the arpet. At the top of the stairs he did not turn right toward neir own room but took her to one of the guest rooms, which happened to be the one that she had shared with ne Arabs. It still smelled faintly of the oil they had used nd she was immediately reminded of her night spent in xual ecstasy. Henry flung her down onto the bed and, one too gently, he pulled at her clothing; ripping the ems that didn't undo easily. He did not remove his own othes; he simply unzipped his fly. He pushed her legs art bending her at the waist and took her with speed and olence. He spoke and acted in a rough aggressive

517

manner. Brooke whimpered, her body ached, her knee and wrists hurt, her mouth was bruised from his rough kisses, and she loved every minute; she was in ecstasy, sh though she would die with the thrill of it.

Afterwards Henry zipped his fly and stood by th side of the bed. 'I think we both know where we stan now, don't we, my little tart?' He spoke through clenche teeth.

Ten minutes later she heard his car drive away.

CHAPTER SIXTY-SEVEN

Henry drove as far as Royston where he pulled into a Little Chef. He ordered coffee and sat gazing into its brown depths. He was frightened; he had practically raped his wife, and it had excited him. He couldn't remember being that turned-on before, except perhaps . . .

It seemed to him that he'd been married to a stranger. Brooke and he had first met in seventy-five. He'd been invited to a convention in New York and had been introduced to a US Senator, who happened to have Brooke draped on his arm. There was no doubt about it, Brooke had certainly come on to him in a big way, especially when she heard that he belonged to the English aristocracy. That's when it had all begun; from then on he'd been fascinated by her. He seemed to bump into her at every function he went to, and like as not she was with a different escort. That didn't matter; she was a very attractive woman and it was natural that she should have a string of admirers. She'd made no secret of the fact that she'd slept around; after all, this was the age of the sexual revolution, why shouldn't she? It hadn't repelled him. In fact, the descriptions of the antics of other lovers excited him, and made him want her even more – made him want exclusive rights over her, and that's how he felt now, he wanted her only for himself. And yet the thought of her with other men still excited him and he wanted details – graphic details. For Henry, a tinge of jealousy added spice to the meal of love.

He asked for more coffee, realized that he hadn't eaten at all that day, and ordered a large all-day breakfast. After yet more coffee he made a move. He looked at his watch as he left the restaurant. There was no point in him going to work that day; by the time he reached London he'd hit the evening rush hour. He climbed into his car and turned northeast toward Norwich. When he reached the city he took the ring road and drove toward Pennington, but on the way he saw the signs to Hulver and once again changed direction.

He met Josh on the drive, the ever faithful Fen at his heels. Henry stopped the car and opened the window.

'Henry! What a surprise!'

'I came to apologize for the other night. I'm afraid I was a little out of line.'

'Were you, old chap? Can't say I noticed.'

'Josh, you are such a gentleman. Where's your good lady? It's her, to whom I ought to be giving my apologies. And where's this wonderful grandchild of yours – I hear she's quite a stunner.'

' Yes, she is rather special,' Josh said proudly. 'The ladies are in the house, do go up. I promised Fen I'd give her an airing.' He bent over the car window and lowered his voice. 'And I want to see what this new keeper chap's been up to in the north wood.' He looked from left to right as if afraid of being overheard. 'You'll excuse me? Only I don't quite trust these city gents. Real city dwellers – not like you, I mean. You understand?'

'Oh, I understand, all right,' Henry laughed.

'I'll be up in ten minutes. Tell Vinnie to put the kettle on.'

Henry found Lavinia in the kitchen. She had Zoë's baby, Elizabeth, on one hip and she was stirring soup with her free hand. Zoë was nowhere to be seen.

'Henry! How nice to see you. Is Brooke with you? I expect you've come to see Josh – he's just popped out with Fen – officially to take her for a walk, but he's in a state about the release pen in the north wood.'

'Yes, I saw him. But, in fact, it was you I wanted to see.'

'Oh?'

'I came to apologize about the other night.'

'You'd drunk too much, that's all, Henry.'

'I behaved like a buffoon, and I'm sorry, Lavinia.'

Lavinia smiled. 'Have some tea, Henry. I'll put the kettle on.' She took the soup off the Aga and maneuvering Elizabeth onto her other hip, she filled the kettle and placed it on the hob.

The child gave a little whimper and laid her golden head on her grandmother's shoulder. Her eyes were closing.

'Ah, good, time for a nap. The twins were home at the weekend and they spoil this little one to death. No one can do anything with her when they go back to school.' She laid the baby in the crib that was situated in the corner of the kitchen.

'You're very good with her, Lavinia. Zoë is a lucky girl. Is she going to finish her degree course now she has you to look after the baby?' He'd made a fist with his hand and was screwing it into the palm of his other hand.

Lavinia's hair had, at some time in the day, been twisted into a French pleat. Now her brow was damp, her cheeks flushed, and little wisps of hair escaped from the once sophisticated hairstyle. She looked the perfect picture of domesticity, an apron tied around her waist, the soup simmering, the baby sleeping, the kettle boiling on the hob.

He saw her mouth tighten, she sat down at the

table and stretched her back. 'Henry, you don't understand. I'm helping Zoë right now because she needs me. But I can't go on, I don't want another child. The boys are practically off my hands, and Tiggy will be at university next year. My life should be getting easier, not harder. If I had wanted more children, then Josh and I would have had them.'

'But you look so content. I wish Brooke was domesticated like you – this place is so homely, so right, so welcoming.'

'And you *are* very welcome, Henry. It's nice to have you here. Just don't misread what you see. I'm actually finding everything rather a trial.'

Henry looked puzzled.

'I'm not enjoying it. I hate the bed and breakfast. I hate the dinners, even more, and I hate not having any freedom.'

And then he said it. The words sounded strange to him; so strange it was as if he were listening to someone else speaking. 'My wife quite enjoys the bed and breakfast, or at least, she certainly enjoys the bed bit.'

Lavinia stared at him, she had the teapot poised in mid air, it was as if the moment had frozen in time – a video halted with the pause button.

'She told me that you knew. She said that you had tried it yourself once. But that you had frightened yourself.'

Lavinia was white-faced.

'So you see, she's no more faithful to you than she is to me.' He swallowed noisily as he saw the pain on Lavinia's face. This wasn't what he had planned to do. Hurting Brooke's friend did not lessen his own hurt, indeed it seemed to increase his sorrow.

Lavinia sat down at the table. 'Oh, Henry,' she said. 'I'm so very sorry.'

Henry wasn't quite sure what Lavinia was sorry for, but the stricken look on her face deterred him from asking.

'I thought something had happened the other night.'

'He shaved her, her punter. That's what you call your clients isn't it? Punters? Well, he decided to shave her.'

'I don't have clients, Henry. And I wouldn't know what to call them.' Lavinia seemed perfectly calm, but he could see the tension in her jaw.

But Henry was in full swing. 'Was it Brooke's idea or yours? Don't tell me, it was Brooke's, of course it was. I bet she's good at it too. Is she? Has she told you if she's good at it?' Henry crossed his legs, what was happening to him? He was beginning to get an erection.

'How many? How many men does she take in a week? Does she just take singles or does she do special rates for gang-bangs?' Talking about his wife in this

524

derogatory way made him feel sick with desire. 'Is it just men or does she take couples, provided the price is right?' Lavinia's white face was now turning red. 'Henry! You came here to apologize for your rudeness of the other night, but your acting even —'

Henry interrupted her. 'How much do you charge, Lavinia. Do you give discounts for old friends?'

The blow she struck landed with such force that he almost toppled off his stool. He put his hand up to his face and, when he removed it, he felt the tears trickle down his cheeks.

Lavinia pulled herself to her feet. She looked extremely weary, as if she had played this role before. She pulled Henry's head against her breast and held him while he sobbed and sobbed.

'There, there, Henry, you're hurting now, but it will work out, you'll see. Brooke only did it for you. If you really think about it, deep down, you know that. She did it for you.'

Josh entered the kitchen and catching Lavinia's eyes, and seeing the tableau, backed away, indicating to her that he was going to his study. A few moments later Zoë did the same, she too backed away and pointed to the ceiling – she would be in her room.

Lavinia rocked Henry back and forth, just as she had rocked the child an hour earlier. 'It's all right, Henry,' she soothed. 'Just remember, Brooke did it for you.'

'And you Lavinia? You did it for Josh?' He was still softly sobbing.

'Yes. Yes, I did it for Josh,' she said wearily. Then very softly she added, 'At first, at first I did it for Josh.'

'CHAPTER SIXTY-EIGHT

Lavinia turned to Alex, her face held a mixture of love and regret. 'But what if Henry tells Josh?'

'Best if you tell him first.'

'Alex, I can't do that, I just can't.'

Once again, Alex launched into the familiar speech he always made. 'You have no choice, Vinnie. I love you, and I know that you love me.'

She shook her head. 'Alex —'

'Hear me out, Vinnie. Please?'

'But, Alex, be sensible. Try to understand. Josh and I go back too far, we have four children. You're right, there's no choice to be made.'

'Please, Vinnie, listen.' He held onto her wrists and stared intently into her eyes. 'I love you. I love you more than you can imagine.'

'Josh says that to me every morning,' she said. But

that wasn't strictly true anymore. She was often out of bed before he was even awake, or she was too busy to listen to him.

'Sure he does, just before he sends you into the kitchen to cook the breakfast and wash the dishes for a load of paying creeps.'

'It's my choice,' she replied.

'In the beginning it was, but is it still your choice?'

He was right of course. It had been her idea in the beginning – in fact she had felt exhilarated by her own success, she was proud of her ability to provide for the family. She had saved the day; she alone had saved Hulver Castle. Her hard work had kept the money and the property in the Elliot name. She hadn't paid the Lloyds debts of course, the Estate income and bank loans had done that, but she had put food in their mouths, and a roof above their heads. What right had she to complain? How could she blame Josh for expecting her to carry on doing it? She had been a success, a raging success; she'd even got a mention in the Michelin Guide – not bad going for someone who used to get completely flustered at the thought of a shoot lunch.

So what had changed? She looked back at Alex – her priorities, of course. In the beginning she'd been prepared to do anything for Josh, for his estate, for his children's inheritance. She'd even been prepared to sleep with Alex for money. But now; now she gave herself freely and in giving herself she had deprived Josh of his wife. It was a subtle thing, in order to give, she had to take; she still woke in Josh's bed, she still ran his house and earned money, he had all that, but he no longer had her. She had moved away from him; a gradual but definite migration, and now she resented him. She resented the fact that he was taking the shoot back in hand and that he seemed quite content that she should continue to take in paying guests. She resented his assumption that she was happy and felt fulfilled doing what she did. She resented the assumption that she was of the same mind as he regarding the boys schooling. She was tired; she struggled with her thoughts. Then there was Zoë and the baby; that was another thing; another burden placed on her shoulders, another irritating grain of resentment. She was punishing Josh of course; that's what it was, that's why she was in Alex's bed.

'I'm punishing Josh, you know,' she said. 'I'm using you, Alex. I'm using you to punish Josh.'

'Nonsense! That would only work if he knew about us.'

'How do you know that he doesn't?'

'Because I stay at Hulver at least once a month, and even Josh wouldn't be able to stomach me being there if he knew.' He rolled over onto his back and stared at the ceiling.

'What do you mean? Even Josh?'

'I don't think you need me to explain that, do you?'

She buried her head into his shoulder. 'I don't think you should come to Hulver any more. It's not right, Alex. How many times had she said that to him over the months and years?'

He smiled. 'I see. Then why is it that you sneak out of Josh's bed and into mine when I visit?'

'I'm not proud of that.'

'I don't think pride comes into it. Vinnie, I love you. You have to leave him, you have to come and live with me. We'll be happy – you know we will. We're made for each other.' He rolled over onto her pushing himself between her legs. 'Feel me, Vinnie. See how well we fit. We belong together. We were made for each other. Don't throw it all away.'

'I can't. Not now. It's not the right time. Maybe, when I've seen this thing through.'

'What thing? Surely you don't mean when you've paid off the Lloyds debt?'

'The end is in sight, Alex. In a year's time we'll have the opportunity to make a final settlement, close all the open years and — '

'And when you're worn to a frazzle, and Josh has his precious estate back inline, and your boys are educated to the level of English County Gentlemen, and maybe, when you have Tiggy married off, and perhaps your granddaughter settled at a decent prep school, maybe then, you'll consider my offer?'

'Maybe,' she said and laughed.

He rolled back down to her side. 'Vinnie, I love you so, so much. I'll wait – of course I'll wait – you know that. I want to give you an ultimatum, but I can't, I'm too afraid of losing you.'

She frowned. 'It's strange. It used to matter to me so very much, the estate, the castle – saving it for future generations. I don't know why, but I seem to have changed my mind about things, a shift in priorities.'

'Because you love me, Vinnie, that's what's changed.'

'It's because things are tough now, with Zoë and the baby, and I'm so successful with the B and B's that I don't get a minute's rest. It's because it's all so hard, that's why I've changed.'

He rolled back onto her. 'No, Vinnie. I'll show you why you've changed.' He parted her legs with his hips. 'It's us, Vinnie – it's what we have. That's why you've changed.'

CHAPTER SIXTY-NINE

Lavinia was ironing when Josh returned from taking Fen for a walk. Fen sniffed at the hem of her skirt.

Josh tapped his thigh with his hand. 'Come on old girl, time for your supper.'

Fen, who was now almost ten years old, followed her master with a slightly arthritic gait. When Josh returned to the utility room he was carrying two mugs of tea. 'Here you are. Thought you might like a cuppa.'

She took the mug from him, placed it on the side and took another linen napkin from the overflowing laundry basket.

'Can't you break for a minute and drink your tea?' He said.

'They have to be ironed wet,' she said. 'If they dry out, I'll have to starch them again.'

'Oh, oh I see.' He leaned back against the worktop and sipped at his own mug. He slurped a little as he drank, and Lavinia felt irritated by the noise.

'Can't you drink quietly?' She snapped.

'Oh, right. Sorry darling.'

She knew she was punishing him again. The harder she worked the more she resented him; not openly, it wasn't something she could control, she wasn't even conscious of it herself, most of the time. But when she really thought about it, deep down she knew, and then she would make her apologies; 'I'm sorry, Josh,' she'd say. 'I'm tired.' But even that statement was a perverse form of punishment.

Josh took another sip of his tea, quietly this time.

From the window overlooking the park a couple could be seen wandering hand in hand.

'Ha-ha,' Josh said. 'Young love?'

'They're on their honeymoon.' Lavinia informed him. 'They're staying here just for tonight and flying off to Venice in the morning.'

She looked wistfully out over the park. She was thinking of her own honeymoon. They too had gone to Venice. Halfway through the week Josh's parents had decided to join them. She'd never really liked Josh's parents. They treated her as if she were a child. She smiled to herself. They were right, of course. She had been little more than a child. They were dead now, as dead as the way of life she had married into.

Josh nodded toward the couple. 'Wishing it were

us?' He said.

She smiled. 'No. No, I wasn't.'

'Venice,' he said. 'I promised you a return trip to Venice, didn't I?'

She shrugged her shoulders. 'Yes,' she whispered, the word was hardly audible. She folded another napkin and put it with the others. 'But Lloyds put paid to that, like a good many of our plans.'

Josh took a step toward her. 'Me,' he sighed. 'Not Lloyds.' He nodded toward the couple in the Deer Park. 'If only we could put the clock back,' he said. 'Is that what you're thinking? Wishing it were us on our honeymoon and we were just beginning our lives together?'

'No,' she said, but rather wistfully.

'Then, what were you thinking?'

'I was thinking that I couldn't bear to think of all the disappointments that lay ahead of them.' She looked toward the young couple.

Josh's face looked haggard. 'Lord, Vinnie, you are cynical this evening.'

She had not planned to wound him, but she knew that she had.

'Pass my tea, darling, would you,' she said.

'This is life saving,' she said after she had taken a gulp of the near cold liquid. It was the closest she could come to an apology.

Later than evening, when they were getting ready for bed, Lavinia said, 'Who am I, Josh?'

She was sitting at the dressing table staring into the mirror.

Josh came over to her and kissed the top of her head. 'What do you mean? Who are you?'

'Just that. Who am I?'

'You're my wife, of course.'

In the early days, when she had first met Alex, she had blossomed; everyone had said as much. Now she was burdened down with the weight and worry of her love. Emotional baggage filled with deceit that did not sit lightly on her shoulders, she felt the weight of the burden every hour of every day.

Josh patted her shoulder. 'You need a good night's sleep, Vinnie,' he said. He left her and, getting into bed, he opened his book and started to read.

Lavinia slipped off her rings and her bracelet and put them in a little red lacquer bowl that she always kept on her dressing table. Josh had bought it for her in Venice along with her set of coloured glass bottles; it seemed a thousand years ago.

She rubbed moisturising cream into her face and neck. Her nightdress had slipped from her shoulder, exposing part of her breast. The stretch-marks which she had rarely noticed before looked prominent in the glow of the attic lighting. She wondered if Alex had ever noticed them. Josh gave a little snort. She looked over at him; he had fallen asleep, his book still on his chest.

She smoothed a little cream into the lines on her breasts; wishing as she did so, that the potion could remove both the marks, and the shared history they represented.

She went over to the bed and removed Josh's reading glasses and his book. 'Dear, dear, Josh,' she said. He looked so content and peaceful; sleep seemed to rub out the years. He almost looked like the Josh of old. She kissed his cheek, slipped out of her nightdress, got into bed and snuggled up to him.

She slid her leg over his, then her arm, so that she was almost lying on top of him. He stirred and turned away from her. 'I'm sorry, Vinnie. I'm really not in the mood.'

She swung over onto her back and sniffed. 'Well, it seems a shame,' she muttered. ' It's the one pleasure we have left that's free.'

He tried to put his arm around her, but she pulled away. 'My darling,' he said. 'Can't you understand how impotent this business has made me feel?'

Lavinia closed her eyes and offered up a silent prayer. Dear God, don't let him stop loving me. No matter how badly I treat him, please don't let him stop loving me. She had no way of knowing that Josh was offering up a similar prayer.

CHAPTER SEVENTY

'Take a look at this,' Josh said, handing a large sheaf of papers over to Lavinia. 'See if you can make head or tail of it.' It was the first week of August and a thick tome entitled *Reconstruction and Renewal* had arrived at the castle that morning. She was ironing again, taking pleasure from the rectangles and squares of crisp, white, Irish linen, wondering how much longer the task would fall to her hands. For she had made up her mind; she would go to Alex. She would follow her heart

The first page had *Settlement Offer* written in bold white print on a maroon background. It was a complicated read and although Josh tried, he could not make any sense of it.

She pushed her reading glasses onto her nose and studied the documents. Josh's agent had done his best to explain the settlement offer to him, but he still didn't really understand exactly what it entailed.

Lavinia sat down and carefully read the chapter entitled: *Benefits and Risks, New Central Fund and Personal Stop Loss*. Josh stood patiently by her side as she read. But all Lavinia wanted to know was exactly how much Josh was going to have to raise. She turned the pages and studied the chapter entitled: *Payment and Finality Bill*.

As far as I can make out, Josh, you have until twelve noon on 28th August to accept the offer, and then you'll have until the 30th September to raise the money.'

Josh took the papers out of her hands. 'Can you imagine, Vinnie. What it will feel like to be free?'

'Free?'

'Of the debt.' He was smiling broadly.

'We still have to pay it,' she said. 'How can we possibly raise that kind of money?'

'The Bank will settle it, of course,' Josh said.

'How do you know the bank will pay?'

'Because they've guaranteed to do so, they charge enough for the arrangement. But they're going to want a structured plan to indicate how we're going to pay them off.'

'We?' She said. 'How can we? The interest on a loan that size will be astronomical, we'll have to sell something. We won't be able to furnish such a loan.'

'Yes we will, we can get a mortgage over twenty-five years or something.'

Lavinia pursed her lips. 'So you expect me to do B and B's for the next twenty-five years?' She folded her arms in front of her. 'I suppose you could get me a specially adapted zimmer frame, one with a tray fixed on the front, so I can stagger out to the dining room in my dotage.'

'Oh, Vinnie – look, I'll see Brian Bamford tomorrow, and he can tell me how much it will cost us. It may only be a thousand or so a month – you can make that in a weekend – you know you can.'

'I can't make that sort of money in a weekend Josh. I can take that much, but most of it gets swallowed up in overheads. Food and light and heat. Where do you think all those things have been coming from?'

'I know, Vinnie. I know. You've kept Hulver going.'

'Kept it going? Kept it going? No, Josh, I've done more than that. I've breathed new life into it.'

'You speak as if you're the only one that has made sacrifices, Vinnie. I've been here too, I've been working alongside of you.'

'What? What sacrifices have you made?'

'The shoot, for one.' He chuckled. 'That reminds me, I meant to tell you. I rang the tenant this morning and told him that I wasn't going to renew his contract for next season. He was pretty damned mad, I can tell you.'

'You've done what? But that money would have gone some way to paying the bank off.'

Josh waved his arms about, they were both shouting at each other. 'But what's the point of living at Hulver if we can't have the pleasure of it? You can't begrudge me the shoot, Vinnie, surely you can't, what with all the other sacrifices I've made, all the other things I've given up. Even Steve Jarvis has a shoot.'

'What things? What have you given up?' Her voice was loud and harsh.

'You,' he said simply. 'My wife.'

'Me?'

'I had to give you up a long time ago,' he said quietly. They were facing each other, their eyes locked.

She blushed. 'Don't be silly, Josh – I'm here aren't I? I work hard, I get tired, you know that, but you still have me.'

'Do I, Vinnie?'

She didn't answer him but turned her back and walked through to the kitchen where she put the kettle on the Aga. He followed her; she pushed back past him and made her way to the utility room. 'I have some ironing to do, if you'll excuse me.' He stood at the kitchen door and watched her go.

Later that day she telephoned Alex's chambers. 'I'll be with you as planned,' she said. 'One o'clock the day after tomorrow.'

'   'Darling, Vinnie,' was his only reply.

CHAPTER SEVENTY-ONE

Josh threw the newspaper to one side. He'd expected to feel elated when he saw the announcement in back and white, but he didn't, he felt tired. Tired was too mild a word; he was exhausted, the mere thought of the past five years exhausted him. Years that had seen his sons grow tall; his daughters reach maturity and had even made him a grandfather. Yet Lavinia, despite all the changes, despite all the hard work, had blossomed. She had become a radiant and confident woman. He had always thought of her as beautiful, always loved her cat-like grace, but now she carried an air of mystery about her. She fascinated him; it was as if he didn't know her anymore. He shook his head; there was something else? A hard edge perhaps? Or had she merely grown a protective shell. Sometimes he thought that she had grown away from him and that he didn't know how to reach her. She no longer depended on him; that was certain. But that was surely a good thing, he was older than she was; it was good that she should be able to carry on if he were no longer around. But he had once been the centre of her life, and now he dwelt on the perimeter, a mere addition; no longer the focal point.

The Lloyds crash had not only destroyed wealth, it had taken lives and wrecked marriages. Although some marriages seemed even better for it; Henry and Brooke's for instance. It was an embarrassment to have them for dinner these days, they couldn't keep their hands to themselves, always touching each other and sharing private little jokes. Even poor old Philip's demise had made way for a new strong partnership between Ailsa and Steve. A good man Steve had turned out to be; he'd certainly saved Ailsa from financial ruin. Pity he and Zoë had never made it together, they'd have made a perfect pair. And thinking of marriage, Lloyds had certainly destroyed Lavinia's brother's marriage. Poor old Rupert, Rosie had really taken him to the cleaners; what Lloyds hadn't taken, Rosemary had procured. Mind you; that was a marriage that was doomed from the very beginning.

Not everyone had lost by the Lloyds crash either. Hillary had made a thriving little business for herself, a business that she really enjoyed. And if it hadn't been for the crash, Hillary and George wouldn't have stayed at Pennington on that fateful night, and poor old George probably wouldn't be dead. And that in turn would have meant that Hillary would have gone under, what with

Lloyds and the cost of keeping George in a home. But George's insurance would pay off all their debts and leave a little over. So sometimes, it really was an ill wind that blew nobody any good.

In some ways, the last year had been the hardest. They'd settled to a sort of routine, Vinnie going off shopping twice a week. Zoë, who now lived with his grandchild in the lodge, often coming to the Castle to hold the fort, giving Lavinia a little more freedom.

Lavinia's business ran like clockwork; and from Easter to September the guests, and with them, the money, rolled in. So why was he so discontent, why was he not elated to get the confirmation of the settlement? He looked at his watch, it was almost four o'clock; he ought to take Fen for a walk. In the old days he had so enjoyed walking her and coming home to find Vinnie in their bedroom waiting for him. He smiled to himself, remembering how he used to take a tray of drinks up to her; he felt a warm surge of nostalgia for the Marks and Spencer dinners that she used to cobble together for him. Now she cooked from Raymond Blanc and The Roux Brothers, wonderful, exciting food; so why wasn't he excited by it?

A pile of mail lay on the kitchen table; he sorted through it. There was a letter from Tiggy; he put it to one side for Lavinia to open. Tiggy was doing her first year at

Edinburgh, and thoroughly enjoying it. Her letters always cheered Lavinia up. The rest of the post consisted mainly of bills and circulars, but in amongst them was another handwritten envelope addressed to both he and Lavinia. He tore it open; it was an invitation to Ailsa's New Year Shoot. He pushed the invite back in amongst the pile of letters and shook his head.

He looked at his watch again, the hands had barely moved. He wondered when Vinnie would be home, they had no guests due at all that week, so she'd probably stay out late. She'd probably go and see a film in Norwich before she came home. She had become so independent. In the old days, she would never have dreamed of going to the cinema alone. Now, she seemed to rather enjoy her solitude. And why shouldn't she? Surely he couldn't begrudge her a little time off, a little time alone; she worked hard enough for it, didn't she?

Josh pulled on his outdoor shoes and called Fen. Her arthritis forgotten, she bounded down the library corridor wagging her tail and almost knocking Josh off his feet with her exuberant greeting.

'Calm down, calm down,' he reprimanded.

He had his hand on the doorknob when the telephone rang. He thought he wouldn't bother to answer it, but then he realized that it might be Lavinia and he ran through to the kitchen and grabbed the receiver.

It was Hillary. Josh explained that Lavinia had gone to Norwich shopping and he wasn't quite sure at what time she'd be back. 'It's funny,' he said. 'I was just thinking of you.'

'Nice thoughts, I hope, Josh?'

'How could they be otherwise? Yes. Yes, I was just thinking how clever Lavinia had been in making such a hit with the paying guests and then I thought about you and –,

'And?'

'And, well, to tell you the truth, I was thinking about poor old George and how you'd got the show on the road since he died, and how if you hadn't stayed at Pennington that weekend . . . I mean, if George hadn't died when he did —'

'I'm sorry, Hillary. It was tactless of me to mention — '

'No, no, not at all, I often think the same. I still really miss him, that special relationship. You know what I mean, don't you, Josh? Being able to share everything with another person. All your hopes, and your fears, and know that they won't love you one jot less, no matter what you say or what you've done.'

'I know what you mean,' Josh said. He frowned; it had been a long time since he'd had that sort of relationship with Lavinia.

'You know, it's easier now he's dead. People understand how I miss him now. But I missed him a long time before he died. He went away from me a long time before he went off to the forest. The shell of him was with me, but he wasn't. When they were looking for him, I wanted all the time to tell people that he had left us a long time before, but no one seemed to understand.'

'I understand,' Josh said. 'I miss Vinnie.'

Hillary sounded alarmed. 'I thought you said she'd gone to Norwich. She's not ill or anything, is she?'

'She has gone to Norwich. That's not what I mean. No – she's not ill, not like George was or anything, but she's not with me anymore. She's so busy all the time. She's always somewhere else.'

Hillary laughed. 'Oh, Josh, she works so awfully hard. Don't be so hard on her, she must be exhausted most of the time.'

'But you do B and B, you're the same.'

'No, Josh. I'm not the same. Lavinia has you and the children to worry about. It's different for her. Besides, she's much busier than I am. I've only got three guest rooms. Lavinia has loads more to do than me. This is my life, the paying guests have replaced George, in a way, it has given me a purpose in life.'

'I just want my wife back,' Josh whispered.

'What?'

'You know they've accepted the deal?'

'What?'

'*Equitas.*'

'Oh. Oh yes. I had a letter from George's Agent. You must be mighty pleased.'

'Yes, I just want things to be as they were before.'

'Josh, dear, I don't think things will ever be the way they were before.'

'No. That's what Vinnie says.'

Fen jumped up and down with impatience, she gave a couple a low growls. 'I was about to take the dog for a walk, Hillary. I must go – she's getting impatient. I'll tell Lavinia you called. I'll ask her to phone you.'

He replaced the receiver, but instead of making his way to the door, he flopped down on a kitchen chair. The dog, with a confused look on her face, came over to him; buried her soft head in his lap, and whimpered.

Josh put his head in his hands. Fen became even more alarmed and nuzzled up to him. He smiled at her. 'I want my life back, Fen,' he said. 'I want my life, and my wife, back.'

CHAPTER SEVENTY-TWO

So it was over. Josh had it all worked out; a loan from the bank, which would be paid off with the Estate income. Lavinia could do a few more years of bed and breakfast to cover the cost of running the house and educating the boys. Zoë seemed settled and Tiggy was doing well. Simple wasn't it? That's what Josh had said, 'Simple.' Well, it was simple as long as he wasn't the one having to cook and clean and entertain; of course it was simple.

Lavinia rolled over onto her back. They'd talked far into the night. What was it that Josh had said – he just wanted his wife back — how dare he? How dare he expect her to work the way that she did and still be the subservient wife of five years before? But no, that wasn't the trouble, the trouble lay with her . . . her promise to Alex. 'Yes,' she'd said. 'Yes, I'll come to you. Now Josh has reached the end, now there's a settlement, I'll come.' She lay and mentally rearranged the furniture in Alex's London house. It was a beautiful house, a solid, elegant, Georgian town house; it was fashionable, and close to his chambers. She certainly wouldn't miss Hulver Castle. Alex was free, his divorce had been as painless and as uneventful as his marriage, or so he had told her. She wondered if hers would be the same.

Josh sighed in his sleep, she put her hand out to touch him and then withdrew it. What was she doing? Tomorrow she'd be living with another man; she couldn't embrace Josh. She hadn't told him about Alex, she'd intended to but she hadn't. How could she explain? How could she tell him that she had thought of selling her body, explain to him that that was how she had met Alex. Surely that would rob him of his last vestige of self-respect?

Why, oh why, couldn't she be more like Brooke? No, that was wrong. She didn't want to be like her friend; indeed she had no understanding of her at all, and even less understanding of Henry.

'I love it,' Brooke had said. 'I love it that I'm the lady of the manor and I'm so prim and proper, so untouchable and yet . . .' she laughed. 'You know what, Lavinia. I like it, I like it very much. It's fun, I tell you. You should try it, it's fun, it's exciting.'

'But what if someone hurts you?'

'Sometimes it's exciting to be hurt a little. Sometimes a little pain can be very stimulating.'

'No, I mean really, really hurts you.'

'There's always someone close by. I could call for the staff.'

'But what if they told Henry that it's still going on?'

'Henry! Oh Lavinia, I though you realized, Henry knows all about it. He watches, discreetly of course – it turns him on, he gets madly jealous but madly sexy. We do all right, Henry and I. And the men, they're very funny, you know, most of them don't seem to notice the American accent. They pay to fuck an English lady in an English stately home and they almost get what they pay for.'

'You've changed, Brooke. You've changed so much.'

'How do you know I've changed? It proves you never really knew me. I haven't changed – I just get paid for it now. Don't look so shocked, Lavinia!'

'But Henry —'

'When Henry and I married it was a straight swap, his title for my . . . shall we say – skills. Henry gave me something I couldn't get on my own and, in return, I gave Henry something he had never had before.'

Lavinia began to sweat as she recalled the conversation.

'I like men. I like fucking. It's fun and it pays well. Do you know that I earn in a night what you can earn in a month? Sex is very profitable and it's fun, you should try it.'

'I have,' Lavinia had retorted. 'I do it with my husband.'

As she remembered the conversation the old familiar mantle of guilt settled on her shoulders and, once again, she felt the weight of it pressing, even though she lay flat on her back.

'No, I don't mean dear old Josh, although I'm sure he's a real goer between the sheets. I don't know why you ever let that Alec guy slip through your fingers.' Brooke had laughed then and Lavinia had felt offended. Alex she had wanted to say, his name is Alex; and at the same time she'd felt protective of Josh, and had spoken in his defence. Brooke would be surprised when she heard news of Lavinia's defection. She had told her that she had given Alex up months ago.

'The thrill, Lavinia. The thrill of someone new. The thrill of not quite knowing what they're going to be like. Not knowing what they're going to do. How they're going to fuck you, how they'll feel inside you. It's real control. You wonder how they'll be when they come,' she was pacing about the floor. 'Will they make a little noise? Will they hold their breath? Will they cry to God or, with my clients, more likely to Allah? One of my men cried like a baby. It's a pure power trip.' She smiled. 'Some hold their breath so long you think they're going to faint. It's a wonderful feeling to have them at your knees.'

'But don't you see, Brooke. They're using you, you're a commodity to them.'

'No, Lavinia, quite the reverse, it's thrilling, it's exciting, and what's more it's spiced up our marriage. Our sex life is on another plane.'

Lavinia turned over on her stomach; she thumped the pillow with her fist. Was what she was doing any worse than what Brooke was doing? She'd destroyed her marriage with her affair with Alex, whereas Brooke claimed to have added another dimension to hers. Brooke had saved her husband's wealth with her infidelity, which was certainly not the case with Lavinia.

Tomorrow it would all be over, tomorrow she would go to Alex. What would her children say? Would they forgive her? When she was gone would they miss her? No, she wasn't giving her children up; she would still see them _ in fact, she'd at last have time for them. She closed her eyes and imagined what it would be like to be free. Free of all the responsibility, free of Hulver, free of the day to day worries, free of the wretched bed and breakfast guests that made such huge demands on her time.

Josh turned over and flung one of his arms over her shoulder. She pushed it away from her; he snorted and turned away.

She'd tried to explain it to him, but he hadn't understood. 'I'm tired, Josh,' she'd said. 'I need some time. Time on my own.'

'But you were in Norwich all day Monday, you were on your own then,' he'd replied.

She hadn't been on her own, of course, she'd spent the afternoon in the arms of Alex Kirby. 'No, Josh, real time, time for myself,' she'd said.

'It'll be all right now. We have the settlement, the end's in sight, it's simple – soon we'll be clear.'

But Lavinia had already made her decision; she had already decided to go to Alex. She'd seen Josh through to the end, and now she was going to take what life had to offer her.

'I have something to tell you,' she'd said.

'And I have something to tell you,' he'd replied. 'I love you, Vinnie, and I do appreciate all that you've done for me. You've always been a perfect wife and a wonderful mother. I haven't always understood what sort of sacrifices you've made over the last few years – the toll it's taken from you, but I need you to know that I've always appreciated everything you've done. I know I haven't always shown it and I've often put other things before you _ I'm truly sorry for that, and I'm promising you now, that I'm going to make amends. I'm going to make it all up to you, you see if I don't.' He'd smiled then; his face looked soft and gentle and he looked astoundingly vulnerable.

She could have told him in anger; told him when her resentment was boiling over, but not now; not when he was filled with gratitude, and proclaiming his love for her.

'Now, what were you going tell me?'

'Nothing,' she'd shaken her head. 'Must have slipped my mind. I've forgotten.'

And so the evening had gone on, Josh planning their future and Lavinia planning hers, and Josh not realizing that they were in any way different. Now Lavinia lay in their bed for what she knew would be the very last time and she felt sick with shame and guilt and anticipation.

CHAPTER SEVENTY-THREE

Josh had left the house early. He had, he said, important business to attend to. He'd kissed Lavinia and told her he loved her, and now here she was, sitting at the small desk in the morning room, writing a letter to him. A letter that, once read, would change his view of her entirely. A letter that would alter his whole life. A letter that would shake the very foundations of his being.

She penned the note carefully, she tried to put the words kindly; she was careful to blame only circumstance, and not Josh, for the pressures placed upon her. She told him that she had fallen in love with Alex. Then she tore the letter up and started again, and yet again. No matter how she put the words, they still sounded harsh and accusing. No matter how much she blamed herself, the blame seemed slanted toward Josh; and his loss of money seemed to be the reason for her loss of love.

Eventually she wrote a letter that she felt could not be improved upon; the harsh reality could not be hidden or softened with selective words. She was leaving him for another man. She was sorry for the pain she knew she would cause him. She hoped that one day he would find it in his heart to forgive her. She didn't love him less; it was just that she had fallen in love with someone else.

She packed some things in a small canvas bag; she would send for the rest of her possessions when she was settled. She looked at the little lacquer bowl that she kept on her dressing table, Josh's honeymoon present, the one she had kept her jewelry in overnight for the entire length of her marriage. She picked it up, hesitated for just a moment, and then replaced it. She ordered a taxi and, whilst she waited for it, she walked around the castle. She went into every room of the house thinking that was exactly what it was, a house, a place to reside, it was no longer a home; it had been violated by the hundreds of pairs of feet that had paid to enter it. She felt no regret at leaving it. She told Doris the cleaner that she was going out, and did not expect to be back for lunch. She asked Doris to leave by the side door and drop the latch behind her. She propped her note on the little shelf by the side of the Aga, knowing that Josh would see it there when he came in. She patted Fen on the head. 'Look after him, Fen,' she said. 'He's a good man.'

The dog whined and Lavinia was convinced that Fen had read her intentions. She sighed, 'I'm sorry, Fen. But

I have to do this – for me.'

The taxi arrived to take her to the station. She pulled the front door shut, locked it, and pushed her key through the letterbox. She dusted off her hands. There, she thought, there's no going back now.

She had arranged to meet Alex at a restaurant close to The Royal Courts of Justice; he was in the midst of a murder trail. She arrived long before him; she checked her overnight bag into the cloakroom and sat down to wait. The longer she waited the noisier the room got, the volume level seemed as if it was trying to compete with the noises in her head. There was a long mirror on the wall opposite. For a while Lavinia did not recognize the confident woman looking in her direction. Then she realized that it was her own reflection; and she was alarmed to think that she had changed, even beyond her own recognition.

Josh had told her that he would be out all day, she wondered what time he would get home and when he would see her note. What would he do? Would he try to find her? Would he ring Zoë or Tiggy? She decided that he'd probably take Fen out for a walk, then he'd probably ring Henry.

She stared at herself in the mirror; who was she? If she didn't know herself, then who did know her? Did Alex? Did Josh know her, had he ever known her? What if

Josh had asked her the same question? What would she have answered? 'You're my husband,' is that what she would have said? She thought of Josh's gentle nature, the way he was never shy of admitting that he was in the wrong, the way he always made an excuse for her anger. Josh, with his gentle country ways, preferring to be called Mr Elliot than Lord Hulver. Josh, who could be pig-headed and obstinate and, at the same time, so very kind and gentle. Josh, who was always straight and would harm no one. 'Josh is my friend,' she said aloud. He's the one person in the whole world that would forgive me anything. The one person who would never, ever, let me down, she thought. 'He's my friend,' she said again.

Meanwhile, Alex paced around his small chamber, he was running through his final argument, the speech that would sum up his client's defence. He was defending a woman accused of murdering her husband, a drunken, abusive man who'd made her life a misery for most of the ten years that they had been man and wife.

He rested his hands on his lapels, coughed and said aloud, Ladies and gentlemen of the jury. It's difficult for any decent law-abiding person to imagine the sort of abuse Gary Smith subjected his wife to.' He coughed again. No, far better not to mention the dead man's name; far better for the victim to come across as a vicious impersonal brute. He tried the speech again, this time replacing Gary Smith's name with 'this drunken abusive lout'. But his mind wandered and he thought of Lavinia. He'd done all he could to discredit Josh in her eyes; using all his training and experience, applying all his logical barrister arguments. Hoping to persuade her that her place was not at Hulver, but with him. The truth was, he liked Josh, how could anyone not like him? He was a gentle benign soul, but he didn't appreciate Vinnie, that was for sure. Alex would have given anything for Vinnie to love him the way she loved Josh, but he knew in his heart of hearts that she never would. But he wasn't beaten yet, he was trained to build up the underdog by demolishing the one with the upper hand, and that is what he'd done and would continue to do. It wasn't immoral; it was what he did every day of his life, and this time the prize was the highest prize in the world.

Alex Kirby had started life with nothing except a good brain and a powerful ability to persuade others into his way of thinking. Josh Elliot was no match for him, if push came to shove, Alex would leave Josh standing in the shadows wondering exactly what had hit him. From his humble beginnings Alex was now a force to be reckoned with. His Saville Row suits and hand-made shoes had all been courtesy of Sarah, a fact that had never sat happily with him. But to have the ex-Lady Hulver as his wife and soul mate would show Sarah, and the whole establishment, what a powerful and important man he really was.

He was late, his thoughts had robbed him of the time. He pulled his wig and gown off and threw them in the corner of the room. He took a deep breath and composed himself. She'd said she'd come, why should he doubt her?

He sucked in his bottom lip as he walked down The Strand. She would be there, she must be there; he had to believe that.

He saw her reflection in the mirror long before she saw him, and his heart rejoiced. He strode purposefully across the room.

'Darling. I'm sorry I'm late.'

She smiled up at him. She noticed that his knuckles were clenched and white as he held onto the back of the chair opposite her.

'You're not coming to me, are you?' He said.

And, at that moment, realization dawned on her, and she knew that she wasn't.

He flopped down on the chair opposite her.

'I still can't give you what Josh can give you, can I?'

She smiled sadly. She covered his hand with her own. 'No. No, you can't. I'm sorry, but you can't.'

So you're going back? Back to Hulver, back to where property means more than people?'

'Alex, you don't get it, do you? You see. I know what Josh is about. I understand him. You don't. He's always felt so privileged to have Hulver, and he took it as a point of honor to fulfill what he thinks of as his responsibility to it. He wants to hand it over to the next generation in as fine, if not better, shape than when he inherited it. Surely that can't be so very wrong, can it? And he chose me, he chose me to share in his task.'

'Come on, Vinnie. Who are you trying to convince?' Alex beckoned the waiter to bring them both a drink. 'Josh has sold you into slavery for the sake of Hulver.'

'No, Alex,' she smiled. 'I went willingly.'

'Willingly? Have you forgotten how we met?' He spat the words at her.

'No, Alex. I haven't forgotten. How could I ever forget? I don't regret it either, and I'll always be glad that it was you.'

'Huh!' He threw his head back. 'You're as bad as Josh – you deserve each other.' His mouth twisted with his words.

'Josh is a good man. I shall take that as a compliment.'

'Vinnie, don't throw what we have – our love – away.'

'What have we got? How long have we known each other – three years? Four? Hulver and the likes of

561

Josh go back for generations. I've grown into it – it's too late to part us now. You remind me how we met. I won't forget, and it serves to remind me just how far I was prepared to go, to save what Josh and I had. I can't throw it all away, now.'

He shook his head. 'I knew you could never leave Hulver. I always knew you'd go back to it.'

She gave a half smile. 'You're wrong, Alex. I could leave Hulver tomorrow, if I had to, but only with Josh by my side. I'm not going back to Hulver. I'm going back to Josh. I'm going back to what we have, what we've shared – the good times, the bad times, the things that have happened to us, the things that have made us who we are _ our shared history. Don't you see? Josh and I are inseparable, even my affair with you has been conducted with Josh in the background. It's as if he's part of it.'

Alex snorted and beckoned to the waiter again. He ordered another drink.

'So that's it, is it? Thank you very much, Alex. We're out of debt now and I don't need you, or your distraction, any more?'

'That's not fair. For one thing we're far from out of debt. We just know how much the debt is now, and that it won't go on forever. It still has to be paid off.' She covered his hand. 'You were never just a distraction.'

' Wasn't I?' He closed his eyes and shrugged his

shoulders. Their drinks arrived; he almost gulped his down in one.

'Vinnie, I love you. I divorced Sarah for you.'

'I'm sorry, Alex. I understood that your marriage was over anyway.'

'It was — it is.' There was desperation in his voice. 'Vinnie, please. Please don't —.'

She pushed her chair away from the table. 'I have to get back,' she said. 'Goodbye, Alex. I'm so, so sorry.'

He tried to catch her hand but she wriggled from his grasp. 'I'm sorry, Alex, I have to get back,' she said again, this time with urgency. She rushed from the restaurant, completely forgetting that her small canvas bag was still in the cloakroom. It was suddenly imperative that she retrieve the note she'd left for Josh.

She took a taxi to Liverpool Street where she was informed that the signalmen had downed tools and gone on strike. She took another taxi to Victoria and joined the queue for the next coach that was bound for Norwich. The bus was delayed, but then she thought, she was used to waiting, waiting for guests to arrive, waiting for the time to pass so that she could see Alex, waiting for the settlement; waiting for it all to be over. She'd be too late of course, Josh was bound to have opened the note by now. And she didn't really know whether Josh would still be waiting for her.

CHAPTER SEVENTY-FOUR

But Josh had returned home before lunch. He spotted the envelope straight away, lifted it down from the shelf, and played with it between his fingers. He bounced it on the table then held it between his lips. He turned it over several times and then put it back onto the little shelf. He'd had a busy morning and he still had things to do.

He had visited Max Sowerby, the Estate Agent; he had been to his bank to revise his plans, and he had seen his accountant. He'd also been to the wine merchant, the florist and lastly, the travel agent.

When he arrived home, Doris told him that Lady Hulver had left by taxi; she had overheard her tell the driver that she was catching the London train.

Josh went into the morning room and retrieved Lavinia's accommodation book. He began working his way through the visitors due to arrive at the castle over the next few weeks. They thanked him for his call but told him that Lady Hulver had already telephoned explaining that she would not be available and therefore they would not be able to stay at the castle. Many voiced the hope that Lady Hulver was quite well.

Yes. Yes, his wife was all right – but owing to circumstances beyond their control, they were unable to accommodate them.

It was all right, wasn't it? It had to be all right, he had to make it all right. He'd been a fool, but it wasn't too late, was it? It couldn't be too late.

He retrieved three empty cardboard boxes from the gun room, set them on the floor of the library corridor, removed the set of Bloomfield's Norfolk and carefully stacked them in the boxes. He rearranged the books on the shelves, placing an old set of Encyclopedia Britannica in place of the Bloomfields.

He took one of the books through to his study and, with a razor blade, he carefully removed the painting by John Sell Cotman, and placed it in a clear plastic folder.

He thought all the time of Lavinia, and remembered the day she had vetoed selling the books, and he thought of the way she had worked to save Hulver. He patted the painting. 'This is for you, Vinnie,' he said. 'Whatever happens, Lloyds aren't getting this or the

Bloomfields. These are yours. This is my thank you.' He shook his head. He had laid such store in the Bloomfields, as if they represented all he held dear, and he'd placed such little value on Lavinia.

He carted the boxes through to the hall, went back to his study, picked up the telephone, dialed Sotheby's number, and asked for the rare books department.

'They're packed up ready for collection,' he said. 'And the Cotman's ready as well, and if, as agreed, your private collector could make the cheque payable to my travel agent, I'd be most grateful.'

Josh replaced the receiver and looked at his watch. He had a little over an hour before the books and the watercolour were to be collected.

He took a large plastic clothesbasket from the utility room and climbed the stairs to the attic bedroom. Once there, he filled it with Lavinia's and his personal belongings. He had to make several dozen journeys up and down the steep staircase, placing everything in the master bedroom, desperately trying to recreate the scene of five years before. Forty minutes later, the Sotheby's agent collected the Bloomfields and the Cotman. Thirty minutes after that, Josh drove into town and finished his day's business. He then returned to Hulver and continued his move from the attic to the first floor. It was gone four when he had finished moving the very last item –

the little Venetian lacquer bowl that Lavinia kept on her dressing table.

His task complete, he placed the flowers in water and took them up to the bedroom. He put two glasses on a tray and stood them just inside the butler's pantry, ready to add the chilled champagne.

He took the letter down again and played with it against his lips, fetched a knife from the kitchen drawer and stabbed the point decisively under the flap. Before he was able to slice it open the front door bell rang. He replaced the note along with the envelope he had collected from the town, and went to answer it.

'I got myself locked out,' Lavinia said. 'Did you know that there's a train strike?' She hastily went on. 'I had to catch a bus, can you imagine?'

She pushed past him into the kitchen. The note still stood on the little shelf alongside another envelope. He followed her eyes to it and for a moment their eyes locked together.

He drew her eyes away from it. 'Look at this,' he said. He handed her the invitation to Ailsa's shoot. 'Look. Mr and Mrs Steven Jarvis, would like you to join them for their annual shoot —'

'She's pregnant again, you know,' Lavinia said.
'Who?'
'Ailsa'

'But she must be ... what? – Forty ...' he was counting on his fingers.

Lavinia interrupted him; she put her hand on his arm. 'Very happy, Josh. She must be very happy.'

Josh smiled and nodded his head. 'Look,' he said, 'I'm just going to take Fen for a run, you go up and have a bath, and I'll bring a drink up in half-an-hour or so. We're in our old room by the way.'

She looked puzzled; she glanced again at the envelope still sitting on the shelf beside the Aga.

'There's a surprise for you up there,' he said, looking in the same direction. 'I've had rather a successful day, Vinnie. I know I should have consulted you first, but well, you weren't here and so – '

'So?'

'I went to see Bamford, and my accountant. And I've put three of the cottages on the market. The ones on short leases – they're worth a lot more that I dreamed, and the bank will see us through until they sell – and – and –'

He put his hand out but didn't quite touch her.

'And I'd like to claim my life back,' his voice broke as he spoke.

The tree of resentment that had grown and flourished inside her was suddenly starved of nourishment. Its roots, she realized, were shallow and lacked foundation, and it withered and died.

She took his hand, and she smiled, but the smile was feeble. 'I wonder,' she said, 'if it's still there waiting to be claimed?' She looked immeasurably sad.

He smiled. 'Not quite the same life, my darling. But a good life.' He nodded his head. 'A worthwhile life. In some ways, a better life. So let's make a start by claiming our bed back, shall we?'

He snatched both the envelopes down from the shelf and handed his to her, keeping the one she had written in his hand. She raised her eyes to his, took it from him and tore it in two.

'It's a criminal offence to destroy someone else's mail,' he said.

She gave him a very sad smile. 'It's a moral offence to destroy someone else's life,' she replied, and ripped the note again in half.

He smiled as if he understood.

'Won't you open your surprise?' He said.

She ripped open the other envelope.

'Oh, Josh.'

'Venice,' he said. 'I know it's a year or two late, but – '

'Oh, Josh,' she said again. 'The Danielli.'

'For our anniversary,' he said. 'How many glass bottles do I owe you?'

Lavinia swallowed, remembering all the times, and

all the ways, she and Alex had made love. 'You don't owe me anything,' she said.

'Oh, no, Vinnie. A man must always pay his debts.'

'The slate's clean, Josh.'

'I'm forgiven then?'

'Am I?'

'We always did understand each other, didn't we, Vinnie? I'm so sorry I lost you.'

'You didn't lose me, Josh.'

'Maybe not – maybe for a while I just misplaced, and undervalued you.'

'No, Josh. I undervalued you.'

Fen gave a sigh, and waddled back to her basket. It seemed that her walk was to be postponed to a more convenient moment.

Afterwards, as they lay in their own bed, Lavinia said, 'I do love you, Josh.'

'I love you too.'

'No Josh, you don't understand – I mean, I really do *love* you.'

Read on for a taste of

Enmity's Nurse

the new novel in
THE HULVER TRILOGY
from
SUSANNAH CAMPBELL

PROLOGUE

It was almost eleven o'clock when the knock came on the door. Zoë sighed as the familiar faces greeted her. She thought Inspector Harper looked rather sad, his face laden with doom and despondency, but then he had always looked that way to her.

The other one, Barnes, looked excited, as though he was particularly pleased with himself; but then he usually looked pretty cocky.

'Come in,' Zoë said with resignation. Bracken gave a muffled growl.

'Quiet, Bracken,' she snapped. She immediately felt guilty; the dog was only doing what dogs were supposed to do.

She ran her fingers through her hair, a gesture uncannily like that of her mother.

'What is it now?' She said, none too politely. She was tired – she'd been up half the night.

Afterwards, when she ran and reran the scene through her head, she thought she'd seen Barnes snigger, but she couldn't be certain. The older one just looked extremely troubled, but then she knew he fancied her. He wasn't going to enjoy the mission was he? Even a hardened copper wouldn't have liked the thought of fancying a murderer.

The two policemen looked at each other: Barnes raised his eyebrows and Harper nodded.

'Zoë Louise Elliot, I'm arresting you on suspicion of murder. You do not have to say anything but — '

She heard no more, the carefully structured sentences merged into a long stream of babble. Two words, just two, repeated and resounded in her head, words not unfamiliar in the day to day ordinary run of things, but odd, disjointed, frightening words when applied to Zoë Elliot: arresting – murder – arresting – murder – arresting – arresting – murder – murder – murder. The words screamed through her skull, and at the sound of them her world fell apart, caved in on itself and crashed about her ears, surrounding her with a deafening destructive explosion, as all she held dear toppled around her and fell into oblivion.

A foul, terrifying sense of decay assaulted her body, seeping into every bone and every joint, sweeping into her brain and robbing her of all logical thought; creeping into her mouth, swelling her tongue and making it tarnished and dry; invading her throat and robbing her of speech; oozing down to her lungs and depriving her of breath; spreading into her heart making it beat fast and erratically; attacking her hands and making them shake and tingle. Finally, it poured into her legs and robbed her of the strength to support her exhausted, quaking body.

She sat down heavily and put her hand up to her face. All that she valued, all the things that mattered to her, evaporated and drained away. Then came a second attack, a second wave; her normal bodily functions slipped into a higher gear; she thought she might vomit, or worse, lose control of her bowels or her bladder. Her breathing quickened, her stomach churned, her hands trembled.

She realized that Theo was in the room. She heard him say something like 'Wait a minute.' But his words were lost to her, overshadowed by the two words that still screamed around her head: arresting – murder – murder – arresting. She needed to go to the lavatory; any minute now, she would disgrace herself, and yet she couldn't move; her muscles simply wouldn't obey her brain. Arresting – arresting – murder – murder. Her chest was so tight and so painful that, even if she'd had a coherent thought, she could not have voiced it.

Theo was still speaking, or was it the policeman? She couldn't tell; whoever it was seemed to be a long way away. She squinted, trying to concentrate on what was being said, trying to rejoin the others in the normal world.

Her world still kept moving, folding in on itself, crashing and toppling into a fragmented wilderness. She had no control, there was nothing she could do about it; there was no one to help prop it up, no one to help her rebuild it.

She couldn't communicate, couldn't cry out or express her fear and her pain. She was suffocating, dying, literally falling apart. Couldn't they see that she was disintegrating before their eyes? Didn't they care? Was no one willing to help her?

Her stomach gave another sharp jolt, she was going to be sick. Couldn't they see that she was going to vomit; didn't they have an ounce of pity in them? The words, the two obscene words still played and replayed in her brain – murder – murder. O God, she'd never see her child or Theo again; it was the end for her, she was dying. Arresting – arresting – murder, the words throbbed through her brain, murder – murder – murder.

'But . . . ' she managed to say.

Theo was talking again, but she couldn't hear properly, and her vision was blurred and distorted. He was saying something about a lawyer as he picked up the telephone.

'But . . . I,' she stuttered, ' I didn't . . .I didn't . . . '

Enmity's Nurse

is to be published in paperback shortly.

For details of this and other novels from
SUSANNAH CAMPBELL
please contact ;
DESIDERATA PRESS
POBOX 112
Cambridge PDO
CB4 3SU